REVENGE GROWS HARSH

GRAHAM HEYWOOD

Order this book online at www.trafford.com
or email orders@trafford.com

Most Trafford titles are also available at major online book retailers.

Printed in the United States of America.

ISBN: 978-1-4669-3380-4 (sc)
ISBN: 978-1-4669-3379-8 (hc)
ISBN: 978-1-4669-3378-1 (e)

Library of Congress Control Number: 2012909068

Trafford rev. 05/17/2012

 www.trafford.com

North America & International
toll-free: 1 888 232 4444 (USA & Canada)
phone: 250 383 6864 • fax: 812 355 4082

I would like to thank Sarah, Lucy and Elsa
for being there for me always and Kathryn for the
encouragement and support.

Then murder's out of tune, And sweet revenge
grows harsh.
—Othello. Act 5, Scene 2

INTRODUCTION

MANCHESTER, 1991

MAUREEN MADE HER WAY HOME, slowly, leaning forward against a pressing wind. Grey. The whole day had been varying shades of grey. She had left home at 8:00 a.m. The boy was packed off to school after a struggle to get him up and fed. Husband was already at the workshop by then of course. He always got in early. He worked hard. But life was a struggle.

She had to work to keep the house ticking over. Their living was scraped off the soles of the shoes of the better off.

She had always wanted to be the one to break out. She had four sisters and three brothers, all traditional blue-collar workers or making a living in a tabard. She was always the leading light. Prettier than her sisters, more intelligent than her brothers, and more ambitious than the rest of the family as a whole, she had always seen herself reaching the 1930s semi-detached middle class, children in grammar school, perhaps a new car occasionally and dinner parties.

After leaving school, she had trained for secretarial work at the college in the centre of Manchester. It was not as though that was the limit of her ability, but coming from the back-to-back terraced housing of Moss Side and only having one parent living, it was the best she could do whilst trying to contribute to the upkeep of the family home. Working weekends at Lewis's department store on Market Street helped and only served to make her more determined to succeed.

She would serve the city's bank managers and solicitors and their well-kept spouses and think that they were no different and certainly no better than her.

That was where they had met. He had come in with his then girlfriend, wandering around the store, not buying, trying to look as though he belonged. She had tried the perfume Maureen was selling and pretended not to be appalled by the price. He had just stared at her with those piercing blue-grey eyes. Maureen had blushed. She was seventeen, and at that stage, she had experienced no more than a quick kiss behind the bicycle sheds at school.

By comparison, his face said he knew much more. He left without saying a word, but an hour later, he was back alone, and this time, he spoke quietly so nobody else would hear. The closeness of his lips to her ear created crackles of static that coursed through her reddening neck.

That evening, he escorted her home after work. He was funny. He was confident bordering on the brash. He had that self-awareness, knowing that others want to be around them, want to be them. What a man he was! But that was then in 1961, before it all changed. Everything seemed possible back then.

Two years later, everything seemed to be going their way. A young man was the president of America, working-class kids were taking the world by storm—actors, musicians, even some politicians. Doors that had seemed forever closed to the proletariat were opening, and it felt as though they were going to change the world. Maureen finished college and got a job working for a solicitor in Spring Gardens, the professional centre of Manchester. There was no factory for her; she went to work clean and came home clean. They were married in a small ceremony. He had no family. Her dad gave her away. Her elder sisters warned her it would all change; they knew his sort. He was working hard at the garage; they were saving for their own house, living upstairs at her dad's house. The plan was that he would set up his own garage business, running the workshop. She would look after the books and run the administrative side of the business—an equal partnership in every sense.

Maureen fell pregnant, and her life changed forever. As the years of peace and love turned bitter, so did her marriage. As soon as Mary was born, he seemed to withdraw. They no longer had money to put aside for a house or the business, and he seemed to blame Maureen for that.

He was home less and less. She was looking after the baby. The house was damp; they were due to be relocated to a new council estate ten miles from town. They would at least get a home on their own—three bedrooms and a garden. It was another step forward.

Mary was coughing more, and Maureen took her to the doctor; nothing to worry about he said, but she didn't get any better.

By the time they moved into the new house, all their possessions packed into the oily van from the garage, Mary was in hospital. Two weeks later, she was gone. Even now, the memory cut deep.

Their fire had been extinguished. He had started to drink; she had become a machine—work, home, housework, sleep, work.

She found out the savings were gone and lined the pockets of the bookie on the estate and the landlord of the pub at the centre of the sprawling overspill. He was happy here, surrounded by the very people that they had been trying to break free from, seemingly dragged back at the moment they seemed destined to break free.

Maureen crossed the road. She was hurrying now; the chips would be getting cold. Every Thursday was chip night. The boy loved his chip night. The one shining light that was left for her was her son. His beginnings were nothing to be proud of, a drunken assault by the man she had once loved and worshipped. But the boy, Jack, was everything she had hoped she would have in a child. He was so clever attending the grammar school and so protective of his mum. He told her he would be a solicitor himself one day, and she could be his personal assistant, not his secretary.

She adored the boy. He looked more like her than her husband. He didn't have such a heavy build as his father, but the shoulders were powerful. He was the star of the school football team. One or two professional clubs had invited him to train. He was fast and skillful she was told. There was the occasional flash of that temper he had inherited, but he also had her fierce desire to succeed. He would do well, she knew.

She had retained her fine cheekbones and nose and her slim figure, although the years were showing around her eyes. She still looked good, she thought, if a little tired.

At the top of the estate, by the pub, the wind grew stronger, and Maureen bent her head forward to keep the chilling air from her face and from watering her eyes. As she hurried by the pub, she saw them. Two teenagers were sheltering from the wind around the corner. She knew them and had seen them around the shops. They were not good kids, not like her boy.

'You sharin' them chips, luv?' She looked down and just kept walking.

He leant against the side of the pub, dropped his cigarette, and ground it out with his foot. The wind was biting, and his shelter did little to protect him as it whipped around the sides of the building.

He knew his brother wanted to go home, or to the pub, but he was determined to stay out. She would be here soon. Besides, he had to learn, had to teach his brother to become more of a man.

He had seen her most nights. He saw the way she avoided his gaze. He knew that she wanted him. She could see the new-found strength within him, the power that was growing stronger each month. He saw the desire in her eyes as she looked the other way.

Like all women, she wanted to be taken. He understood the certainty of this fact as he got older. It built day by day, bubbling away under the surface like a soon-to-erupt volcano. As the tension within him began to grow, he got more agitated. He needed his release, and she would give it to him. She wanted to.

He saw her coming out of the fish and chip shop with coat ruffled in the wind. Older women just could not resist his hard, young body. He saw her look at him. Now was the time, his first time. Despite that, he had never been more certain. He stepped forward; the excitement was making his muscles tremble in anticipation. He was already hard.

'You sharin' them chips, luv?'

As she rounded the corner at the top of the street, where she lived, she heard the footsteps behind her, only a hundred yards from home. Then she fell forward; she dropped the bag and the dinner. Her hands were grazed on the pavement. Lights exploded in her head as she was punched on the temple, and she felt herself being turned over. An oily hand covered her nose and mouth, and she gagged.

She felt her tights being ripped, and she kicked out, connecting firmly. But one of them was on top of her. He grabbed the hair on the top of her head, pulled her head forward, and banged it back against the pavement with a sickening crunch.

Maureen felt a sharp pain in her cheek, and she could feel the blows to her face,

'You sharin' anything?' The voice was rough with a thick Mancunian accent.

She could not struggle; her body would no longer obey her desire to fight. She knew her life was in the balance, and she wanted to scream and kick and bite, but she could not; she thought about her boy, Jack.

PART I

CHAPTER 1

MILTON KEYNES, 2011

THE ROOM WAS UNCOMFORTABLY WARM. The air conditioning was turned off, and there was no opening window. The light came from both the tubes overhead, which seemed to produce heat and light in equal measure, and the wall with the door, which was entirely glass, and which overlooked the reception area of Hanson LLP, the firm of solicitors who were hosting the meeting.

Glass jugs of water and short, fat, heavy glasses were spread around the light oak table, which was highly polished to demonstrate wealth and solidity. Files having disgorged their paper were scattered around most of the table in front of the two men and one woman sitting together on one side with two laptops whirring before them.

Alan Dawson was trying to remain focused. He was the barrister instructed by Surgical Defence Mutual, his two colleagues the solicitor, Jane Smailey, who had instructed him, and her client, Lee somebody or other from the insurer. Alan liked Jane and was planning to buy her a drink after the meeting, hopefully to celebrate an advantageous settlement, provided they could lose the ubiquitous Lee with his shiny suit and Dr Martens Air Wear shoes.

Why, **Dawson wondered,** *are all insurance people so abjectly devoid of any style, wit, or intelligence?* This was a case that should have been resolved years ago. It should never have reached this stage, one month before a final hearing and a settlement meeting, where the claimant's lawyer knows that you need to settle before a judge, who is bound to sympathise with a vegetable of a claimant and decides what you have to pay.

Despite all that, Dawson felt the meeting was going his way. They knew the surgeon who had treated the claimant was negligent. They knew he had not followed the prescribed procedure when removing the tonsils of the claimant, a twenty-eight-year-old mechanical fitter called Hayes. They knew the hospital had a poor record in maintaining the appropriate level of cleanliness. They knew it, but could the claimant's solicitors prove it?

In the most basic terms, Hayes had his tonsils removed with a blunt and dirty knife. He contracted an infection whilst still in recovery (either from the knife or some orderly who provided him with drinks from a less than spotless container) and two days after the operation was in the coma that kept him in suspended animation for nearly two years. When he did eventually come around, he could not walk, he could not go to the toilet without help. Cognitively, he was effectively a child and would remain so for the rest of his shortened life.

On the evidence of what they had seen so far, the answer to the question of whether the claimant could prove negligence was 'unlikely'. Dawson had made a nuisance offer of £40,000. Take this sum, and we won't cripple you with costs when it gets to trial, your client walks away with something (not literally in this case) and you get your costs paid, which was always the clincher, he felt, with claimant's solicitors.

His worst-case scenario settlement was £7.5 million, but there was nothing to suggest that the lawyer before him (Dawson disliked using that term for an unqualified legal clerk) had the wherewithal to persuade them to get anywhere near that sum.

On the other side of the table, with the whole length of the table to himself, sat one man; he appeared to be in his late twenties or early thirties. He had short hair, light brown and not really blond, thick and strong that stood on end apparently without the aid of any products. He was of medium height and build and had no papers, no water, just an iPad propped up like a mini lectern within its own black case.

He looked relaxed and confident, but Dawson assumed it was his bluff. He had a face that was difficult to read, quite a young face, round but not fat, a strong nose and grey eyes, cold eyes. He was not exactly handsome, but not ugly too. He had a heavy chest and shoulders, not overweight but not lean either. Dawson could see the veins in the backs of his hands, which suggested little body fat. He did not appear to have the charisma of a top lawyer; he should have employed a barrister who would have been more of a match for Dawson.

No, Dawson felt sure he would be having a nice, cool gin with Jane within the hour. Ryan Airwear, as he had privately dubbed the insurance clerk, could rush back to the office with the news of his savings, and Alex Harris would have to deliver the disappointing news to the Hayes family.

Across the table, Alex Harris looked closely at Alan Dawson and saw the damp look around his forehead—the distant look in his eyes. Dawson was losing concentration. Overconfident. Jane Smailey was sitting with her head buried in her laptop, hoping not to have to speak. The guy from the insurers, whose name he had forgotten or, to be more accurate, had never really allowed to sink in, was sitting smiling, almost worshipping Dawson. He would have nothing to add to this meeting.

He sat back in his chair, a standard light green meeting room chair that neither swivelled nor tilted. It was chosen, along with the others, to be hard and uncomfortable. What was the point of making yourself comfortable if you were supposed to be concentrating in a meeting? The senior partner of the firm, Christopher Hanson, did not like the idea of lengthy meetings that may eat into the chargeable time of his fee earners. Meetings were all very well provided they could be charged for. On this basis, all meeting rooms in the firm's well-appointed offices were Spartan. There was no pretentious artwork on the walls, like in many boardrooms throughout the legal profession. There was nothing to distract you from the job at hand.

Christopher would be happy with this meeting. It was all chargeable time for his most successful fee earner. Alex was the top fee earner in the firm every year without fail. Sitting in this meeting, he was £20,000 short of his annual target of £250,000 with six months to go to year end. When he settled costs on this case, which he would in the very near future, and without the need for the satellite litigation that insurers seemed determined to indulge in on all injury claims, he would exceed his target by almost £100,000 with most of the financial year to go. He would speak to Hanson regarding his plans for an extended winter break once the cheque came in. Any such request was always received with more sympathy when accompanied by a significant cheque.

Dawson was waiting for his answer. Like most barristers, he had this seemingly inbuilt confidence. Some people considered it arrogance, but Alex saw it as confidence— the ability to think quickly, to assess the strengths and weaknesses of your opponent and their case. The ability to persuade people that what you are telling them is fact, not opinion. Charisma.

Alex didn't have these skills. He had not had the benefit of years of training at the Bar. He had never even been to law school. What he did have was the gift of meticulous preparation, patience, fierce, feral intelligence, and an unquenchable desire to win—to beat the system, to triumph for the ordinary man over the unthinking or unfeeling establishment or rapacious corporate beast. It was a feeling that was never articulated, nor was it acquired; it was just hard-wired into a working-class lawyer.

Alex looked directly into the eyes of the barrister. 'Your offer is rejected. I hold instructions to make a formal offer under Part 36 of the Civil Procedure Rules to settle my client's claim for an all-inclusive figure of £7.5 million.' He paused to assess the reaction. Dawson was smiling trying to look amused and patronising with a slow shake of the head. Smailey was anxiously looking at Dawson and back to her laptop. The insurance boy, mouth open, vacant eyes.

'Plus costs of course,' he added with a smile.

'There is no reason for my client to even consider such a figure.' Dawson was still smiling. 'You have precious little evidence regarding liability for this tragic incident. We are confident that we can demonstrate to the court that my client's took all necessary precautions and that this was just an unfortunate series of circumstances. Whilst we have sympathy . . .'

Whilst Alex Harris had the great attribute of patience in preparing a case; he felt that his main weakness was a temper that was liable to flare at the slightest provocation, that he struggled everyday to control. At the first sign of injustice, it raged within him. Over the years, as he started to mellow a little, he had begun to develop the ability to use this apparent loss of control to dramatic effect.

'Oh yes, Mr. Dawson, your client has so much sympathy for Johnny Hayes that they are attempting to right, royally fuck a broken, shattered man even though they have already taken his right to a normal life.'

Dawson was shocked. 'Your language is unbecoming of the situation, sir . . .'

Alex stood abruptly. The three on the other side of the table all flinched in unison. They had no idea what he was about to do. Dawson, recovering his equanimity, smiled inwardly. Harris had lost it, his composure and the case. Smailey was frightened. The raised voices shook her; she was not used to this sort of behaviour in her professional life. Insurance man looked at Dawson for guidance on how to handle the situation.

Alex pushed his iPad to the middle of the desk.

'Let's cut the crap. On there is my copy of the original report from your hospital's cleaning contractors. By original I mean the one that the chief executive of the Health Authority buried. You will also see the original statement from the anaesthetist, Rizwana Begum, the one taken by your insurer client one week after the incident, not the one filed at court. Finally, there are the operative notes, filled out by the consultant, signed by him. You will see that my copy of the notes has the full three pages, not just the two that your insurer client disclosed to me.'

Looks were exchanged.

'There is also a breakdown of my costs. I'm leaving the room for ten minutes to allow you time to confer with your client. If you cannot accept my offer and agree my costs, the meeting is over, and we will make our application to the judge to have these items included in the trial bundle. I am sure he will be interested to find out why they weren't there before.'

Alex turned to his right and walked purposefully to the door, yanked it open, and pulled it sharply behind him. The glass wall shuddered satisfactorily.

It was warm and close as Alan Dawson stepped on to the pavement, leaving the offices of Hanson. It felt like it might rain.

After Harris had left the room, he had looked at the iPad. The documents were all there. Of course he had warned his clients regarding the rules of discovery, but they had never believed that these documents would see the light of day. They had pre-planned the argument that they were just drafts and were privileged as a result, but when it came down to it, that would never wash. Besides, the complicity of Jane Smailey's client, in the actions of the chief executive, was enough to force a resignation if made public, and there was no way Jane wanted to go back to her firm and report that she had brought down the CEO of their primary insurance client's biggest policyholder.

The discussion was short. Airwear wanted to try to knock them down on the offer and do a bit of bartering; Jane wanted to pay and leave as quickly as possible. Dawson had to advise them both that they needed to protect their position. The best they could hope for was a settlement on the claimant's financial terms but with a hastily drafted confidentiality agreement regarding the settlement. This was where Dawson earned his fee, thinking on his feet and drafting a watertight agreement and a court order asking the judge to approve the settlement in a matter of minutes.

Harris returned to the room; Dawson pushed the handwritten draft agreement over the table. Harris typed it up into the iPad and printed it from the printer on the receptionist's desk. It was signed; Harris handed it to the receptionist and instructed her to send it to the court by fax. It was all over in minutes, none of them spoke to each other. As they trooped through the door, which Alex Harris held open for them, he wished them all a safe journey, and as Airwear stepped on to the pavement, he heard Harris say, 'Nice suit.'

Dawson had always felt Milton Keynes was a barren, heartless place.

He turned to look back at Harris. 'My client will need to have original identification documents and bank account details for the payment. I assume the money is to be paid into a trust fund so if you could let Ms. Smailey have the details . . .'

'Yep!'

The door closed. They were left on the street. No taxis, no buses, just a long walk to the train station. Jane had already started calling the office, and Airwear was marching off down Silbury Boulevard towards the station. There was no point in asking Jane for a drink, that opportunity was now passed and, frankly, he wasn't sure of his chances now anyway.

He hiked his laptop bag high on to his shoulder and began his purposeful march towards the station. The pavement was away from the road. All the buildings were surrounded by parking, which was between the pavement and the dual carriageway. All the paths ran under the roads on the infamous grid system using a series of underpasses. Dawson had been to Milton Keynes a number of times. Despite the underpasses and the wide 'boulevards', people just didn't walk here. The new town was designed for the car, and everybody here embraced the principle.

The trees, planted in regimented fashion down the middle of the dual carriageway, were starting to sway in the stiffening breeze, like the crowd at some pop concert, with arms high in the air. It did feel like rain.

On the bright side, he would be home early that night.

Manchester.

Duncan sat at his desk. There was light drizzle outside. The city was starting to reawaken, little by little, as the rush hour approached. Everybody was cramming into buses and cars and crawling out of the suburbs. Leaving the city centre were the evening revellers. Manchester was always moving.

The young professionals, the young trades people, the young tourists would be hitting the city that evening for a long weekend of nightclubs and bars. They mingled in the city centre, where there used to be alehouses and the ubiquitous 'blob shop', and there were now slick themed bars selling coloured alcopops to the masses.

The blob shop, for the uninitiated, was the poor working-class forerunner of the wine bar. Yate's Wine Lodge, a whole string of them throughout the northwest, but in unbelievable density around Manchester, was a spit and sawdust affair. There were no tables and chairs, a long bar behind which were various wines, some of them served hot, all of them able to rot the guts of a factory fitter. Each serving was called a blob—a serving, not a glass. There were no glasses in the blob shop. You went to the blob shop for one reason—to get pissed, not just drunk, pissed, arseholed. The people who went there varied. The primary customer was the homeless tramp who could rustle up thirty pence for a hot blob on a wet winter's night; who would sit on the floor in the gob and the dust.

You had the young lads and apprentices who could not afford a night of serious drinking in town, so had to get 'trolleyed' for a few quid before heading into the proper clubs, where the drinks were outrageously priced and weak as cat's piss.

Later in the evening, it would be the serious drinkers who were running short of cash and were not nearly as anaesthetised from their tough, miserable working-class lives as they wanted to be before picking up a steak pudding and chips on the way back to a grumpy missus.

But the blob shops were now gone. The working classes no longer wanted their own, suitably priced venue. They wanted to appear to be upwardly mobile and sophisticated. They wanted what they thought the upper and middle classes had. They didn't realise that they were still drinking in their own environments and that the people whose apparent style they aped had moved on into the hotels and bistros. They were paying higher prices to drink in a blob shop disguised under leather and chrome.

Duncan took a swig of tea from the plastic cup on his desk. It was vile. He continued typing up his report which he was able to do whilst gazing out of the window over the Manchester City Centre skyline towards Salford.

Another busy weekend on the way—groups of drinkers in town, special constables (not full-time policemen) were wandering around in groups of two or three, hoping their presence would keep the party people on the straight and narrow. It was a much less violent city than it had once been. It had always been hard. Like any industrial conurbation, people worked hard and played hard and fought hard. In the poorer areas, there had always been fights and fist fights when he was a lad. Now it was all knives and guns, and a fist fight seemed out of fashion.

Back then, Friday night would mean a plenty flare-ups, scores settled, and friends made and lost—violent but in a far more acceptable way. He didn't like the new way with weapons instead of heart and sinew. Now the cowards and weaklings could win because they had the guns. In his day, you respected a man who would fight his way through the weekend. Now you avoided him because he was most likely an inadequate, who needed a weapon to steal fear as a substitute for respect.

Those were the people Duncan enjoyed putting away. Those were the people who he knew would suffer in Strangeways Prison, where the hard men of old still preyed on those who lost their bravado when the guns and knives were confiscated.

He had been working in the Crime Squad for more years than he cared to remember—two marriages worth. He knew he was a good copper in the old tradition. The odd favour was gratefully received from the odd character, but to the real villains in Manchester, he was a nightmare. He was only thirty-five, and his body was still lean and fit, naturally so, as he was not much of an athlete. His dark hair was thick and cropped short, but his face was lined and drawn, making him look older than he was. He had strong features; his eyes were a little deep-set but a straight angular nose and high cheekbones. Two creases ran vertically down his cheeks, like crevasses, highlighting the lack of body fat.

As a chief inspector, he got the good cases. Violent crime, organised crime, murder; if it happened in the city centre, it would cross his desk at some point.

Once this report was finished, and another cup of tea downed, he would look at the new case—a man found beaten to death in Canal Street, the centre of the city's gay community.

He was found by a gay couple heading out for an early breakfast. He was wearing a T-shirt and jeans, no shoes and had apparently been carrying a bag of chips. Duncan's interest was piqued—chips and no shoes.

Alex sat back in his office chair, tilted slightly so that he looked up at the window set high in the wall. He always told people he was like the Bird Man of Alcatraz. His office was like a cell with just the small window that a person couldn't fit through at a height that meant all you could see out of it was a small square of sky.

He pushed a button on the phone on his desk and the ring tone boomed out of the speaker.

'Hello.' The voice was female.

'Diane, it's Alex.'

'Hello, Alex love, how are you today?'

'I'm good, Diane. We had our meeting today, Diane, the settlement meeting. I've got an offer, and to be honest, I've already told them we will take it.'

'That's all right, love, you know we trust you and you know we don't have a clue what it's worth, so if you say it's a good offer that's good enough for me.'

Alex smiled. 'Diane, you are the client from heaven, you know that, don't you? Look, I'm going to need Johnny's passport, driving licence, any proof of ID for the other side so we can get a trust set up. The money will be paid in, and you will be able to draw on it to provide for Johnny. It will provide an income to keep you and him comfortable for the rest of his time.'

'That's great, love. I haven't a clue where that stuff is. I don't think Johnny has a passport. I put all that stuff away when it was obvious he wouldn't be needing it again. I'll have a look at the weekend, and I'll pop it down to the office for you.'

'That's great, Di, thanks.'

'OK, Alex. Will you be popping down to see Johnny? He likes your visits.'

'Yeah, there's loads of paperwork to be sorted out yet, and I'll need loads of your autographs yet. You will be sick of the sight of me soon.'

He could hear the smile in her voice. 'That's great then, just give me a call before you come. I'll see you soon, Alex.'

'Diane? You still there? Diane . . .'

He disconnected the call and let out a short laugh that turned heads outside his office. Shaking his head, he said to himself, 'She didn't even ask how much.'

Alex got up and walked to the south side of the building to the corner office. Christopher Hanson sat in the spacious room behind a large modern desk. He had a large head on a formerly athletic body ruined by good wine and cheese. Silver hair swept back; he looked more like an ageing beach bum in a suit than a senior partner in a law firm and a deputy district judge.

Alex opened the door and sat opposite the Silver Surfer, as the staff liked to call him, when he was out of earshot.

'Come in, Alex, I'm not too busy.' Heavy sarcasm was standard.

'You want to know this, Chris, so I assumed you wouldn't mind me interrupting your MI reports.'

Hanson ran his practice like a well-oiled machine constantly checking the management information produced by his practice management software. It was what kept him as profitable as he was. Some people said he wasn't a great lawyer, but the truth was he had been a superb lawyer. But the thrill of running the business had overtaken his love of the law.

'Is it about money?'

He hadn't looked up. Alex paused and waited for the glance that he knew was coming, then gave up waiting.

'I've settled the Hayes case and got my costs agreed.'

Hanson looked up from his screen. 'And?'

'And I've got him a fucking brilliant settlement. He's set for life now and . . . ,' Hanson interrupted.

'The costs, Alex, what are the costs?'

This time when Alex paused, he knew he had Hanson's full attention. '117,000.' Hanson was smiling. 'Plus VAT and disbursements, that's a 117 grand net, Chris. How many more ivory backscratchers will you and your partners buy with that?'

Hanson laughed. He could accept the occasional acerbic barb from the man who did more to keep him in ivory backscratchers than anyone else.

'Well done that man. I might even buy you a pint unless I can interest you in a more civilised drink. I think we should take the team out to celebrate this evening. It's not every day we get a result like this. Get them organised for five-thirty, my treat.'

Alex got up as Hanson picked up his phone. He closed the door as Hanson was speaking to the firm's accountant. *He didn't even ask me how much Johnny got,* he thought.

'What do you think? Shall we up the game?'

The older man looked at his watch; it was nearly time for the car to collect him. He had given up driving two years ago. A minor heart complaint gave him the excuse he was looking for to get a driver. Dainius was a good driver but a better bodyguard. Six foot four of hard Lithuanian muscle plucked from the numerous eastern Europeans who drove the trucks that made him a wealthy man.

He spoke quietly, a soft, gentle voice with the faintest of Irish lilts.

'If he's as good as you tell me, Ryan, is he the right person for what we want?'

'He's exactly right, Dad, he's into the money big style. I know him and his type. Besides, his boss will come to rely on the money we make them, so it's not just his choice.'

Another glance at the watch, a quick view of the yard outside—grey and wet—it was time for him to get out. He had been here too long. Another six months and the business would be ready to hand over to his son, and the cash would be transferred to his account. He would retire to the sunshine, the house in Nassau was nearly built; it should all come together nicely.

'OK. Get in touch, sound him out but be careful. I don't want anything to slow down my plans.'

He got up and walked around his desk, took his cashmere overcoat from the old rack in the corner, and shrugged into it. He was heavily built, broad in the shoulder, and barrel-chested. He still looked relatively fit for his advancing years, and the black hair dye at his temples helped. He opened the door into the anteroom with his enormous hands with thick manual worker's fingers. His secretary was sitting, tapping away on the keyboard before her.

'Dainius is outside, sir. I called your wife to say that you are on the way.'

'Thank you, Dawn. I will see you next week. I want to know if we hear anything from Piotr or Davis, but just text me.'

He strode into the yard, where the Mercedes was waiting, engine running with Dainius in the driver's seat. He opened the rear door and settled in the back seat. The newspaper was on the back seat, and the headline in the *Manchester Evening News* was about a man being beaten to death outside a gay club in the city centre. He felt a little uncomfortable. Of course the car was luxurious and had every extra imaginable. It was not that. It was just that memory, buried deep, that had just stirred from a lengthy slumber. He didn't like it. He didn't want any connections to the past, not that part of his past anyway. Not when he was so close to getting out.

As the Mercedes pulled out of the yard and into the early evening traffic, the feeling melted away as his thoughts turned to the reception this evening and his meeting with the delegation from Germany. If they got the contract, the business would be set for the next ten years, and they could phase out the business in the Balkan states and

Ireland and concentrate on the legitimate side of things, and he would finally be free—six more months.

The rain came as the car headed towards his Cheshire home and one of his fleet passed in the opposite direction. 'Frank Maguire, King of the Road' it said on the side of his truck.

Manchester 1991

Maureen lay still. She was cold, icy cold. It crept up through her fingers, and it started to spread through the forearms, past her elbows, leaving a hopeless numbness behind it. She knew it would reach her heart, and she knew that when it did, her time was up.

She was a fighter though, and she always had been. She had fought every day of her life to make it better, and she would fight now for the sake of her boy.

The ice was still moving, gripping her upper arms and shoulders. She tried to move herself but nothing seemed to be responding. She wanted to prop herself up on her elbows and the thought was transferred to the arms, but they remained motionless clutched around her head. She was feeling the ice in her toes, and she could feel she was in foetal position, but she was unable to stretch her legs out to allow herself to roll over.

She could hear herself whimper, almost a sob. She had to get through this and had to get back to her boy. How would he manage with just his father?

Anger flared in her. His father was strong, violent, and hard, but where was he when she needed him most? How could he care for the boy?

Maureen could hear voices. They seemed to be far away. Had they come back? Panic rushed through her; an irresistible desire crept in her mind to get up and run—run back to her home, be safe, keep her boy safe.

It must have been the rush of adrenaline that made her roll over on to her back. She felt the viscous liquid run down the back of her neck and was comforted by the warmth. She couldn't really see where she was. There were shapes, but it seemed like a misty film of cloud had descended over the estate, and it was hard to make out the buildings. It was getting darker and darker, and the voices were getting nearer.

Why would they come back? They had taken everything she had—everything she could give them and more besides. She felt herself getting up. She was almost standing, kneeling on one leg and pushing herself up with the other. It suddenly seemed as though all her coordination were restored. She was moving freely; her mind was clearing; her sight was restoring itself. It seemed the weather was brightening; it was getting warmer, and the sun was breaking through.

Maureen was on her feet. She had no shoes on but that didn't bother her; she seemed to be running on lush grass. Her body movements were fluid, and she felt strong. The voices were right behind her, but she was in flight and felt she could outrun anybody. She had never moved with such power and control. She lifted her head and increased her speed even more. She was elated, almost laughing. The breeze in her face made her eyes water, but she was running so fast the tears ran off in streak horizontally towards her ears before flying away off her face in the warm air.

She would make it home to her boy and everything would be fine; she was stronger than ever, and she would take him away and make him into the man she knew he could be. She kept running.

The two men approached the stricken woman. She was on her back; she had no shoes on, and her coat was open. Her dress pushed up around her waist, and she was naked beneath. Her hosiery ripped in tatters around her ankles. Her eyes were open but glazed and unseeing, but she was breathing in short gasps; her chest was rising and falling rapidly. Her face was bruised and bloody; she had what appeared to be a hole in her cheek, which was covered in blood and gaping flaps of jagged skin around it.

There was a spreading pool of dark red blood forming a grim halo around the back of her head. Her lips were thick and bloodied; her neck was red and raw. Her fingers and toes twitched constantly.

'Jesus Christ, it's Maureen from over't road, run home, son, and call the police and an ambulance. Get your mum to come and give us an'and.'

The younger man set off immediately. His father took off his old overcoat and placed it carefully over Maureen.

'God love, what happened? Who did this to you?'

Her breathing seemed to get quicker; her twitching was more pronounced. He sat on the ground and took her hand, which he held in his calloused workman's palm, covered by his other rough mitt. He held her like this for what seemed like hours but was, in reality, just a few minutes.

She was cold and her fingers still twitched. He looked up at the sound of running footsteps and saw his wife with a clutch of the neighbour's and his son. In the distance, he could hear the wail of a siren, and he wondered if they would make it in time. She seemed to be fading fast.

'Hold on, Maureen love, help's on the way, just hold on.'

Maureen was running freely; she felt warm and happy. The voices were louder now but indistinct. But she was not afraid. They were reassuring sounds, comforting. It felt like the sun was out; it was bright, although she was just sensing this as she was running with her eyes closed. She would soon be back to her boy.

Tommy was in the pub The Wordsworth, named after either the poet or the street it was situated on; he wasn't really sure and didn't really care. His pint of Boddingtons Bitter was nearly finished. The Wordsworth didn't serve the best pint, but it wasn't the worst. *Time to head home for tea any road,* he was thinking. His mood was turning, irritated by the youngsters in the bar, for they were boisterous and disrespectful. Now wasn't the time to take them outside for a lesson in manners. He had done that before and was treated with respect and no small amount of trepidation by the teenagers on the estate as a result but not tonight.

It was the lads from the fairground family, coming in the pub, eating chips bought from the chip shop across the road. They were loud and laughing. The old chaps moved from the bar to the tables to keep out of their way. They shouted at the barman for service. They wouldn't get much change out of Terry with that sort of behaviour, and Terry was more than capable of sorting them out without Tommy's help. Terry had been a paratrooper, and he could certainly handle himself.

Tommy saw old Bill Jones and his son, Little Bill, who stood a good six feet four, slip out of the door with a disdainful glance back. He took a long swig of his beer and put the empty glass down on the table. A quick leak and off home; he should time it right so he was back just before the wife. Time to get the plates warm and a cuppa on, show her he was trying.

When he came out of the toilets, the taller of two youngsters was banging on the bar, demanding service whilst Terry had his back turned, looking over the frosted glass at a flashing blue light outside. As he walked behind the lads towards the door, Tommy saw that it was a woman's shoe that he was hammering on the bar, holding the toe and hitting the flat heel on the wooden bar top. Terry turned back to the bar; he didn't look happy.

A good time to get out, **thought Tommy,** *before it all kicks off.* Anyway, he wanted to get home before Maureen.

CHAPTER 2

MILTON KEYNES, 2011

ALEX LOOKED AROUND FOR JULES. The team was all there; Christopher was holding court with a clutch of the younger fee earners, all keen to be on friendly terms with the big boss. He didn't blame them. Christopher was a charismatic speaker and everybody seemed to want to be around him. It was one of the reasons Alex had been persuaded to join Hanson's.

There was another group of his team at the bar, three young men who rebelled against the team ethos. Alex called them his 'irregulars' borrowing the term from Conan Doyle. Good fee earners one and all but negative and fractious. Had they been working in industry, he could easily imagine each of them as a Trotskyist shop steward.

The young girls from the team were seated at one of the tables or rather two tables pushed together. The pub was large with lots of light, open spaces, and almost entirely glass, other than the wall behind the long bar. The high ceiling was curved so that from the outside it looked like a huge wave—for the Silver Surfer perhaps.

Jules stood behind the girls in the team, talking to one of the employment lawyers. She wore a fitted dark blue suit that accentuated her slim, athletic figure. She was the least sporty person Alex had ever met, and he doubted she had ever set foot in a gym, yet she looked like an Olympian.

She was not as tall as people thought; high but discreet heels and a towering intellect gave the impression that others often categorised as Amazonian. Her black skin was flawless and her cut-glass English intimidating for many. Alex, however, knew she was from Wolverhampton and that the accent was the result of many years' elocution lessons that her father felt would be an essential part of his West Indian family's success in integrating into England.

He tried to catch her eye. He was ready to head home, but they could not just leave together. Their relationship was a secret in the office, and he preferred to keep it that way. He did not want personal relations with him to hold her back. She was on the verge of an equity partnership and had made significant progress in her commercial litigation practice. He had helped her by introducing her to a former client of his who happened to be the chief procurement executive of a large manufacturing company, and their growing business had led to a boom in litigation. He did not want that connection to diminish her chances or water down her achievements. She was a top-notch lawyer, but she was too shy when it came to marketing or self-advancement.

He was debating heading to the toilet to text her when she looked up and gave an almost imperceptible nod. He walked to Christopher and made his excuses, can't hold his drink, early start, etc. He waved his goodbye to the Irregulars, left the bar, and turned left on to Midsummer

Boulevard walking towards the huge shopping centre, which was deserted by now, closed for the evening.

When he reached the crossroads with Saxon Street, he turned left walking through the car park in front of the Church of Christ the Cornerstone with its dome lit up and the columns of its entrance giving off a milky whiteness in the bright moonlight. The church was the epitome of what a modern cathedral should look like, only it was not a cathedral as Milton Keynes was not yet a city and possibly never would be.

There was a time when the dome was the highest building in the town. When it was built in 1992, the council at the time had intended for it to stay that way as some sort of a religious statement. Subsequent councils, however, were tempted by the offers to build big hotels and the Xscape building, a huge slug-shaped glass monolith that tapered away at the rear, which housed a cinema, numerous bars, restaurants, and shops but, primarily, the real snow ski slopes.

Alex wondered whether the eclipsing of the church by an indoor ski slope was a metaphor for religion in the new town and the country as a whole. He was not especially religious and thought the idea more pretentious than profound and had a quiet laugh at himself.

When he reached Silbury Boulevard, he waited before the underpass to the modern shopping centre, which was the central focus of the town. Once the largest covered shopping centre in Europe, it had since been eclipsed by many of the 'out of town' shopping malls in the United Kingdom. It is, however, still a busy thriving centre, and it is firmly placed at the epicentre of the town's well-known grid system of roads and walkways.

When he had moved to the town, the shopping centre had been unlike anything he had seen before, but as a whole, Milton Keynes had been like a ghost town. Nobody really lived in the town centre, except those, like Alex, who were given small, cheap, low-rise flats to rent by the then Milton Keynes Development Corporation. The bulk of the population lived, and still does, in housing estates shielded from the main transport arteries by trees and wide verges. Unless you knew where you were going, you would be hard pushed to find a residential house as a stranger to the town.

The only centre for entertainment had been the glass pyramid called 'The Point'. Now the town had a theatre district, a restaurant area known as The Hub as well as the Xscape Building. It was a busy, youthful town commercially successful and full of ambition. It wanted its city status. It had even hijacked a professional football team from South London and relocated them in a new stadium and with a new name, MK Dons.

Alex had hated the sterile town when he first moved here but now loved the convenience of it all, the cleanliness and the business-oriented set-up of the town. It was a town designed for the motor car in the 1960s but with the foresight to provide miles of pedestrian and cycle paths, known as redways, which crisscross the grid of the road system and allowed safe travel for the green-minded individual who did not mind arriving to work with a bit of a sweat on.

The town still looked incredibly modern, and the continued expansion showed that both residents and business agreed with Alex. The town was situated between the M1 motorway and the ancient Roman road, the A5, which was now a modern dual carriageway. Both roads headed to the heart of London, as did the rail link, which had you in the capital in thirty-five minutes—all this in the middle of the beautiful Buckinghamshire countryside.

A blue BMW pulled up in the car park and the central locking clunked as the doors were unlocked from the inside. Alex walked over to the car and opened the front passenger door. It shut with a satisfying thud, and Jules put the car in gear and headed on to the dual carriageway.

Five minutes later, the car was in front of the ground floor garage of the three-storey townhouse in Campbell Park, just to the east of the shopping centre.

Alex and Jules settled on the sofa with coffee, soft classical music playing on the Bose sound system driven by Alex's iPhone.

'Christopher says you are off to Manchester for the MASS Conference,' Jules almost whispered. 'Will you go and see him?' MASS was the acronym for the Motor Accident Solicitors Society.

'No.'

'You should think about it. He is not getting any younger.'

'No. There is nothing to think about.' Alex drained his cup and got up.

'Time for bed.' And he was gone up the spiral staircase, leaving Jules curled up on the sofa. She would give him five minutes to calm down and then slip in beside him. She worried about him and his refusal to confront his past.

She did not know what lay there, which was probably just as well.

Alex lay in bed. Sleep would come to him soon. He knew Jules would join him in a few minutes, and he hoped he was still awake. He wished he could tell her everything about his past. He wished he had never told her anything.

He knew they had reached that point in their relationship where he had to share himself totally, but the thought that it might end it all paralysed him. He could never find the right time. He could never build up the courage to put his life in her hands. He had spent nearly all of his life alone, not physically but mentally—a solitary existence. His innermost thoughts and feelings firmly locked away, too dangerous to share.

But Jules had slowly worked her way in. It had been a purely physical attraction in the beginning. She was so exotic and exciting. She was the coolest person he had ever met. Not in the California sense of cool, but in the English way, detached and aloof. She was a challenge that he could never be sure he had ever conquered. Even after she had finally given herself to him, he felt that there was a part of her he didn't quite reach.

He suspected she realised the same of him. They had both, after that first time, been explicit about their physical desires, and they both found themselves completely compatible. Intellectually they were well matched. He felt that she was more considered and analytical than he, qualities he admired. She found his self-confidence and worldliness filled the gap in her own psyche. He could be rash and spontaneous, both good and bad traits. She was reserved and cautious, both in a positive and negative way. Together they balanced each other out. He often joked that together they made one really good person, adding, with a smirk 'with a great tan'.

He knew all about her childhood. He had met her parents last year. The pride in their daughter was obvious. Winston and Rose Everett had sacrificed a lot to have Juliette educated privately, and she was repaying them handsomely with her success. There was no sign of any disappointment in his appearance as the first boyfriend she had ever introduced them to, although Alex was sure that they had probably hoped for a surgeon or a politician. But they were good people, and he admired them both, and they had welcomed him into their home unreservedly.

There lay the difference. Alex had never taken Jules back to his home town. He never denied having a family, but he never spoke of them, and the thought of introducing her had never really been considered. He liked his life now, as it was, and had no desire to go back, even for a short visit, to his past.

He heard the dishwasher open and close and knew she would be with him shortly. He thought about his father. He had told her he was alive but that they didn't get along, but no more. He considered going to see him and decided against it. The past, as he had once read, was a different country, and to Alex, like Australia, it seemed to be too far away to make it worth the trip.

He heard her footsteps on the stairs. He rolled over to the cold side of the bed; he liked to warm her side. He watched her slip out of her skirt and blouse; her feline movements were arousing him. When she was naked, she slipped in beside him, and they embraced.

'Why don't we have a go at making that one person?' He smiled.

'Well, we should at least practice for it . . .'

CHAPTER 3

MANCHESTER

DUNCAN LEFT THE POLICE HEADQUARTERS on Bootle Street. Based just off Albert Square by the magnificent gothic town hall, Bootle Street had been police HQ since it was built in the 1930s. It was always known as Bootle Street Station even though the grand Portland stone facade was on Southmill Street. Bootle Street, a narrow side street, ran at right angles to Southmill Street, down what appeared to be the side of the Regency style building. The impression that this was the side of the building was confirmed by the fact that, other than the facade on Southmill Street, the rest of the building was constructed in a dull, uninspiring brick. Yet it remained commonly known as Bootle Street Station.

Once on Bootle Street, you would find the huge archway halfway down the building, leading into the open square in the middle of the construction. You could drive straight through to the other archway on Jacksons Row, if it was open both ends. Duncan left from the Bootle Street arch and turned left up to Southmill Street.

Bootle Street had been replaced as HQ for Greater Manchester Police by a modern, purpose-built building in Old Trafford, just near the Manchester United football ground, a few miles outside the city centre. But Duncan felt lucky to be one of the detective team left behind, working the city centre almost exclusively. He liked the character of the old building—the imposing nature and the almost military impression given by the cavalry barracks' appearance of the arched courtyard.

In addition, it was right in the heart of the city. From the front door on Southmill Street, you could look left and see the circular Central Library, also built of Portland Stone, with the Town Hall just behind.

To the right, you could look towards Peter Street, where the old Free Trade Hall had been before it was ripped apart behind the facade, which remained, and turned into a modern and characterless hotel. He had never understood how such a historically important building was allowed to be gutted and, but for one wall, replaced. The first suffragettes held their meetings in the Free Trade Hall, and it was central to the birth of Trade Unionism. It had long been the home of classical music in the city. When he was a youngster, his school had held its annual prize-giving ceremonies known as 'Speech Night' there, and he had a fondness in his heart for the old place.

It was literally a few minutes' walk to the main shopping streets of Deansgate and Market Street and the upmarket boutiques and bars of St Anne's Square and King Street West. Castlefield, with its renovated mills and warehouses converted into apartments for the upwardly mobile, was just to the west. The quiet backstreet had everything on its doorstep.

The weather was typical—windy, a few spots of rain, dull. Duncan walked to Peter Street, turned left, and up to Oxford Road. He passed the cinemas and turned left on to Portland Street and carried on down to the junction with Princess Street, where he turned right and headed towards Whitworth Street. After a short distance, he turned left on to Canal Street by the New Union pub. Canal Street was now mainly pedestrianised and took its name from the adjacent Bridgewater Canal.

Canal Street was the heart of what Manchester called its 'Gay Village'. It was nothing like any village Duncan had ever seen being mainly surrounded by modern apartments or converted mills. On a fine summer's day, one could almost believe you were at a canal side cafe in Amsterdam, overlooking the locks on a pleasant tree-lined avenue. Almost. But there were precious few fine summers days that Duncan could remember.

Duncan could see the crime scene ahead of him, a small white tent surrounded by blue and white police tape. Two uniformed officers were at the southern end of Canal Street, and they stepped aside when he produced his warrant card.

He ducked under the tape and looked back up the street. Early in the morning, when the body was found, he felt sure there would be clubbers and revellers around. The nightlife in the Gay Village was certainly lively and the clubs and bars were teeming most nights of the week. Last night had been a Thursday, but even so, Duncan knew it would be busy.

He stuck his head inside the tent and saw three people in white overalls, hoods pulled up, oversize goggles, and gloves. They looked like they were investigating some sort of viral outbreak, and he half expected one of them to be Dustin Hoffman.

'You took your time. Body's gone, mate, went hours ago.' The tallest of the three spoke in a Liverpudlian accent.

'Hi, Jim, what can you tell me?'

'White male, aged about twenty-four, Steven Redford, born in Blackley, still living there, well, not now obviously with his mum and dad, had a Transport Workers Union card in his wallet but no bank cards. Severe head wounds, massive trauma to the back of the head, likely cause of death between one-thirty and two-thirty in the morning. Road was dry under the body, so we can be pretty precise. No defence wounds obvious at first glance. He had a cigarette burn on his left cheek by the look of it, but we will take a closer look at that, not run of the mill. We are looking for the shoes and scouring connecting streets for his chips. He had one in his hand and one in his mouth, so we assume a bag of chips was taken from him, other than that, nothing else at the moment.'

'Cheers, Jim, who's door knocking, is it Drew?' Drew was Detective Sergeant Terry Drew. Duncan worked with him a good deal and tolerated him. Thorough and humourless, Drew was an excellent second in command but was unlikely to lead his own investigations. His lack of imagination and his dour personality would make him a poor leader. He might be chief constable one day though.

'Yeah, laughing boy himself. He is off frightening the Indians.'

'OK, I'll call him, get hold of me on my mobile when you have more, see you back at the ranch.' Duncan ducked back out of the tent and heard a 'yes keemo sabi' behind him as he headed back towards Oxford Road.

Along with Drew, he would have Lynn Melbourne and Steven Miles on his team. He typed a group text to arrange a meeting for 5.30 back at Bootle Street. Lynn confirmed that she would be back from Blackley by then, Miles acknowledged with a 'yep', and Drew sent a 'yes, Boss'.

Duncan regretted walking the half mile to Canal Street when the heavens opened above him. He flagged down a Taxi whose driver couldn't hide his disappointment at the request to return him the short journey to the Peter Street and who was even less impressed to be asked for a receipt, tut-tutting audibly as he scribbled almost illegibly.

As Duncan was going back through the doors of the station, he already knew which file he would be reading for the next couple of hours. He had read it many times before.

He knew they would eventually find the shoes when the bar reopened. He had watched Duncan arrive and then scurry away. He hoped he was receptive to the message he was sending. Things would be a lot easier if he was.

He put on his shirt—silk, very expensive. He liked expensive clothes.

The trousers were Versace, black; black suited him, matched his hair. He looked at himself in the full-length mirror. *A boxer's physique,* he thought. He smiled at the reflection and winked.

He turned back to the bed. She was on her back, hands tied to the bedpost with a scarf, together above her head. Her thick red hair spilt over her face and on to her shoulders. She was naked, of course. Her heavy, pendulous breasts were now flattened by gravity. Her soft, rounded stomach looked white in the morning light. With wide hips and large thighs, she was a real woman.

She turned her face away from him when she realised he was looking at her. He knew she wanted him. She had wanted him last night, despite her protests. He could always tell. They all want a young, virile man—the stronger, the better.

He had demonstrated just how strong he was.

As her face turned, he saw her right eye was closed and already purple. He reached into the pocket of the designer trousers and pulled out his wallet, throwing crumpled notes on the bed.

He slipped on his Kurt Geiger loafers and left closing the bedroom door quietly behind him.

CHAPTER 4

MANCHESTER, 1991

TOMMY SAT DOWN ON THE floral print sofa. A cup of tea was pushed into his hands, but he did not seem to acknowledge it. The police constable had asked him questions about where he had been and who had seen him there, but Tommy was not really listening. Bill Jones vouched for the fact that Tommy was still in the Wordsworth when he and his son left. This seemed to satisfy the constable.

Bill's wife was busying herself making cups of tea and reassuring noises. Tommy stood and made for the door, putting his tea down on the glass and chrome coffee table. Bill stepped into his path.

'You can't go yet, Tom. They've not finished with you. Besides, your lad will be home in a minute, yer don't want him finding out from a stranger, do yer?'

It was then that they heard voices outside. The front door exploded inwards, and there was the boy. He was fifteen now, not as tall or as heavily built as Tommy but athletic, like a middleweight to Tommy's light heavyweight. His blond hair was long, shoulder-length and swept back— like a girl's hair, Tommy had said. He wore his school uniform but with the disdain borne of a rebel. Tie was crooked and a long way south of his collar and shirt was outside his trousers, which appeared to be black jeans masquerading as school regulation trousers. Jacket was ripped at the shoulder and the school crest was hanging by a thread to the breast pocket.

His eyes were wild, darting around the scene in his living room.

'What are you doing here, you didn't even go with her?' The accusation stung.

'Steady on lad, your dad wanted to go but the rozzers wouldn't let him,' said Bill.

'Who the fuck are you, get out the lot of you, just piss off,' he roared the last two words, making everybody in the house stop where they stood.

Tommy spoke for the first time since Maureen had been placed carefully in the ambulance. 'Jack, let's me and you go to the hospital, Bill will look after the place, we need to go and be with your mum.'

The constable took a step forward, and Tommy and Jack both turned to confront him. 'I'll er . . . get a car to take you.' He had calculated the path of least resistance and danger and turned his back on the two of them and began muttering into the radio on his tunic.

Tommy guided his son to the front door. A gaggle of neighbours were in the front garden and stood around the gate. All conversation stopped when the two of them came out of the door. A police car started up its engine across the street and switched on its blue lights as father and son crossed the street and got into the back of the car.

'How bad is it, Dad?'

'It's bad, Son, real bad.'

'They're saying it's them pikeys did it. They had mum's shoes in the pub. If it's them, I'll kill 'em.'

Tommy said nothing as the car squealed away from the kerb. He had seen them in the pub. He knew them, and he knew about them and their family. He had no anger in him, however. He could only feel his despair. What would he do now? How could he raise the boy? He had never cooked, never cleaned, and he had barely spoken to his son in the last four years and knew nothing about him.

He turned his head to the side and watched the traffic melt away as the police car sped towards the hospital.

When they reached the infirmary, Jack took up a seat outside the operating theatre. Tommy paced up and down the corridor slowly. Neither spoke. After two hours, they were ushered into a room, where a doctor told them that Maureen was alive but that she was unable to communicate. She would live for as long as they chose to keep her alive, but she had suffered such massive head injuries that she would never regain consciousness.

Tommy sat staring vacantly ahead. The doctor was not sure he had heard what was said. Jack cried uncontrollably. He asked if he could see his mum, and the doctor had a nurse show him through to where Maureen lay. Tommy watched him leave, then shut the door behind him and turned to speak to the doctor.

Jack sat with Maureen. He talked to her, pleaded with her to wake up, and begged her to come back to him; he talked about their future plans, how he would set his mum up in a semi-detached house in Cheadle. She had always wanted to live in Cheshire. He would make it happen if she would only come back.

Then he was still and quiet. Eventually he slept, emotionally spent.

When he woke, his father was in the room standing at the foot of the bed.

'It's time to say goodbye to your mum, Son.'

'No! Don't you touch her, don't you dare.'

'She's already gone, lad. I'm not having them drag this out. It's time to move on.'

'No. No, I won't let you do it. You've no right.' Tears were welling up; he was struggling to keep himself together. The desperation in his eyes was obvious to anyone; Tommy wasn't looking.

'Say goodbye. Then let's go home.' He turned and left.

Jack stood by his stricken mother's bed. He was struggling to comprehend what had happened. He just could not accept that he was about to lose the person in his life that he cared most about. He sat back down and took his mother's hand. He talked to her about holidays they would go on and about his football; she always wanted to know how he was getting on. He talked about his friend Joe. She had teased him about the time they spent together, how Jack spent all his time at Joe's house. She had gently mocked his schoolboy crush on Joe's elder sister. Jack asked his mum if he could bring Joe round for tea, Joe would be worried about her; she was like a second Mum to him, Joe had said.

The doctors and nurses arrived. Jack's one-sided conversation became more frantic. He rambled almost incoherently as his desperation grew. He was asked to leave for a few minutes, but he refused. He wouldn't let go of Maureen's hand, and eventually, they had to prise him free of her and physically restrain him in the corridor. He was coming apart; his mental grip on events was slipping away.

After a couple of minutes, they let him back in. They told him she would slide quietly and peacefully away, and he should comfort her.

The pain was too much for Jack to bear. He wailed and cried; he fought when they tried to remove him again. In the end, he slumped into the seat by the bed when he could fight no more. A nurse gave him a tablet, which he swallowed. He knew that sleep was coming again but that when he woke up, his mother would be gone. He held her hand and leant next to her and whispered in her ear.

Maureen felt happier. Her boy was with her. She could hear his voice. She couldn't quite make out the words; they seemed to be muffled, but she knew it was him. They were walking in the sunlight in a flowered meadow. There was a door, and it opened; she felt that it was time for her to walk through. But as she began to cross the threshold into the dark, she realised he was not coming with her. She panicked but couldn't call his name. He let go of her hand, and she was propelled into the abyss beyond.

Maureen seemed to be breathing harder—rasping, sharp breaths. As Jack began to slip into unconsciousness, he felt his fingers being squeezed hard and then released. She was gone. He let himself slip into a welcome oblivion.

Jack had been working hard at school. He had the odd run-in with the teachers. He was something of an outsider—the only kid off the council estate to make it to the grammar school in his year. When he got his exam results and confirmation of his scholarship, he was torn between delight at making his mum proud and despair that he would go to a school, where he knew nobody and where they played rugby rather than football.

He had known he was going to be technically good enough to play professionally even at eleven. He was just so much better than his peers. He played with lads of sixteen and seventeen and was not only strong enough but more skilful. He had all the tools he required, allied to a ferocious desire to succeed. He played every game in an almost blind fury, however, and rarely remembered anything but the score and his own highlights.

Whenever he got on to the pitch, he was gripped by the rising rage within him, fuelled by the adrenaline released by the excitement of the competition. It was common for his rage to get the better of him, and his football career was littered with dismissals for violent behaviour.

His lack of self-control was what would prevent him from making a living from the game, and at fifteen, he had already realised that. He could earn decent money being paid his 'expenses' by top level amateur clubs, but he would never reach the heights that his natural ability deserved.

Joe played with him. He was a good goalkeeper, but he didn't have the fire in his belly that would allow him to make the most of his talents. Joe enjoyed the game. Jack loved it, and it often pressed him into crimes of passion.

Joe was a calming influence on Jack. They were in the same class at school, but that was the only class they shared. Jack was from the council estate, Joe lived in a double-fronted Victorian detached house overlooking the park with its wrought iron bandstand and it's war memorial.

Joe was tall and wiry, affable, funny, but a deep thinker. Jack was impetuous, arrogant at times but quick-witted with a sense of humour like a bacon slicer. Jack didn't take prisoners, but Joe was never at war.

Joe liked his pop music and chart stuff mainly but also had a long-term relationship with The Smiths. They had the local connection, and he loved the dark humour of Morrisey's lyrics. Jack, however, liked his Ska music, both original and the eighties revival, and The Clash. He loved the music of the sixties and worshipped John Lennon and Hendrix.

Together they had a natural understanding of each other. They had fought, laughed, and cried together, but mainly, they laughed.

Joe was at home when he heard the news. A neighbour had called around to talk to his father about his tax problems. Joe's father was an accountant and often helped his neighbours, up to a point, with their financial issues. Whilst having a cup of tea, the neighbour had recounted the story of the woman, on the council estate, who was raped and murdered and how it had always been on the cards ever since they pulled all the people out of the slums of central Manchester and dumped them on their doorstep.

It was the mother of that lad who had trials with United.

Joe knew immediately it was Mrs. Ladd. Jack had never had trials with United, but he led people to believe he had and the myth was readily believed.

Joe was up straight away. He had to get to Jack. He couldn't imagine how this would hit him, but he was worried about what he might do. He grabbed a jacket and was off at a run, covering the ground quickly in long, lanky strides. It was two miles to Jack's house, but Joe covered the distance in no time. He was red-faced and out of breath when he knocked on the door.

The door opened on his second rap of his knuckles on the hard wood; it was as if Jack had been standing behind the door waiting for somebody to knock.

'You'd best come in.' His voice was thick, and his eyes red rimmed. Joe followed him in and straight up the stairs. Jack's room was at the front of the house, so it was straight up the stairs, which ran up the middle of the building, turn left. The room was a mess, clothes were everywhere. Under a mound of clothes was a bed apparently and Jack threw the clothes into a new pile and sat on the bed.

'We're mates, right.' Jack was abrupt. Joe was concerned.

"Course we are, Jack.'

'I'm gonna tell you what's gonna happen. I'm trusting you not to tell anyone, and I'm gonna need your help.'

'Help with what?'

Jack looked at his best and only real friend long and hard.

'I'd do anything for you, Joe, you know that. But I don't expect you to go as far as I'm going. I just want some help to disappear when I'm done.' His tone was even and flat.

'Done what, Jack?'

'I know who did it Joe, and I know exactly what they did. Little Bill told me everything. They saw them in the Wordsworth. They raped my mum and then went for a pint across the road. Right across the road, she lay there all mashed up . . . ,' Jack's voice was rising, and tears were dampening his eyes. He took a deep breath.

'Everyone saw them, Joe. Everyone. Nobody did anything and nobody's telling the filth what they saw cos their old man's put the fix in.'

'Jack, I don't know what you're on about.'

'It's the pikeys, Joe, them lot off the fairs. The two brothers did it and their dad has been offering folk money to keep quiet. Little Bill told me he'd been round to his dad, but you know what Big Bill is like, he told him to shove it. But the rozzers ain't listening to Bill and nobody else is coming forward.' He lowered his voice, and his eyes flashed in anger. 'Not even those who have nothing else to lose.'

Joe had no idea what that meant, but he was starting to get a picture of where the conversation was headed.

'Jack, two things—if you're thinking of doing what I think you are, you need to stop right now. First, the pikeys are hard. They're tooled up. Everyone knows they carry knives, Jack.'

'You know me, Joe. You know what I can do.'

Joe knew. He had seen Jack fight at close quarters. If they weren't such friends, Joe would be terrified of Jack. He had seen him break a grown man's arm, gouge out another's eye. He was there when he was attacked by two lads from a rival football team after a game. Jack had floored them both before Joe had realised what was happening. But what frightened Joe was that Jack wouldn't stop. He beat his attackers until Joe could get between him and them. Joe remembered the look on Jack's face that night and shuddered—fury, yes; anger, of course. However, it was the excitement that scared Joe. Jack was enjoying himself.

'But there's two of them, Jack. You can't take them both.'

'I can, but it will be easier to take them separately. What's the other thing?'

Typical of Jack; he seemed be making the most irrational of decisions but was still listening to advice and willing to consider all possibilities.

'If you do this, what happens after? Where do you go? How do you live and . . .' Joe paused and looked into his lap, ' . . . is it what your mum would want?'

Jack looked out of the window. It was grey and damp again. He seemed lost in thought, and Joe wondered whether to say anything else.

'Yes, she would want me to do this. But she would want me to get away. If I get away, I can start again.'

'Jesus wept, Jack, you're only fifteen. How will you live?'

Joe was seriously worried now. He could see that Jack had made his decision.

'Joe, thanks, mate, I'll get by. I will need a place to stay for a couple of nights, and if you could lay your hands on a few quid, that would be handy. I've got some but more would be better.'

Fuck. Joe realised he was duty-bound to help. Jack was like a brother, only closer.

CHAPTER 5

MANCHESTER, 2011

THE MIDLAND HOTEL IS SITUATED on Peter Street in Manchester, just around the corner from the Bootle Street Police Station but a world away. Whilst Bootle Street is a narrow seldom-used thoroughfare, Peter Street is one of the main streets in the city centre.

The hotel was originally built at the turn of the century and was opened in 1903 by the Midland Railway Company. It was situated next to Manchester's Central Station, subsequently the GMex indoor exhibition centre and arena, now Manchester Central Conference and Exhibition Centre, and was intended to capture business from the travellers using that busy terminus. At the time, Manchester was the centre and birthplace of the worldwide industrial revolution and the Midland was its prima hotel.

It's red brick Victoriana exterior, reminiscent in style of the Harrods department store in London, and is a Mancunian landmark. It forms part of the fabric and heritage of the city being inextricably linked with the time when Manchester was 'Cottonopolis' and one of the most influential and powerful cities in the world. It is the place, where Rolls first met Royce. Monarchs and presidents have all stayed at the Midland.

Alex Harris walked through the lobby of the hotel with its marble floors and dark columns to the Octagon Lounge, a remarkable room within a room, with dramatic high arches and, to his great relief, a well-stocked bar.

The conference had been uninspiring so far. The usual outrage at the government's desire to bend over for the insurance lobbyists' desire to ban solicitors' payment of referral fees or commissions for anyone passing over a claim and to either reduce solicitors' fees or, preferably, make it socially unacceptable for an injured party to even consider claiming compensation. As usual, it would be the little man and the independent law firms, not those who relied upon the insurance companies for their living, who would suffer from the government's proposals. All dressed up as an attempt to bring down the cost of insurance but without the insurance industry making any commitment to do so.

The beneficiaries would be the wealthy, the shareholders and directors of the insurers, many of whom, coincidentally, are in the government.

Alex made his way slowly to the front of the queue at the bar. As he was about to order, he was tapped on the shoulder. He turned to see Amrit Singh smiling and holding out a glass of white wine.

Amrit was an ENT consultant who had set up a medical agency in 1989 using his contacts in the profession to provide medico-legal reports to claimant solicitors. His business had grown exponentially. Solicitors realised it was far more cost effective to send instructions for a medical report to Amrit than to contact the doctor themselves. Insurers obviously railed against the cost but then realised that they too could use an agency and, even better, receive commissions from them due to the economies of scale they controlled.

Amrit kept his hand in as a surgeon but was now a businessman, the medical equivalent of Christopher Hanson.

Alex had used Amrit's company for many years and often met up with him at these conferences.

'Alex, here, have a glass on me. Come over here. I've got somebody who wants to meet you.'

Alex took the proffered glass, looking longingly back at the beer pumps.

'Ammy, look, I'm not really up for a marketing spiel. I've got plenty of work, and I'm not changing any of my suppliers . . . not unless they pester me with sales talks.' He winked as he said this.

'Alex, you will thank me for this. I've just made contact with the best client you could hope for, and he is keen, after my sales pitch, to meet with two or three firms I recommend. I recommended you, and they want to meet you.'

'Jesus, can't a bloke ever get a quiet pint.'

Amrit pulled Alex in close. 'Alex, this is big, don't piss about. If this goes well for you, I will have made you a millionaire, just because I like you. So don't give me any of your shit, OK.'

'Steady, Amrit,' Alex patted his arm and gave him a quizzical look. 'Who is it you want me to meet?'

'It's Steve Holland. He is a solicitor and barrister, and he works as in-house counsel for Maguire Transport.'

'Frank Maguire, King of the Road?' Alex looked shocked. Amrit felt pleased that the penny had dropped.

'That's right. They are effectively self-insured. They are looking for somebody to do their claims management, recovery of repair costs, business interruption when a wagon is off the road, injuries to the drivers. But that's not all. They want the same business to do their third-party assistance, traffic accidents, accidents at work, etc. I've told them you can do it, but I know you are not that big. Can you handle it? There is some cat work in there.'

Cat was the common abbreviation for catastrophic injuries—Alex's speciality. Third-party assistance was the now common practice of insurers contacting people who may claim against their policyholders and introducing them to a law firm, from whom the insurer received a referral fee. Despite the fact that they were effectively promoting claims against themselves, they worked out they were better off, as most claims were likely to come in anyway, so they might as well make a few quid off it. Independent solicitors called it third-party capture, rather than assistance, since unrepresented claimants, or those represented by the insurers' pet firms, had a tendency to receive less in damages, not surprisingly.

'If the government gets rid of referral fees, what is the benefit to them of third-party capture?' asked Alex.

'That's just it. The big man, Frank Maguire himself, is keen on being seen to be fair. He likes his man-of-the-people image. The fees are small and, if they do get banned, Frank will give the work for nothing.'

'Is he here? Do I get to meet him?' Amrit sensed anxiety in Alex.

'No, not yet. Come and meet Steve. Let's not put the cart before the horse, eh!'

Steve Holland was at least six foot four. He looked fit; he had a light suntan that complemented his blond, naturally curly hair. He had blue eyes, a thin nose with arched nostrils, and a thin mouth that invariably seemed to be fixed tightly shut. The combination of the shape of nose and mouth gave him the appearance of always having a distasteful smell around him. The skin, taut over his cheekbones, belied his ferocious exercise routine.

He was sitting in the French Dining Room, an opulently decorated room with circular tables and chandeliers, reminiscent of many a French palace and even more French restaurants. He was drinking mineral water and had a large coffee pot and minute cups laid out on the table.

He stood to greet Amrit and Alex as they approached, smoothing out his immaculate Yves Saint Laurent suit. He looked very much at home in these surroundings. Alex immediately thought that if he were an actor, he would be typecast as the evil SS officer. He just had that look.

'Alex, this is Steven Holland. Steven, Alex Harris from Hanson's. We talked about him earlier. Alex is very much the personal injury man at Hanson's.'

'Yes, Alex, I've heard a lot about you.' His voice was somewhere south of baritone with an indistinct southern accent, typical home counties.

'Nice to meet you, Steven, how is business.' They shook hands—two iron-like grips. Holland pressed his thumb down on the back of Alex's hand as they shook, a mason. Alex ignored the gesture. Holland appeared not to notice.

'Perhaps, before we talk business, you could tell me a little about yourself, Alex. We are a family business, and we like to get to know people before we invite them to become part of the family.' He gestured to a chair. 'Have a seat. Coffee?'

He started pouring, and Alex considered refusing just to see if he would take the coffee for himself. Before any answer could be given, the thimble of coffee was placed before him and another before Holland. Amrit looked around a little uncomfortably and then excused himself claiming to have just seen a possible business opportunity in the bar. Alex was impressed that Holland had the authority to dismiss Amrit so coldly, but, at the same time, took an immediate dislike to him for doing so.

'To be frank, Mr. Holland, if we are to manage claims against your employer, then we should never be considered part of the family. We will represent the claimant and his or her interests, and there could be no consideration of the interests of your company. Whilst we would be happy to enter into a referral arrangement, I would brook no interference or influence over the way in which we work, no agreements not to litigate, no discounted costs, no influence over medical experts other than what a court would ordinarily allow a defendant. If that is a deal breaker, then it's better to get it out in the open now, and you can pour coffee for somebody else.'

Holland laughed. 'That's not exactly the opening gambit I expected from somebody hopeful of getting a substantial amount of business, Alex,' he made a point of using first names, 'but I can see immediately that you are looking for exactly the type of relationship we are hoping for.'

He sipped at the steaming black coffee. 'Frank Maguire is an old-fashioned man. He comes from an underprivileged background. He feels the pain of the working-class man, and he wants somebody to right any of the wrongs that he may commit, vicariously, in the course of his business. If he wanted a lapdog, there are many of them here today, and they all have larger and better equipped organisations than yours.' A compliment and a put-down all in one. Holland was clearly trying to re-establish himself as the senior partner in this discussion after Alex's opening statement.

'Thank you for understanding my position.' Alex felt a coldness towards Holland, but he knew, within himself, that this was the opportunity he had been waiting for all of his adult life.

'I think it's important to be able to speak one's mind and be honest with those you intend to do business with.' Holland smiled. That appeared to be the decision made. Alex picked up the cup and took a swig of the coffee. It was strong and bitter but better than the wine.

'Now, about you. For starters, I did not have you down as a Pinot Grigio, man.' Holland nodded towards the wine.

Alex laughed. 'No, I am a beer drinker, typical Northern man.'

'Is that right, I assumed you were from Milton Keynes?' Holland said with a raised eyebrow.

'Nobody my age is from Milton Keynes, Steven, everybody moved there. I originate from the North West, just near Stockport. But I moved away at a fairly young age, spent some time in London, and eventually pitched up working for an insurance company in Milton Keynes. I was approached by Christopher Hanson to help him set up his personal injury team, and from starting with just three fee earners, we now have twenty-five doing bent metal recoveries (which I believe is part of what you are interested in), ten doing pre-litigation personal injury work, and five doing post-litigation work. We do some medical negligence work, but that is only a small part of the business. The core work is road traffic and employers liability PI. I try to steer clear of the slippers and trippers.'

'I see, which insurer did you work for?'

'Cloverleaf. They specialised in non-standard risks, so drivers with convictions, high-performance vehicles, and high-profile policyholders, any high-risk business really.'

Holland smiled. 'And where did you study?'

'All my studying was done once I started working, Steven, home learning or part-time college work. I never went to university, and I am not a solicitor myself.'

'Good. Forgive me, Alex. I find many unqualified lawyers try to disguise the fact that they are not solicitors and that was just my little test of your character.' Internally Alex riled.

Holland picked out a silver rectangle from his inside jacket pocket. He pressed the two ends, and one side of the rectangle slid up and opened slowly. Inside were business cards and he handed one to Alex and snapped the case shut. 'Call me on Monday, and we will make an appointment for you to come to the office and meet the team. We will the want to come and see your offices and meet the money men, make sure you can contend with the challenges our work brings. It's been a pleasure.'

Holland proffered his hand, and Alex took it. He stood to leave and reviewed the surroundings.

'It's a grand room, Alex, and I can certainly vouch for the food. We will eat here when you come up to see us. If all goes well, you can get used to it.'

Alex gave a weak smile. 'Thanks, Steven, see you again soon.' He turned and was gone. He walked straight to the lobby and out through the doors on to Peter Street. There was no point in attending the rest of the conference now. He would get in his car and drive straight back to MK.

The Audi TT was parked in the car park of the GMex, which still looked exactly like the Victorian railway station it once was. Alex loved the car. Dark blue, black alcantara interior, lots of chrome and dials. It was the 225 bhp Quattro rather than the V6. He preferred the sound and the feeling of the engine working when he drove it hard. The V6 was too smooth, not raucous enough. He fired up the engine and drove through the car park and into the traffic, heading down towards Deansgate intending to drive out on the Chester Road and get on the motorway at Stretford.

As he drove towards Old Trafford, he flicked through the playlists on the iPod-controlled stereo, settling on Twisted Wheel, a Manchester band, he considered how the city had changed whilst listening to the acoustic refrains of 'Bouncing Bomb'. He barely recognised the area around the Manchester United football ground. It was all retail parks, where once it had been heavy industry and back-to-back terraces.

Times change, he thought, *we all have to move on.* But there was no conviction in the thought, and he knew it.

On Bootle Street, Duncan walked into the office, where his team was already waiting for him. Terry Drew sat at the head of the table, Lynn Melbourne to his right, and Steven Miles to his left. Drew looked older than his thirty years. His hair was cropped but unable to disguise the thinning circle at the back. He was a little heavy, not many hours in Bootle Street's gym. He wore a grey suit, pastel pink shirt with white collar and cuffs, and brighter pink tie.

Lynn wore a red vest top with a white blouse over the top, jeans, and trainers. Her blonde hair was cut in a short bob. She looked like she spent all her waking hours in the gym. She had tanned forearms and face. She wore subtle make-up. She had a natural look about her, almost Scandinavian. She was thirty and unmarried. Given her musculature, there were inevitable locker room rumours about her sexuality, which none of the officers at Bootle Street could confirm or deny.

Miles was nothing like a police officer should look. His dark hair was cut short at the back and sides but manufactured into a slick quiff at the front, like a 1950s pop starlet. He wore a check flannel shirt with the sleeves rolled up, black jeans straight in the leg and turned up at the bottom, and heavy boots.

He was twenty-seven and very bright. He stood a well-proportioned six feet and was, by all accounts, something of a heart-throb with the female officers and 'civvies', the administrative staff. Duncan had heard that he was in a relationship with the head of human resources at Old Trafford but found that hard to believe as she was nearly fifty and not exactly in his league. Miles was classically handsome; he had a firm jaw with a cleft chin, had chocolate brown eyes, and had white straight teeth, which were often seen in his ready smile. If the top brass could get over their attitude towards his clothes and hair, they would see he was the perfect recruitment poster boy.

Drew was talking and had stopped when the door opened. He looked at his open file of papers somewhat sheepishly.

'Started without me, Terry?'

'Just trying to get some of the obvious stuff organised before you got here, Boss. Sort out who is doing what.' He coughed nervously.

'OK, where are we up to?' Duncan did not sit down. He closed the door and then leant back against it. He knew his height intimidated people, and right now, he was hoping it would work on Drew.

'Well, Lynn is going to Redford's workplace tomorrow. Miles will do the bank records and mobile records, and I will resume the house to house.'

'No.' Duncan jumped in. Drew looked up, obviously annoyed that his authority was undermined. 'I want Steve doing the door-knocking. He looks more at home in that part of town whereas you look like a copper.'

'I'm not sure you can say that boss, political correctness and all. Are you saying I look gay?' Miles was smiling; he winked at Lynn, she rolled her eyes.

'Yes.'

Miles was taken aback. Lynn laughed out loud. He had expected an explanation along the lines of how he looked younger, more approachable. He should have known better. Duncan had an innate knack of catching people off guard; it was what made him such a good detective. He always threw out the unexpected and then sat back and gauged the reactions. It was well known that he had a degree in psychology from Cambridge no less.

Some, though, doubted it. Why was he working as a copper if he was that clever they would ask? Nobody really knew the answer.

'Lynn, what did we learn about Redford today?'

'Well, chief, he worked as a forklift driver cum warehouse operator, down at Trafford Park. He was twenty-four, single. He had been working there for four months, before that, he had been working at the big transport depot in Ardwick, seemed like a normal sort of lad. Played a lot of football until a back injury at work, which was also the reason he changed jobs his mum said. We have asked for the medical records. He had a girlfriend, she is interesting. She is Charley Richardson, daughter of our old friend Michael.'

Michael Richardson was one of a family of four brothers who ran a string of amusement arcades, slot machines, and other forms of electronic gambling. Nothing wrong there, but there was a family history of violence, many arcades had been opened despite planning objections that melted away as the residents and small business owners befell accidents. Nothing terminal, but you would be surprised how many people walk into doors or fall down steps.

'Now then, that is interesting. You need to speak to her before getting on to the employers.' Duncan looked at Drew, 'What do we have from the door to door?'

'We have one old Queen who heard some shouting around two-thirty but nothing he could distinguish. He had been asleep and had got up for a leak. Other than that, nothing at all.' Duncan winced as Drew answered.

'OK. Here is what I want. By the time we meet up tomorrow, we should have bank records analysed. I want his complete work history on my desk, personnel files and all, and I want you, Terry, to have got his phone records and to have spoken to whoever he was calling, other than the girlfriend. When is the PM report due in?'

'We expected it tonight, but it looks like it will be tomorrow now,' said a somewhat crestfallen Drew.

'OK, we need to trace his movements the night he died, hopefully phone and bank records will help, but we need a presence in the clubs and bars tonight. Any volunteers?'

Miles put up his hand. 'As I look gay, I suppose I am the obvious choice.' Duncan and Melbourne laughed. 'That will be enough for now. Steve, you head home now and get some free time in if you like. I will see you tomorrow.' They all stood, Duncan pushed himself off the door and opened it. As Drew filed past him, he said, 'Good work, Terry, thanks.' He clapped Miles on the back of the shoulder as he went through the door. As Lynn walked by, he touched her arm to stop her.

'Before you go tonight, put the details of his employers, past and present on my desk, will you?'

She looked at him quizzically. 'Sure, why?'

'Well, you will have your hands full with the girl tomorrow. I don't expect that to go smoothly if her dad is there. Make sure you take some uniforms with you, but leave them in the car. We don't want to go mob-handed. She hasn't done anything wrong as far as we know. But I don't want you there on your own, and I have a feeling that any interview may end up being done down here.'

'OK. See you tomorrow.'

Duncan headed back to his office—a somewhat dated box with a view of the central courtyard. The blinds were half down and twisted; the desk was supposed to be mahogany but was varnished a ridiculous shade of orange that screamed 1975. The chair creaked as he sat in it and creaked again as it swivelled to face the desk and the door.

He looked out towards the open plan 'pit' as it was called. There were two groups of ten desks divided into banks of five with a broader walkway down the middle. There were offices like his around the outside of the pit overlooking the courtyard and Bootle Street and a door out to the corridor that led to the stairs and the interview rooms, one of which he had just vacated.

The pit was quiet that day; late afternoon it often was. His team of three was busying themselves at their desks. Miles was tidying up before leaving, Melbourne was on the phone, and Drew was typing furiously, hammering the keyboard.

At times, the pit would be a cacophony of noise as phones rang, officers called to each other, white boards squealed. It reminded Duncan of what he imagined a newspaper office to be like, run by J. Jonah Jameson perhaps—too many comics in his youth.

He picked up the old, tattered buff folder from his desk. It was remarkably slim for a murder case, especially as it was marked with a large red 'Unsolved' stamp.

He opened the folder and looked at the ageing photograph of Maureen Ladd.

Frank Maguire was enjoying a late breakfast at his favourite cafe, the Koffee Pot on Hilton Street. The cafe overlooked Stevenson Square, once a major shopping area now reduced to a run-down backwater off the main commercial streets around Piccadilly. It was just around the corner from his old yard on Tariff Street, where he still spent most of his time.

The company had flagship offices on King Street, opposite Ship Canal House, designed to impress potential clients and to house the accountants and the like who would never be attracted to work in an old warehouse like Tariff Street. But Frank liked to spend most of his time in the place, where he built his empire. He felt at home there, and he liked to keep in touch with where he came from, so that he could appreciate where he was going.

The Koffee Pot was a prime example of this trait. It was ostensibly a greasy spoon cafe. It was on the corner of Hilton Street and both sides of the building were covered in urban art, Graffiti to Frank.

The secret to the Koffee Pot, however, was that the owner was a chef of high quality who had worked in many top class hotels and restaurants throughout the country. Quite why he had pitched up in the run-down backwater of Stevenson Square was not clear. But Frank was delighted he had. His breakfast was a masterpiece and an essential start to any day that followed an evening reception at the town hall.

It was around lunchtime when Frank finished his last sausage and sat back to enjoy his perfect coffee. The reception had gone well, and the Germans were impressed with his national and international coverage.

Frank was hoping to benefit from the success of the BMW Mini. Having originally introduced a state-of-the art retro car based loosely on the old Alex Issigonis designed car, BMW had continued expanding the range with numerous variations. The cars were assembled in the United Kingdom in the midlands of England and shipped all over the world in ever increasing numbers.

This was where Frank came in. He had the ability to ship parts from Germany and France to any country in Europe or any port ready for shipping to the United States and the Far East. He had a yard just off the A34 near Oxford, handily place for the factory and on a direct road down to the shipping containers at Southampton.

The contract would be for five years. It would pay for an overhaul of the Oxfordshire yard and provide a massive cash injection and guarantee the future of the business for at least seven years. The deal would be sweetened by the council, who wanted more local jobs. Frank already employed three thousand people, and this would mean at least another one thousand jobs, although not as many in Manchester as the councillors seemed to think.

The injection of cash would provide Frank's retirement bonus. He would buy himself out of the business with the Irish. They went a long way back, his families were immigrants. His great-grandfather had come over to Manchester as a navigator. A navigator was a labourer who dug out, by hand, the Manchester ship canal. The title of navigator was shortened to navvy and became a term commonly used for all labourers.

He had left behind the crushing poverty of his homeland to work ten hours a day for the modern-day equivalent of £16. At its peak, the construction of the canal had employed seventeen thousand men. The Big Ditch, as it was colloquially termed, was a monumental feat of engineering that was both extraordinary and divisive. People in Manchester took the canal for granted now. Frank knew the canal inside out. It was part of his family's history. He knew, for instance, that it was only slightly shorter, at thirty-six miles long, than the much more famous Panama Canal.

It was divisive in that it caused substantial acrimony between the cities of Manchester and Liverpool. The merchants of Manchester felt the charges for exporting their goods through the Liverpool docks were too high to the extent that it was often cheaper to take goods to the port of Hull on the eastern side of the country. So, resourceful as ever, the paragons of 'Cottonopolis' decided to create their own port in the centre of Manchester, thirty-six miles from the sea.

That decision alienated the whole city of Liverpool and the powerful Railway companies, but connecting Manchester to the sea created massive employment in the area during the Long Depression of the late 1800s and saved the merchants of Manchester more than two-thirds of their port and transport costs. At its peak, Manchester's inland port was the third busiest in the country, behind only London and Southampton—testament to the economic powerhouse that the city was at the beginning of the twentieth century.

Frank's great-grandfather survived the canal but not without cost. Health and safety laws were practically non-existent, and he became one of the thousands of men who sacrificed limbs during the construction, losing an arm. He was, however, found work by the Ship Canal Company, who had the foresight to look after their own as Frank tried to do now. The chief engineer on the Ship Canal was Thomas Walker and those who were left maimed during construction were given the rather brutal nickname of 'Walkers Fragments'. *Typical of the Mancunians, thought* **Frank,** *blunt, insensitive, and yet caring and fiercely loyal to each other all in one.*

Frank hoped that he maintained some of the old principles of looking out for his own, but in truth, he had most in common with the Manchester Merchants who had trampled over others to achieve what they wanted.

The Maguires had settled in the city, but it was not until Frank started using his father's lorry to ship entertainment equipment, then a second lorry, and a third that the family was able to move out of their council house. Frank's brother Jimmy had returned to Ireland just as the business was taking off, and he helped with his connections over there to expand the business. Jimmy knew people. Both of Frank's boys were destined for the family business until Sean disappeared. Ryan was now Frank's operational director.

The business grew and grew, the Irish connections encouraged the trade with Eastern Europe, and Frank was perfectly placed when the continent was opened up and millions of euros were ploughed into the former eastern bloc. He now had business interests throughout the Balkan states.

Frank waved his farewell to the waitress. The cafe was empty other than a young man with blond hair, huddled into a parka and nursing a cup of coffee and, probably, a hangover. Frank never paid. The cafe sent a monthly bill to his accountant's, which was paid without question.

He walked the short distance to the yard and did a quick tour, inspecting the workshop and exchanging banter with the fitters. He made his way to his office, where his son, Ryan, was waiting.

Ryan was a taller, more muscular version of his father. Both had black hair and blue eyes. Both had broad shoulders and were barrel-chested. Frank stood at around five feet ten, Ryan just breaking six foot. He was obviously slimmer than his father, but at thirty-six, he was thirty years younger.

He was sitting on the edge of Frank's desk tapping away at his Blackberry. His expensive shirt was looking a little creased.

'We are all set with the insurance business. Steve has it sorted pretty much. He will have it tied up in the next month, and we start shifting more cases. We expect to turn over around a couple of million in the first year, all going through the Caymans. Two years from now, five million a year.' Unlike his father Ryan had none of the lyrical Irish brogue. His accent was harsh Mancunian.

'I'm not comfortable with such a long-term plan. I don't see there'll be any need for it by then.' Frank sat down. Dawn had already switched his computer on, and the software designed by his own IT team was showing the whereabouts of every King of the Road wagon and what it was carrying and to where.

Ryan stood and moved towards the door. 'Don't you worry about it, Dad, you'll be out of here long before then, and it'll all be down to me. I can deal with it.'

He opened the door. 'I'll be back next week, off to Belfast tonight for the weekend, any message for Uncle Jimmy?'

'Tell the old bastard it's time he gave up,' growled Frank. He meant it. Ryan laughed and closed the door behind him.

'Dawn, get me Davis on the phone,' he shouted through the door to his PA in his usual fashion. He never used the intercom system.

The door opened. 'It's the middle of the night there, Mr. Maguire. Shall I put the call through at around two o'clock, Davis will be in his office by then?'

Frank grimaced. With the amount of money Davis was making out of him for building his house, Frank thought that a call at 5:00 a.m. was not unreasonable. The look on Dawn's face told him otherwise, and he relented. 'Very well, patch him through later. But tell him I want to see the pictures.'

Frank went to his window and looked over the yard. Another wagon was rolling in. He glanced back at his computer, which told him that the wagon had just arrived from Turkey via Holland. He watched as it entered the large 1960s-built workshop at the back of the yard and the huge concertina doors were closed behind it. He saw Ryan speaking to his workshop manager.

This workshop was separate to the main modern service and repair building. The main workshop, which was very different to the one the lorry had just entered, was huge, could hold six lorries at once and was so clean you could eat your lunch off the floor. It was full of computers and diagnostic machines.

The old workshop, the one Frank had started with, was a step back in time. It still had welding equipment and inspection pits that were always an inch below the water level. Frank never went to the old workshop these days; he left that to Ryan and his business.

His lad was doing OK. He had often worried that Ryan had no head for commerce. He had always been a bit of a rogue, but he had developed the same kind of natural street savvy that Frank had when he was younger. But Ryan was more reckless than Frank and that was his main worry until he was clear of the business and enjoying his villa in Nassau.

CHAPTER 6

MANCHESTER, 1991

Jᴀᴄᴋ ꜱᴀᴛ ᴀɴᴅ ᴡᴀɪᴛᴇᴅ. Hᴇ watched them cross the car park outside the Wordsworth—every week night, the same routine. They would have a few beers in the pub, would be back home for tea, and would then be back to The Wordsworth for last orders. Every night they stayed together. Only Fridays and Saturdays broke the routine. On those nights, they headed into town and were often separated.

Jack had been watching them for three weeks now. He had been to town on the same buses, sat outside pubs waiting for them to come out, and got the night bus home. One night, he was worried the younger one had taken an interest in him and recognised him, so he let them get the last bus and resigned himself to the seven-mile walk home. He didn't mind. His rage, whilst diminished, had become cold and hard within him. He could survive anything with the feel of cold steel in his very fibres and tucked into the waistband of his jeans.

The next day, he had gone to the barber's. He had his head shaved, cropped so short that you could barely see his blond hair. He wanted to be a different person to the one they had seen the night before.

He was in no real hurry. He enjoyed the sense of power he felt from knowing that they did not realise he was stalking their every move and that they were being hunted. He was determined to see this through, but he was equally determined to come out the other side. He would keep watching and waiting. His desire for revenge consumed his waking hours; his slumber was haunted by the visions of his mother's death. He could take his time.

CHAPTER 7

MILTON KEYNES, 2011

'THAT'S THE DEAL, CHRIS. IT is quite a big investment in terms of staff, but we have the technology, and the additional software licences are not expensive. We are talking about one hundred cases per month of the routine injury matters. That's £135,000 per month in fees, just over £1.6 million a year. We also get paid for the recovery of their own vehicle damage in non-fault accidents. If it's over five grands' worth of damage, we get hourly rates, so that's great. If it's less, they will pay us a flat rate per case plus, at the end of the financial year, ten percent of what we recover. Worst case scenario is we clear £2.5 million in fees, from that I think we can squeeze profit of £1 million, at worst £600,000.'

Hanson was looking over his desk for the relevant pages of the contract. Alex passed it to him.

'We take on school leavers to do the recovery work. We train them up, and they graduate on to the injury work. We have a conveyor belt of our own talent. We don't pay agency fees. We don't have fee earners who come to us with preconceived ideas. They work the way we tell them.

Provided we do actually promote from within you will have a loyal and highly trained workforce that is competitively priced. On top of that, we can roll this product out to other businesses, car hire firms, fleet managers. It's an opportunity we can't turn down, Chris.' Alex's enthusiasm was infectious, but Hanson was only interested in the hard currency.

'I agree. We are on a sound financial footing. The risk of financial overexposure from this is minimal, go ahead and do it. I expect you to manage it all, Alex. That means taking fewer, significantly fewer cases. You will be a head of department. You will manage the budget, and you will share in the rewards.'

Alex smiled. 'Are you offering me a partnership, Chris, a non-lawyer partner at Hanson's?'

'I suggest you stop being so smug before I change my mind. The contract will be on your desk by tomorrow, the management committee has already agreed it.'

Alex laughed. The management committee did as they were told. Hanson ran the practice as a benign dictatorship, mostly benign.

Alex picked up his copy of the business plan and stood up. 'I'll get HR sorted out and speak to the software people about the licences. The people at Maguire's want to come and see us to seal the deal. Shall I arrange it for this month?'

'Yes, talk to Alice in marketing. We want this announced with trumpets.'

Alex walked back to his office. A partnership in Hanson's was, effectively, his golden ticket. He would most likely be financially secure for the rest of his life unless things went horribly wrong.

The investigation into Steven Redford's death was not going well. Great excitement had ensued when they found his shoes in the New Union Hotel toilets, a small pub-cum-hotel at the end of Canal Street. Scene of crime officers had descended on the place like a biblical plague and came away with nothing but the shoes.

Miles had turned up nothing of any real note.

Drew had located a significant payment to Redford eight months before his death—ten thousand pounds exactly from a firm of solicitors. Duncan assumed it was from some sort of civil case and had tasked Drew with speaking to the law firm to get all the details. He also wanted him to check with the banks and building societies to see if he had anything other than his current account, which was a possibility, given he had received one lump sum.

Lynn had failed in her attempts to question Charley Richardson. She was being looked after in a local retreat, supposedly overcome with grief at the death of her young Romeo. Her father had lawyers crawling all over them, refusing access until she was fit to answer questions.

Melbourne had made it clear that Charley was not a suspect, but Michael Richardson had a history with the police, and to say there was a lack of trust was something of an understatement.

Lynn's report, however, contained one fact of note. Michael Richardson had badly grazed knuckles on his right hand, not enough to get him in for questioning, but Duncan made a mental note.

Duncan reviewed his notes of the post-mortem. He found he remembered more of what he read if he wrote it down, so he was a copious note maker. Redford was beaten badly, mainly about the head, primarily to the left side front. There was bruising on his upper arms, consistent with him being held by two people, one either side with both hands on his biceps. There were no chips in his stomach contents despite there being a chip in his mouth and one in his hand. The wound to the cheek was post mortem.

If he was held whilst being beaten, why was he still holding his chips?

The modus operandi was inconsistent with the Maureen Ladd case. Yet there was the wound to the cheek, the removal of the shoes that are later found in a bar, and the missing chips that Maureen had bought five minutes earlier from the chip shop only yards from where she was attacked.

As an experienced detective, Duncan disliked the thought of coincidence. It was just so unlikely. Yet the only other reason for the coincidences he could come up with was that they were deliberate clues. Clues to what though? That also raised the spectre of a killer who was killing people in order to send a message to the police or, even more disturbing, to Duncan himself.

He sat back and looked at the grubby cream ceiling. A thought occurred to him, and he shuffled the papers on the desk until he found what he was looking for—Lynn's list of past employers. Current employers were Hyde Trucks, a truck dealership, where he worked as a fitter, doing servicing and warranty work and upgrading the standard specifications on newly ordered trucks. He had only been there a few weeks, and Duncan wondered if the ten grand was some sort of employment payout from his previous employer. He turned to the next page.

Duncan got up from his desk and walked to the window. He opened it. He needed fresh air. There it was on the page in front of him, the name that linked Steven Redford and Maureen Ladd. Sweet Jesus. He ran his hands through his short, cropped hair, then physically flinched when the phone on his desk rang.

His mind was racing, and he let the phone ring. He couldn't deal with anything now. He had to calm down and think this through. He sat back down and checked the last page again, no mistake.

His mobile rang. The caller's number was blocked. Somebody was determined to reach him. He picked the phone off the desk and answered it.

He heard a low voice, mumbling, as though trying not to be overheard, an indistinct accent that was familiar but that he could not quite place.

'You got my message then.'

CHAPTER 8

MILTON KEYNES 2011

THE MEETING WITH MAGUIRES WENT ahead as planned. Steven Holland attended with the company secretary, a small balding man in a suit bought from British Home Stores. Alex estimated the cost to be approximately £90. He was unsure how a man like that could hold a position of such importance with a multinational company. The number of times he agreed with Holland perhaps provided some insight. Christopher got his fanfare, a reporter from the local paper attended with a photographer. Alex slipped away when the photos were being done, much to Hanson's annoyance, who wanted a shot to announce his partnership.

The deal was done, signed, and sealed. Hands were shaken, and the cases started to arrive within the week.

Alex worked long hours and built his team for the Maguire's work. He took inexperienced people, young people who were receptive to the training he would give them. They were first taught the skills of establishing who was responsible for a traffic accident, looking at previous cases decided by the courts in Binghams Motor Claims

Cases, learning from the Highway Code and just the common sense approach to deciding who had failed to drive with the appropriate care required.

From there, they were taught the process of recovering damages. What was a reasonable claim and what was not. How to manage their time and how to prioritise work. How to identify the person you will sue, their employer if they were driving a business vehicle. They were taught to use the Motor Insurers Database to trace the insurer of a vehicle by inputting the registration number and date of the accident.

Alex trained them on how to submit claims through the ministry of justice web portal, using the firm's case management software, which was compatible with the portal and transferred the relevant information at the push of a button. Once information was on the portal, it formed part of your claim and could be relied upon by the defendant at court. It was essential, therefore, to be accurate with your inputting.

The staff were trained on what sort of evidence they had to gather to prove their claim, whether it be for vehicle damage or, in the case of an injury claim, what type of medical expert would be used to provide a medical opinion on the extent of their injuries.

How to value an injury claim was something that needed experience. To begin with, all valuations and offers would be done by Alex. Only when he was satisfied that the fee earner was doing the correct research of previous case law and was regularly recommending valuations that Alex agreed with, would they be allowed to 'fly solo'?

The final piece of the jigsaw that each fee earner would aspire to would be the drafting of court documents and the management of a case through the courts all the way to a trial. It would take a few years for an inexperienced fee earner to be trusted to do this without supervision, and they would learn these skills by shadowing the more experienced fee earners or attending hearings just to take notes of what happened and to sit behind the barrister.

All of these skills could be added to a person of reasonable intelligence with an attention to detail. What made a top-notch fee earner, however, was personality. You could have all the legal skills in the world, as many of the trainees straight out of law school could demonstrate. But in personal injury work, you had to have the mentality to want to argue your case, the guts for a fight, the bravery to take a financial risk on your assessment of your client's ability in the witness box, or your own ability to present their case. You had to have the bravura to negotiate the best settlement you could, whether it was fair was not the issue at that stage. Your client would judge you on your ability to exceed expectations. You needed that competitive instinct. Alex was interested in people with that drive to succeed, not just to win cases, but to be the best fee earner in the firm. Those who had the fire in their belly, which made them want to outperform their teammates.

Alex's skill was his ability to consistently identify those people in a thirty-minute interview. Some may fall by the wayside but not many. He would pay more attention to their performance at interview than their academic qualities. As he was fond of pointing out, you don't get the best settlements by relying on the theory, you have to wring them, kicking and screaming, from the grasping hands of the insurer. A good fee earner to Alex was the one who celebrated a settlement, where every little victory was savoured. If they liked to win, chances are, they could become addicted to it.

Alex had, as Amrit had suggested, started to pick up some significant injury claims. He retained those, but the majority of cases were straightforward whiplash claims. When a Maguire's truck reported an accident, the company would contact the innocent party to admit liability and offer them the opportunity to put forward their claim through Hanson's.

If they were happy to do so, then the call was transferred directly to Hanson's, hot keyed they called it, and the fee earner at Hanson's would discuss the terms of the contract between client and solicitor. A no-win-no-fee agreement would be e-mailed to the potential client, whilst they were still on the phone, using software that allowed them to type in their name by way of an electronic signature. The agreement would be explained in full and the client is shown where on the document to sign. As soon as they have done so, the document is immediately e-mailed back to the fee earner, and they print off the agreement and countersign it.

From that point on, the contract is binding. The fee earners would then book a medical appointment online, so in the course of one telephone call, the client has had the no-win-no-fee agreement explained to them to the satisfaction of the Solicitors Regulation Authority and in accordance with the Courts and Legal Services Act, and they have a medical appointment booked and directions for the medical appointment e-mailed so they know where the doctor's consulting rooms are. Inside of thirty minutes, the case is signed and evidence booked. The majority of clients were, quite rightly, impressed by the efficiency of the firm, when most people's perspective of solicitors in England was of a slow-moving, technologically backward business. All quill pens and wigs.

The case would then be allocated to the appropriate fee earner which, if it was a sizeable claim, would be Alex.

In month one, he had fifteen multi-track cases (a case with a value of over £25,000). This was great news. The multi-track cases paid significantly higher, uncapped fees. It also meant that, with his management responsibilities, he would need more experienced fee earners, so he began to recruit from the existing staff. Those who had been with the firm a few years and had developed the relevant skills but were not getting the right amount of exposure to the work were promoted.

Within the first six months, Alex had taken seven hundred cases and the fees were starting to flow.

Everything in the garden was rosy; at least that was the view from over the garden wall.

Alex turned his TT in to Crownhill. It was a modern estate in Milton Keynes, where all the roads were named after dead singers and actors. It was a good address to have in Milton Keynes, a sought-after estate. There was very little of the housing association or low-cost housing that other estates had. It wasn't the most expensive, but it was certainly a place some people in the new town aspired to.

He took a left into Hendrix Drive and the first right into Chevalier Grove, a winding cul-de-sac. He stopped outside a detached house with terracotta roof tiles and a large conifer on the small front lawn. It was a house much like the others on the street, although the one obvious difference was the wheelchair ramp to the front door.

He rang the bell and waited. Diane Hayes opened the door. *She is around fifty,* **Alex thought,** *but she still seems young and vibrant in her outlook.* **As always she was dressed as though she was in a nightclub—a silk** blouse with perhaps one more button undone than was strictly necessary, a black pencil skirt, and black stockings; the only incongruous item being her Lion King slippers. She was a very attractive woman. Her hair was auburn coloured; her figure was of the hourglass variety, and she always had a light tan. Her eyes had a tinge of green and the lines at the sides gave lie to both her age and her disposition.

'Come in, Alex, love. I was expecting you a bit earlier, Johnny is in the living room, go through.'

Alex walked through into the living room, chintz sofa and matching curtains with pelmets. In his specially designed chair, Johnny Hayes was sitting watching television, sucking a drink through a straw from a cup gripped by one of the cup-holders attached to the wheelchair. He didn't notice Alex come in; he was engrossed in an episode of *Scooby Doo*.

'Sit yourself down, love. I'll make us a cup of tea.'

Alex sat to the right of Johnny's chair. He could look through to the kitchen, where Diane was putting the kettle on, and to the right of the kitchen door, to the former dining room, now converted to a bedroom with full en suite facilities for Johnny.

Of the money recovered from the insurers, the court had allowed release of an interim payment of just over £500,000 for home improvements and modifications. Diane did not want to move to a bungalow; she wanted Johnny to stay in the house they had lived in for the last twenty years.

Johnny's father was a builder. He had moved out since the accident. He found it hard to share his wife with his dependent son. Alex knew him well. He found it too painful to see his broken and damaged son every day and not be able to help him. He had done all the building work, and

Johnny now had everything he could possibly need in the two rooms that were his.

Alex knew that Johnny's father had not charged for anything but materials for the building modifications and the extension that he built, and Alex had talked Christopher into letting the firm do the legal work at a discounted rate, including the setting up of a trust for the management of the money.

'Johnny, how's it hangin'?'

'It's hanging loooong, Al.' The long elongated for effect.

It was the usual greeting. Johnny laughed every time. Alex smiled as Johnny continued to watch Scooby and Shaggy eating hot dogs. They were similar in looks. Johnny Hayes had the same light brown hair, perhaps not as thick as Alex's, but a full head. He was four years younger and, when he had been working, was more powerfully built. But his relative inactivity had made his features a little flabbier, which made him look a little older.

Diane had cut his hair in a similar fashion to Alex's. They could easily pass for brothers. Diane, during the hundreds of meetings they had together in this very room, had often referred to the two of them as the 'naughty twins' on account of their joint inability to take anything too seriously.

Johnny was often like he was now, little more than a child, with simple needs and desires. He liked to be occupied but a simple story would often keep him enraptured for hours. He would listen to the tale, and then be compelled to go off and turn it into cartoon form. His drawings were skilled, for the mental age he had, and he would formulate the story as a comic strip but without the words. He had trouble forming the words, and his reading was limited. His neurologist explained that he saw everything in pictures, and he struggled to express anything in any other form.

Alex had taken Johnny to Whipsnade Zoo a few times, just to give Diane a break. They didn't talk much on the first trip, and Alex did not know how to talk to children, so he talked to Johnny like an adult. They would discuss women and football, like two teenagers bunking off school. Alex felt a huge responsibility for Johnny. His was the first case that had affected him emotionally. They were just such nice people who were handling Johnny's tragedy with such stoicism. Alex admired Diane and her never-ending supply of good humour and optimism. He was also touched by their unreserved trust in his ability to help them. They were the nearest thing to a family that he had.

Diane returned with a tray of tea and biscuits.

'You look tired, Alex. It's either too much work or your girlfriend is keeping you up late.'

'It's definitely the work I'm afraid, Di.' Alex smiled. 'You know I'm single.'

'Don't give me that, Alex Harris. I've known enough men in my time to spot one who's not getting any, and you are not one of them.' Alex felt himself flush. It was like being fifteen and discussing your first girlfriend with your sexy aunty—uncomfortable and embarrassing and a little bit exciting.

'But it's more than tiredness, isn't it, Alex? What's the matter?'

'Nothing really, Di, I just came to pick up the passport and birth certificate you promised. We need to get that money invested and the other side needs the documents for the trust fund.'

He was looking at the carpet and had to force himself to look up and into her eyes.

'I'm sorry, I couldn't find the passport after all, so I went and got some photos done, and we got a new one. I'll get it.'

She got up and went upstairs. Alex looked back to Johnny. In profile, he looked even more similar, the nose was the same shape. His eyes were more blue, whereas Alex's were grey.

Diane returned with the passport, and Alex opened it up and looked at the photograph. It was almost like looking at a photograph of himself, and he stared at it for a long time.

'Spooky, isn't it.' Diane had been watching him.

'Yes.' Alex coughed and shut the passport up and put it in his inside jacket pocket.

'You don't seem yourself, love. You know you can always talk to me if you need to. We both owe you everything, Alex, and we will do anything we can to help you. You know we've got more than enough money if you need help.'

Alex was shocked. 'I'm fine, Di, really, I don't know what you're on about. Did I tell you I'm a partner now? I don't need any money, besides which, that's Johnny's money and it's needed for him.'

'S all right, Al, you can have some.' Johnny called over his shoulder.

Diane smiled at him and put her hand on his shoulder. 'He loves you, Alex, we both do. Just so you know. We will always be here for you.'

Alex got up and made his excuses about being under pressure at work and must head back. When he was outside, he took a deep breath of air, and he blinked back the rising tears.

Summer was over, autumn was blowing to a chilly end, and the winter months stretched out long and dark ahead of him.

He felt shaken. He had genuinely believed that he was keeping everything within himself that nobody would have any idea of the pressure building up within him. He opened the TT and decided he needed to get back to the office. He would arrange for Jules to come over tonight, and he would have the talk he had been postponing for some time.

He assumed now that she may also have seen a change in him, and he needed to try to resolve things with her.

The TT roared into life and pulled away slowly, heading out of Chevalier Grove and back towards Central Milton Keynes. It was just after three, and already it was looking close to dark.

'So what happened then?'

Jimmy Maguire sat in the bar on Grosvenor Road, Belfast, a thick layer of cigar smoke hung just below the low ceiling so that if you would stand, your head would be in the clouds. He was in his late sixties; he was a former shipbuilder and still looked strong enough to build a liner single-handed. His massive hands were loosely curled in fists on the table between the two men. His fingers, as thick as an Irish sausage, held the cigar. His huge head was tilted to one side, and his shock of white hair framed the ruddy complexion.

He carried a deep scar above his right eye that curved around the brow and down on to the cheek, pulling the skin tight, making the right eye appear smaller than the left, as though squinting, and making it seem as though his eyes were constantly narrowed in suspicion.

The smoking ban didn't really apply in his bar. It was formerly a barber's shop in an arcade of burger bars and off licences. It now had a bar down one side and four small round tables, each with two chairs. It looked neither homely nor welcoming, and it did not play music. No police ever came in here, nobody would ever complain about smoking in Jimmy's bar. Only his friends and neighbours came in here and, not to put too fine a point on it, they valued their kneecaps.

He was sitting opposite his nephew. Ryan looked uncomfortable. He sipped at his Guinness. Jimmy assumed he didn't drink pints at home. He was too soft this kid, too flash. He had never really known the harsher side of life, not like him and his brother Frank.

Jimmy had returned to his mother country in the 1970s. He had seen the troubles on TV and, not to put too fine a point on it, he wanted in. He was not a particularly political or religious man, but he obviously had taken a side. What he wanted was the chaos and lawlessness. He saw an opportunity, and he took it.

He had planted bombs, shot at soldiers, intimidated witnesses, and lived on the run moving from safe house to safe house. He had worked his way into the organisation's trust, and they had put his plans into place to raise funds to buy arms and political protection.

But the troubles were now over, or at least, the violent struggle was. However, his fund-raising plans were still working. The big difference was that he was now the beneficiary, and the money it raised was no longer spent on the cause.

'Well, he quit his job and refused to hand over the money. I sent some boys round to discuss it with him and, well, it seems they went a bit too far.' Ryan's voice wavered a little.

'Is that it? They went too far? The dumb fuckers lost us our money. Corpses don't pay debts, Ryan, do they? What sort of shitheads have you got working for you?'

'I gave it to someone reliable Uncle Jim. He's done loads of these jobs for me.'

Ryan's eyes flicked around nervously.

'Right. Whoever did the job, they owe me. They pay, and I have a memory lapse about how fucking stupid they are. They don't pay, and my boys will be on that ferry to Holyhead, do you get my meaning?'

'Yes, Uncle Jim, but there is no way they can lay hands on that sort of money, and the bottom line is, we don't know where the money is. We've spoken to the lad's parents about it, but they don't know anything, and there's certainly no sign of them having come into money.'

'It is your responsibility. My cut of that deal, once it was all washed, was going to be four hundred grand. I don't expect that sort of leakage.'

Ryan was starting to sweat. 'The lads who went to him, Uncle Jim, they say he swore he had already paid the money back. They say he took a real beating and wouldn't break. If we can get his bank records, we might be able to find out where the money went. I know you have people on the inside. I'm sure you can get what I need.'

'This one time, Son, I'll give you a hand. But I don't expect to have to recover your mistakes. Once I get the information, I give it to you, for a fee, and you get me what's owing, do you understand?' Ryan nodded. 'What's this lawyer like, how is he doing?' Jimmy's eyes were fixed on his nephew who literally wilted under his gaze.

'That's all taken care of, the lawyer's moving cases, and we've got three big ones on the way, but it will be tight to get them paid by the end of the year . . .'

'Don't start giving me excuses kid. You said you could do this. I trusted you. Now you had better deliver.'

'You got my message then.'

He terminated the call. He didn't wait for Duncan to respond. He just wanted him to know he was here. They didn't need to talk just yet, but they would, and soon.

It was time to start work again; this one was going to be more difficult than the last.

CHAPTER 9

MANCHESTER, 1991

Jᴀᴄᴋ ᴡᴀs ᴄᴏʟᴅ. Iᴛ ʜᴀᴅ been a long night. He had tracked them through the streets of Manchester from bar to bar. He had never followed them into the bars; he was too young, and he would be too conspicuous. He had spent the whole evening shuffling from one frozen foot to another outside numerous pubs and clubs.

It was another Saturday night, and he had finally found a weak point. Heading home on the last bus, top deck and right at the back, Jack pulled his second-hand parka around himself with his hands thrust deep into the side pockets and rested his feet on the seat in front.

He had certainly been surprised by the turn of events. The younger brother had separated from their group and made his way to a narrow side street. He had been standing under a street lamp by the canal retaining wall, and waited.

Jack remained still and quiet; he huddled into a doorway, shrouded in darkness, but from where he had a view of the whole street. He sat against the door and shrank back into his coat. If he was seen, he would be mistaken for a tramp, sleeping in the shelter.

Under the streetlight, there was some movement. The brother had straightened up and was joined by another man. They spoke together, but Jack could not hear what was said; then they linked arms and crossed the street, walking towards Jack. He froze. Involuntarily he held his breath. He could not move without drawing attention to himself. He kept his head low whilst trying to see the second man.

They walked to the doorway, where Jack was hunched into a corner. His heartbeat was faster. His mind raced, and he braced himself. But they continued past and did not even glance in his direction.

Jack stayed where he was. He did not move for some time. He had recognised the second man, who was not really a man at all. He was no older than Jack. He was a pupil at the Comprehensive school on the estate, and he lived in the block of flats at the top of the road that Jack lived on by the Wordsworth.

His name was Raymond, shortened to Ray. He lived with his father in the flats; his mother had died some time ago of cancer. His surname was Ladyman. His father, Keith Ladyman, was a coach driver. A big man with a spectacular expanse of stomach; he wore country—and Western-style clothing, pointed cowboy boots with garish patterns and drove an American car, a Camaro, with the same paint job of the rebel flag as *The Dukes of Hazard*. He was known locally as American Keith, although he had only ever left Britain on day trips to France, carrying booze-laden shoppers to Calais and back.

Ray, however, had a somewhat different nickname. He was quite obviously and openly gay. He was fine-boned, slim, reserved, all the things his father was not—quite feminine. It all explained why, in the usual caustic way in this part of the world, his friends called him Ladyboy. It seemed to cover all angles.

Jack knew Ladyboy well. They had played together often as young children as they lived practically on the same street and went to the same junior school. Jack had often protected the smaller, more sensitive boy from those who sought to tease or bully him for his disinterest in physical pursuits as children do.

When Jack went to the grammar school, they had grown apart somewhat. Jack had his own circle of friends from school, and his fanaticism about football whilst Ladyboy became more solitary and withdrawn.

But they remained friends. They would often meet outside the shops. Jack had introduced Ladyboy to Joe. Like most people, Ladyboy was comfortable with Joe. He inspired confidence and exuded reliability. Ladyboy had articulated his sexuality to Jack and Joe one winter evening when they were sitting outside the newsagents. He had never been open with anyone before but felt safe with Joe. He knew there was no risk of Jack reacting as he expected his father to when he told him, not when Joe was around.

Jack had just shrugged and told him that he had always assumed he was gay, so nothing had changed. When Ladyboy had mentioned his fear of telling his father Jack had volunteered to go with him and provide moral support, which is exactly what he did.

Keith Ladyman did not take the news in quite the way Ray had expected. He had looked at Jack, back at Ladyboy, and asked if they were 'bumboys'. Jack had laughed aloud and assured Keith that he was not gay; he was just there to make sure that Ray had some moral support. Keith had told Jack it was none of his business. He raised his voice, shouting that he had no right to interfere in their family business and that he ought to leave before Keith threw him out and not through the door.

Jack looked at Ray, who nodded that it was OK for him to go. Keith had walked to the front door of the flat and opened it.

As Jack left, he had spoken quietly to Keith; Ray could not hear what was said, and Keith had slammed the door behind him.

The next day, the three had met, as arranged, outside the same newsagents. Ray explained that his father had not spoken to him for four hours but that, eventually, he had told his son that he was all he had, and he would stand by him. Ladyboy had asked what Jack had said to his father as he left, but Jack said he couldn't remember; it was nothing important obviously.

From that point on, the relationship between the boys was unbreakable. They still moved in different circles, but there was an unspoken bond, as often happens, when teenagers go through traumatic events together.

Now here was Ladyboy with one of the people who had raped Jack's mother. It didn't really make sense, but it did give Jack an idea as to how he might take retribution.

As the last bus pulled into the estate, Jack had his plan worked out. He would see Ladyboy and Joe tomorrow, and then next Saturday, he would extract some degree of justice.

As he got off the bus, he looked up at the block of flats. It was a cold, wet night, a freezing light drizzle soaked through his clothes. His skin was cold, but it was nothing like the cold that ran right through to his soul.

CHAPTER 10

MILTON KEYNES 2011

Aʟᴇx ᴡᴀs ɪɴ ᴛʜᴇ ᴏꜰꜰɪᴄᴇ reviewing the medical records for his largest claim from Maguires. His client was a fitter in the King of The Road workshop in Manchester. The employers' records confirmed his version of the accident circumstances. He had been working under one of the vans used as rescue vehicles for the lorries when they suffered a breakdown. It was cheaper than using the manufacturers' extended warranty to have your own field force, who knew the vehicles inside out, particularly when you had so many rigs on the road at one time.

As he was under the van, the hydraulic ramp had collapsed. Alex's client had been trapped under the weight of the van; his cervical vertebrae crushed. The X-rays confirmed the fractures to the vertebrae and discs in the neck as did the MRI scan. The notes suggested that there was nothing much to be done for him. A fusion of the vertebrae and disc excision may help with the pain but would affect his mobility. He would never return to any form of heavy manual work and would be limited to sedentary employment.

Alex calculated his loss of earnings claim. He was twenty-four. He was likely to work for another forty-one years. His current salary was £24,000, which seemed pretty good for a relatively inexperienced mechanic. The likely loss of income was multiplied by a multiplicand pulled from the Ogden Tables, a book of multipliers and multiplicands used to calculate the appropriate discounts for early lump sum payments, likely salary increments, and work life expectancy.

His claim would be discounted by any amount he was capable of earning. A claim for past and future loss of income, loss of pension rights and claims for medical expenses, and pain and suffering and loss of amenity was estimated at around £1.2 million.

Alex pondered the electronic file before him. He felt something was not quite right about the case. Holland had been on the phone the day after the case came in. He wanted this case dealt with as a priority. It was a serious incident, and Maguires did not want any adverse publicity from it. The hydraulic ramp had failed an inspection prior to the incident, and they anticipated problems from the Union if the case were publicised. They were admitting liability, and they wanted Alex to quantify the claim and put forward an offer on behalf of his client straight away.

In the normal course of events, a claim like this would take at least three to five years to resolve, possibly longer. The Maguires were looking to sort this one out in the same number of days.

Alex knew things were wrong but proving it was going to be difficult. The radiology was conclusive, there was a significant injury, but the haste with which Holland was moving was an indicator that all was not well with this case.

Alex contemplated his options. He knew that the path he was heading down would cause irreparable damage to his current life and to those around him. He had been waiting for this moment—in part with dread, in part with excitement.

He felt relieved that it was finally all happening.

He had called his client and advised him of the content of the medical records and that Maguires were looking to settle before he got any medical evidence. He warned his client that with injuries of this significance, he should get a neurologist's and orthopaedic surgeon's evidence together with a report from an employment consultant. Alex needed to know if he would need surgery in the future and how much it would cost to be done privately. He suggested that the client should seek the guidance of a disability advisor, who could guide him into the right sort of employment, in order to maximise his future income. Alex warned him that he would not be able to value the claim properly without this evidence.

He was told, brusquely, that he already had a part-time job, doing a bit of sweeping up in a garage down the road. He was earning £25 per day, four days per week. He just wanted it all over and done with and no 'fannying around'.

Alex pondered the situation. He was duty-bound to take his client's instructions, even if the client was wrong. Any young man who was claiming he was not able to work should surely be looking to secure his financial future and not rush into a settlement.

It was a dubious call to make, but Alex called his investigation agents. He normally used them to provide reports on accident locations, to take statements from independent witnesses, and to investigate liability for an accident. What he did not normally do was investigate his own clients.

He was not sure where the firm would be, ethically, if he was found to have had video surveillance on his own client, but he needed to know the truth as it could dictate his whole future.

He made the call and then went to see Christopher Hanson. He was the money laundering officer for the firm.

All law firms are required to report any clients they feel are possibly laundering money and that includes those who are putting forward fraudulent or exaggerated claims. They are obliged to do so without tipping off their clients. This statutory duty overrides their duty to client confidentiality, something which virtually all solicitors' clients are unaware of. Even in cases where the amounts involved are relatively small, if a suspicion is not reported, the lawyer could face up to seven years in jail for being complicit or even just negligent in not spotting any financial malfeasance.

Hanson was in his office. Alex knocked and was waved in.

'Chris, I think I've got a dodgy case on the Maguires account, and I think we need to report it under the money laundering regs.'

Hanson sighed. 'Bollocks. Do you have any idea how much paperwork is involved?'

'I've attended the seminars, Chris. I'll do the forms for you, and you can send them off. That way, you can stay out of prison and keep your arsehole the same size as it is now,' and under his breath, 'about as tight as a water rat's.'

'Thanks, Alex, succinctly put, as always.'

Dover

The huge doors dropped down on the ferry, and the daylight flooded in. After a few seconds, once his eyes had adjusted to the light, Jakov realised it was a grey, half light that had risen over the harbour. He could see the cliffs, but they were not as white as the song claimed. The chain was removed from across the front of the ferry, and he started his engine.

The Scania roared into life. He was carrying machine parts as usual. It was a regular run from Warsaw to Manchester, traveling through Lodz and Poznan in his home country, skirting south of Berlin, and heading west to Hanover with an overnight stop in Duisberg, not far from the Netherlands' border. From there, it was through Eindhoven, Antwerp, Ghent, sliding south of Bruges, and on to Dunkirk, where he had another long stop before the crossing at Calais. The Netherlands was his favourite part of the journey, before the sea crossing, which he never really got used to, and the gridlocked motorways of the United Kingdom.

The final hurdle was about to come as he went through the UK border control. He didn't know what additional materials he was carrying, and he didn't know where. He wasn't supposed to know that he was carrying anything else at all. But he had become suspicious the last time he arrived in Manchester, and his wagon was taken into the repair shop and the doors firmly shut behind it. He was sent to a hotel in town, where he had all the comforts he needed (including some company) on the organisation's account. Then, when he returned home, the wagon was taken off the road again for three days whilst he took his accrued time off with his family.

He didn't like being a mule for anybody. He was a good citizen, honest and hardworking. But he had a duty to look after his family, and if he gave up this job, he would earn a lot less or nothing at all. He was a proud man. He simply did not have the strength of will to admit to his family that he had been used. That he could no longer put the bread on the table.

He rolled the giant vehicle off the ferry and towards the customs shed, where he was guided into one of the inspection sheds, open at both ends but covered. Nothing unusual about that, they would sweep for explosives as they always did.

Today, however, there were dogs. He was asked to leave the cab whilst it was swept with the explosives' wipes, the same to other areas of the wagon and trailer. He saw the border guards spray the wipes with the chemical agent that would show whether there were traces of explosives, but as far as he could see, none of the wipes changed colour.

The dogs were busy sniffing around underneath the truck and around the axles. Jakov watched nervously. The dogs circled around each of the axles around and around. He began to feel a tightness in his chest, and his stomach felt hollow. Then the dogs moved on to the wheels, where one of them cocked its leg and urinated over the tyre.

Jakov was motioned to get back in the cab, and minutes later, he was through the port and on the motorway heading towards London.

The money was good, but he couldn't take many more journeys like this. Something would have to be done. The stress was too much for a man like Jakov.

Later that day, as the drizzle set in and the light faded even further, Ryan watched Jakov's wagon rumble past him into the workshop. This was the delivery he had been waiting for. The machine parts had been removed from the trailer by the forklift drivers, and Jakov was on his way to an evening of hotel porn films, sausages, and beer.

It would be a couple of hours until he had the merchandise out of the axles and into the back of the vans that were parked at the back of the workshop.

It would probably take less time to shift it on the streets of Moss Side, Hulme, Longsight, and Gorton. Ryan's people controlled the trade in the southeast quadrant of the city from Princess Road, which headed south out of the city centre to Ashton Old Road, heading east towards the Penines. To the west of Princess Road the Salford gangs ruled the roost and to the north of Ashton Old Road, there was something of a battleground, gangs from Middleton, Collyhurst, and Ancoats struggled for supremacy and occasionally strayed south of the boundary into his territory, where they were dealt with mercilessly.

A map of fatal shootings in the Greater Manchester area showed the highest concentration was in the Ardwick, Gorton, and Longsight districts, all in Ryan's sphere of influence and all bordering Ashton Old Road.

The city centre itself stayed remarkably incident free as it was generally agreed as a free trade area, provided that trade was kept unobtrusive. It didn't pay to have a turbulent war in the tourist areas of town as it would both reduce business and heighten police activity.

If anybody did get out of hand, then they were dealt with outside of town and by the mutual consent of all interested parties. It would be wrong to say that it was an organised crime syndicate that would be suggesting a greater degree of cooperation than truly existed. But a loose collection of shared interests attempted to enforce a fragile status quo.

Ryan made his way to the back of the workshop, where a small door opened into an office. Two men waited by the vending machine, drinking the terrible coffee.

'OK, the stuff will be in the van by 6:00 p.m. Get it out to your boys so it's on the streets tonight. I want fast turnaround on this load. I've got debts to pay.'

'Sure thing, guv.'

Ryan left the office, leaving the door open. The drizzle was starting to soak through over the collar of his leather jacket. He got in his car to head home. As the engine fired up, he placed his mobile in the cradle for his hands-free kit. It buzzed as an e-mail came through. He opened the mail and then the attachment.

'Cheeky bastard,' he said quietly to himself, then, banging the steering wheel with his palm, he continued, 'the cheeky fucking bastard.'

Duncan sat in the meeting room. Miles, Melbourne, and Drew sat around the table with open files and laptops.

'OK, Steven, no joy on your night out then. Lynn, when do we get the Richardson girl in?'

'We think next week, probably Tuesday, with her dad and her lawyer,' general groans around the table.

'Drew, what have you got on that payment?'

Drew sat forward leaning his forearms and palms flat on the table top. 'I spoke to the law firm. They were prepared to confirm that Redford was a client of theirs but would give me nothing more than that. They say that they have no evidence that their client is dead and, even if he is, the confidentiality between client and lawyer goes beyond that. The file they have belongs to the client, and if he is dead, it belongs to the estate. So I spoke to Mr.

and Mrs. Redford and asked them if they could get the file for me. They said that they would. I figured it would be quicker than a court order.'

'Probably,' Duncan confirmed.

'And Mrs. Redford told me that he suffered an injury at work, something fell on him and hurt his neck, and he made a claim. Apparently, he fell out with his employers about it, they didn't like the idea of him claiming against them, so that's why he packed in the job and went to work at . . . erm . . . whatever place he was working at when he croaked. So that explains the ten grand. I'l let you know when I get the full file.'

'What about the phone records?' Duncan hadn't looked up.

'Well, just prior to his death, he had called his girlfriend twice but got no answer. We are told he left no message, and the call duration time would suggest that is correct. In the days leading up to his death, a couple of calls to his parents' house, one to William Hill bookmakers (he only gambled small amounts infrequently and in keeping with his income) and one to his friend Ralph Small. He has no form and appears to be a friend from school days who Redford did his drinking with. Incoming calls, one from his insurance broker the week before (car insurance quote), a couple from his girl; to be honest, there is nothing unusual in there.'

Duncan looked around the table. 'OK, good job. Now, I've something to report to the rest of you, which is a bit, well, off the wall. But I can't ignore it, and I think there is a possibility it is relevant.'

He dropped a pile of papers on the desk with a hefty thud, Lynn jumped, Miles smirked, and she punched his thigh. Miles winced.

'Right, this is the unsolved murder of Maureen Ladd. She was raped and brutally beaten in 1991 on the Haughton Green housing estate in Denton. She later died from the massive head injuries she had received. She had sustained an injury to her left cheek, identical almost to the one on Steven Redford. She had her shoes removed, and they were located later in the bar of the Wordsworth Pub on the estate, only just across the road from where the attack took place. Maureen had been to the chip shop on the estate and had bought fish and chips and steak pudding, and chips for her husband and son for their tea about five or ten minutes before she was attacked, but the chips were not on the body when she was found.'

Drew was flicking through the report on Maureen Ladd. 'She was raped though, boss, and the rest of her injuries are nothing like Redford's. We know he was held by two men and beaten. This looks like your standard rape, one perpetrator got a bit too carried away.'

'A bit carried away, Drew, Jesus, you are one insensitive prick, that's almost an apology for the scumbag who did this.'

Lynn was furious. Duncan intervened, 'I agree, but let's keep our focus here. The injuries on Steven Redford that relate to those of Maureen Ladd were inflicted post-mortem. He had obviously not been eating chips whilst he was being beaten. No potato in his stomach but one, unchewed chip, in his mouth and one in his hand, so the chips were added later. If he is attacked by three men who beat him senseless in a sustained attack, why did they take his shoes? If he is being held up to take his beating, it indicates that they wanted him awake, so I am assuming they wanted him to talk so, again, why take his shoes, which we know were nothing special, and why then leave them in the bar of the pub, which seems a strange thing to do, especially as you would have to break in to get them in there?'

'I agree it is odd, but are we saying it's the same killer?' questioned Miles.

'No, I don't think so, but I don't know. I think, and I can't really back this up that somebody was leaving a message trying to bring the Maureen Ladd case to our attention.'

Drew put his arms out in front of him. 'Whoa, hang on, that's a bit of a leap, isn't it. How would they even know we would locate these connections, if that's what they are, I mean, I've never heard of Maureen Ladd.'

Duncan paused. He hadn't thought this through properly, and now he didn't know how much more information to give. 'I know the Maureen Ladd case, and I think whoever did this knew I would be involved in this case.'

Drew again said, 'So it's all about you then? What you are suggesting is that someone killed this kid to send you a message, is that right?'

'No,' Duncan said firmly, 'the boy was killed for some other reason and somebody seized the opportunity to send me a message.'

Lynn looked up from the file and almost apologetically said, 'It does seem a bit far-fetched Guv. Besides, what is the motive behind the message? Come to that, what is the message?'

Duncan spread out his arms, showing his impressive wingspan. 'If I knew that I wouldn't be sitting here asking you guys to consider it as an option. Look, I didn't want to muddy the waters but familiarise yourselves with the Maureen Ladd investigation and just keep an eye out for any connections. I am off to see the employers in the morning, let's reconvene here on Monday at four and let me know if anything crops up.'

Alex returned to his house. He had left work early and driven to Newport Pagnell, about four miles east of Milton Keynes. Newport was not a very inspiring town, but it was well known for two things: the motorway service station on the M1 and being the home of Aston Martin, the great British sports car manufacturer.

The factory was now gone, moved north to Telford to become more automated, but there was still a large service and sales centre in the town. Where the factory had been was now an empty lot waiting for a new Tesco supermarket.

The town centre itself was a curious mixture of Georgian coaching inns and latter-day charity shops. There was a nice church and an historic iron bridge over the River Lovat, the smaller of the two rivers running through the town.

Alex parked in the middle of the town, outside Boots Chemist and walked to the bank, where he had an appointment to open an account. He was ushered into the manager's office, and after discussing his financial needs and presenting the passport and birth certificate as identification, and was thanked for his custom and assured that both credit and debit cards would be on the way.

From the bank, he walked up to the post office at the northern end of town, where he completed his form for replacement of a lost driving licence. He presented the form with the photographs authenticated by the signature of the senior partner of Hanson's solicitors. The form was verified by the miserable, rude, and balding clerk, who seemed to see himself as a higher species because he was on the right side of the glass. Alex ignored the weary sarcasm, intending to leave no impression whatsoever.

He called in at his lock-up garage on the way home. He maintained a beautiful 1965 Volkswagen Karmann Ghia, type 1. It was guards red with a white roof and, having been imported from California, left-hand drive and rust-free. The pillarless coupé styling was evocative of the cafe culture of the 1960s, and the two angled air intakes on the front gave it a rakish 'face', like a pencil mustache on Errol Flynn. It had an original 1300 cc engine that buzzed willingly, like all Volkswagens air-cooled engines.

The Karmann only came out of the garage on sunny weekends. It was an item of automotive beauty. It was essentially a Volkswagen Beetle in a fancy Italian suit. Performance was no more than adequate, but for a car that was well on its way to being fifty, it was unbelievably reliable and ran as smoothly as many a modern car. It was soundproofed much better than the old Beetle, so the clattering air-cooled engine at the rear did not interfere with the driving experience.

He started the engine and let it run, checked underneath for leaks of any kind. He had the car maintained religiously by specialist air-cooled mechanics. It was always ready to go. He had not driven it much over the last few months as he had been working virtually every day, but it gave him a sense of achievement just to look at it in his garage.

As a child, he had seen one every day on his way to school. He had no idea what it was at the time, but it was the most exotic thing he had ever seen, and he had made a promise to himself that one day, he would be able to afford such an item. As it turned out, the Karmann only cost him $3,500, plus $1,700 for carriage to the UK. Since then, he had spent thousands of pounds rebuilding it and repainting it. The whole interior had been refurbished and all to the original specification save one item. His cheeky little secret was a DAB radio with iPod connection that looked exactly like the period radio it replaced.

After checking the oil and making sure his lights were fine, he rolled the car forward out of the garage in to the fading, pale winter sunshine. He took it for a quick turn around the estate, where he kept his lock-up and then parked it carefully back. He covered the car with the bespoke car cover and locked the garage. Then he drove the short distance back to his house.

It was pretty much dark when he parked the TT in the garage, leaving the driveway clear for Jules. He wasn't sure whether she was driving straight from work or whether she was walking round from her flat.

He put a Marks and Spencer's pasta carbonara in the oven, opened a bottle of Pinot Grigio, poured the contents into a carafe, and put it in the fridge to cool.

He wasn't sure yet how he was going to explain his life to Jules, or how he would justify his future. He was torn. He didn't want to lose her. He had realised over the last few weeks since he had been contemplating his fate that he loved her. At least, he thought he did, but Alex was a stranger to the concept of love, so it was impossible to be sure. He knew that she was the one person in the world he wanted to trust. Perhaps that was what it was, love.

On the other hand, he didn't want to hurt her and he certainly had no intention of dragging her into what would be his world from here on in. He contemplated just breaking up with her. Sure it would cause short-term heartbreak, but she would soon get on with the rest of her life, and without him dragging her down, she would soon achieve all of hers and her parents' ambitions. It was better for her that way. But Alex, as strong as he was, did not feel strong enough to give her up without a fight. He realised he was too selfish to do so.

Five minutes after the bell-signalled dinner was ready, Jules arrived home. They sat and ate in the kitchen, talking about work. As Alex was filling the dishwasher, Jules asked, 'Where did you get to today?'

He closed the door and set the machine off. He picked up their glasses and walked into the lounge, putting the glasses down on the side table, he sat on the long sofa; Jules sat next to him and held his hand. 'I think we need to have a talk, don't we,' she said quietly.

'I think we do. There's a lot to talk about, Jules, but I want you to know, before I start, that you are the only person, other than my mum, that I've ever loved, really loved. I don't want to lose you, but you might not want me after I've told you everything.'

'That's a bit melodramatic for you, Alex. What have you done?'

'I don't know where to begin, Jules, but you have to know. I am the man you know. But there is another me that you've never met.'

'I'll start at the very beginning'. Alex did, and he told her everything.

CHAPTER 11

MANCHESTER 1991

JACK SAT IN THE DARK of the hallway. They would come through the door to his right and turn to walk away from him down the hallway to the living room. That was when he would make his move.

He was nervous, but he tried to calm himself. He had found, before a major football match, that his nervousness sapped his energy. He would constantly be moving, tapping his feet or his hands, constantly drumming, all the time, his power being dissipated by the constant movement and the pounding of his heart. So he had developed the art of bringing down his pulse rate by thinking of his favourite songs. He sat in the dark, eyes closed, seeing The Kinks playing 'All Day and All of the Night' in his mind's eye. He was reliving a video clip he had seen, so his imaginings were in black and white. Ray Davies was singing, wearing his guitar like a fashion accessory, he could see the gap between his front teeth. He was relaxing now, in his own world, playing the guitar solo with Dave Davies, that was where all the power in the track came from; Dave's oversized Harmony Meteor guitar and bastardised amplifier, which he thrashed into a magnificent growling and wailing.

He heard the key in the door. The door opened. 'It's all right. He's working away. Come through.'

One person through the door, then a second, pushing the door shut behind him as he walked away from it, looking in the opposite direction to Jack. As the door was clicking shut, Jack noiselessly rose to his feet.

As Ladyboy disappeared in to the room, Jack exploded from his position at the end of the hallway. He hit him before he had even registered Jack's footsteps. Months of pent-up fury erupted and found its outlet in Jack's fists. He was upon him, pounding the sides of his head with both hands, fists a blur, punches raining in like a jackhammer gone berserk.

He fell to the floor, face first. There was a crack, and Jack stood over him breathing hard. It was all over in seconds.

'Shit, I think you killed him.'

'Don't be stupid, Ladyboy, get me a chair and let's get the twat in the kitchen, on the lino.'

Duncan pulled up on Tariff Street. The whole area was almost unrecognisable. Certainly some of the old warehouses and mills were still standing, but now they were ritzy apartments with German machinery parked outside. There were modern apartments too, large portions of them in garish colours with lots of wooden cladding and unusual angles. Duncan wondered why modern architects insisted on having wood cladding on a building in an area completely dominated by Victorian brick.

The one incongruous structure was the place that Duncan was headed to. A 1960s style workshop and office building set back in a large yard with enough room for around twenty heavy goods vehicles. The building was painted white and, despite a relatively recent coat, it looked tired and decrepit.

It was hard to believe that this was once the head office of Maguires Transport. The company was a colossus and certainly the largest road haulage company in the UK and possibly in Europe. Duncan was aware of their glamourous offices in King Street, but he also knew that Frank Maguire was based here with his son Ryan. Despite its size, the business was still privately owned and had resisted the lure of a public listing some years ago. Duncan wondered how they managed to compete with some of the more forward-thinking businesses they must be pitted against.

As he walked through the huge gateway, wide open for a steady stream of vehicles coming and going, he was approached by a walking muscle in a suit that was too tight and a shirt that seemed to be struggling to contain the neck that was reminiscent of an elephants leg.

The head was shaved, and he carried a walkie-talkie. When he was within five yards of Duncan, he spoke in what the police officer could only describe as an eastern European accent. He could be no more precise than that.

'Can I help you, Boss?'

Duncan took his warrant card from the back pocket of his grey flannel trousers and held it in front of the small, round eyes. 'Police, I'm here to talk to Mr. Maguire.'

'Do you have appointment, Boss?'

'No, I don't have an appointment, but the Greater Manchester constabulary would appreciate it if Mr. Maguire could assist us in our enquiries. Where do I go?'

'Sorry, Boss, you don't go nowhere till I speak to the big man.'

With this, he placed a flat hand on Duncan's chest stopping him from walking any further. Duncan was a good head taller and was willing to bet he had quicker reflexes. But on reflection, he decided it was better to play it cool and wait for the appropriate moment to assert himself. He also thought that he could probably hit this man with one of the trucks in the yard and still struggle to move him.

The Pole (for that was how Duncan had decided to categorise him) turned his head away and spoke into the walkie-talkie in a language that was neither English nor French, which was a problem as those were the only two that Duncan could understand.

Duncan was counting the rolls on the back of his neck when he turned his head.

'You're OK, Boss, straight ahead to the door and wait, the big man will meet you there.'

'You're very kind.' Duncan smiled, trying very hard to appear flippant. He walked to the glass door in the main building. Beyond the door, he could see a large potted plant, a couple of chairs, and a staircase. There was another door, wooden, with a chrome handle and a keypad for security. Duncan pushed the glass door, which did not move, so he stood and waited.

A tall man with blond, curly hair came down the stairs—clearly not a Maguire. He touched the keypad on the inside of the glass door and it clicked open. He pulled the door inward and stepped to the side to allow Duncan in.

'Chief Inspector Duncan, I wonder if I could have a word with Mr. Maguire?'

'Good morning, Mr. Duncan, I am afraid that Mr. Maguire is off site at present. I am Steven Holland, the group head of Legal, is there anything I can help you with?'

'Perhaps, Mr. Holland, does head of Legal have human resources under his remit?'

'Well, to a degree, yes. Tell me what is it that you want, and I will endeavour to help you, but may I see your identification?' Holland spoke lightly. Duncan felt this was forced, which meant he did not feel relaxed. He reached to his back pocket again.

'Of course, my apologies.' He handed over his warrant card for inspection. Holland took out his iPhone and tapped in some details off the warrant card before he passed it back.

'One can't be too careful. We are very security conscious here, despite appearances.' He turned towards the stairs. 'Please, follow me, Mr. Duncan.' Duncan let the failure to acknowledge rank slide for a second time. He did not want to antagonise or arouse suspicion of his motives. He followed Holland up the stairs, solid concrete stairs with threadbare blue carpet, which turned right before coming out on to a large landing with a square window on the front wall, overlooking the yard. To the right was a door, slightly ajar, and Duncan could see a large desk within with a very well-groomed and professional looking young woman sat behind it.

'That's Mr. Maguire's office and his PA, Dawn Marshall. My office is this way.'

There were three other doors on the same wall, and they were headed to the one furthest away. Holland opened the door to a replica room to the one glimpsed down the landing. A different PA sat typing furiously. Not quite so professional looking and not nearly so attractive.

Holland carried on to the next door immediately opposite; he tapped his finger on the desk as he passed it, three times quickly. He did not introduce his own PA. Duncan wondered if the tapping on the desk was codified message 'three minutes, then call me'.

They went into Holland's office, which took Duncan by surprise. It was sparse to say the least. There was a desk with computer monitor and keyboard, a standard office chair, two slim wooden armchairs with thin fixed cushions facing the desk and a large grey metal filing cabinet. There was literally nothing else. No blinds or curtains on the window, no personal items on the desk, and no sign of the type of activity you would expect from a man of his lofty position.

Holland was behind his desk. 'Do take a seat.' He seemed to read Duncan's expression. 'This is my second office. I work from King Street mainly and only come over to the yard occasionally. Now, what was it I can help you with?'

'We are investigating the murder of Steven Redford, a former employee of yours. He worked for you up until a couple of months ago when it appears he left quite suddenly. I wondered if we could look at his employment record, see if there is anything in there that would be relevant to his death.'

Holland had his fingertips placed together making an arch shape with his hands.

'Well, strictly speaking, you would need a warrant or a court order to get access to our employees' records. But . . .' He paused for effect as though considering the legal implications, 'I am sure that in the circumstances, the somewhat tragic circumstances, we can make an exception. Of course, should you need anything for the purposes of a trial, you will need to make a formal request and have all the paperwork in order. I wouldn't want to leave us open to criticism, you understand.'

'Of course not, thank you for your understanding of our urgency. We will ensure that Maguires are not exposed to anything of the sort, I can assure you.'

Holland smiled. He looked at Duncan for a long moment, sizing him up, Duncan thought. Had he picked up the hint of sarcasm?

'Good.' He tapped at his keyboard and then leant forward to turn his screen around so that Duncan could see what was on it.

'Please feel free to make notes, but I can't print anything off for you, I am sure you understand.'

Duncan scrolled through the usual basic details, name address, date of birth, and national insurance number. He saw his sickness record, which was generally exemplary. There was a record of the accident, a copy of the accident book from the workshop—notes taken from his exit interview. Redford had felt it was time to move on; he felt uncomfortable after making his claim, like the lads in the workshop didn't think he should have made a claim that he was some sort of pariah as a result. It seemed that he left on good terms with his superiors, and there was a note suggesting that he was worthy of consideration should he ever apply to come back.

'There is not much in there that will be of any real use to us. Is there any detail of the insurance claim that was made, Mr. Holland?'

'Well now, I don't think so. All of that stuff is dealt with by our insurers and then, in turn, by our insurance team at King Street. They would find out the settlement details but nothing more. Purely for renewal purposes, we need to declare all claims and their cost.'

Holland turned the screen back round to its original position. 'I can have a look and see what information there is.' He tapped away, glancing at the screen as he clicked the mouse.

'All I can tell you is that the case is settled and that Mr. Redford received £10,000. I have no other detail than that I am afraid.' Holland smiled, clicked the mouse, and sat back; his body language saying that his cooperation was complete.

'Thank you, that ties in with his bank statements. Could you let me know who your insurers are? I think I will need rather more information, just to be complete in my report. I am sure you understand.'

Holland's face said that he didn't. 'Of course, our insurers are BGA.'

Duncan frowned as he wrote a note. 'BGA? I don't know them. Do they have a local office?'

Holland laughed. 'Only if you are a native of Grand Bahama, Mr. Duncan, they are based there.'

Duncan looked puzzled. 'Isn't that a bit unusual, an insurer based in a foreign country?'

'Not at all,' Holland said, rising from his seat. 'We are a multinational company, Mr. Duncan, and we have many financial interests, one of which is an insurance business, which happens to be very profitable. The regulatory system over there is as rigorous as our own. Did you know that there was no corporation or income tax in the Bahamas?' Holland was around the desk and heading towards the door, a sure sign that Duncan should leave.

He rose from the chair and walked slowly to the door. 'No, I didn't know that, it's not something that really affects me in my line of work. My investment portfolio is limited to a new mobile every two years and a new car every ten.'

Holland opened the door and smiled as they passed in the doorway, a 'never mind', patronising sort of smile.

Duncan did not like Holland. It was time to fire a warning shot.

'By the way, it's Detective Chief Inspector Duncan, I would appreciate it if you could remember that for next time we meet.'

Holland said breezily, 'I most certainly will. Heather, could you let Mr. Duncan out please.'

Duncan balled his fists, and the muscles visible in his jaw tightened. *You will remember, Mr. Holland*, he thought to himself as he headed down the stairs, *next time, you will.*

Ryan Maguire watched Duncan leave from the window of his father's office. He knew him, or at least knew of him.

He would have to speak to Holland. He didn't want him reporting this visit to his father; the old man was getting jumpy enough as it was. The last thing he needed right now was the old man pulling the plug on his deals, at a time when he needed to repay Uncle Jimmy.

He had to get these next few cases through and keep the flow of merchandise going. If he really pushed it for the next few months, he would be clear with Jimmy and be able to pay off the old man into his retirement. Then the business would be his, and he could sideline the Irish. There were other markets to open up, and he could see no reason why he would share that with psychotic Uncle Jimmy and his prehistoric allegiances.

He was hopeful that he could get Jimmy's money back, now that he knew, or was fairly sure he knew, who had it. That would certainly oil the wheels.

He picked up his phone. 'Yeah, Mickey. Look, bud, I've got a job for you. You know that job you fucked up on? Well, call it what you want, but I call it fucked up. Well, this is your chance to put it right my friend, and I want it done properly this time . . .'

Jules sat alone in her flat. She was thinking and had been crying. She had no idea what to do. She had nobody she could talk to about her dilemma, not without running the risk of seriously compromising Alex.

But why shouldn't she compromise him, had he not done the same to her? Everything he had told her put her in the position where she knew too much—every revelation more shocking than the previous one.

But she loved him.

She didn't really know him. His whole life was a charade, lie woven on to lie, with just a thin strand of truth holding it all together. He had literally unravelled himself before her. He was completely exposed, and she was horrified and compelled and yet compassionate. He had finally opened that last door into his psyche. Was that not what she had always wanted? To make him let go and to release his innermost being to her so that she could know him absolutely. Yet it was fair to say she had not realised that his closed heart was going to be a Pandora's box.

Still, sitting here, in the darkness of her flat, she still loved him.

But could she live with what she knew? Could she ever trust him? It was true that he had placed the ultimate trust in her. But how could she ever really know. Would she ever know what he was thinking? Would he be able to carry on as he was or would he have to take off? Would the burden he had laid upon her crush their relationship? Had it already? She had never doubted Alex, never questioned his integrity, and now she knew that his whole life was a deception.

She picked up her mobile and sent him a text message. She needed time to digest all of this. She was not sure that her love was enough. She was not sure whether his was.

Alex lay on his bed, fully clothed. He had intended to go to sleep, but his mind was racing. He had done it. He had honestly believed that he would be able to work his way past it all and that he would be able to keep Jules, that she would understand him, stay true to him, help him to unburden himself, and to come out the other side.

It was only when he was revealing the truth about himself, and when he could actually hear what he was saying out loud, that he realised that it had always been a forlorn, fantastic hope that their relationship could survive.

His mobile sounded, like the horn on a clown car in the circus, a honking sound. It was a text from Jules. He grabbed the phone off the bedside chest of drawers.

I don't know what to think. I don't know what to do. You are safe, but I need time to decide. Don't contact me. I will ring you when I know. J.

He put the phone back and put his hands behind his head. Well, it was the best he could hope for. She was always going to take her time, that was just Jules.

He made his decision there and then. He would try and have everything done by the time she had reached her decision. By then, he would be free, one way or another, and she would either have no choice to make or he could offer her a better choice than he had so far.

He would get things moving in the morning. He had greater motivation now to bring things to a head. It meant confronting his past. He would have to go and see him. But he had already made the first step with his confession that night, and he had no doubt that was the one that he would regret the most.

He closed his eyes and lay still. Sleep would not come, not that night. It was all back with him, resurrected from the depths of his subconscious, which brought into the light for the first time in twenty years. He was compelled to take a fresh look and reassess himself. If he was going to come through this, he needed to regress back to the person he used to be. But he was afraid of that person, afraid that he would feel too comfortable in that skin and that he may never find his way back.

CHAPTER 12

MANCHESTER 1991

Jack had tied him to a kitchen chair using an old washing line from the balcony and some gaffer tape. His arms were behind his back; his hands were taped together. His feet were together and taped at the ankles. The washing line was tied tight against his chest and fastened to the slats on the back of the chair, tied around and around, so tight that the skin was white around the line, where it wrapped around his biceps.

He had been bleeding from his nose, which was clearly broken but that had now dried. His right eye was swollen and almost closed from Jack's ferocious attack. Red marks were around his face, where the punches had hit home. His jaw looked swollen.

Jack stood before him wearing just his black jeans. His body was taut, ripped, a slight sheen over the hairless chest. He was not heavily muscled, but he carried no excess. In his right hand, he held the knife.

He looked into the wild, frightened eyes.

'Tell me about Maureen Ladd. I want to know what happened, and I want to know who did what,' Jack spoke quietly. 'If you don't tell me everything, this will go very bad for you.'

There was a laugh and blood was spat on to the floor. 'It's not exactly going fuckin' great so far, is it, you little prick? How old are you? When my brother gets hold of you, he'll gut you, rip you right up the middle, and empty you out like an old fuckin' bin bag.'

Jack's right hand arced through the air. There was an audible disturbance of the atmosphere around them, then came the warm feeling of the blood flowing down over his stomach, and after that came the stinging pain. The white T-shirt started to stick to him and change colour.

'That is just a scratch, slightly more than a paper cut. You will tell me, or I swear I will start cutting bits off. And when I'm done, there'll be no more fudge packing for you, gay boy.'

Another guttural laugh, Jack could see the blood on his teeth. 'Fuck you.'

Ladyboy was standing in the doorway. His eyes were wide; his breathing was coming in short, sharp gasps. 'Jack, can we have a word?'

'When I'm done.'

The voice raised an octave. 'Jack, we need to talk now.'

Jack took his eyes away from the man in the chair, and seeing the urgency in Ladyboy's eyes, he walked out of the kitchen and into the hallway.

Ladyboy turned and spoke quietly, 'He's not going to tell you anything, Jack, you can hit him and cut him as much as you want. He won't tell you a thing.'

'Now isn't the time to get squeamish, Ray. He will tell me everything, it just takes time.'

Ladyboy looked at the floor. 'Jack, let me do it.'

Jack looked at him in amazement. 'Are you joking?'

'No, I'm not joking. I know him better than you, Jack. I know what will make him talk. But you'll have to do as I say and don't interrupt me. You won't like it.'

'Jesus, Ladyboy. I've attacked a man, tied him to a chair in your kitchen, and sliced him with a fucking kitchen knife. And you think you can shock me?'

Ladyman nodded. He went down the hallway and into his bedroom. When he came out, he was carrying an enormous black vibrator and a video camera. 'I think you'd better take the camera.'

'No shit.'

Two hours later, they sat in the living room. 'Ray, you'd better turn that music up.' Jack wanted to drown out the sound of the sobbing coming from the kitchen.

Jack had found out everything about the attack on his mother. If the story was to be believed, the elder brother was entirely responsible for the rape and the injuries. Jack was inclined to believe the story he had heard. From what he had just filmed, he doubted that the man in the kitchen was either interested in or capable of raping a woman.

He claimed to have received a kick to the genitals as Maureen was wrestled to the floor, which rendered him inactive throughout the attack.

The full story was willingly told without any further violence. Ladyboy had untied him from the chair, leaving his hands and feet taped up, undone his jeans and pulled them, and the boxer shorts as low as they would go before the tape got in the way, then kissed and caressed him into a state of arousal. Then he had inserted the vibrator. He had moaned in obvious agony and ecstasy. Ladyboy had brought him to climax while he begged to be taken roughly. All the while Jack had been sitting on the kitchen floor filming on the Sony camcorder.

Then he had played the video back, and Ladyboy told him that he either told them everything or the tape went through his father's letter box that very night. At that point, he had broken down and told the whole story.

He was now sobbing in despair alone in the kitchen whilst Jack and Ladyboy sat in the lounge, stunned by what they had just done.

'What now, Jack?'

Jack didn't look up. 'I don't know. I was gonna kill the bastard, but he didn't do it, did he?' Jack seemed lost in thought.

'Jack, he was there, and how did he get a kick in the balls if he wasn't going along with it?'

Ladyboy got up and walked across to the stereo by the hallway door.

Jack mulled over his predicament. Ladyboy had a point, but Jack felt that the other brother was the main perpetrator. Maybe he should just send him home? He would not go to the police. They still had the tape, and they could make sure everyone knew what was on it and that his family would see it. Chances are he would not even mention this to his family; the shame would be too great for him to bear. But he could warn his brother, and if he did that, Jack might never get to him. And Jack really wanted him. There would be no talking next time.

'Get me the tape, or I will cut this bastard's head off right now.'

Jack reached for his knife, but it was not on the sofa. He saw it on the window sill behind Ladyboy. Ladyboy stood with his chin held high, the forearm beneath it keeping it his head tilted back, the knife in the hand touching the side of his face.

He stood behind Ladyboy, holding Ray's right arm, twisting it high up his back with his right hand, the left held the knife. A thin line of blood started to appear on Ladyboy's face.

Immediately Jack was trying to calculate how he could get to him, but he could not reach his knife as they were between him and it. If he tried to take him unarmed, then both him and, particularly, Ladyboy would be cut badly.

He still had strips of tape on his wrists and ankles, but they were free. Jack got up slowly. The miniature cassette was on the floor between them. He bent to pick it up, never taking his eyes off the knife.

He held it out towards the hand with the knife. He was thinking he may be able to get the knife away from Ladyboy's throat.

Ladyboy's right arm was released from the grip, but the free hand came immediately up to his forehead, and the point of the knife was thrust into Ladyboy's neck. Ray screamed. But the knife did not go all the way, and he whispered, 'Take the tape and pass it back to me, or I finish you.'

Ladyboy held out his hand towards Jack, pleading with his eyes. Jack didn't hesitate. He handed the tape over and said, 'Let him go. If you let him go, you both get to live. If he dies, you die. You know I can get to you.'

Ladyboy was passing the tape backwards bending his arm around. In the next moment, he went tumbling towards Jack, propelled forward, the tape snatched from his hand, the knife drawn across his throat as he fell. The man behind him turned and ran for the door as Ladyboy hit Jack pushing him back on to the sofa; his blood spilt on to Jack's shirt and his hands clutched his throat.

Jack shifted his weight and rolled him so that Ray landed on his back on the sofa, and then he was up and running and grabbing the knife as he passed.

He flew out of the flat and into the corridor as the lift doors at the end of the narrow walkway closed shut; Jack turned the other way and yanked open the fire door to the stairwell. He set off down the stairs taking the top three or four and then jumping to the half landing, rounding the corner and doing the same again.

It was eight floors, two staircases, and a half landing per floor, but he needed to get to the foyer before him. He pushed himself on as his lungs were burning with the sudden exertion. There were six more floors. It was taking him too long; then five and four. His thighs and calves were feeling the strain of the jumping and running; then three. He started to gamble, once on the landing, he took hold of the banister and propelled himself down the whole flight—no running, just a single leap. He hit the landing and staggered but turned the corner and did the same again. Two; he hit the half landing; his right ankle gave way, and he yelled out in agony and jumped again, and again. One; he pushed himself off, the pain in his ankle forced him to land on his left leg and then use his right to steady himself; he winced as his right foot hit the landing, and then he pushed off again, losing his balance on hitting the concrete floor as the damaged right ankle gave way, and he crashed into the door.

He pulled himself up and tore open the heavy fire door and ran awkwardly. The wide foyer was empty; his heart sank, and he stopped, bent over, his hands on his knees whilst he gasped for breath, his thighs trembling, the knife hanging loosely in his left hand. He leant back against the wall.

Then he heard it—the lift grinding to a halt; the heavy metal doors rumbling open; and out he came, full pelt for the front door of the flats. He hadn't seen Jack, who had been leaning flat against the wall when the lift doors had opened. Jack was after him, the rush of adrenaline erupting through his legs and chest. As the first man reached the heavy glass door, he slowed, grabbed the long brass door handle, and pushed. It stuck. The doors opened inward. Jack hit him from behind, and the knife sank deep into his lower back; he arched his back and started to scream. Jack pushed his head forwards, and his face was smashed into the thick glass of the door, killing the scream almost before it had begun. Jack pulled out the knife and plunged it in again, upwards, under the left arm. At that moment, as the point of the knife pierced his heart, Sean Maguire died.

'Joe?'

Joe yawned. 'Yeah?'

'It's Jack.'

'I know it's you.'

'I need your help, mate.'

'What with?'

'Meet me at Ladyboy's flat. It's urgent, Joe.'

'Jack, do you know what the time is?'

'No. I need you, Joe.' The phone went dead. Joe whispered under his breath, 'Christ'. How was he supposed to get out of the house at 11:00 p.m. without his parents noticing?

Thirty minutes later, Joe was tapping on the door of the flat. He had said goodnight to his parents and headed upstairs, only to grab his coat and head straight back down, as quietly as he could.

He had crept through the kitchen to the back door, which he had left unlocked. This was the crucial moment;

he had to open and close the door, half-paned door, without his parents hearing.

He stood by the door. They were in the lounge right next to the kitchen. He listened, heard the sounds of the television, and guessed there was some political debate, probably *Question Time*. His father never missed *Question Time*.

At that point, he had heard his father speaking angrily, unhappy with the answer of one of the guests—a socialist more than likely. Joe opened the door, the creak of the handle and click of the latch drowned out by the sounds of heated discussion and applause. Joe assumed there was a left winger on the panel as they always got his dad a bit heated.

He stepped outside and slipped on the shoes he had left on the step after Jack's phone call.

He listened again to the muffled sounds of the presenter saying goodnight and the loud applause. He had to get away now as the door from the lounge would be opened any minute by his parents taking their teacups to the dishwasher before heading up to bed.

He pushed the door shut and ducked down below the glazed half of the door. He saw the shaft of light from the opening of the lounge door and saw it disappear as the switch in the lounge was flicked off. Then the garden was flooded with bluish light as the bulbs in the kitchen spotlights came on.

He was stuck; he crouched below view, praying that nobody came to the door to look out. His heart sank when he realised that the door would be locked. When his father came to lock the door, he could not fail to see Joe on the step.

He listened, calculating wildly how he could explain this away, and decided he could not. He heard his mother asking if the door was locked, and he prepared for the worst.

'I did it earlier,' his dad had said.

A moment later, the light was out and the garden was all shadows and was swaying dark shapes that were the laurel bushes by day.

Joe ran to the end of the garden, between and behind the laurels, where he reached the fence. He pulled himself up, careful not to let his feet bang against the fence panel, until he was prostrate, straddling the top of the fence. Then he just let himself slide over the other side.

From the path that ran behind his garden, he could get back on to the road, and from there, he could run the two miles to the flat. It was a distance he had been running since he was eight years old, since he started playing with Jack after school or in the summer holidays.

They played football together of course. Joe had concluded early on that their friendship was based on the fact that he was a goalkeeper. When they played, Jack did not have to take a turn in goal, like he did when he played with the other kids.

But as time went on, they became inseparable. Joe realised that Jack was not just the tough kid from the overspill estate. He was bright, funny, and often surprisingly sensitive. He was also deeply embarrassed by his background. The fact that his parents did not own their house and that they were not as wealthy as other kids' parents. That his dad was a drinker and violent and was always driving around in some rust bucket of a car that he had picked up from the garage because it was ready for scrapping. All of these things burnt in to Jack.

Joe also knew the conflict within Jack. He was clever; he wanted to be a professional—no job where he had to get his hands dirty. He wanted to earn real money. But he could not be seen to turn his back on the roots that still bound him. His whole family was working class; he lived amongst working-class people on the estate. He hated the thought that those people would see him as some sort of traitor if he achieved his potential.

Having passed the exams for the grammar school for instance, Jack had to be convinced that he should go. His guilt at what he saw as his betrayal of his blue-collar surroundings made him want to forsake the biggest opportunity he would ever have to achieve his goals.

Joe had always thought this was why he put so much into his football. The only way to retain your working-class credibility and yet earn enough money to set you apart from the norm, as Jack saw it, was to be a footballer or a pop star. You could then be a 'local lad made good.' Jack listened to John Lennon's 'Working Class Hero' over and over. Something he thought he would never be if he became a lawyer or an accountant. In that case, he would just be that kid who thought he was better than the rest of us.

It was Maureen who gave him the strength of mind to reach for what he wanted; to cut himself free from the grind of their daily lives. She made him feel that it was good to dream of a better life, even if it was only a little better. There was no treachery involved. He owed the estate nothing. She would even go so far as to tell him that he must not let them drag him back to their level. He was better than them, and he should be proud of the fact and embrace the possibilities that brought.

Jack was devoted to Maureen. She was always there to assuage the guilt, to smooth his path towards the middle classes. She encouraged the friendship with Joe. She wanted Jack to pick up on the style of life that Joe had. His family was not wealthy, but they were comfortable.

Joe's Dad had a new car every four years and read the broadsheet newspapers. Joe's Mum didn't work. They drank wine with their meals. There had never even been a bottle of wine in Jack's house. To him, it was something that was drunk on television in period dramas.

Maureen's aspirations for Jack were subtly reinforced by the boy's friendship, and Jack had changed over the years.

There had, though, always been the dark side to him—the fights, particularly, at grammar school. As the sole representative of the council houses, he felt it was his moral duty to be harder than all the 'middle class softies'. He felt pressure to revert to the stereotype that was expected of him and often relented to that pressure, fighting, rebelling in class, playing the surly teenager from the wrong side of the tracks.

Maureen had kept chipping away. She had made him go to the martial arts classes to channel the aggression that was inherent within him, to relieve the build-up of anger and frustration, and to act like a safety valve. Jack had embraced it to begin with; his natural athleticism making him an outstanding student. But the discipline they demanded of him was more than he was prepared to give, and gradually he drifted away.

Maureen's loss, Joe felt, had destabilised Jack completely. He had been dragged back like a lost soul hauled back into Hades.

Jack opened the door of the flat.

He looked at Joe, then turned and walked back into the flat. Joe followed him to the lounge.

'Christ.'

Joe had never seen anything like this. There was a body on the floor in the middle of the room, glazed eyes open, seeing nothing. On the sofa was Ladyboy. He had a towel wrapped around his neck. It was soaked red with blood, which was dripping on to his chest. His face was white, and he looked close to death.

Jack stood next to the body on the floor; his hands were red and his hair damp. His T-shirt was stained with blood and the sweat from his underarms. He was looking dazed.

'Jack, what have you done?'

Jack looked up. 'Sorry, Joe, I didn't want to get you involved in all this, but it all went a bit tits up. We had him tied up in the kitchen, but he got free when we were in here. He cut Ladyboy's throat and ran. I went after him and caught him in the lobby.'

'You dumb fucker, you tied him up and left him in the kitchen. Where the knives are?'

Jack just shrugged.

Joe surveyed the scene again. The original shock was wearing off, and he was already computing the possibilities of them actually getting away with this.

'OK.' He was talking to himself. It was the only way he would know if what he was thinking sounded plausible. 'He,' Joe said, pointing at the ailing Ladyboy, 'needs a hospital, now. Get him out of here, take him to the park round the back of The Wordsworth, and leave the towel here. Make a huge racket, wake everybody up, and tell them he was attacked. You saw Sean Maguire, no you saw a man run away. When you describe him, you describe Sean Maguire.'

'OK.'

'Ladyboy, you're gonna have to tell the police that you were having it off and got into an argument, over money, and he cut you and ran. Ladyboy, can you hear me?'

Ladyboy grunted.

'Right, I'll get rid of him whilst you are out, and I'll get this place cleaned up as best I can. Whatever happens, don't let anybody come back here, you understand. *Jack!'*

Jack started, 'Yeah, I'm listening, nobody back here.'

Jack helped Ladyboy off the sofa, and they headed to the door. Jack came back and bent down by the body.

'What are you doing?' Joe held out his arms with incomprehension.

'I need his shoes, Joe. Them bastards have to know why he's not coming back. I want them to know.'

'Jack, you can't take them now, the police will be in the park. I'll keep them safe for you. Get going, or Ladyboy won't make it.'

Jack half led, half carried the stricken Ladyboy out of the flat, and Joe watched them struggle to the lift. When the doors closed behind them, he returned to the flat. He stared at the scene of carnage. He wept. *This is the point at which the rest of his life will be defined,* he thought.

He dragged the body through the hallway to the front door, tears still clouding his vision.

He left it slumped by the door. He was already out of breath. There was no way he could carry it to the lift, and he couldn't drag it because it would leave a trail behind. He had to find another way to get it out of the flats.

He went into the kitchen and got all the cleaning materials he could find and started on the kitchen, where there were splatters of blood on the floor and the cabinet doors. From there, he moved to the lounge. The sofa was covered with a throw, which, when removed, revealed a large stain, but it was an existing food stain, not a blood stain.

The carpet had blood soaked into it. Joe thought it would be easier for Ladyboy to explain to his dad why he had spilt bleach on the carpet rather than blood. So after he had soaked up as much as he could, he applied the bleach liberally. He knew from the crime programmes, which his parents watched, that the bleach would destroy the evidence. But he was more concerned with making it look like there was no evidence.

When he had finished, there was large patch of carpet that was much lighter in colour than the rest, but he saw no sign of any blood. He opened a window to relieve the cloying stench of blood and bleach.

He stood in the doorway and examined the room. There were no obvious signs of what had gone on that night.

He had spent two hours cleaning. He had heard the sirens and was keen to get out of the flat just in case anybody turned up to investigate the lad's story. He had visions of the police coming through the door, just as he was dragging the body out.

So when he heard the door open, he froze.

'Hi, Joe.'

Jack sauntered in as though he had just been for a walk in the park, which, to be fair, he had.

'Is Ladyboy OK?'

'I think so. He's in the hospital, and they said he had lost a lot of blood, but there was no major damage. He might have some difficulty talking for a while, which is probably no bad thing. I've got something that might help.'

Joe followed him back out into the corridor, where there was a wire shopping trolley. 'One of the advantages of living on a council estate, Joe, is that you are never very far from an abandoned shopping trolley.' He smiled.

That action lifted Joe's spirits immediately. He saw Jack's macabre and black humour despite the situation, and, now he was no longer alone with the problem, his energy was renewed. They went back inside and lifted the body and struggled through the door. It was back-breaking lifting it high enough to get it in the trolley, especially as the trolley kept moving as they tried to push the inert weight into the top of it. Eventually, it dropped in and was left in a lopsided seating position.

Jack explained that there were a few people about after the commotion in the park, so they took one of Ladyboy's jackets hanging in the hallway and put it on the body. A green parka with fur-trimmed hood—they pulled the hood up and zipped the front of the jacket as high as it would go.

'If anybody sees us we're three pissed-up mates larking about with a shopping trolley,' said Jack.

They filled the trolley with the throw and a blanket off Ladyboy's bed and put all the cleaning equipment under the blanket in the trolley. Jack threw in his T-shirt and came out of American Keith's room wearing a traditional American Country and Western shirt, light blue but white across the shoulders with white piping and metal tips on the collar.

'Jesus, Jack, couldn't you have found one with tassels on the back?'

Jack was smirking. 'You need to see that man's wardrobe, mate, this is tame. Yee ha.' He slapped his thigh.

They pushed the trolley as quietly as they could to the lift. It was now two in the morning, and the whole block of flats seemed to be asleep.

The lift doors rumbled open and they went inside.

'Where are we taking him?'

Joe was pensive. 'I was thinking up to the canal.'

'What, just push the trolley in and watch him sink? Don't bodies come back up after a while cos of the gas?'

'Yeah, they do. I don't know, Jack. I've never disposed of a body before, you know.'

The lift pinged and the doors opened slowly. They held their breath, praying there was nobody inside. It was empty.

'Right, let's head up there anyway. We'll go through the village and down Gib Lane, and we'll decide what to do from there, once we are in the woods. If anybody sees us, just say Penny for the Guy.' They both laughed.

They went through the foyer and opened the door, and before heading out, they cleaned the door and the floor, where Sean Maguire had met his death. Then they turned right outside the flats and headed past the bus terminus, which was in reality nothing more than a large lay-by, where the buses from Manchester and Ashton under Lyne turned around for their return journey. They wheeled on past St. Mary's Church and up the slight hill into Haughton Green village.

Before the huge council estate was built in the early 1960s, Haughton Green had been a small village on the outskirts of the larger town of Denton. There had been a tram stop and a number of small shops on the main street of Haughton Green Road. The village bordered the River Tame, and on the other side of the river was the Peak Forest Canal, which runs between Ashton-under-Lyne, a suburb to the east of Manchester, and Whaley Bridge in Derbyshire, where it had picked up limestone from the quarries in Derbyshire to be transported into Manchester.

The village had an industrial past, having had some coal mines in the late eighteenth century, then a hat factory, which later became a paint factory, situated between the river and canal.

Jack and Joe pushed the trolley up the deserted Haughton Green Road and passed the terraced houses at the old tram stop and The Jolly Hatters pub opposite.

Reaching the heart of the old village, they turned right, down Gibralter Lane, commonly called Gib Lane, a narrow road that began with small Victorian terraced houses, but, as they went down the hill towards the bottom of the river valley, more modern, detached houses, until when they were in sight of the bridge across the river, and the road turned into nothing more than a track, the houses returned to being a single row of brick Victorian workers' cottages.

When they reached the bridge, the houses could no longer be seen. They pushed the trolley across the bridge amid the deafening roar of the weir a few yards upstream.

Upon reaching the other side, Jack stopped. 'Joe, remember when we were kids when the paint factory was just over there.' He pointed straight ahead where the remaining base of the old factory could just be made out through the trees in daylight but which was invisible to them in the near total darkness. 'Yeah, I remember.'

'Well, there was the old mine shaft just behind the factory, remember? It was all fenced off.'

They looked at each other. 'Do you think we can get in?'

Jack shrugged again. 'Dunno, but let's go have a look, shall we? See if it's still there.'

They pushed the trolley up the steep path that wound around the old factory site. The moon was now out, and they could see the remains of the old Victorian mill through the trees—low lines of brick that were once the foundations of a huge building. They turned right, off the path, and cut through the trees. Jack knew instinctively where to look, despite the dark. He had spent most of his childhood in these woods, riding around on his bike during the summer holidays. The bike that he and Joe had made was pieced together from the parts of other bikes that they had liberated from back gardens and unlocked sheds throughout the estate and the village.

It was heavy going now. They were tiring; the rush of adrenaline received from their being reunited at the flat was wearing thin. There was no formal path, just a bumpy narrow track between the trees. The trolley hit tree roots and was bounced around by the uneven earth. Then, it was in front of them, exactly as they remembered it. On a mound of black earth, the remnants of what they had always called slag, the useless deposits of coal from the original excavation, was the fence, which was at least six feet high. The gate was padlocked. Through it, they could see the large slab of concrete over the narrow shaft.

They had never realised it as children, but this was nothing more than a breather shaft. The main shaft for the miners was further up the river. The breather shaft itself was narrow, but it would certainly serve their purposes.

Jack walked around the perimeter of the fence. He came back to Joe. 'Massive hole round the other side, we can just walk in there.'

They pushed the trolley around and through the gap, but it would not go up the small slag heap. The shards of coal on the ground were loose and the wheels would not turn, so they turned the trolley on to its side and hauled the body from it.

When they got to the top, they pulled at the concrete slab. It moved about an inch. Jack sat on the floor and put his heels against the edge of the slab, with his legs bent, and pushed, trying to straighten his legs and shift the block. Joe followed suit. They strained and grunted, and just when they felt they would have to give up, the slab shifted with a terrible echoing scrape. They slid forward and pushed again. It was easier this time, and the shaft was half open. That was enough.

They both stood, and Joe's thighs tingled from the effort. They each took an arm and dragged the body to the gaping shaft. They laid it down with the head over the edge, then walked to the feet, picked them up, and pushed until the weight of the body started to pull itself over the edge. They let go, and Sean Maguire's lifeless corpse slid into the abyss.

Jack stood by the shaft waiting to hear a noise, but he heard nothing. He walked back to the trolley and took out the contents. He threw the cleaning products in next, the empty bleach bottles and sprays. He could hear them bouncing off the sides for a little while but then nothing.

'I've no idea how deep it is, Joe. But I'm buggered if I'm going in there after him.'

'OK, throw the rest in, and we'll chuck the trolley off the bridge.'

They threw the blanket and the woolen throw from the sofa down the shaft and then sat down again to push the slab back into place.

'Joe, thanks, mate.' Jack's voice was thick with emotion. 'I'm sorry about this. I just wanted to do them both, then clear off. I thought I might bunk at yours one night and then disappear for good. I never meant for you to be this involved.'

'Forget about it,' said Joe in his best New York gangster accent.

They laughed and started for home, ditching the trolley off the bridge as they went. They watched it sink out of sight in the black, fast-moving water. They could just make out their outline reflected in the water.

'You're going to need to disappear, Jack. Now. Forget about Ryan Maguire. He killed your mum. You killed his brother. You're quits. If you go now, you've a good chance of starting a life somewhere else. If you stay, you will either be dead or the chances of you getting away with this again will inevitably be diminished. Two brothers disappearing and the filth will look to who had a motive to make that happen.'

Jack stood quietly. Gazing into the inky river below, the weir thundered relentlessly behind them.

'Don't forget, you've got Ladyboy in a right mess as well. If you go after the other one, what are the chances that they will connect him to this, or if their dad gets wind of it, then you and Ladyboy, and probably me as well, are all up shit street. You know what they say about him.'

Jack continued watching the river. 'All right, Joe. Do me two favours. First, can I have any money you can spare?'

'You know you can.'

'Second, take this tape,' he said, handing Joe the compact video tape from the flat, 'and his shoes and deliver them to the Maguires. They have to suffer more. If you promise to do that, I'll go right after I've seen my dad. He has to pay for switching her off.'

CHAPTER 13

MANCHESTER, 2011

DUNCAN STRODE PURPOSEFULLY DOWN TO the interview room on the ground floor at Bootle Street. Lynn was waiting outside the room.

'We've got Charley Richardson, Michael, and Martin Palmer, Charley's lawyer.'

Duncan looked through the one-way glass. 'Michael's lawyer.'

He opened the door and went in, Lynn followed, closing the door behind her. Duncan sat opposite the two men and the young girl. Michael was a big man. Not as tall as Duncan but powerfully built. He wore a short-sleeved shirt that exposed the tattoos on his arms and hands—a dragon with a tail that curled around his thumb, the body twisting around the forearm of his right arm, a serpent on the left. Duncan knew that they met face-to-face on his upper back. His head was shaved, but from the stubble pattern, it was obvious he was balding at the back. His face was round, his nose flattened and twisted, and his mouth thin-lipped and in permanent sneer.

The lawyer, Martin Palmer, was quite different. He was smaller and thin with narrow, sloping shoulders. He had thick, brown wavy hair, neatly trimmed. He wore a dark blue suit, light blue shirt, and blue and silver striped tie. Whilst Michael Richardson looked comfortable, Martin Palmer looked a little nervous. When Duncan proffered his hand across the table, he hesitated looking at his client before he took it. Duncan mused that it was like shaking hands with his dried out dishcloth.

It was Charley Richardson who surprised Duncan. She was not what he had been expecting at all. She had mouse-coloured straight hair, shoulder length and full. She had large blue eyes and a straight nose with a slight upturn at the end. She had full lips, sporting very little lipstick. She had a natural look about her, and Duncan thought her quite striking, although not classically beautiful. She wore a green woollen three-quarter-length coat and had matching green gloves on the table before her. She appeared confident and in complete control of herself, and Duncan could not imagine this self-assured-looking young woman falling apart in the way that had been described to him.

She seemed so far removed from her father in appearance and demeanour that Duncan felt obliged to begin the interview by asking, 'Are you Charley Richardson?'

She looked straight back at him and answered with a firm 'Yes'.

'Could you confirm your address for me?'

'Flat 22, The Old Rope Works, Medlock Street, Manchester. Do you need the post code?'

'No, that's fine. You don't live with your parents then?' Duncan knew that Michael Richardson lived in Ancoats, a grim, run-down area adjacent to the city centre.

Charley Richardson gave a tired, world-weary look. 'I am twenty-five, Detective Chief Inspector, not fifteen.' Michael Richardson smiled; Lynn covered her mouth to hide her own smirk. Duncan looked at her blankly. 'Thank you, that was the answer to my next question. We carry on like this, and we'll be done in no time.' *Good recovery,* thought Melbourne.

'I'm not sure why you felt the need to bring your lawyer, Ms. Richardson. This interview could have been done at your home. We merely want to get to know more about Steven, find out how he was before his death, what was happening in his life, who his friends were, that sort of thing. You are not under caution, and the interview will only be recorded for the purposes of making a transcript at a later date, that you will have the option to amend before you sign. Is that OK?'

She nodded. 'It was my dad's idea.'

Michael Richardson shifted in his seat. 'I have more experience of dealing with you people. I know you can't be trusted.' His thick Mancunian accent made every word sound like some sort of threat.

'Thank you, Mr. Richardson, but we are taking a statement from your daughter and, as she is an adult, your presence is not required, if you could wait outside, please. Mr. Palmer, if you are instructed by Ms. Richardson, you are free to remain.'

Palmer stuttered, 'Well, I . . . erm . . . that is . . . yes, I am, and I will stay.'

Duncan stood and walked over to the door, which he held open. 'Thank you, Mr. Richardson.'

Michael Richardson stood and looked at his daughter, who remained looking straight ahead at Duncan. He looked at Palmer, who spread his palms upwards as if to say, 'What can I do?'

Richardson walked to the door. He stood face-to-face with Duncan, looking up slightly to the taller man, his face close. 'I know you. Just remember that.'

'You won't need a business card then.' Duncan held his gaze. Richardson went out, and Duncan closed the door behind him.

'Now then, let's get on.' Duncan opened a file on his desk. 'So, Ms. Richardson, when did you meet Steven Redford?'

'We first met four years ago at a club in town. I was living at home then. We went out a few times and things progressed from there. We started seeing each other regularly and went on a holiday together. We got on really well. He was kind and good fun to be around. He made me laugh a lot.'

'I understand he had an accident at work recently.'

'Not that recently. It was last year he had the accident, but he got a settlement quite recently. We planned to use the settlement to start our own life, away from Manchester and our families. We intended to move to London.'

Duncan raised an eyebrow. 'Really, on ten thousand pounds?'

Charley looked puzzled. 'What do you mean? He got £10,000 as an interim payment, but there was more to come, much more. We also had the money from my flat. We were looking at moving down there with something like three-quarters of a million.'

Duncan made hurried notes and passed a slip of paper to Melbourne. 'I'm sorry. I was under the impression that the ten thousand was a final payment. That's what his parents seemed to think.'

Charley smiled. Her face changed completely, and she seemed much more attractive whilst smiling. 'I don't think

Steven was planning on telling his parents he was coming into money. The plan was to just up sticks and go.'

'Did your dad know about the plan?'

She looked across at Palmer nervously. 'Well, no. He didn't. I don't think he would have liked the idea. I suppose he will know now though.' Palmer shifted in his seat.

Duncan tried to reassure her. 'We will not be discussing it with him unless it becomes essential to our investigation, and Mr. Palmer here is bound by his professional conduct rules over client confidentiality, and if he were to tell your father,' Duncan said, looking at Palmer, who visibly wilted, 'you could report him to the Law Society, and there is a strong possibility his practising certificate would be revoked.'

Palmer leant forward, and in a meek voice, he confirmed, 'That's absolutely correct, of course. I would never divulge anything.' He sat back, apparently relieved to have got that off his chest.

Duncan continued, 'Is there any reason why this information could become pertinent to our enquiries into Steven's death?'

'Only if somebody had killed him for the money because they knew he was going to do a bunk.'

Duncan looked closely at her, trying to read her emotions to gauge her own reaction to her remarks.

'Did Steven owe money, Charley?'

She exhaled deeply. 'I don't know. I think so. He wouldn't tell me anything about it, but I got the impression that he owed some money to someone from work, and they knew about his claim.'

'How would somebody from work know about a claim he was making against his previous employers?'

'I mean somebody from his old work. I think that was part of the reason Steven wanted us to disappear.'

Duncan turned a page in his notes. 'OK, on the night that he died, he rang you a few times, and he left a voicemail message for you.' This was something of a gambit as Duncan could not know for sure that any message had been left. 'Where were you and what was the message?'

She looked straight into Duncan's eyes; her gaze was steady, her hands still. She seemed completely in control. 'I was out with my girlfriends. We went to Castlefield to the comedy club, and I couldn't hear my phone. I didn't get any message as such, just sounds. I assumed he had dialled me whilst the phone was in his pocket.'

'Do you still have the message?' Duncan tried to keep his own voice steady as though the question was inconsequential to him.

'Yes,' she said softly and took her Blackberry out of her coat pocket. She scrolled through the screens and then pressed a button with her thumb, turning up the volume as she did so. The recording played back, and it appeared to be nothing more than rustling. It lasted around one minute and then stopped. Duncan looked at Lynn and inclined his head towards the phone.

'We are going to need to borrow this for a while so that we can try and decipher what is on there. If I take it to our tech guys now, I should be able to let you have it back before you go.' Lynn picked up the phone using an evidence bag from her pocket as a glove, then turning the bag inside out, leaving the phone in the bag untouched.

'Please yourself. I will need it back though.'

Lynn was already on her way out of the door. Duncan waited for those left to settle down from the quick disruption.

'Finally, Ms. Richardson, do you know who killed Steven?'

'No,' she said quietly. 'I have no idea who and no idea why. Can I see him?'

'I'm sorry, Ms. Richardson, you can't see the body unless you have formal permission from his parents. I'm sure that, in the circumstances, they will oblige you.'

She laughed to herself. 'Yeah, sure.'

Alex sat back in his chair and looked around his office. He had just taken the call from Steven Holland. The offer had been accepted. The money would be transferred to their client account before the close of business that day. It was all too easy. He looked at the report that had come back with the video from his surveillance.

He had the evidence to destroy the claim. He was duty-bound to report the matter to the Serious Fraud Office; otherwise he would be the one going to jail. If he failed to report it, the firm as a whole would be in difficulties, and the Solicitors Regulation Authority would be crawling all over them looking for reasons to shut them down. There was only one decision to make. Alex didn't make it.

He inserted a disc into the computer and downloaded the whole file, including the video surveillance and his call with Holland, which, like all calls in the firm, was recorded.

He picked up the phone to call his client.

'Hello?'

'Hi, it's Alex Harris from Hanson's. I've got some very good news for you. The offer we made has been accepted.'

'Cool, man, when do I get the money?' Too easy.

'It will be paid into my firm's client account later today. We will then pay it into the account that you designated.'

He decided to take his chance. 'We will have to meet up on the day that you get the money. You know what the arrangement is. I am the person designated to take control of the funds. I will give you the account details and go with you to the bank to see the payment is made.'

'OK. When is it safe for me to take my two hundred grand out?' There it was—confirmation. Alex could feel his heart beating faster. He had to struggle to keep the excitement out of his voice.

'Just as soon as you have paid us, you can withdraw your money. I will meet you at ten on Thursday outside the bank. When we meet, I will call the office to transfer the funds. Once they are done, we will go into the bank together and finalise the transactions.'

'Nice to know that Ryan doesn't trust me.' There it was again. He had the name, the one he had wanted. He felt the elation and the excitement rising within him. He now had everything he wanted.

'Thursday at ten, don't be late, or the money doesn't come.' Alex put down the phone and sat looking at his computer. He could still pull back from this. It was not too late. The forms for the fraud office were in his drawer.

He logged out of the system, got up, and turned off the lights in his office. It was dark outside, but the sky was clear through the tiny square of glass.

He has prepared himself well, he thought. Once he had done what he had to do, he would find a home for the evidence he had gathered. He already knew where. But he had to go through with it.

As he left the office, he sent a text message to Jules.

*out of office for few days. would like to c
u when i get back. it may all be over by then*

and we can talk about where we go from here. no pressure.

He set off up Silbury Boulevard towards his house at Campbell Park. The house was paid for, and the Audi was leased. If he decided to walk away from everything, he could do so leaving him with his clothes, his iPhone, his iPad, and his beloved Karmann Ghia. The house could provide an income. Rental opportunities were extremely popular in Campbell Park. The thought was quite attractive. It would be more attractive if he was taking Jules with him.

Frank Maguire was in the back of the Mercedes. He had a portfolio of photographs of his house in Nassau. The main build was complete. The images showed wires hanging from ceilings, windows without glass, hardboard, where there should be doors. Where he hoped to have a beautiful manicured lawn, there was a builder's yard with cement mixers and work benches. The swimming pool was half tiled, but the surrounding deck was complete. All in all, he was pleased with the progress that was being made.

He spoke loudly, 'It all looks like it's coming together, Davis, how long before it's ready for me and Mrs. Maguire?'

The familiar American twang of Davis Paul came booming through the ether on hands-free, Bluetooth technology, 'I think we're looking at a month if the weather holds good and we are heading into our dry period here.'

Frank looked out over a wet, dark Manchester winter. People rushed by with umbrellas and hoods, leaning forward into the teeth of the icy rain. A month was good, but it couldn't come soon enough for Frank.

'OK, Davis, do what you can. I really need to keep this on schedule.'

'Sure, will do. We are going to need an injection of funds this week, Frank. Work gets done quicker here with well-paid labour.'

'Don't worry, Davis, the money is already on the way. You just keep them lazy sods working.'

'Ha-ha, it's done, Frank. Speak to you soon, buddy.' The line went dead, and Dainius reached forward to press a button on the steering wheel with his thumb.

'Buddy, what the fuck is that about.'

The car rolled through the Manchester evening, winding its way towards Frank's Cheshire home, where the cold and wet never seemed quite so bleak as in these streets. In four weeks, he could be out of this place for good. No more Jimmy, pushing his contracts through the business. The whole thing would become a thoroughly washed, legitimate concern. He would pull the plug on Ryan's activities. The business would be his pension fund. He would look to sell within six months of moving. Ryan would not want that, but Ryan could not stop it. Frank was the majority shareholder, and he was already working on his exit strategy. He had been sounded out by an Indian consortium; they wanted to look at the books. He would make Ryan very wealthy, just not leave him in control of his baby.

A few more weeks, and they would all be clean— Ryan gets a very nice golden handshake, Jimmy gets his percentage to sit on into his old age, whilst Frank retires to the sunshine to play golf and fish.

He had never done either before, but he was sure that was what he wanted to do.

'So, Boss, when do you go to the Bahamas?' Dainius rarely spoke unless spoken to, but Frank understood that he was concerned about his role once Frank left. He had heard the call, so his question was pointless other than as a vehicle to enter into a conversation about his future.

'Well, Dainius. It looks like we will go in three or four weeks' time. Have you ever seen the Bahamas, Dainius?'

Dainius's voice fell a little. 'No, Boss, I've never been out of Europe.'

'Well, you know. I will still have my dodgy ticker in Nassau, Dainius, so I will still need a driver. You are welcome to come if you can persuade your lovely wife to leave these beautiful surroundings.' Frank waved his arm at the scene outside of the luxury motor car.

'Thank you, Boss,' Dainius had got the bounce back into his conversation. 'She will want to come to the sea side. She lived by the sea at home, and she cooks very good fish.'

'Good.' Frank smiled. 'That's sorted then. You had better start making plans.'

CHAPTER 14

MANCHESTER, 2011

DUNCAN HAD CALLED THE TEAM into the meeting early. He was sure that the answers to Steven Redford's murder were tied up with the claim against Maguires, and he wanted the manpower resources he had, devoted into that area.

Drew was sitting on one side of the table, Melbourne and Miles on the other side with Duncan at the head.

'Terry, I want you to get on to the insurers. I want full disclosure of their file. I want to know what they paid out to Redford and when, and I want to know where the money went. They must know which bank it was paid into. Lynn, I need you to trawl through the banks in town, see if they can confirm whether Redford had opened an account. Then we can get an order to get the details. Steve, I want you to talk to all of Redford's workmates, find out who knew what. I think the key to this whole thing lies in the money trail.'

'Are we just swallowing everything that the Richardson girl has told us?' Duncan sighed inwardly. Drew was questioning the direction of the investigation again. 'Are we not considering the possibility that she found out Redford was cruising the gay village for a bit of man love and had her dad give him a good hiding. After all, she seems a bit out of the lad's league in any event. Perhaps she wanted shot of him, and dad went a step too far?'

Duncan considered the ramifications of putting Drew down and telling him to just do as he was told. He concluded there was little to be gained from alienating him in front of the more junior officers, but he was convinced that the case was inextricably linked to Maguires.

'OK, Terry, it is a possibility we need to consider. You can make enquiries into Michael Richardson's movements, look into the girl's finances, but the insurers information is top priority, OK?'

Drew spoke up again; he seemed keen to push his point. 'You seem to be pushing the insurance thing too far, Chief. It is far more likely that this is a domestic gone wrong. Redford has no record, and there is nothing to suggest he has any involvement in any sort of fraud.'

Duncan took his time answering. He had not mentioned any sort of fraud; he had merely asked the team to find out what had happened to the money. He considered Drew. He was looking down at his notepad, avoiding Duncan's gaze.

'Right, Steve, you talk to the insurers. Terry, I want to know what's under Michael Richardson's fingernails. I want everything about him. If he is going to be in this investigation, then you need to do a proper job on him. I will talk to the workmates. If Redford was playing for both sides, then there is one person in the village who will know. I will go and see the Queen.'

'Thank God for that. I thought I was going to get landed with that job. He gives me the heebie-jeebies.' Duncan looked at Miles. Lynn was trying to hide her amusement.

'I can't help it, he does. That weird voice of his, he just freaks me out.'

Duncan shook his head in mock dismay. He had always intended to see the Queen himself in any event. He may have some answers regarding both this murder and the Maguire connection.

The Queen was the doyen of Manchester's gay village. He had been in residence in the Northern Quarter for nearly twenty years. He was an active gay rights campaigner and had been the public face of the gay movement in the city for a number of years.

He was often the liaison between police and community, especially in the late 1990s when there was significant tension between the two, as the Queen called them, camps.

Duncan had known the Queen for many years.

He would have to meet him; he knew that, but he had a creeping dread about the meeting. Unlike Miles, it was nothing to do with his sexuality. It was what he might find out that filled him with trepidation.

Michael Richardson watched Piccadilly Station slip away through the window of the train. He had two men with him; both worked his arcades and both provided muscle when required, violence on tap: Fat Tony and The Lizard.

Fat Tony had been with Michael for fifteen years. He had been a bodybuilder who worked the club doors in the city to pay for his steroids. He was now over forty but spent every waking hour, thinking about his physique. He was built like a bull, heavily muscled and sculpted. He had a large head, stubble on top, and a neatly trimmed goatee, small eyes; indeed his whole face seemed too small for his head. He had earned the nickname after a drunken party-goer had called him a fat bastard when refused entry to one of the clubs Tony was working. It was part of underworld lore that Tony had ripped off his jacket and shirt and demanded that the poor drunk tell him again how fat he was, whilst Tony beat him to an unconscious pulp. Thereafter, the Fat Tony moniker stuck.

The Lizard was Lenny Woodward, not as big as Tony but very strong. He stood with an erect posture, an abnormally straight back, making him look like he was constantly standing to attention. He had an acne-scarred face and slicked back black hair. He constantly licked his lips. In short, he looked like a lizard, and with a name like Lenny, there was a certain inevitability in his nickname.

Both men were not much more than strong-arm characters, who did as they were told and got paid accordingly. They generally worked together, but occasionally alone, and sometimes with Michael.

It was rare for them to work outside their home town. They were strictly local in the main. Michael had no business interests outside of Manchester. He required ever more assistance from people like Fat Tony in his own area. Times were hard, the recession was biting and the bills were getting paid slower and slower. His margins had been slipping for a good six months. That was why he had started to take on outside jobs—work that was even less legitimate than his own borderline business.

He didn't consider himself a gangster. He was a businessman who had to be aggressive to achieve what he wanted. To compensate for his lack of skill and qualifications, he employed violence and intimidation. That was the way he had grown up. He and his brothers were all brought up the same way. If you want something and you can't buy it, you have to take it. If you are going to take it, you have to be stronger than the guy you are taking it from—simple law of the jungle.

He was aware that there were bigger and more dangerous animals in the jungle than him, but he tried to keep a distance between him and them and to keep out of their territory. By and large, he succeeded.

As the train headed south, past a saturated Levenshulme and Longsight and on towards Stockport, he reflected upon the meeting with the police and his daughter. He was not happy with how things stood. He didn't like Duncan, not one bit. He was a dangerous copper—one of those holier-than-thou types, not easy to influence, not like some of them.

He did not like the fact that his daughter had refused to discuss the meeting with him. She was getting too uppity. She got a job, made a bit of money, and thought she was something special with her flash pad in the city centre and her designer clothes. She needed a reminder of where she came from, just to bring her back down to earth.

He hadn't liked her mingling with Redford. He was not to be trusted. He was out for whatever he could get, and not just in the usual way of young lads. He was looking to improve his liquidity. That was a good word used by his accountant quite a lot.

It was always a bit of a mystery, why his snobbish daughter was mixing with some grease monkey. It was not as if she was ugly and could do no better.

Palmer had turned out to be worse than useless as well. He refused to tell him what had been said and spouted some rubbish about professional ethics as if lawyers had any ethics, particularly ones like Palmer, and the one he was on his way to see.

As the train screamed through the Cheshire countryside, The Lizard and Fat Tony started to nod in their seats. The sun was starting to creep through the grey and small patches of blue that appeared behind the dissolving cloud.

Get this job done properly and things might start to brighten up for him all round, he thought. The train slowed down to pull in for a scheduled stop at Crewe before moving on to Rugby and then Milton Keynes.

CHAPTER 15

MANCHESTER, 1991

TOMMY WAS SLOUCHED IN HIS chair. He had fallen asleep with the TV on again. A whisky bottle stood on the coffee table with an inch of golden brown liquid in the bottom. Next to it was a crumpled white envelope. An empty glass sat on the arm of his chair, and the TV screen was blank.

He rubbed his eyes to clear his vision and tried to defog his mind, then listened. He could hear movement upstairs—Jack's bedroom. He was walking around opening and closing drawers. What time was it? He looked at the clock on the video which told him it was 3:00 a.m., just as well he was not in work tomorrow. It seemed likely that he would not need to be in work for some time.

He replayed in his mind the events of the early evening. He had returned home from The Wordsworth a few pints to the good. No Jack, but that was hardly unusual these days. He had fixed himself a sandwich and settled down in front of the television when there was knocking at the door.

He had contemplated ignoring it, but on the second knock, he had pulled himself from the chair and lumbered to the door.

On the other side stood Frank Maguire.

'Good evening to you, Tommy. Might I have a word?' He was all smiles. Tommy had never seen him in a suit before; he normally wore overalls when they nodded greetings in the pub. Frank wore a white-collared shirt and a blue tie. His dark hair was neatly parted and trimmed but not the unruly locks he normally sported. He had played a few frames of snooker with Frank from time to time but did not consider him a friend. Tommy looked back stone-faced.

'What about Frank?'

'Let's go inside and discuss it, Tommy, not out here on the doorstep.'

Tommy stepped back and waved his arm to invite Frank in and point him towards the living room.

'What is it, Frank?'

'Do you mind if we sit, Tommy?' Tommy went back to his armchair, and Frank perched on the edge of the sofa.

'It's a delicate matter, Tom, and it affects us both. I'm terribly sorry for your loss by the way. Me and Mrs. Maguire have said our prayers for Maureen,' Frank said as Tommy stiffened at the mention of his wife's name, 'and for you and the boy. Is he here by the way?'

'Jack's out, football training.'

'Sure he is. He likes his football the lad. I hear he is really good. Might turn pro I'm told.'

'Might.' Tommy was terse in his monosyllabic response. He didn't like the familiarity about his family from somebody he barely knew, and he had a good idea why he was here like this. He had been talking to Bill Jones. He knew what the Maguires were doing.

'It must be expensive running the lad around to training, buying boots, and the like, and with Maureen tragically lost, times must be hard.'

'Yes. What's it to you?'

'Come now, Tommy. We are neighbours. We live on the same estate. I was hoping that you would let me help you. You know my transport business is going well. I've nearly ten trucks now.'

Tommy raised an eyebrow. 'Is that right, I thought you were still spinning the waltzers.'

'Ah well, we still have an interest in the fairground, but it's not my core business these days. I've been lucky and picked up some big contracts.' He reached into his inside jacket pocket and pulled out a business card. 'Here you go, that's my business. Now if you are ever looking for work, Tommy, I can always use another good mechanic.'

Tommy studied the card and put it down on the coffee table. 'Very kind, Frank, but I have a job.'

'Sure, I know that. But the offer's there. Look, Tom, I'm sure you've heard these wild stories on the estate—about my boys, and the night Maureen was attacked.'

'Yeah, I've heard them.'

'Well, it's all just tittle-tattle and misunderstanding, and I wanted to come and see you, face-to-face, to explain that my boys weren't involved.'

'Is that right, Frank? Only I was in the pub when it happened. I saw your boys come in. They had a woman's shoe and were banging it on the bar when I left.'

Maguire pointed his finger. 'You see there, Tommy, that's exactly the sort of misunderstanding that I'm talking about. Now, I'll hold my hands up and admit that my boys might have found Maureen's shoes, by the pub, on the way in, no doubt dropped there by the heinous bastard who did this. But my boys didn't do this Tommy, they weren't involved. I've spoken to a lot of people on the estate.'

'Yeah, I've heard that.'

'And they all say that my lads were in the pub, and they were noisy, but nobody saw them do anything wrong and nobody has found these shoes, so we don't even know if they were your Maureen's shoes. Basically, Tommy, there is nothing to link my lads to this attack and I've spoken to them, and they deny knowing anything about it.'

'Really?' The sarcasm dropped like a stone. 'So why are you going to such lengths to convince people not to talk to the police?'

Maguire's smile had disappeared. His brow furrowed. 'You know how it is with us people, Tom—travellers, pikeys. We are an easy target. If the police get even a sniff of suspicion about any of us, we will be locked away before you can say innocent until proven guilty.'

'My heart bleeds.'

Frank leant forward from the edge of the sofa. 'You know, as well as I do, how the police work here, Tommy. All I'm doing is protecting my family from false accusations. If I have to grease the wheels a little here and there to ensure my boys are not persecuted, then I will.'

Tommy stared at him for a long time.

'Grease the wheels you say?'

The smile was back on Maguire's face, and his eyes seemed to have come alive. 'Tommy, like I said, I've come here today to see if me and Mrs. Maguire can help you and your boy. You are in our thoughts. Now, I don't want to insult you, Tommy. I know you are a proud man, and you don't want any charity, and I certainly don't want to offend a big strong fella like yourself. But we had a bit of a whip-round at work, and as the business is going so well,

I thought I would top it up for you.' Maguire stood and took a crumpled white envelope out of his back pocket.

Tommy frowned. His voice hardened. 'What's that?'

'This, Tommy, is a token of our understanding of what you and your lad are going through, and please accept it. We hope it will make your burden a little easier to bear.'

Tommy's temper began to rise. 'You know nothing about my burden, Maguire. I suggest you get out now before I take the opportunity to demonstrate what a "big, strong fella I am".' Tommy rose out of his chair; his fists were already balled. Maguire was already moving towards the door; he threw the envelope, and it landed on the coffee table. Notes spilled out, a lot of notes. Tommy looked down at the huge amount of cash and heard the door slam shut behind Maguire.

Tommy had stood and looked at the table for a long time. The lines on his face seemed more deeply etched than they had been before. He went to the kitchen and came back with the glass and the whisky bottle.

Now he had woken up, he realised that the envelope was empty.

He walked to the bottom of the stairs and shouted up, 'Jack, get down here.'

He walked back to the living room; he picked up the bottle and began to drain it when he heard the heavy footsteps on the staircase. Jack appeared in the doorway; he had a khaki duffel bag in his hand, packed into a full cylinder shape, and he flung it towards the front door, where it landed with a dull thud. He was wearing black jeans and a fishtail parka, an old 1960s parka that he had bought from a charity shop. He looked gaunt; his face was noticeably thinner, and he had shaved his hair again. It was now so short as to be merely a colouration of his scalp.

'Where's the money, Jack?'

'He gave it to you, didn't he, Maguire? He gave you fifty thousand quid to keep quiet about the fact that his sons raped my mum. And you took it, you lousy bastard. What the fuck happened to Tommy Ladd, the big man on the estate? Eh? What happened to him? You're just a coward.'

Tommy downed the remnants of the bottle and threw it against the wall. It smashed by the side of Jack's head.

'Who do you think you are talking to, you little shit?' Tommy fired out the words, spittle flying as he shouted. 'I can't prove who did what. I can't do anything about it. I can't go down there and beat the crap out of those little bastards cos then I'd be locked up, and you'd be on your own. I've got responsibilities now and your mother would have wanted me to look after you.'

Jack's eyes narrowed. 'I don't need you to look after me. You can't even look after yourself. Look at you. I've never needed you. The only person I needed you switched off. You might be too scared to sort out them Maguire boys, but I'm not.'

Tommy laughed. 'You? You're gonna be the big man now then, are you? You've been watching too many films, Son.'

Before the last syllable was out, Jack was upon him— fast, hard blows to the face, left and right eye, jaw, and nose. Tommy had fought many times in his life. He had been hit harder and by bigger men, but he had never faced an attack with such ferocious speed and with such unforgiving, pitiless accuracy.

He had been drinking and was sleepy and that was why he had been unable to even raise his hands in self-defence, he would convince himself later, before he was propelled back and down into the chair, and his foot rising upwards as he fell crashing through the glass table.

Once he was in the chair, his son rained the punches down with increased ferocity. Tommy felt his lips splitting; he felt the warm flow of blood from his nose, and there was swelling around the eyes.

Then it was over. Jack walked away, his footsteps crunching over the glass-covered carpet.

He turned at the door. 'You never should have done that. That was never your decision. She was my *mother!*'

Tommy spat the blood from his mouth. 'Fuck off.'

'I'm going, and I will never see you again.'

'Where's my fucking money, you little bastard?'

Jack picked up the bag and opened the front door. He turned and walked back to the living room doorway. He spoke calmly to his father, who was still slumped, bleeding in his armchair.

'You said you had a responsibility to look after me, so I assumed it was for me. If you want it back, try to find me and take it back. If you're brave enough, you'll deserve it. Personally, I don't ever expect to see you again as long as I live, which is longer than at least one of them Maguire boys. I can promise you that.' He turned, slung the bag over his shoulder, and left.

CHAPTER 16

CHESHIRE 2011

ALEX PASSED JUNCTION 16 ON the M6, the exit for Crewe. The TT was on cruise control, set at a comfortable 80 miles per hour, purring through the Cheshire plain. Alex's iPhone buzzed in its cradle and was then followed by his ringtone, London Calling by The Clash, playing through the Audi's speaker system. He pushed the call button on the steering wheel. 'Alex, Harris,' he spoke loudly so that his voice was picked up by the microphone in the sun visor.

'Alex, it's me.'

Alex involuntarily sat straight up in his seat when he heard Jules's voice. 'Hi, Jules, you OK?' He didn't know what to say and thought what he had said was insensitive and stupid.

'Yes, Alex. I'm fine. Are you going to be away long?'

'No, I don't think so. I've just got some business to tie up with one of my Maguire's clients. I will probably stay over tonight as it's such a long drive, so I will be back tomorrow, late afternoon probably.' He was going to ask why, but he didn't. He didn't want to lead the conversation in case she thought he was trying to push her in a particular direction. He wanted her to decide what the call was going to be about, and he was happy to follow her lead.

'OK. I want us to have a talk, Alex. I think what I'm saying is I need to talk to you. I want to know where we go from here.'

His immediate reaction was relief. If she wanted to know where the relationship was going, then there was at least some future in it.

'Jules, I'll talk to you whenever you want. I'm just relieved that you still want to talk to me.'

There was a long pause. He waited; his mouth was open and his heart was beating loudly in his chest.

'You don't put me off that easy, Harris. Look, I'll be at your house when you get home. Ring me when you are an hour away, and I will get some dinner ready.'

Alex was smiling to himself. 'Yep, I will do. Thanks, Jules.'

'Don't thank me yet. I might just want to dump you over a nice dinner.'

'Tell me you're joking, right?'

'I'll see you tomorrow night. I've missed you.'

The line went dead. 'You beauty.' Alex whopped and banged the steering wheel. The call meant a change of plan; his end game now had to be different, and he was relieved. He turned up the volume on the stereo and pressed the next track button, also located on the multifunction steering wheel of the Audi. Jangling guitar came over the speakers, followed by a wolf whistle. Alex laughed loudly as The Undertones launched into 'I Don't Wanna Get Over You', and he sang along, drowning out the tremulous tones of Feargal Sharkey, at the top of his somewhat tuneless singing voice.

Duncan put down the phone. It was just after 6:00 p.m. He was sitting at his computer in his flat in Chorlton Mill, a former factory mill on Cambridge Street, once part of the well-known Dunlop rubber factory. The building retained the huge chimney stack and the traditional grim, forbidding exterior for an early nineteenth-century mill building. Inside, however, it had been converted to numerous apartments using all the features now familiar with such conversions, brick walls and original floor to ceiling windows. Originally, the mill was the largest in Manchester and was a cotton mill connected to other mills on the same street by underground tunnels with train tracks to ensure materials were moved from one part of the factory complex to the other without delay. In the 1860s, the mill had been bought out by Charles Mackintosh and Company for the production of his rubberised waterproof clothing, for which his name became synonymous.

Duncan had been fortunate to be able to afford such a place. When the conversion was first completed, prices were high, and a number of properties were soon repossessed when the housing market collapsed, leaving many young professionals with negative equity and living above their means. The converted mills were a just an expensive fashion accessory to many.

Duncan's apartment was one such example. It had been taken on by the bank after the previous owner had defaulted on the mortgage. Duncan had heard about the property from a colleague at work, who had been present at the repossession. He had contacted the bank and offered to take the property at a greatly reduced price so that they avoided the cost of cleaning and decorating and, of course, of estate agents. Duncan was a cash buyer, having just received the proceeds of his father's estate following his death from a heart attack. His mother had died some years earlier, having failed to catch the cancer soon enough to make treatment a viable option.

The bankers were happy with the deal, and Duncan found himself owning a very desirable flat for a fraction of the market price.

The flat was open plan with cast iron pillars, infilled brick arched ceilings and original broad oak floorboards. It had two bedrooms and two bathrooms and was really too large for Duncan's needs. But he liked the history attached to the place and had a feeling of being part of Manchester's industrial heritage. Plus, it was a fantastic investment and was already worth double the price he had paid.

He needed some financial security, having been left without any capital by his second wife, Sharon. His first marriage had been a wonderful experience whilst it lasted. He had met Helen at university. She was studying Mathematics; he was studying psychology. They were soulmates; they shared the same political and social ideals. After graduation, they had decided to move to Zimbabwe to teach.

They spent an idyllic year together, teaching underprivileged children in Harare, before it all turned sour for them. In one of his lessons, Duncan had made some unguarded remarks about the Mugabe government and their claims to have built roads and dams that were, in fact, already in place when the country was a British colony. Within a week, his salary was stopped. A week later, so was Helen's. In order to raise money for food, Duncan had decided to sell some furniture, items he had brought from England. They were confiscated along with their passports and an arrest seemed imminent. They were literally living on bread and water.

Duncan crept out one night carrying his video recorder and stereo in a canvas bag. He sold the items in downtown Harare, and in the morning, he went straight to a travel agent and booked a safari.

Two days later, he and Helen walked over the border into Zambia, having left their safari in the Zambezi National Park. From there, they were flown home by the British Consulate. But their idealism had been shattered, and their connection with each other seemed to have been loosened. They both needed to find work as they had returned with nothing. He applied to the Greater Manchester Police with no clear idea as to what he wanted to do but with the thought that he could at least try to do some good. That seemed to be the last straw for Helen.

She ended the relationship, which he tried desperately to keep alive. It was only later that he realised that she had been right and that he had just been afraid to close the door on his youthful, idealistic love. Duncan returned to his parental home and decided to rethink his life plan.

Having been through training, he was sent out on to the streets, where he soon found he had a knack for calming people down and a steely determination to do right. It was something of an old-fashioned attitude in what was fast becoming a results-driven, statistically measured profession.

He worked hard and was soon promoted to detective constable, plain clothes work, getting involved in the groundwork for the more complex cases, taking statements, and general routine investigation work that contributed to the bigger picture. He was methodical. He soon realised that most investigations began with a trickle of information that became one of a number of tributaries that then grew into a river, which then became a flood that could not be contained. There were those where the stream dried up and those where the flow was stopped, but he was dogged, and he knew that if he could just dig the trench of information that little deeper, he could revive the flow.

His superiors identified his calm authority and organistional skills, and he quickly moved through the ranks.

He had met Sharon, his second wife, at a Christmas party. It was a purely physical attraction he now realised. She was five years older than him and ambitious. She would become one of the first women to reach the rank of assistant chief constable. He was attracted by the sheer strength of her personality and her voluptuous physique. She would bounce ideas off him and bounce on top of him in equal measure, sometimes at the same time. Duncan now felt that he had simply been a stepping stone in her career. He had taken something of a back seat, attended dinners with her, supported her, but when she decided to move on, she was ruthless and left him without ceremony. It had caused friction at work, and when the Detective Division moved to Trafford Park, he was deliberately left behind at Bootle Street.

It had left him wary of entering into any further relationship. He had been left by the only people in his life that he had ever loved, and Duncan had decided that it would never happen again.

He had been happy to be considered peripheral to the main detective bureau. He liked to work his way, and he was left pretty much to his own devices, reporting weekly to his superior officer, Superintendent John Hall—the epitome of the career, pencil pushing officer.

Since the breakdown of his marriage, Duncan had felt emotionally detached from the force. He was still a romanticist when it came to his function as a police officer. He still felt duty-bound to serve the society he worked for, but he felt that responsibility in its broadest sense. He was never an officer who felt the collective responsibility of the force or who saw the force as an organism or society within a society that needed to be cherished and protected. He took his civic duty very seriously whether that was to the benefit or detriment of the force was incidental to him.

He had no personal friends in the force and preferred to keep his relationships strictly professional. He was very much a loner. He did not enjoy his solitude, but he was comfortable with it. He liked to leave work and to have the time to think. He often considered that his lack of a private life was what made him a good detective, and he was a very good detective.

He had just spoken to Terry Drew. Richardson had gone to ground, and Drew could not trace him. Drew was now convinced that Richardson was doing a runner because the investigation was closing in on him.

Duncan thought otherwise. The connections to Maureen Ladd confused him, and the direct link between Maguires, Redford, and Maureen Ladd played on his mind.

Miles had reported that the solicitors and insurers were refusing to disclose any information on Redford's claim. The person dealing with the claim was away from the office, the solicitors had said, and was not expected back for two weeks. The insurers just plain refused to give out any information, and Miles explained, they had openly invited him to try to get a court order to force them to.

Duncan knew there was something he was not seeing. He felt like he was walking in a forest, looking for breadcrumbs, knowing that the birds had been out before him.

He clicked the mouse and turned off the Mac on his desk. He grabbed his grey three-quarter-length overcoat from the rack and left. From Cambridge Street, it was a short walk up Whitworth Street West to Princess Street. It was raining and dark and Duncan carried his umbrella to protect him from the worst of the weather. When he reached the junction with Princess Street, he turned left. Up ahead, he could see the New Union Hotel, where Redford's shoes had been found. On the left-hand side of Princess Street was Asia House—a baroque-style former shipping warehouse, now one of the city's premier addresses. Noel Gallagher was a former resident, in his earlier Oasis days, which had afforded a certain cache to this particular building.

Duncan walked into the grand lobby, all-veined marble and stained glass, and stepped into the cage lift. He pulled back the iron concertina grate and pressed the button for the sixth floor, the top floor.

When the lift jerked to a stop, he pulled back the handle, and the door folded away. He turned left into a dramatic green-tiled corridor with arched and square windows to one side and a black and white tiled floor. He saw a young man leaning against the door of the end apartment. He straightened up as Duncan approached.

'What do you want?'

'Good evening to you too. I am here to see an old friend. What are you doing here?' Duncan could see the dilated pupils, the unkempt hair, and the crumpled clothes of the addict.

'Got nowt to do with you, pig.' The young man snarled the final word and gave a triumphant look. He had correctly identified Duncan as a policeman without the need for introductions.

'That's very good. Now can I suggest that you run along before you get into any trouble. I'm here to see the Queen, not his courtiers.'

'He don't want to see you. He don't talk to the filth.'

Duncan grabbed the young man and twisted him around, forcing his arm up his back and pushing his face against the tiled wall of the corridor.

'Are you seriously planning on obstructing a police officer in your state?'

'Put him down, Duncan.' The unmistakeable wheezing growl of the Queen drifted down the corridor. Duncan looked up to see him standing at the door to his apartment. He was only in his late thirties, but he looked fifty. He was larger than life in every respect. He stood at a similar height to Duncan, but he carried a few stones extra, quite a few. He wore light grey, loose-fitting drawstring linen trousers with open sandals, a cream silk shirt open down to his expansive waist and the perennial silk scarf around his neck, long and hanging down to his waist but pulled tightly around his throat. He was completely hairless. He wore eyeliner around his round, dark eyes and lipstick on his thin lips.

'You don't know where he's been.' The Queen turned and waddled slowly back into his apartment leaving the door open for Duncan to follow.

Duncan let go of the boy who immediately ran down the hall. He turned and shouted 'pig' before getting into the lift.

Duncan closed the door behind him and wandered into the main room of the apartment. It had windows to two walls making it light and airy. The furniture was modern and functional with very few colours. As Duncan looked around, he noticed that there was a galleried bed deck built above the kitchen with steps up to it in the hallway. It was lavishly decorated with Indian textiles and cushions, and it provided the only splash of colour in what looked like an archetypal bachelor pad.

The Queen lay on his sofa looking out of the window. Duncan could see the clock tower of the Palace Hotel on Oxford Street and the chimney from his own building at Chorlton Mill.

'How have you been?' he asked.

The Queen's rasping voice came back. 'What do you care how I've been? You don't keep in touch.' He turned his head away from Duncan in an extravagant gesture of hurt.

'I know, we should talk more, but it's difficult for me. You need to stop selling to these kids and clean your act up, then we can talk more. I can't be seen with you when you're operating on the other side of the law, you know that.'

The Queen turned his head. 'And I thought that you just didn't fancy me any more.' His voice was like a drum full of marbles.

Duncan laughed. He pointed at the neck, covered by the wrapped scarf. 'How is it?'

The Queen touched his scarf. 'Same as ever. I thought I might offer my services to a satnav seller, doing impersonations of that butler in *Hart to Hart*.' He put on a Brooklyn accent, ' . . . don't turn left, the traffic is murder.' They laughed together.

'I need your help. I am trying to find out a bit more about Steven Redford, the young man that was murdered on Canal Street.' Duncan handed over a photograph. 'I thought if anybody knows what's going on in the village, it's you. I need to know whether he was a fellow traveller as it were.'

'Very delicately put, Chief Inspector.' The Queen studied the photograph closely. 'No, he's not batting for our team this one, though he is a regular down here. He does the odd deal here and there, nothing big, just a little bit now and again. Maybe selling off his own surplus you know.'

Duncan viewed the wet Manchester skyline through the huge windows. 'Was he doing enough to get him into trouble?'

'Oh no, nothing like that, strictly an amateur, a hundred quid here and there, once in a blue moon. No, he was not a serious player and not worth the trouble it would cause to stop him.'

Duncan took back the picture. 'Did you ever meet him or do any business with him?'

The Queen laughed, 'Really, Chief Inspector, what do you take me for, some sort of criminal? No, I saw him in the bar now and again, in The Navigation, but I've never spoken to him. He never had anyone with him, and he didn't really mix.'

'OK, thanks.'

'Was I any help?'

Duncan shrugged. 'I don't know yet. I'll let you know when I've worked it all out.'

'Well, don't leave it so long next time. Pop in and see me again. It would be nice to have a talk about the old days.'

Duncan turned to leave, he looked up at the bed and it's Eastern decor. 'Do you actually use that thing?'

The Queen laughed—a gravelly choking sound. 'No, it's just to unsettle squares like you, the main bedroom is to the right.' Duncan smiled and walked to the front door. As he opened the door, he turned. The Queen was sitting on his sofa looking out across the town again. 'See you soon, Ray,' he shouted and then closed the door behind him.

As Duncan left Asia House, the rain pelted the streets around him. The lights reflected back off the road surface, and all around was the sound of rainwater running into the gutters. He started to retrace his steps back to Chorlton Mill and then turned around and went back up Princess Street, heading back towards Bootle Street. There was another file he needed to look at, the file on the disappearance of Sean Maguire.

Alex arrived at his hotel, the Premier Inn on Medlock Street. Christopher Hanson did not believe in extravagant hotels for his team; he had an account with the Premier Inn and, if you wanted to avoid paying for a hotel yourself when you were away on business, this was where you stayed.

He parked the TT in the car park and checked in, dropping his bag off in the room, he immediately headed down to the bar, hoping he was not too late to get something to eat.

He sat at a table by the window, overlooking Medlock Street and having ordered a steak and chips with pepper sauce. He thought it unwise to be too adventurous in such simple surroundings. He had a cup of coffee and sat to wait for his food.

A large weary-looking man at the table opposite him raised a glass to him. 'Na zdrowie.' Alex picked up his coffee cup and somewhat apologetically said, 'Cheers.'

'Jakov Zenczakowski,' the big man said. 'I am Polish, I drive truck.'

'Nice to meet you, Jakov, Alex Harris, I am a lawyer.'

'No, really, lawyer? Well, let me buy you drink, Alex Harris. I have much to say to you.'

'No, really, Jakov. I am just about to eat and then I really must have an early night, busy day tomorrow.'

Jakov was already sitting down opposite Alex. He placed his beer down in front of him, wrapped his huge mitts around the pint glass and looked at Alex, his head tilted to one side. 'Alex Harris, I am a good man, I look after my family. Can I trust you with secret?'

Alex looked around the room, hoping that a fellow truck driver would be coming to rescue Jakov, but there was only a couple in the corner who looked like they may be having an illicit tryst, possibly boss and secretary. He didn't think they were with Jakov.

'I am a lawyer, Jakov, if I hear anything illegal, it is my responsibility as an officer of the court to report it to the appropriate authorities.' Stock answer when you don't want to hear something.

'This is good. I tell you, and you tell authorities, this is good.'

Alex groaned inwardly. It was going to be a long night.

CHAPTER 17

MANCHESTER, 1991

JOE WAS RUNNING LATE FOR school. He hurried through the front door without any breakfast; he didn't want to sit in the kitchen in front of his parents. He knew he would have the feeling that every time they looked at him, they would know what he had been doing last night. He was not entirely whether the whole thing was real or a dream. He was running towards the bus stop now, but he felt almost as though he was watching himself from above, waiting for the police car to pull up next to him, for him to be dragged into custody and locked in a cell.

He told himself it was the lack of sleep that was making him feel this way. He had returned home at three, creeping in through the back door and getting undressed in the kitchen. He thought he could then explain he had got up for a drink; it never occurred to him how he would explain the bundle of clothes under his arm. He had made his way up the stairs, on his hands and knees, to spread his weight and to avoid making the stairs creak. He climbed into bed, cold and shivering, and then the reality of what he had done had hit him.

He had buried his head under the pillow to muffle the racking sobs. He had cried because he was losing the only real friend he had in the world. He knew that Jack would be gone within a day or two.

As he approached the bus stop, out of breath, he slowed down. He was in time for his bus; the usual kids were all there in uniform, huddled in their usual groups.

One figure was sitting apart, leaning on the low garden wall of the Victorian terraced houses on Stockport Road. With Bulky parka and duffel bag, Joe approached, passing through the queue, to sit on the wall next to Jack.

'All right, mate?'

'Yeah, I'm good, Joe. How are you?' Jack spoke quietly, but he was calm. He looked the same as ever, as though the only thing that had happened to him since the previous day had been a haircut.

'Like your hair. You look a bit Travis Bickle.'

Jack smiled. 'Yeah, we have lots in common, me and Travis.'

'Yeah, he's a fucking nutter too.'

Jack looked up. He laughed. 'Cheers, Joe. Mate, thanks for everything. You saved me last night, and I needed to come and see you to say thanks before I go.'

'Go where? Do you know anybody who can help you? Why don't you stay here, you can crash at mine for a bit and we can try and get you some money together.' Joe was trying not to sound desperate and was struggling to keep his voice even.

Jack pushed himself up off the wall. 'I don't know anybody who would ever be a better friend to me than you, Joe. I don't need any money. Honestly, my dad has given me a huge wedge. I've got fifty grand in me bag. Maguire tried to pay us off, and Dad kinda gave me the cash.'

Joe looked closely at Jack. 'How is your dad, Jack?'

'He's doing OK. He's still walking if that's what you're worried about. I'm not a complete psycho, you know.' Jack winked at Joe. They both smiled. 'Yeah, right,' said Joe.

'Here comes your bus, Joe. Look, I've got to disappear, but I will keep tabs on you, and I will get in touch when it's safe for me. Those things you've got, you have to deliver them to Maguire, but only do it when it's safe, Joe. I don't want you taking any risks for me. You've already done more than enough. I want you to help Ladyboy. I've got some money for him so he can get himself sorted out.'

'Jack, don't go. If you've got that much money, we can hide you here, and you'll always have somebody to help you.' Joe had dropped any pretence of being cool. His voice had raised an octave, and it trembled with emotion.

'I can't stay. You know what will happen if I stay here. I won't be able to stop, and I will go after Ryan and I'll go after his dad and I will end up in prison, and so will you.' Jack held Joe, both hands gripping Joe's upper arms. A solitary tear rolled down Jack's cheek. Even though he was holding Joe, he said, 'I've got to go, Joe. Please, let me go.'

Joe stood up, away from the wall. He looked down on Jack, who still held his arms. 'You'd better go then.' His voice was thick; his throat was constricted with the emotion. 'But you'd better let me know you're all right as soon as you can. And stop crying, you big poof.'

Jack laughed again. He let go of Joe's arms and wiped the tear from his cheek. The bus pulled up at the stop behind them, and kids filed slowly towards the doors as though they were taking a train to Buchenwald.

'You'd better get on the bus, you lanky twat.'

Joe walked to the back of the slowly moving queue. He turned to look at Jack, who had hoisted the bag on to his shoulder. He was holding out a sock, filled. 'Give this to Ladyboy for me.'

Joe took it. He could feel the cash inside, thick wedges of banknotes. 'Jack,' he cut off as Jack held up his hand. 'Don't, Joe. I'll ring you, OK?' With that, he turned and walked towards the centre of town, his parka pulled around him. As he walked, he pulled a knitted hat from the pocket of his coat and put it on his shaved head. Joe showed his pass to the driver and headed to the upstairs of the double-decker to get a window seat. The bus was moving by the time he sat down. He craned his neck to watch Jack as the bus drove towards him. As the bus came level, Jack raised his right arm above his head and gave a short wave without lifting his eyes towards the bus. And then the bus had passed him, and he was out of sight, and that was the last time Joe saw or heard from Jack Ladd.

Joe opened his school bag and shoved the sock deep into it. He turned his face back to the window so that the rest of the passengers would not see his tears.

CHAPTER 18

2011

'OK, WHAT I'VE LEARNT SINCE the last meeting is that Redford was an occasional dealer down in the village—nothing big time but fairly regular. We now need to widen the scope of this investigation. Could his drug deals be behind his murder?'

Duncan looked around the team. Lynn was sitting opposite him in a thick woollen jumper with a large roll neck. She looked straight back at him, eyes clear and wide. 'Of course, it could be linked, but where does the information come from?'

Duncan looked at Miles and Drew. 'The Queen.'

'Jesus, we're taking tips from that old fag now, are we?' Drew again. 'How can we possibly believe anything he says, and besides, if Redford was dealing in the village, then the Queen would be one of our prime suspects surely,' he challenged.

'Yes, Terry, one would think that, but then surely he would have just told me that he had never seen Redford. I think, to be honest, we need to keep an open mind on this investigation. It is amateurish to only go in one direction because we prefer that explanation.'

Miles looked at Melbourne and winced. Duncan was looking directly at Drew. Drew sat back. 'I'm telling you it's Richardson and all the rest is you trying to complicate the investigation. We know you like a juicy case, but this isn't one of them, a straightforward domestic.'

'Terry, if you feel my leadership of this investigation is in any way substandard, then it is something we should discuss in private. However, as you have brought the subject of personal competence into the public domain, what happened to you tailing Michael Richardson? How the fuck can you lose him when he's the centre of your universe at the moment? He is your prime suspect in the investigation, and you let him wander out of your field of view. Were you out buying another new suit or what?'

Drew flushed. Duncan glared. 'I suggest you get off your arse and find him, and quick.'

'Yes, Guv,' Drew muttered under his breath.

There was a moment's silence. Duncan was still glaring at Drew; his eyes were burning like cold blue flames. 'Well, you're not going to find him sitting there.'

Drew looked up, and it finally dawned on him that he was effectively dismissed from the meeting. His cheeks still burnt as he stood abruptly, shoved his papers together, and stormed out of the office, leaving the door open behind him.

Miles looked at Duncan and then got up and pushed the door closed and sat back down sheepishly.

'Right, perhaps now we can make some progress. Lynn, I want you to go through bank statements again. Where is the money coming from and going to? Are there any regular payments in that might equate to his dealing?'

'Yes, sir.'

'Miles, what is the position regarding the law firm?'

'Well, the person dealing with the case seems to have done a bit of a runner, sir. I can't get hold of him at all. He's still working for the firm, but he seems to have more holidays than a teacher.'

'Keep after them. I need to know what's going on there. I wonder now if the big payoff that Redford was promising Charley was coming from a drug deal rather than his claim. Maguires, tell us he got ten grand only and that ties in with the bank accounts. Perhaps he was keeping that from her. Lynn, do we know anyone in the drug squad who would give us any indication as to where our boy was getting his supply?'

'I do,' volunteered Miles. 'I've got loads of mates in there.'

'OK, get some digging done. I want to know where the merchandise is coming from.'

Duncan stood up. 'OK, that'll do for now, same time tomorrow.'

Miles got up and headed for the door, Lynn hung back. When Miles was at his desk in the Pit, she looked at Duncan. 'You need to watch him, Boss.'

'What, Miles. Why, is he spreading vicious rumours about my fashion sense?'

She laughed. 'You know who I'm talking about, and you know he has Hall's ear.' Duncan looked wearily at her. 'I know, Lynn, but he is one awkward bastard, and I struggle to contain myself around him. If he wants to stir up trouble with Johnny Boy, then let him, I've dealt with that sort of thing before, and I'll deal with it again. What are they going to do, move me sideways again?'

Lynn put her hand on Duncan's arm. 'Just watch him, he's been a bit too cocky lately, and if I end up working for that prick, I'll never forgive you.'

Duncan was looking down at her hand, which was slowly removed by gently brushing down to the crook of his elbow.

'Right, thanks.'

Lynn went back to her desk. Duncan stood for a moment. Had he read the right signals there? Christ, that was all he needed. He stalked back to his office.

Alex stood outside the bank on King Street and checked his watch. His client was late but was now strolling towards him.

'You're late.'

'Yeah, well, I figured you would wait for me.'

'OK, let's get inside and get this done.' Alex turned towards the heavy oak doors of Renoud, the private bank that was to be used to transfer the money from Hanson's client account. As they went through the doors, Alex was on the phone to the office to get confirmation that the sum of £1.2 million had been transferred to the account at Renoud's for his client. By the time they reached the immaculate receptionist, fitted blue suit, probably Yves Saint Laurent, hair in a severe bun, he had the confirmation he required.

The client handed over a note to the receptionist who showed them into a small office with a round table and four chairs, a telephone, and two bottles of water and glasses. They sat down, and the door was closed behind them.

'All that needs to happen is that you ask them to confirm the money has transferred and then ask them to move the million to this account. The rest of the money stays in your account here, and you can do as you please with it. However, you need to leave it in there for a week at least.'

'If it's my money, you can't tell me what to do with it, can you?' Alex said nothing. 'No, I didn't think so.'

Alex considered the young man before him. Too sure of himself, in way over his head, and he has no idea who he is dealing with. 'What do you intend to do with the money?' Alex asked.

'I'm going into business myself. Fuck, Ryan.'

'Are you talking about competing with Ryan? You know about the trucks then, do you? And the stuff he ships in?'

'Yeah, I'd have to be some sort of prize idiot not to know. I was in the workshop, remember.'

At that point, the door opened and another immaculately presented young woman walked in same suit, same hairstyle, and same frosty look.

'I can confirm that the money has arrived, and I understand that you wish to transfer the money to another account?' She was looking at Alex. Alex pointed to his client. 'Oh, I'm sorry.'

'That's right, love. Here's the account and the amount.' He handed over the piece of paper that Alex had given him. Twenty minutes later, they left the bank with the transaction completed.

'You tell Ryan to leave me alone now, OK? I'm done with him and his business.'

Alex looked up at the thickening cloud. The sky always seemed heavier here, almost like it was crushing the city slowly. The first spots of rain had started to arrive, and Alex decided it was time to head back to his hotel.

'Be lucky,' he said as he skipped across the road, flagging down a passing taxi.

CHAPTER 19

MANCHESTER, 2011

JACK STOOD IN THE DOORWAY of the hotel. It was the same doorway he had sat in twenty years ago, watching Ladyboy meet Sean Maguire. It had been a long road back. But he felt he was now truly back.

It was dark, and he could not be seen from the street as the lights were out in the hotel. He watched. He wore a black waterproof jacket and black jeans. The chips he had been eating were spreading warmth through their paper wrapping and into the pocket of the jacket. He would finish them later. He looked at the text message on his iPhone and checked the time. He should be here by now.

He heard footsteps approaching and shrank back deeper into the shadows, a natural reaction until he was sure who was approaching. He could see a single figure, but he was too far away to be recognised. The yellow street lights gave the scene a slightly hazy effect, created by the moisture in the air. The man ambled down the street towards him, unaware that he was being watched from the doorway but furtively searching the street for signs of activity. He froze and listened. Jack was reminded of a deer in a forest scenting the hunter—head held high, twisting side to side.

Jack was about to step from the shadows when he heard the footsteps—more than one person. Through the damp sodium gloom, he saw three men approaching. As they got closer, they spread out as if to block an escape route. Jack held his breath fearing that the mist from his warm expulsions would give away his position.

The three men closed the gap on the man Jack was supposed to meet—three tall men, one particularly bulky. Two of them stood either side, the one in the middle spoke to the man, who looked tense and afraid. Initially, he could not hear what was said but then the voices became agitated and louder, and Jack understood immediately what was happening. He decided that he was best served by remaining in the blackness and observing what was to unfold.

The two men on either side grabbed an arm each, and the third man started to throw punches—wide and sweeping blows arcing down on the head and body. Innocence was pleaded, forgiveness sought, but the punishment was pitiless.

When the beating stopped, the two men either side let go of their prisoner, who wobbled like a drunk. One last punch was thrown, catching him on the temple, and the injured man crashed to the floor. It was obvious he had lost consciousness before he hit the pavement as he made no attempt to break his fall. When his head hit the flagstone, there was a crack, a noise not dissimilar, Jack thought, to that when you break open an Easter egg. The body lay motionless.

The three men looked down on him and then ran.

Jack stepped out of the doorway. He had heard enough to know what he should do. He walked over to the dead man and checked his pockets. He took his mobile phone and the piece of paper with the note Renoud 10:00 a.m. and a bank account number on it. Jack took off the man's shoes. He took a match from the pocket and lit it. Then he placed it on to the flaccid cheek of the dead man. He burnt a small area. He lit another match and then another until he had made a small hole in the cheek.

He took a look at the body of Steven Redford. He remembered the chips in his pocket. He placed one in the dead man's mouth and one in his hand then set off at a slow trot. He wanted to get inside before it started to rain.

A few hours later, he stood motionless in the bar of the New Union Hotel. The door to the rear kitchen had not been as secure as it might. He had learnt many years ago, in France, how to enter a locked door silently.

He saw the forensics team arrive and then the detectives. He peered through the clear writing on the frosted glass as they milled around. Then he saw him arrive. He was tall and heavier than he remembered but unmistakeable. Jack watched as he ducked under the tape and hailed a taxi.

Now it would begin—the end at last.

Alex had arrived back in Milton Keynes by three. It was cold but dry. A light wind rustled the bare Poplar trees in Campbell Park, and he could see the water on the canal was a stony grey. He had been to check on the Karmann and had a drive out to Woburn and back. It was a nice, wide country road, deserted at this time of day, heavily wooded on either side. The Karmann had buzzed through the countryside and looked perfectly at home parked in the Georgian market town, outside the antique shop. He had filled up with petrol and checked his oil and tyres on his way home. He had left the car under its protective cover in the garage and felt satisfied that all was well.

He had called in at the bank in Newport Pagnell on his way home from Woburn. When he was back in the house, he had turned on the iMac and logged into the bank website. From there, he had transferred the money from the bank in Newport to three other banks.

He had opened his post and put his new driving licence in his wallet, checking the photograph.

After an hour, Jules had arrived. Alex had coffee ready, a latte for Jules and a cappuccino for him.

She sat down in the thick sofa and kicked off her heels; her long legs were stretching out, pointing the toes gracefully. She wore a similar suit to the receptionist at the bank. Only she filled it better.

Alex kissed her on the cheek. 'Thank you.' She smiled and stretched again. 'OK, what happens now? Do you intend to stay at Hanson's? You've made partner, surely you are not going to walk away from that?'

'I have to, Jules, my position is compromised. I introduced the Maguire's business, and the claims are fraudulent. Not all of them but the large ones are. If I don't go, then I could bring the rest of the business down. The Solicitors Regulation Authority will not be happy as it is, us having dealt with some huge bent claims. When I go in tomorrow, I will start putting the case together for the Serious Fraud Office and submit it. I will resign with immediate effect. With me gone, and with the information in the file, Hanson's will survive and the Maguires will be brought down.' He smiled as he massaged her feet. 'We will book a holiday—a long one. Then life returns to normal.'

'I don't think that a holiday is a good idea, Alex. How will we afford it? You have to face the fact that once you come clean on the Maguires' cases, you will be blacklisted. You won't be able to find another job. I will support you, but I don't think a holiday is a good idea, at least until you've sold this place.'

Alex sat next to Jules and took her hand. 'We don't need to worry about money ever. I've got more than enough for us both to give up and do what we want. We don't need to work at all. This house is paid for anyway out of my bonuses and my equity from my old flat.' He moved in closer to her. 'But things are not finished yet. I have to go back to Manchester.'

'No, Alex.' He held up his hand apologetically. 'I do, Jules, just one more trip to tie up the loose ends. But it's not what you think. This time, it is all going to be above board. The police will be involved. I am going to expose them, get them put away. Once they are locked up, we can move on together. That will be the end of it.'

Jules stared deep into his eyes, looking for answers and seeing only the same grey eyes she always saw. She worried that she would always be looking into those eyes for truth and never be quite sure whether she had found it.

'You promise me this is the end?'

'I do.'

'And it's all legal.'

'Yes, it is.' At least, he hoped it would be.

'OK, I'm going to trust you on this. But if you break my trust, that will be the end for us, you know that?'

Alex put his arm around her slender shoulder and pulled her in close. 'Jules, I love you. When you said we could talk, my whole life plan changed. You've saved me, and I'm not throwing that away.' He kissed the top of her head. 'Let's go to bed. I've got a big day tomorrow.'

They both got off the sofa. 'Alex, just how much money have you got and where did it come from?'

'Well, you know I always like to have a plan?' She nodded. 'Well, I have been saving for a long time, and I invested well. I've got enough for us to go and live anywhere in the world and be comfortable—not super rich but comfortable.'

He didn't like the idea of lying to her, but he didn't feel he could stretch her trust in him any further than he had already. He would tell her the truth but only once this was all done.

They held hands as they went upstairs, and Alex was already thinking about how he intended to bring down the Maguires.

'I want this sorting out, and I want this sorting out quickly, do you hear me, lad.'

Ryan grimaced. He hated talking to Jimmy on the phone. Perhaps because he found it harder to disguise the fact that he was afraid of him. He could not transmit his faux nonchalance without body language.

'I know, Uncle Jimmy. I know. The man lives two hundred miles away. I've got people down there now, and they are looking for him. It's not a big place, and we know where he works, so it will just be a couple of days. Trust me, Uncle Jimmy, we will have this all tied up in a few days.' He knew he sounded nervous; he hated himself for being afraid of Jimmy.

'Call me three days from now. I expect to find out where my money is and when I will get it back, and I want this fucking lawyer made an example of, do you understand?'

'Yes, Uncle Jim. I will sort him out. He's just a greedy lawyer. We just underestimated how greedy he was. When I've got your money, and mine, we will leave a very public message for everyone, so they know we don't piss about.'

'Three days, Ryan or I'm coming over there with my boys, and we will take our money from you if necessary.'

'Yes, Uncle Jimmy, I will ring you.'

Ryan put down the phone. 'I hate that mad old bastard,' he muttered.

'You should have steered well clear of your uncle Jim, didn't I tell you so?' Frank Maguire had walked in to Ryan's office unnoticed. 'Don't you think it's about time you told me what your mad bastard of an uncle already knows. I am your father.' Frank sat down on the edge of the desk.

'Look, Dad, you'll be out of this soon. It's best that you don't know anything.'

Frank stood up and yelled. 'It's still my company. If you have done anything to prejudice my plans, you will still have to answer to me, and God knows I'm a worse enemy to you than mad, old Jimmy, do you understand me?'

Ryan was shocked. He blinked and sat upright in his leather chair. 'OK, Dad. It's the cleaning job. We have had a bit of a hiccup. The insurance company paid money out to one of the boys, through the lawyer, Harris. I sent my lads out to arrange the payback of the clean money. It was a lot. He told us he had already paid it back to the lawyer. My lads didn't believe him, and he got roughed up a bit and, by accident, he cracked his head open.'

Frank Maguire spread his arms. 'Jesus, Ryan, that young fella who was murdered in Canal Street, it was in the papers. That was your boy?'

Ryan looked down into his lap. 'Yes.'

'And does the lawyer have the money?' Frank sounded exasperated.

'I think so, he called Redford on his mobile just before the money was paid in, and Redford called him after we had asked him for the money. So I think it's pretty certain he has it.'

Frank glared. 'How do you know about the phone calls?'

'Jimmy's contact.'

'OK, and how much of this money is Jimmy's, and how much of it is mine?'

Ryan's eyes flicked sideways and upwards. 'About two hundred is yours.' Frank slapped his palm on the desk, the loud bang made Ryan flinch involuntarily. 'That is my house money. How much in total has this little prick taken?'

Ryan mumbled, 'Four hundred of Jimmy's money and four hundred of mine.'

'Jesus H Christ Ryan, a million. You've got that much coming in, in one shipment? That's stupid, Son. This business makes a lot of money for no risk. You can do a steady trickle, to keep the cash flow up, but big transactions like that attract attention. On top of that, why the fuck is Jimmy making more than me?' Frank reached over the desk. He was quicker and more agile than his appearance belied, and he slapped Ryan across the cheek, leaving red finger marks, where the skin burnt from his touch. 'You pay that fanatic of a brother of mine more than your own father?'

'I'm sorry, Dad, but Jimmy put up more of the stake money. I knew you wouldn't want to get involved in a big score, so . . .' His words trailed away, and he flinched as

Frank raised his arm again. He left his arm there, poised to strike, and then withdrew it.

'You've made your bed, Son, you and Jimmy can sort this out between you. But I want my money, and if there is any shortfall, I want the first cut, and you can look after Jimmy from your end, understood?'

'Yes, Dad. Look, I've got men down there now. We should have him and the money in a few days. But I need to get Jimmy off my back, Dad. He's talking about coming over here, and we can't have that Republican head case running amok in Manchester.'

'Then you'd best get the man his money then.'

'Dad, he's insane, you know he is. If I don't get hold of that money in three days, he will be here taking my knees off, or worse. You know what he's like. Can you lend me the money, just for a few days?'

'Son, I would, but I don't have the money available. I've been moving all my assets to the Bahamas, as you know, and that house out there is draining my cash. I can't get hold of that sort of money. I will speak to Jimmy if you don't get the money. He won't hurt you if I'm here. We are still family, but he will hurt somebody, so have your scapegoat ready, if not the cash.'

With that, Frank left, leaving only the scent of his aftershave behind him. Ryan picked up the phone and dialled Michael Richardson's mobile. He would have a scapegoat, all right.

CHAPTER 20

MILTON KEYNES 2011

Alex was shut in is office. He had been for most of the last week. He occasionally came out for coffee, but he had made it clear to the team that he was not available for queries or technical referrals. In a normal day, he would devote at least half of his working hours to the referrals of junior fee earners, helping them to draft court documents, providing valuations on medical reports or just doing the random file reviews that were required from a quality control or training perspective.

All of those jobs had been delegated to the more senior members of the team. Alex was preparing his files for the Serious Fraud Office, the SFO. All solicitors and their employees are obliged to report, regardless of their client confidentiality responsibilities, any cases of potential money laundering. This overrides their obligation to their client. They are not allowed to notify their client that they have reported a case that would be considered tipping off and is punishable by a prison sentence. They must report any suspicions that they have, not just when they are sure of a case. If they fail to notify the SFO of any suspicions, they are deemed to be aiding and abetting, which carries a maximum sentence of five years.

When reporting any suspicions, they have to go through a nominated money laundering officer, appointed internally by every firm. In Hanson's case, that person was Christopher Hanson himself. Alex knew that he would be pedantic in the extreme, ensuring that the forms were completed with precision. Whilst Christopher was driven by the financial rewards of running a practice he was, deep down, very typical of most lawyers—law abiding and infused with an old-fashioned morality. He, like the overwhelming majority of legal practitioners, treated his obligations to uphold the rule of law gravely.

Alex put the final pieces of evidence into his file. The whole thing was scanned in to his system and put on to four discs: one for the SFO; one for Christopher's file; and one for Alex to keep; the fourth disc was put in an envelope and addressed, and Alex placed it in his leather satchel.

To the satchel, he added a further disc that contained the details of his conversation with Jakov Zenczakowski, which included a recording made on Alex's iPhone by way of a statement.

Alex took the two discs he intended to give to Christopher Hanson together with his letter of resignation. He was weighed down by the thought that he was throwing away everything he had worked for. It pulled at his chest, making his movements slow, reluctant. He felt close to tears. He had struggled from nowhere. No family had offered him support; no school or university had succoured him. He had started at the very bottom and had to fight to prove himself every step of the way to his partnership. Now here he was about to give it away, and for what?

He had that hollow feeling in the pit of his stomach, but he pulled himself away from his desk and walked through the office to Hanson's room in the corner. This time, he didn't bother to knock.

'Hi, Chris.'

'Alex? What can I do for you?' Hanson sat back in his chair with tie off and shirt open at the top. Behind him, Alex could see his reflection in the windows and beyond the inky blackness of a winter's evening—the lights of Milton Keynes punctuating the gloom.

'I've brought you the SFO forms, two discs as you requested.' His voice wavered as he spoke.

Hanson sighed. 'Is it as bad as you led me to believe?' Alex looked back to Hanson, who suddenly looked older than he had earlier that day. They both knew what was coming and neither of them wanted to go through it.

'No, Chris, it's not as bad, it's worse.' Alex dropped the envelope on his desk. 'That's my resignation. I'm sorry, Chris. I never wanted this to happen, but I don't see how I can stay having introduced this sort of business into the practice.'

Hanson looked at the envelope but didn't open it. He looked back to Alex. 'Alex, you know I would have stood by you, and you know I would have helped you. You've made me and my partners very rich over these last few years. But now you've put that in front of me, I have a duty to my business partners to accept it. Unless you pick it up now, I will and your position will be terminated forthwith.'

Alex made no move towards the envelope. He just stood looking at it, his hands behind his back, as though preventing them from unilaterally grabbing the envelope off the desktop.

Hanson sighed again and picked up the envelope. 'You will be paid six months' notice, like any other partner, but there is no requirement for you to come into the office during your notice period. You will also be paid a bonus, Alex, based on performance. A golden handshake if you like, equivalent to another six months' salary. I really am sorry to see it end this way, Alex. You will get a glowing personal reference from me. I will do what I can. Where will you go?'

Alex cleared his throat. 'I don't have any plans at the moment. I'm going to go on a holiday for a few weeks, straighten myself out.'

Hanson brightened, relieved that the awkward moment was over. He felt a genuine warmth for Alex.

'Good idea. I expect that means I will need to approve some holiday for Juliette?'

Alex laughed. He had done everything possible to keep their relationship a secret at work. Hanson never failed to surprise him. 'You've never lost your touch, have you, Chris?'

'Hmm, I don't know about that. I have not mentioned your relationship to anybody else, and I do not intend to. But if word gets out, the partners will not be happy and that could make her position here untenable. You should discuss it with her. She's a brilliant lawyer, and she will succeed wherever she goes. Look, when this is all done and dusted, we'll go for a drink. I hope there will be no hard feelings, Alex.'

'No, Chris. No hard feelings, not towards you or the partnership. I'm sorry I messed this up.'

Hanson stood and the two men shook hands across the desk. They held on slightly longer than was normal and then Alex released his grip. He turned and walked back to his office. It was six o'clock, and the office was mostly empty, which was, of course, how Alex had wanted it. He did not want long goodbyes.

He picked up the ancient leather satchel and swung it over his shoulder. He took nothing else. He had no personal items at work. He went down to the ground floor and out through the back door into the car park. He got into the TT and put his mobile phone in the cradle. He switched on the ignition and looked back up at the building. He then reversed from his parking space, with his initials painted on the floor, and swung the car around to the exit of the car park.

It was Thursday, December 8, 2011. *Twenty-one years since the murder of John Lennon,* he thought to himself. He always felt sad on this day. Lennon had been his idol as a youngster, a working-class hero. It's something to be.

Alex no longer had idols. Once again, Alex Harris was in transition.

Alex decided to drive out to see Johnny and Diane. He needed to say goodbye to them in person. He called Jules to let her know he would be home at around seven, and she confirmed she would be there. She asked him if he had seen Christopher, and he confirmed he had. 'Come home as soon as you can. I'll be here for you.'

He felt comforted. It was hard enough walking away from his work, but had he lost Jules, he may well have forsaken everything. There would have been nothing left for him to look forward to, and he feared where that would lead him to.

The Milton Keynes traffic was light. Everybody was headed in the opposite direction to Alex and into the centre of town for Christmas shopping. The shops were open with extended hours throughout December to cope with the demand. He was soon parking outside Diane's house.

He walked up the ramp and rang the bell, his satchel over his shoulder.

Diane came to the door. As usual, she looked like she was on her way out; she wore a black pencil skirt and a black blouse with a frill around the neckline, which in true Diane style was low, displaying her admirable cleavage.

'Alex, you didn't say you were coming, come in, love, it's freezing out there.'

'Sorry, Diane, I don't want to interrupt. I won't be long.' He followed her into the living room, which was warm. Johnny was in his chair with the TV on, watching cartoons as usual. Phineas and Ferb were creating winter in their summer holidays; it was called 'swinter'. Alex sat in the chair next to him.

'I'll pop the kettle on,' said Diane. 'Johnny, turn that down, love, Alex is here to see you.'

Johnny groaned, 'You always come in the good bits, Al. I'm gonna pause it and watch it when you've gone.'

'That's a good idea, Johnny. Look, buddy, I need to have a chat with you. I'm going away for a while, and I won't see you for some time. I won't be able to call you either.'

Johnny turned to face him, tearing his eyes away from the static picture on the box. 'Why?'

'Well, I've got a few problems at work that I need to get sorted out, and I can only do that by going away.' Alex was looking at the TV. He didn't look Johnny in the eye.

'How do you sort out work while you're away, that's daft.'

Alex smiled painfully. 'I know. Look, I've got to sort something out. Family stuff, and once I've done, it I will have to go away.'

Johnny continued to look Alex in the eye, his open face uncomprehending. 'Is it your mum? My mum is my family.'

Alex flushed. He looked at Johnny and reached out and took his hand. 'Yes, Johnny, it's to do with my mum.' He felt the tears coming, stinging his eyes. He brushed them away with his free hand. 'Will you look after your mum? Mums are the best, and they need looking after.' His voice cracked.

Johnny had turned back to the TV. 'Yes, I look after my mum. She says she doesn't know what she would do without me.'

Alex was aware that Diane was standing behind him. She put her hand on his shoulder. 'Can you give me a hand in the kitchen, love.'

Alex stood and followed Diane into the small kitchen with worktop and cupboards to three sides and built-in appliances all around.

Diane went to the worktop opposite the door and picked up the teapot. She dropped two teabags in and filled it with boiling water from the clear electric kettle. She turned back to Alex.

He looked at the floor, embarrassed that she would be able to see his red rimmed eyes.

'I had to get you in here, Alex. Johnny will be upset. He will need time to process the information. I know he seems unmoved, but he will be devastated. It just takes him time to work it out.'

Alex was still looking at the floor. 'I know.'

'Alex, are you in trouble?' He shuffled from one foot to the other.

'Yep, a bit.'

'What have you done?'

Alex looked up. 'I'm sorry, Diane. I can't really tell you anything. It's a very long story, and I don't want you to have to deal with it. You've got enough to worry about. You don't need to be worrying about me.'

Diane was leaning back against the worktop, her arms folded across her front, her head tilted to one side, gazing deep into Alex's eyes.

'You told Johnny it was about your mum, Alex, but you told me your mum and dad were dead.'

'I know. My mum is dead, Di, but it is about her, and I can't really say any more. Look, I've resigned from my job, and I'll be leaving in the next few days. I wanted to see you both before I went. I wanted to say sorry.' Alex could feel the tears rising once again.

Diane stepped towards him. 'Alex, you have nothing to be sorry about. Whatever you have done, or are going to do, you have saved me and my boy. You have set him up for the rest of his life. He will have everything he could possibly have, and that is all down to you. So we don't care about anything else. You are part of our family, Alex, and you always will be.'

She moved closer to him and put her arms around his middle and rested her head on his chest. 'If there is anything we can do to help you, Alex, we'll do it.'

Alex broke down. He cried. He cried like he had not cried since he was a child—racking sobs. And Diane held on to him and comforted him like a mother would her grieving son.

When his tears had subsided, she took his face in her hands and bent his head down towards hers, and she kissed his forehead. 'Diane. I've still got Johnny's passport.' She kept his face in her hands. 'I know. We don't need it. You keep it.' She looked into his eyes, and Alex felt as if she understood him completely.

'I'd better go.' His voice was still thick with emotion. 'I think your tea has gone cold.' Diane took her hands from his face. She smiled at him. 'I'll see you out.'

As Alex walked through the living room to the door, he shouted goodbye to Johnny. He didn't turn away from the TV, but he shouted, 'See ya, wouldn't wanna be ya.'

When he got to the door, he opened it and turned around. 'He will miss you, Alex.'

'I know. I will miss him too. And you.'

'Alex Harris, if only I were twenty years younger.' Alex reached and touched her face. 'Age has nothing to do with it, just circumstance, Diane.' He kissed her cheek. 'Thanks for everything.'

As he walked down the ramp towards his car, she called after him, 'You look after that beautiful girl of yours, Alex, and let me know you are all right, OK?'

Alex looked back and laughed to himself. He waved to Diane as she shut the door. He opened his car door, 'Jesus, does everybody know?'

It was twenty minutes later that Alex arrived home. He embraced Jules. 'It's all done. I will start getting ready to go tomorrow. You need to speak to Christopher tomorrow.'

She held his embrace. 'Tell me it will all be OK, Alex.'

He took a deep breath. 'It will.'

PART II

CHAPTER 21

FRIDAY, DECEMBER 9, 2011

ALEX HAD LEFT THE HOUSE early. He carried with him his satchel. It was a bright and sunny morning, no breeze but a light frost on the grass verges. He decided to go to his lock-up on foot to clear his head after his emotional night, so he left Adelphi Street and walked towards Campbell Park. As he turned left out of the cul-de-sac, he looked back at the house, where Jules was standing on the balcony, in front of the large picture window to the lounge, to wave him off.

Milton Keynes is a city of straight lines, but in this instance, when driving to Springfield, where Alex rented a garage attached to a modest house, he would have to drive around the open space of the park. On foot, he could go as the crow flies through the grass-covered amphitheatre and across Avebury Boulevard to the older housing estate of Springfield.

Milton Keynes had been built outwards from the centre. The estates, nearest the shopping centre, were the oldest, and, in the main, least desirable. Campbell Park was the one exception where small numbers of houses and some upscale apartments had been built, around the edges of the park in recent years, on land that had originally been set aside for businesses connected to the shopping centre.

Springfield was one of the older housing schemes. Private houses mingled with council properties. The original idea was that the private housing would encourage the council tenants to maintain a level of appearance that would not be achieved on a purely council owned estate. In many cases, it had not worked, and the private houses were generally owned by absentee landlords who raised an income, letting houses to those who could not get a council property.

On Springfield, however, the experiment seemed to have worked. It was a generally tidy estate. Alex approached his garage. The tenant of the house had no car and ameliorated his rent by subletting his large garage to Alex.

Alex unlocked the door and raised it. The Ghia was still under its cover which Alex peeled back. It was a perfect day for a drive, no salt on the roads yet. Despite it being early December, the weather had been very mild and dry.

He unlocked the driver's door and dropped his satchel over into the passenger seat and lowered himself in behind the wheel. Being an import, the car was left-hand drive, but Alex was accustomed to driving that way. He put the key in the ignition and fired up the willing air-cooled engine.

The bright red car, its chrome bumper and overriders glistening in the morning sunlight, rolled out of the garage. Alex got out, locked the garage, and then set off to find a post office, not too near, so that he could enjoy a drive. He fished his sunglasses out of the door pocket and drove down Child's Way towards the M1 motorway, which he crossed heading towards Newport Pagnell. From Newport, he took the B road to Northampton, stopping in the pretty village of Stoke Goldington to post his envelopes. He and Jules had often driven to the village to park up and walk in the nearby woods, where they would often see deer. For a city boy like Alex, it was always exciting to see wildlife wandering through the woodland. He had never lived in a rural area. He often joked with Jules that the first time he saw a cow he thought it was a bus with no windows. It occurred to him that now might be a good time to start thinking about the countryside as an option.

He had driven about ten miles. The Wolfsburg-designed engine was purring nicely, and he decided to head back. The roads were clear, as the rush hour had passed, and he pushed the Ghia up to 70 mph, which it did comfortably enough.

He had a relaxing morning planned. He would take the car back to the garage and then walk back to the house. He needed to take his tools as he wanted to re-hang a couple of the doors on the kitchen cupboards to take out the dishwasher, which didn't seem to be cleaning quite so well. He suspected he needed a new filter but was concerned about a possible leak from the waste pipe.

He rarely did jobs around the house, other than car maintenance, but felt a certain sense of accomplishment when he did. He assumed that was just a sign that he was heading into middle age and resolved, in his own mind, to stop doing jobs around the house for fear that it would lead to garish sweaters and slippers. He could not correlate his love of Ska music and The Clash with a warm cardigan, a flat cap, and a desire for power tools for Christmas.

After leaving the car, he headed back through the park with his small box of tools. It had a small hammer, a set of screwdrivers, a few spanners, and various nails, screws, washers, nuts, and bolts. He felt relaxed. He had taken a huge step, and a weight had been lifted from him. For the first time, he felt he could consider his plans with a genuinely clear head. He would present his evidence to the authorities and walk away clean, wealthier than when he started.

As he crossed the park in the weak sunshine, he plotted out the remainder of his day. Jules would be at work by this time, and he planned to have all his jobs done by lunchtime. He would sit down with a cappuccino and a DVD for the afternoon. He wanted to catch up with his Pacific boxset. His evidence would be with the SFO tomorrow. He had also posted a disc to the police.

He had discussed his plan with Jules. He felt confident that he could get the Maguires people put away for a few years at least and that would satisfy his needs. In that way, he got to keep the money he had stolen from them, and they paid a price for their criminal activities. More importantly, he could carve out a future with Jules. It meant putting aside his vendetta but gained him a degree of redemption.

He felt content with his choices and felt relieved that he would not need to get involved any further. He would not need to unlock his past. It could remain in the cold, dark place in his mind, where it had been for the past few years, getting further and further away and less and less relevant.

The new plan was to sell up in Milton Keynes and to move away, abroad, for at least a couple of years. Experience something new. Alex had always loved to travel, and he was excited by the prospect. He had always felt like a different person when living in a different country. He had heard the saying that to speak another language was to possess another soul. But he considered that placing oneself in a foreign environment allowed you to recreate yourself in whatever image you chose. It was not just language that allowed you to possess another soul. He was living proof of that.

As he crossed Silbury Boulevard from the park, into Adelphi Street, he had a spring in his step. He swung his toolbox and whistled tunelessly.

He came to the turn in the cul-de-sac; his house was one of two directly opposite the entrance. The house had a wooden and electronically controlled garage door on the ground floor, next to the front door. The lounge was on the first floor and had large windows to the front of the house that opened on to the balcony. The kitchen diner was open plan but situated at the back of the house, overlooking the small-walled garden. The second floor had the bedrooms, one large bedroom to the front with two smaller rooms at the back. All three rooms were en suite. It would sell quickly since it was situated within walking distance of the shopping centre, the theatre district, and the park.

Alex stopped as he turned the corner. He could see the curtains moving through the open door on to the balcony. Jules would never have left the balcony doors open if she was going to work; she was just too careful. He assumed, therefore, she must still be home. Perhaps she had spoken to Christopher already and resigned straight away. He was about to start towards the house when the electric garage door began to swing up. Alex instinctively ducked to his left, on to the driveway of one of the houses, behind the silver Golf parked there.

He saw a man moving around inside the garage, squeezing up the side of the TT, moving items around, picking up cans and bottles and discarding them. Then he walked behind the car and came back towards the front and out of the garage. He was holding Alex's green plastic petrol can, the sort everybody had, bought from a petrol station in times of emergency. Alex always kept his full just in case he needed petrol for the Ghia.

The man stood outside of the garage facing back in towards the car. Alex was unsure what he was doing as he just seemed to standstill. Then the door came down, and Alex realised he had been struggling with the remote control.

The man turned to look down the street glancing left and right and checking to see whether he had been noticed. The street was deserted. It always was at this time of day, all the professional couples at their accountancy firms or legal practices.

He was tall with slicked back hair, pockmarked features, and an unusually erect stance. Alex stared. He recognised him immediately. He knew his plan had just changed. He set down his toolbox and opened it. He pulled out a few tools and closed the box, sliding it under the Golf. He was wearing jeans with a broad leather belt, Converse tennis shoes, and a T-shirt with an image of John Lennon on the front with a sweater over it and a brown canvas bomber jacket. He took off the jacket, placing that under the car and pushed the tools under his leather belt at his back.

He peered around the rear of the car and watched the man closing the front door behind him.

Alex felt the adrenaline pumping inside him—the old excitement starting to rise. It had been a long time.

Duncan sat at his desk, looking at the rest of the team out in The Pit. His mood was dark. He thundered around the building, snapping at anyone who crossed his path. He knew why. The investigation into the murder of Steven Redford had, like an old Ford, ground to a dismal stop.

He had been at his desk for three hours and had reread the files, looking for something that he might have missed. He had gone back through every interview and the notes of all the meetings. He had trawled his own scribbled notes and the jottings on his computer, reassessing even the wildest theories for a glimmer of hope that there was an unseen connection.

The previous day, he had tried to trace Jack Ladd. He felt one person who could have sent him the message that tied the murder into Maureen Ladd was her son Jack, who had disappeared in November 1991, shortly after his mother's death.

Duncan had scanned the Internet for any links to the missing boy, who would now be in his thirties. He found out from the Immigration Service that Jack Ladd had travelled, on his own passport, from Dover to Calais on the now defunct Hoverspeed hovercraft, The Princess Anne, in March 1992. From the time of his disappearance until the time of his channel crossing, there was no record of his movements, no bank withdrawals, no arrests for vagrancy, and no record of him being employed. Nothing.

Duncan had contacted the French police. Jack Ladd arrived in Calais on March 8, 1992, and simply walked into obscurity. There was no record of him returning to the UK. His passport did not appear to have been used since that original crossing and had long since expired. The trail ended at the Hoverport in Calais, and there was nothing to pick up on from that point.

That had certainly blackened Duncan's mood. He did not like failure. He did not like the fact that a person could just walk away from a life never to be seen or heard of again that they could become untouchable by the rest of society and remain so for so long. He felt that the alternative explanation that Jack Ladd had died, unnoticed by anybody, was even less palatable.

He decided to get himself a drink. He got up, slapping the file down on the desk and stalking through The Pit towards the coffee machine. As he passed the desk occupied by Miles, the younger man was finishing a telephone call. 'Thank you, we appreciate it.'

Duncan got to the machine and punched in the code for an espresso. The machine gurgled and fizzed and a plastic cup with a dribble of black fluid was presented to him. He took it and repeated the process. As he was picking up the second cup, Miles appeared next to him. He seemed agitated. 'Boss, I think we might have a development. I'm not sure, but I think it's something you need to look at right now.'

Duncan straightened up and poured one dribble of coffee into the other, making around a third of a cup. He mumbled something under his breath and started back to his office. 'Come on then,' he called over his shoulder.

He sat himself back behind his desk and took a swig from the cup and grimaced, 'Shite.'

Miles came in and closed the door behind him. 'OK, you know you asked me to speak to the guys in Drugs.' He waited for an acknowledgement but realised that none was going to be forthcoming and carried on. 'Well, erm, they tell me that in the last six months, there has been a dramatic increase in the amount of coke on the streets. They say it's coming in from Eastern Europe and from Turkey before that. They are not sure who is behind it, but they say it comes in regular shipments once a month, when there is a huge flood. Whoever is selling it is undercutting everyone else, and they seem to be trying to shift it all in the space of a few days. This causes a problem because there is only a small window for the drugs boys to find out who is selling and then it goes dead for a few weeks and then resurfaces for a few days and is dead again.'

Miles looked at Duncan who was studying the coffee cup. He got no indication that he was even listening. He hated it when the boss got morose like this. It just made his life more difficult than it needed to be.

He got no acknowledgement again, so he carried on. 'They don't know Redford, but when I told them, he worked for a transport firm; their ears were pricked up. They didn't exactly say so, but it was clear that was one line of enquiry that they were following to explain the shipment pattern. So it is possible that coke was being brought in by somebody at Maguires and Redford was one of their sellers. What do you think?'

'It is a possibility. But no more than that,' Duncan muttered.

'OK. What do we do with this? Do we go back and see Maguires or what?'

Duncan heaved a sigh. 'Yes, we will need to get our ideas straight before we do. Anything else?' Duncan downed what was left of the fluid masquerading as coffee and winced again as though drinking pure mountain distilled moonshine from the backwoods of Kentucky.

'One more thing. I tried to get hold of that lawyer again today, the one who dealt with Redford's claim. I was told he has left the practice. It appears he resigned and left with immediate effect.' Miles raised his eyebrows, expectant, waiting to see if this snippet would have any effect on his doleful superior.

Duncan raised an eyebrow. 'That's interesting. Do we know where he lives?'

'Yes, Boss, I've tracked him down. He lives in Milton Keynes. The senior partner at the firm says that if we attend their offices, he will provide us with some basic details on the case, but he must have some guarantees regarding confidentiality.'

'Hmm. Did you tell him to fuck off and just tell us everything we want to know?' Duncan growled.

'Er no, no I didn't.'

'OK, right, go home and pack a bag. I think we will have a drive down to Milton Keynes. I've heard it's a shithole. Be back here by one, you're driving.'

'Er, right, OK, Boss.'

'Before you go, get on to Old Trafford and get them to book us a couple of rooms for tonight and ask Lynn to book us a pool car unless you want to drive yours.'

'Yeah, we'll go in mine, Boss. I can claim some mileage then.'

Duncan put on his overcoat and shut up and locked his office. 'I'm off to get my bag,' he announced to nobody in particular. 'Miles, don't be late back. What sort of car have you got?'

'BMW, Boss.'

'That'll do.'

With that, he strode from the office and headed back towards his flat.

Lynn looked at Miles. 'Since when have you got a BMW?'

'I haven't,' said Miles, smiling. 'But if I tell him I've got a Mini, he'll whinge about there being no leg room or no head room, and he won't let me use it.'

'You know he'll do his nut. He's in a bad enough mood as it is.' Miles laughed, picked up his vintage Donkey Jacket and swung it over his shoulder as he left.

Alex moved slowly and quietly towards the house. He had his keys in his pocket but had decided against simply walking in through the front door. By the time he got the door open, they would be upon him. He was sure there would be more than the man he had seen in the garage, and if he lost the element of surprise, his chances of overcoming any of them was immediately diminished.

He walked up the driveway watching the lounge window in case anybody should be looking out. There was a low wall dividing his drive from the drive of the house next door. On top of the wall were cast iron railings, which were fixed to the front of Alex's house by a metal bar.

Alex stepped on to the wall and then pulled himself up, with his natural balance and agility, so that he would stand on the top of the railings, his feet between the pointed rods. He held on to the wall dividing the two properties as he put his right foot on top of the metal bar fixing the railing to the wall. The top of the bar was only an inch deep, so Alex needed to hold the wall tightly as he balanced.

From this position, he could reach bottom of the balcony on the first floor. He reached over carefully, but aware that his foot could slide from the metal support at any moment. He grabbed the bottom of the balcony with both hands as his foot slipped off the support, and he dangled off the balcony for a few moments.

He swung his left leg up so that his Converse gripped on the platform and wedged between it and the glass balustrade. From here, he was able to get his knee up and thereafter pull the rest of his body up so that he was lying on the narrow ledge on the outside of the balustrade.

He could see inside his living room. The sofa was on the left side of the room, and one man sat there smoking a cigarette. Another man stood by the kitchen at the far end of the room, and the man from the garage stood by the door to the landing and stairs.

In the middle of the room sat Jules on a stool from the kitchen. Her hands were tied behind her back. Her head was forward so that her chin seemed to be resting on her chest. Her hair was covering her face.

Her white silk blouse was ripped at the shoulder and appeared to be open down the front. Alex could see the curvature of her breast and her sternum. She was breathing heavily. She was wearing the blue skirt from her suit and her shoes. Alex assumed she had been caught as she left the house heading for work.

Alex could not see the face of the man on the sofa, so was fairly sure he could not be seen. But the two others would be able to see him if they were to look out of the window. The curtain was pulled across one side, so Alex decided to shuffle along to the left side of the balcony, where he would be able to get over the balustrade hidden by the curtain.

He heard a high-pitched whistle as the kettle on his hob began to boil. The man by the kitchen turned his back to the window to go to the hob. Alex glanced quickly at the man with the petrol can. He was following into the kitchen. Alex quickly shifted himself along using his arms to push himself feet first and, upon reaching the point where he was masked by the curtain, pulled himself upright and vaulted over the balustrade, landing silently the other side.

His heart pounded. His senses seemed heightened. He took a long breath to try and regulate his pulse rate and make sure he was thinking clearly.

He peered through the fine curtain to check whether his movement had alerted them, but they seemed to have been distracted by the screeching of the kettle. The piercing sound had now stopped, and Alex heard a strong Mancunian accent.

'Don't worry, love, we will just sit here until he gets back, having a pot of tea, just like old friends. We can party later.'

Alex looked at Jules, who didn't react to the words and kept her head down. Alex watched each man in turn. They did not appear to be carrying weapons, but he could not be sure they were not secreted. He waited, contemplating the right moment to make his move.

The petrol can was placed down by the side of the sofa, and the man with the slicked hair was walking towards the window. Alex's decision was made for him. He reached behind his back and pulled a tool from his belt. He lowered himself into a crouch and stretched out his right arm.

A foot appeared on the threshold of the door. Alex swung his arm in a wide arc. The hammer smashed into the kneecap, crushing the patella. There was a high-pitched scream. Alex leapt into the doorway. The Lizard was lying on the floor before him howling with pain and holding his right leg either side of the destroyed knee. He began to push himself away from Alex with his left leg, scraping his foot along the floor, but he could get little purchase on the thick pile carpet. Alex reached forward and grabbed his left foot, raising it and holding it in his left hand and raising the hammer above his head. The Lizard squirmed, but he could not wriggle free without causing excruciating pain to his right leg, and he was unable to free himself. He whimpered as he realised Alex intended to smash his left knee and looked imploringly to the man on the sofa.

He had not moved, but he shouted 'Tony' and pointed to the petrol can. The huge muscle-bound figure of Fat Tony moved awkwardly but reached the can. He spun off the lid and the odour of petrol filled the room. Jules looked up and stared wild-eyed at Alex.

'You cut her loose or this fucker never walks again.'

Michael Richardson stood up. 'Tony, pour it on her.' Fat Tony emptied the contents over Jules, soaking her completely. Her blouse stuck to the naked breasts beneath, and she gagged from the smell. Richardson took out his lighter and flicked open the top, putting his thumb on the wheel.

Jules looked from Alex to Richardson. 'No, please,' she pleaded.

'We don't want to hurt you, love. We are reasonable people, it's just that your boyfriend here stole a lot of money from some very bad men, and they want it back.' Richardson looked to Alex. 'We need that money, and if we don't get it, she will burn. And when she is burning, we will make you watch. Then we will beat you until you beg us to take the money. Do you understand?'

Alex looked from Richardson to Jules. He saw the carpet was soaked around her. All Richardson needed to do was strike his light and drop it. He could do that before Alex could reach him. He looked at Fat Tony, who had backed away from Jules and out of reach of the flammable liquid.

Alex spoke slowly, keeping his voice even. 'OK, how do we work this? I can get the money, but it means a trip to the bank. It can't be done instantly, and it can't be handed over in cash. Banks don't carry those sorts of sums in cash.'

He was buying himself time, trying to work out how he could rescue Jules. He was starting to get desperate because no obvious answer would come to him. The Lizard was still squirming, and Alex raised the hammer higher and said, 'Still.' The writhing stopped immediately.

'Well, you transferred the money once, you can do it again.' Richardson was smiling. He knew he had the upper hand. He would get the money transferred and then burn them both. Richardson reached into his pocket and took out a slip of paper. He placed it on the sofa near to Alex but kept his distance.

'I am going over to the worktop over there, and I will get you the phone, then you will call your bank and get the money sent through to that account.' He backed away, keeping his eyes on Alex.

'I've spread the money around to avoid suspicion. It will take a few calls.' Alex was watching both men, eyes flicking from side to side. Jules was emitting soft, whimpering sobs. Her head was down again. She was shivering. She was going into shock. Alex was running out of time and ideas. He knew that once the money was transferred, they would both die. His frustration began to grow; his initial excitement was developing into an underlying rage, rising on a synchronous scale.

Richardson was moving back towards him with the cordless phone, holding it out in his left hand. Alex was struggling to think clearly to contain the violence building within. He knew he could not just let go; he had to have a plan of attack. He took a deep breath and exhaled slowly, calming his thoughts in the process. Richardson bent forward to drop the phone on to the edge of the sofa by the slip of paper. His eyes left Alex for a split second so that he could see where he was dropping the phone, and Alex unleashed his fury.

He threw the hammer at Tony, like a Comanche throwing his tomahawk in an old western, it somersaulted rapidly, looping through the air, before hitting him square in the forehead, and he crumpled to the floor without a sound. Alex had dropped the Lizard's leg at the same moment and reached behind his back. Richardson was frozen as he watched the trajectory of the hammer and that was all the delay Alex needed to plunge his screwdriver into Richardson's side.

Alex lurched forward and grabbed Jules roughly under her arms, dragging her towards the landing door. Richardson screamed 'Bastard' and struck the wheel on the flint of his lighter. A small blue flame appeared, and he dropped the lighter into the soaked carpet. Yanking the landing door open, Alex yelled 'Get out' and unceremoniously pushed Jules through the door. The floor burst into flame. The Lizard screamed, and his hair caught fire. 'Mike,' he screamed. Richardson dragged him to the balcony—Alex's screwdriver still sticking out from his side and blood beginning to seep through his clothes.

The flames began to roar. Alex grabbed Tony by the collar; he remained motionless. Alex pulled him to the door, but he was too heavy as a dead weight to manoeuvre through the doorway.

The wired in smoke alarm started to shriek. Alex could see through the flames that Richardson was pushing The Lizard over the balustrade. The Lizard was reluctant to let go and then was screaming as he was ejected.

Richardson looked back at Alex as he climbed over the glass, then sat on the edge of the balcony, turned himself round, and lowered himself so that he could drop down, feet first, reducing the drop to a manageable height.

Alex turned and sprinted to the door, crashing down the stairs, he saw Jules stumbling through the front door. He realised that Richardson would reach her before him and hurled himself down the stairs and through the open door.

As he broke into the bright light of the morning, he saw Jules struggling to escape Richardson's grasp. The drop had not been as kind to him as Alex had thought it would, and he was bent forward with pain while he clutched at her hair.

Alex closed the gap between them in two rapid steps and drove his fist into Richardson's right side, just below the ribs and just above the screwdriver. The air went out of Richardson, and he opened his mouth in a silent scream of pain, which could not be articulated by his vocal chords. He buckled and let go of Jules. Alex punched him again on the right side of the jaw, and he hit the block-paved driveway.

Alex looked around. The Lizard lay crying, holding a badly deformed arm, his hand at right angles to his humerus and splinters of bone poking through the skin.

Alex bent down to Richardson. He put his mouth close to his ear and whispered to him. He stood up. 'Make sure he gets the message.' Before walking away, he swung a powerful kick to Richardson's groin; he heard him whimper and smiled to himself.

Alex peeled off his sweater. He walked Jules to the driveway, where he had left his coat. He tore off her blouse and put the sweater on her whilst she stood shaking. He picked up his jacket from under the Golf and put it on her. He looked back at the house, the fire was taking hold and alarms had started to go off on the next door property. He could already hear a distant siren. He decided they needed to move, and he set off down Adelphi Street towards the park. He would get them to the lock-up, where he would get the Karmann Ghia, and from there, he could go anywhere.

He coaxed Jules into a jog whilst hugging her. They were halfway across the park when they saw the fire engine.

CHAPTER 22

FRIDAY, DECEMBER 9

'IT'S LEFT AT THIS ROUNDABOUT.' Duncan snapped directions at Miles. He had been in a sour mood all day, magnified by having to fold his long frame into the Mini Cooper S and then by their dismal failure to understand the apparently simple Milton Keynes's grid system. It was hard to understand how you could go so wrong when you were following vertical and horizontal road patterns, but it seemed that every junction was a roundabout and every roundabout offered a different route to the city centre.

Miles was red in the face, trying to contain his frustration and embarrassment. Two and a half hours in a small car with an angry bear of a chief inspector was not his idea of a day well spent. The mileage expenses were simply not worth it.

'That's the shopping centre there, so we need to go left again.' They had come to the sprawling glass monolith that was The Centre MK. The roads were heaving. The enormous car parks around the shopping centre were full with cars parked in every last spare piece of tarmac;

people being dropped off at the doors of the centre were clogging up the thoroughfares through the car parks.

Early Christmas shoppers from all the surrounding areas descended on the shops from the end of November. Miles was surprised by Milton Keynes. It appeared to be everything he had expected from a small American town, but it was deep in Buckinghamshire. A more English setting he could not imagine.

They stopped at traffic lights. The Cooper S burbled, and Duncan shifted in his seat. 'Left at these lights and Campbell Park is straight ahead. Adelphi Street is on the left.'

'What if he's not in? Should we have got some uniforms down here first?'

The lights turned to green and Miles swung the Mini around the corner on to a dual carriageway with the shopping centre to their right and modern office buildings to their left. Ahead of them was a small roundabout. They could see the open space of the park to the right beyond the roundabout. As Miles steered the Mini around the roundabout, the road became single carriageway, and they could see the turning for Adelphi Street just ahead to the left. They could also see the reflection of the blue flashing lights on the three-storey houses that lined the street.

Duncan groaned, 'Looks like somebody might have called them already.'

Miles parked the Mini, and they both got out. The turning into the cul-de-sac had been cordoned off, and a uniformed officer stood behind the yellow and black tape. Duncan approached him and flashed his warrant card.

'Could you just wait there a moment, sir?' The officer turned away and spoke into his radio. Then he turned back. 'Inspector Stacey will be with you momentarily, sir.' He clearly had no intention of letting them through.

Miles could see the muscles in Duncan's jaw tighten. He looked down the street and saw the house with charring around the windows on the first floor. The garage door was open, and it appeared most of the first floor was on top of the car within.

A broad-shouldered man with grey hair and a neatly trimmed beard was walking towards them. He had the look of a squire in his Barbour jacket and check shirt and tie. He appeared to be around fifty and of heavy build all round with ruddy cheeks. He came to the tape and spoke to Duncan.

'Afternoon, sir, Detective Inspector Stacey. What can I do for you, sir?'

'Well, Inspector, myself and my colleague here were on our way to interview an Alex Harris of Adelphi Street. I am investigating a murder, and Mr. Harris was the lawyer representing the dead man and may have been one of the last people to speak to the victim.'

Duncan looked at Stacey, who was almost as tall as he was. 'I am assuming that Harris's house is the burnt-out property, is that correct?'

'It is, sir. Mr. Harris, however, is not in there, and I would very much like to talk to him myself. If you would like to leave your number, sir, I will contact you as soon as we find him.'

Duncan looked beyond Stacey, towards the house. He could see the Scene of Crime officers in their overalls, and the fire investigators were in deep conversation. He needed to know what had happened at the house, and he had no time for petty jurisdictional divisions.

'Stacey. Perhaps you are a little hard of hearing. I said that I am investigating a murder. A man who is at least a witness, at worst a suspect, has disappeared, and his house burnt down, and you want me to drive back to Manchester and wait for your phone call. You have no fucking idea what sort of a prick you are making of yourself. Now, either you let us through and fill us in on what is going on, or you send me away, you wait for the phone call from your chief constable telling you that you are on 'cat up tree' duty forthwith, and you wait for the press to write what a bunch of head-up-arse dickheads Thames Valley police are for withholding vital information from a national manhunt for a murder suspect because they wanted to find the man themselves. Are you beginning to see the situation you are in, Inspector?'

Miles turned away to avoid Stacey seeing his suppressed smile. Stacey stared back at Duncan for what seemed like minutes. He appeared to be completely unmoved. Then he smiled. 'Very eloquently explained, Chief, follow me.' He lifted the tape and Miles and Duncan ducked through.

'Right, sir, what we know so far. The owner of the house is, as you know, Alex Harris. He was a partner in law firm Hanson and Co on Silbury Boulevard. Quite the high-flyer until he resigned, suddenly, yesterday. He lives here alone. The house is bought and paid for, no mortgage, but on his income that is not a big surprise. No wife or kids, but he does have a girlfriend, a,' Stacey flipped open his notebook, 'Juliette Everett. She lives the other side of the park in an apartment on the Crescent, but she is not there, and she did not attend work today at Hanson's.'

Miles interrupted, 'Did she call in?' Stacey looked round. 'No, she did not. We have a very interesting crime scene. The fire was started using a petrol can from the garage. It looks a lot worse from out here than it really is.'

They stood at the end of the drive. Duncan surveyed the whole scene whilst listening to Stacey.

'The damage is localised to a small area in the lounge, which is on the first floor there. We found a man, unconscious, with a serious head wound, by the door to the lounge . . .'

Duncan interrupted this time, 'Do we know who he is?'

'Not yet, sir. He had no wallet or any form of ID on him. He is at MK General now. The paramedics thought he had a fractured skull due to a deep indentation in his forehead. There was a hammer on the floor, or, at least, the head of a hammer, the handle had burnt off. It seems likely that our guy was hit with the hammer.'

Duncan was moving towards the door. 'Careful, sir,' called Stacey after him, Duncan stopped. 'There are blood stains on the driveway.' He pointed. 'Here and here. Somebody dropped off the balcony here.' He was pointing to a spot just near the front door. 'And just over there also, so we know that there were at least three people in the house. There are corresponding blood stains on the balcony, so we know they were wounded before they escaped the fire. Follow me, sir.'

Stacey went through the front door. Duncan looked at Miles and nodded towards the forensics. Miles nodded back and wandered over casually. Duncan followed Stacey into the hallway and up the stairs. He sniffed the air as he walked. He turned into the lounge and marvelled at the gaping hole in the floor.

'There are blood stains on the sofa. There was a chair in the middle of the floor, well, one of those kitchen stools.' He pointed towards the kitchen area. 'My best guess is that someone sat on the chair, someone on the sofa, and the fractured skull guy by the door here. But beyond that, I'm pretty stumped. His nice car is knackered though.'

Duncan peered over the hole in the floor. The kitchen stool was twisted and bent on the roof of the Audi. There was blistered paint all over the bonnet. It appeared to have one flat tyre. It looked a rather sorry mess.

He considered the scene in the lounge. 'So the chair was right here in the middle, otherwise it couldn't have gone through the hole. If the petrol was poured on the floor here, then it was poured on the chair. Why would you do that, Inspector?'

'I don't know, sir.' Stacey looked blankly at the scene and back at Duncan. He shrugged his huge shoulders.

'Well, I'm guessing that someone sat on the chair and the petrol was poured over them, which makes this look like a rather different scene. We have someone on the sofa, which is directly in front of the chair, your man by the door here and the other man who went over the balcony, but we do not know where he was. Plus we have the person in the chair who is soaked in petrol. You need your SoCo's in here, tracing petrol on the stairs and the landing, also checking to see if there is any on the balcony. I'm pretty sure that whoever sat on that chair escaped down the stairs, judging by the smell of petrol down there. They need to check outside for the same thing, but that might be a bit tricky as it's a driveway, but do it anyway. If two people went over the balcony and they were bleeding, then there must be a trail beyond the drive. You need to find it.'

Duncan looked back down the hole. 'This was an interrogation, Stacey, but I doubt it ended well, what do you think?'

'Er, no, sir, I don't think it did. I'll get SoCo's back in here.'

'Right. Can you tell me the way to the hospital?'

The receiver crashed into the cradle. Ryan picked it up and banged it down again. 'Shit, shit, *shit*,' he yelled, hitting the receiver on to the phone each time. He dropped the phone back into its place and put his head in his hands.

He would have to talk to his dad. He would need protection from Jimmy now unless he acted really fast. He picked up the phone and dialled an internal extension number.

'We need the next shipment, and we need it now. I want it here tomorrow, and I want it liquidated within twenty-four hours.' He paused whilst he listened to the response. 'I don't want your fucking excuses. You make it happen, do you hear me? Make it happen.' The phone crashed down again.

Ryan Maguire put his head in his hands again. He might just be able to pull this one out of the fire. Just so long as he can keep Jimmy in Belfast.

He left his desk and headed out and through the building to his father's office.

CHAPTER 23

FRIDAY, DECEMBER 9

THE KARMANN GHIA BUZZED THROUGH the bright early afternoon sunshine on the M6 motorway towards Wolverhampton. Alex, buzzing like the Ghia, glanced across at Jules as she sat with her head on the passenger side window. He was not sure if she was asleep but was not talking to her just in case. Or perhaps because he simply could not find the words to explain what she had been through.

When they had reached the garage, Alex had knocked on the owner's front door and convinced the elderly man that there had been an accident with the petrol can. He and Jules were allowed in to use the bathroom, where Alex stripped her down and put her in the shower, running the water as hot as she could stand it while stripping off himself so that he could get in and wash her completely free of the smell of the fuel.

She hadn't spoken up until that point, but as the needles of hot water pricked her skin, she began to come around. She had recounted how they had ambushed her as soon as she had opened the door to go to work. They had forced her back into the house and up the stairs, where they forced her on to the chair.

They had asked where he was, and she had told them, truthfully, that she did not know but was expecting to meet him back at the house after work. They had slapped her face and ripped her clothes, threatened to rape her, and threatened to torture her until she gave them an honest answer, but she had maintained her story. She assured Alex that she was physically unhurt.

She had been there for what seemed, to her, to be only a few minutes before Alex had arrived. She wanted to know what he had done to make these men come looking for him. She wanted to know why he had told her it would all be sorted out peacefully when it was clearly beyond that stage, and she wanted to know what money they had been asking about.

Alex had lathered her all over until the last vestige of the odour had gone. He answered her questions as truthfully as he could. He explained that he had taken the money from Steven Redford's account by convincing him that he was acting on behalf of Ryan Maguire. He explained that he had already sent his file to the police and the SFO and that he had assumed that all he needed to do was disappear. He had no idea how they could know that he had taken the money as he had transferred it into a private numbered account with a Swiss bank, no names were used. From there, he had distributed it into three other accounts, none of which bore his name. He held her close to him and told her that he had done everything they had agreed and that he had passed everything on to the authorities.

But now the game had changed again.

Alex asked Jules to repeat exactly the questions that she had been asked, which she did, her memory was functioning perfectly as he knew it would. He had become animated when she had recounted the questions about the money. 'We know he took the money. We know he called to arrange to meet Redford, so where has he hidden the money?'

Alex had suggested that she stay where she was, and he would go and buy her some clothes, but Jules had refused, she did not want to be left alone. Alex had borrowed an old jumper from the wardrobe and went to the garage, where he pulled out a pair of overalls from the shelves at the back of the garage, which she had to roll up at the bottom, and a pair of his trainers from the boot of the car.

Jules looked like something from a 1980s Dexy's Midnight Runners video, but she was clean and warm. Alex told her that he would drive her to her parents' house and that she was to stay there until he came for her. She had agreed and had not spoken again since.

Alex had taken a metal box from the garage and put it into the boot at the front of the car. He had thanked the old man and paid him fifty pounds for the jumper and use of the shower. He explained that they were going to stay with his parents in London, should anybody ask after him.

It was an hour and twenty minutes later when Alex parked the car on the driveway of the large Victorian semi-detached house in Wolverhampton, where Winston Everett was pruning the rose bushes in the small front garden.

Jules got out of the car and walked straight past him and into the house. Winston watched her walk by, his secateurs open, hovering over the brown stem of a bush. As she was swallowed up by the tall, angular facade of the red brick house, he turned to Alex.

'Sorry to surprise you, Mr. Everett, but I'm going away on business for a few days, and Jules wanted to come and stay with you.'

Winston continued to look at him carefully. 'Is everything OK, son?' His rich Jamaican baritone belied his concern.

'It will be when I get back.'

'Will we be seeing you over Christmas, Alex? I need to have another man in the house at Christmas, or I'll never get to see any football.'

'I'll do my best, Mr. Everett, tell Jules I'll call her tonight, will you?' With that, Alex got back in his car and started the engine. He reversed out of the driveway and into the road and set off back towards the motorway, intending to head north to Manchester.

As they entered the hospital, Miles was on the telephone. 'Yes, Boss wants to know everything on Alex Harris, A-L-E-X, no alpha, lima, echo, X-ray. That's right. The address is on my folder on my desk, yes that's the one. Everything, we want to know where he is from, his parents' names, his siblings, other jobs, known associates, everything.'

'Picture,' Duncan said over his shoulder.

'Oh, and the boss wants a picture of him sent to his mobile. No, we have no idea what he looks like. OK, thanks, Lynn.'

Duncan was striding to the reception area. He approached a sour-looking receptionist with frizzy hair and a disinterested appearance. She ignored him whilst she typed into her computer.

He waited, drumming his fingers on the countertop. He looked around the waiting room. It was busy for a Friday afternoon on a working week. There was the usual mother and small child, huddled together, a man in working clothes and hard hat holding his arm, and two women in full burka, but Duncan could not make out whether they were even women, let alone the nature of their complaint. There was also the standard emergency room drunk, asleep, and lying across three chairs.

'Would you mind?' The frizzy-haired receptionist was pointing at his fingers, still drumming.

Duncan reached inside his jacket and pulled out his warrant card, which he dropped over the counter and on to her keyboard. 'Now I finally have your attention perhaps you would be so good as to answer me a question?' Before she could respond, he had reached over and retrieved the card. 'An ambulance brought in a man suffering from a fractured skull. He was escorted by a uniformed officer. Can you tell me where to find them? Please,' he added as a deliberately calculated afterthought.

'I'm sorry, officer, I didn't realise. Yes, they took him straight down to X-ray. If you walk down the corridor, there is a yellow sign pointing to the right, just follow the yellow lines on the floor and it will take you there.' She seemed to have lightened up dramatically. Duncan turned away and marched down the corridor. Miles muttered a 'Thank you' and hurried after him.

The corridors were wide and grey with broad coloured lines of green, red, and yellow on the floor. As they followed the yellow line down a darker corridor to the right, the other two lines carried straight on. The corridor opened up into a waiting area, and the sign on the desk to the right indicated that they were in the radiology department. There was yet another receptionist who, like her predecessor, appeared to be completely unaware of the presence of anybody seeking her assistance.

Duncan scanned the room. There were four people in the seated waiting area and three people on gurneys, either waiting to be seen or just abandoned out of sight, Duncan could not be sure. He turned back to the receptionist and was about to interrupt her when Miles leant in close to him. 'Jesus, Boss, have you seen who that is?'

Duncan looked around again. How on earth had he missed him before? Lying on one of the stretchers was Michael Richardson. His eyes were closed, and he was grimacing as though in a great deal of pain.

Duncan walked over. 'So, Michael, how are you?'

Richardson's eyes remained closed. 'Not feeling too good, Doc.' Duncan saw an opportunity.

'So what happened to you again?'

Richardson winced. 'Accident on the site, Doc, I stumbled and fell and my mate's screwdriver stuck in me side.'

'How long have you been working on a building site?'

Richardson opened his eyes. 'Oh fuck.'

'Nice to see you too, Michael. Looks like your meeting with Mr. Harris didn't go according to plan.' Duncan was flying by the seat of his pants a little; he had no evidence that Richardson had been there or even knew of Alex Harris, but the coincidence of his injury and location was too great to be ignored. In any event, if Richardson thought that they knew that he was there, he would immediately be on the back foot and that was when stories started to unravel.

'So he stabbed you with a screwdriver. We wondered where all the blood came from. Where are the other two?'

Richardson was unsettled. Duncan knew from the look in his eyes that he had hit three marks with Harris, the stabbing and two others. But Richardson was an old hand, and he did not cave in easily.

'If you want to interview me, you can make an appointment with my lawyer.'

'Where is Harris now, Michael? Did you really let some mincing lawyer take you and your two boys out? He put you all in hospital? What's that going to do to your reputation? Miles, go find the other two.' Miles turned and walked back to the reception, where he tried to engage the bulldog of the desk.

'I don't know what you're on about.'

Duncan sighed. 'Really. Look, Michael, you're fucked. We have your blood at the crime scene, and you're lying here bleeding all over your nightgown. You have no idea what you have fallen into this time, do you? You are going down and not for a couple of months in an open prison, serious hard time. You need someone to help you, Michael, and I don't mean that skinny-arsed lawyer of yours. Right now, the only way you can shorten the sentence you are looking at is to talk to me and sick up all the details, who and why.'

Richardson closed his eyes again and winced in pain. 'I'm not going to prison. I was working, and I fell on a screwdriver.'

Duncan bent over the twisted frame of Michael Richardson and his drawn face close to his. 'You will talk to me, Michael, you know you will. Because we both know that you are going down for attempted murder.'

Richardson groaned. It may have been the pain, but it may have been the realisation. 'I was just collecting a debt. That's all.'

Duncan was thinking as fast as he could. Trying to put pieces together, but, like any jigsaw, you can never quite find the last piece you were looking at when you need it.

'So Alex Harris owed you money? He was a regular in your arcades, was he? He drove up from Milton Keynes just to play on your rigged slot machines? You are going to have to do better than that, Michael. Steven Redford was his client. You knew Steven Redford, he's now dead. Harris knew Redford, and then you turn up at his house nearly two hundred miles away to collect a debt. Am I supposed to believe that it's just a coincidence? At best, we are looking at attempted murder, at worst, that and the murder of Steven Redford. Start talking, Michael.'

At that point, Miles returned. 'We know about Ryan Maguire, Mr. Richardson. We know he's paying you to get Harris.'

Duncan looked at Miles with wide eyes. Miles smiled back at him and spoke again to Richardson. 'Your mate Lenny, he is in a terrible state. He has had a fair old shot of morphine, and he was just on his way down to be prepped for theatre. They are going to try and rebuild his arm and knee. But Lenny, he is so out of it, he will talk to anyone.'

Richardson looked pale and in more pain than ever.

'So,' Duncan said, stepping in, 'Ryan Maguire wants Alex Harris, and he sends you to do the job, but you fucked it up, seems to me that you might need me more than I first thought, Michael. I don't think Ryan will be too happy, do you? Especially after you fucked up with Redford as well.'

There was another gamble by Duncan—pushing beyond the limits of his knowledge, feeling for the cracks that he can then prise open.

Richardson's voice was weak like an old man whose doom was upon him. 'OK, I need to speak to my lawyer first.' His voice was reedy; his strength was dissipated by the weight of his impending ruination. 'But when I've spoken to him, I'll talk to you.'

Duncan felt the rush; he was close to unravelling this, and he knew it. 'It might be too late by then, Michael. We've got Lenny and . . .' He realised he did not know the other man's name, and he looked at Miles for help. 'Tony.'

'That's right, Tony. They will talk. You know that. By the time they do, we won't need you, and you talking then won't earn you any favours.'

Richardson looked frightened. He was cornered and, without his lawyer, unable to compute the probabilities of Duncan's prediction. He hated Duncan.

'Right. Shit. OK. This is all I'm saying now. I want you to get me back up to Manchester. I'm not staying in this shit hole. Get them to patch me up and get me back home. I want my daughter and my lawyer there when I get there. You give me that, and I'll give you something now, OK?'

'OK, I can arrange for that to happen. What have you got for me?'

Richardson winced and grabbed his side. He looked around as though hoping a doctor or a nurse would be coming to take him away to save him from having to commit himself. There was no such luck, not a doctor or a nurse in sight, fucking National Health Service.

'Ryan paid me to come down and see Harris, like I said, to collect a debt. Maguire was paying Steve Redford for a claim, it's dodgy. Redford gets paid by the insurance company and is supposed to split it with Ryan. Only Steve doesn't cough up. Then he ends up dead. Ryan knows this twat Harris took a call from Redford just before he died, so he figures Harris done him for the money, and Ryan wants the money back.'

Duncan was very still. He felt cold in the pit of his stomach.

'Miles,' Duncan's voice seemed to have lost its edge, 'Call Lynn, we need people down here to take Michael back when he has been fixed up. We can't have Thames Valley sitting on him. Get him his lawyer.'

He looked back at Richardson. 'This Harris. He's taken out you, Lenny, and Tony with a hammer and a screwdriver. And he's a lawyer. What sort of lawyer is that?'

It was a rhetorical question and not one that he was expecting a reply to. But he got one anyway. 'An injury lawyer.'

Miles laughed at the unintentional pun. 'Nice one.' Richardson looked blankly at him.

Duncan frowned. 'Did he say anything?'

'I've told you enough. I need my lawyer before I tell you any more.'

Duncan saw a doctor approaching and gripped Richardson's arm. He hissed, 'What did he say, Michael?'

'Excuse me, who are you?' The doctor was next to them. Miles stepped in front of him immediately and showed his warrant card.

'Michael, what did he say?' Duncan's grip tightened. His intensity seemed to give off an electrical energy. Richardson was frozen; he opened his mouth as if to speak, but the words never came.

'I'm sorry, but this man is seriously wounded. You need to leave and leave now.'

Duncan's head snapped around to face the doctor, who stepped back involuntarily.

'This man is in protective custody. If we leave, he gets up and walks out of here, and you have aided and abetted the escape of a suspect, so just back off.'

He turned back to the patient. 'Michael?'

'He said to tell Ryan he was coming. That's it. Doctor, please, I'm in a lot of pain,' Richardson pleaded to the physician.

'I'm sorry. I need to treat this man. You need to wait over there.' He nodded his head towards the seats in the waiting room. Every head was turned looking at Duncan.

Duncan let go of Richardson's arm, and the doctor waved an orderly over who wheeled Richardson through double doors into the X-ray room.

'Where are the other two?'

'Sorry, Boss, they are both in theatre by now. They're not going anywhere though.'

Miles looked at Duncan. He seemed to have calmed down. Miles realised he had hardly taken a breath during the confrontation, and he pulled in a deep draught of air.

'So is this Alex Harris our killer, do you think? It seems plausible. He is doing bent claims for Maguire and decides he wants his own share of the money. He bumps off Redford so he can't grass him up to Maguire and comes back to Milton Keynes, gives up a very well-paid job, kicks the crap out of Maguire's heavies, and now he's done a runner.'

Duncan pulled his mobile out of his trouser pocket and started dialling. 'Steve, you need to stay here until Lynn has sorted out transport for Richardson. We need him back in Manchester. If the locals come sniffing around, they don't need to know any of this. I need to get the train back. It can't wait.'

'OK, Boss.'

'And I want you talking to the other two. I want to know everything.'

With those words, he was off, striding through the reception area, phone glued to his ear.

CHAPTER 24

FRIDAY, DECEMBER 9

FRANK MAGUIRE SAT BEHIND HIS desk. It was 4:00 p.m. and dark and raining again. He had done enough that day. He was tired and ready to go home.

Home was a large detached property near Wilmslow, not as big as some people might expect. He had done well for himself, that's for sure, but he was modest with his wealth. Of course, he had the high wall and the electric gates, the security cameras and private patrols around the perimeter in the evenings, but so did his neighbours— mostly lawyers, doctors, and other professionals. Immediately next door was an architect one side and on the other an ex-footballer. Frank had more in common with the footballer, but Mrs. Maguire preferred the architect and his wife.

Frank called out to Dawn. 'Get Dainius to bring the car round, Dawn, I will be leaving shortly.' He got up and walked through the ante-room and down the landing to Ryan's office. He didn't knock but opened the door and went straight in.

Ryan had been sitting, head in hands, staring at the telephone but had bolted upright when the door opened.

'Hi, Dad, you off now?' Frank sat in the chair the other side of the desk. He let the silence grow between them, waiting to see if Ryan would be strong enough to tell him what was troubling him. When he realised he was not, he spoke first.

'I take it, things aren't going well, Son.'

'Who told you that?' Ryan said, smiling lightly.

Frank slapped his palm on the desk and Ryan flinched. 'I can see, Ryan, I'm not an idiot. Jesus, what do you take me for? What's gone wrong? Why are you sitting, looking at the phone, eh? You're afraid to call Jimmy, aren't you?'

Ryan ran his hand through his thick black hair and then down over his face. 'Yes. This lawyer who took the money, I don't know what's happening. I sent some boys down there to get it back. I mean, this is just some lawyer, how hard could it be, right? Three big lads, and this lawyer puts all three of them in hospital, all three of them.'

Frank looked down, deep in thought. 'Do you know where he is?'

'No, not right now, but I know where he will be.'

'Explain.'

'He sent me a message through the boys. I've never met the guy, never even spoken to him, and he sends me a message.'

Frank started to get impatient. It annoyed him to see his son rattled like this, scared.

'What was the message?'

'He said they were to tell me he was coming.'

'Ryan, what was the message exactly?'

'Tell Ryan I'm coming back.'

Frank remained still, deep in thought. He spoke softly. 'And you've never met this man?'

'No, I'd never heard of him before we were told he was a good lawyer. I've never been to Milton Keynes. I don't exactly mix with lawyers.' There was an edge of bitterness in his words, and Frank was unsure whether it was aimed at him or the lawyer. He let it pass.

'I think now is the time to call Jimmy. You tell him everything. You don't try to whitewash over anything. You be totally straight with him, and you invite him to come over and help.'

'Jesus Christ, Dad, I can't do that. We don't want mad uncle Jimmy kneecapping everyone from here to Milton Keynes. Jesus.'

'Ryan,' Frank's voice was raised, 'get a grip. You need help. This fucker has robbed you and then done your boys and now he says he's coming to see you. Why take a chance, Son. What if he actually is coming for you, and what if he might just be able to take you? Now is the time to let Jimmy off the leash. There will be a price to pay, there always is with Jimmy, but it's better that than losing altogether.' Frank stood up to leave. 'Make the call, Son. Swallow your pride for once. Jimmy is the most dangerous man you will ever know, and it is no shame to admit that he is better at this than you.'

He turned and walked slowly from the office. Ryan went to the window and then paced back to his desk, turning immediately and back to the window. He patrolled back and forth rehearsing his call. He saw his father leave and get into the back of the Mercedes.

All these years, he had been trying to step out of his father's shadow. Show him what a big man he could be. Prove that he could do everything he had done and more. Try and make up for the loss of his brother.

But here he was, at thirty-seven, being bailed out by his family. Ryan took a deep breath and went back to the desk, dialled the number, and waited.

'Uncle Jimmy, it's Ryan. I've had a chat with my dad. We think you should come over.'

The phone rang in Alex's car. He had the headphones in his iPhone; he was listening to music as he drove, and he touched the control on the headphone wire to answer the call.

'Hello. Yes, I remember. When? OK. Don't worry, I guarantee you will be OK. Yes, I promise. Bye.'

CHAPTER 25

FRIDAY, DECEMBER 9

DUNCAN SAT IN THE QUIET carriage of the Virgin train from Milton Keynes to Manchester. He needed to clear his head, and the thought of being annoyed by the chittering of people taking a phone call on the train forced him to seek refuge in the carriage towards the back of the train.

He had been fortunate to find two seats that were both empty, not as part of a four. He made himself as big as possible to discourage anybody from sitting next to him, and it seemed to have worked. It was more likely the angered expression on his face that had made his fellow travellers too timid to take up the free seat.

The train was careering through the Staffordshire countryside, but Duncan could see none of it. It was pitch-black outside the carriage, and all that could be seen was a reflection of a weary man on the verge of eruption.

He leant back and closed his eyes. He needed to order his thoughts. A lot had happened today, and things were suddenly starting to take shape in his mind. He considered the starting point of his investigation, the death of Steven Redford. He now had a motive. Ryan Maguire and quite possibly Steven Holland were encouraging staff or acquaintances to make fraudulent insurance claims. They then took a significant cut of the damages paid by their own insurance company. Redford had been unable to pay as it would appear that the lawyer, Alex Harris, had somehow convinced Redford to pay him the money.

That tied in with Charley Richardson's assertion that Redford was expecting a significant payday. But there was no money trail, so the proof was just not there.

On his way to the train station, he had called in to Hanson's solicitors and spoken to Christopher Hanson. He told Duncan that the firm had received a payment from the insurers, a significant sum of money he had said—seven figures. They had paid the money into the bank account they were instructed to by their client. It was into a private Swiss bank, a numbered account, and that was where the trail ended.

Hanson had, however, made it clear that before his resignation, Alex Harris had reported to the Serious Fraud Office, his suspicions of fraudulent claims and potential money laundering, which struck Duncan as an odd thing to do if you had just stolen the money yourself.

Here was the paradox of the whole case—Alex Harris. On the one hand, an apparently trustworthy and valued partner in a successful law firm—a man with no criminal history whatsoever, not so much as a caution for drunk and disorderly as a student. And that was another thing. They could not trace him at any university. They could find no GCSE results for him. Lynn had only found one Alexander Harris that would have been the right sort of age, but he had disappeared in 1993 or 1994 whilst backpacking around Europe. Lynn had been instructed to investigate further but nothing so far.

Hanson's had no pictures of Alex Harris, much to the surprise of Christopher Hanson, who had assured Duncan that all the staff had appeared on a publicity shot taken the year before. When the pictures were brought up on his laptop, Harris had managed to stand himself directly behind a tall, black woman. The most that could be seen was the side of his head and his right shoulder.

Despite his reluctance to be caught on film, Harris was apparently well known in the personal injury field. He was mentioned in the Legal 500, a publication that identified the great and the good in the legal market. He was described as a 'rising star' who was 'renowned for his client care' and his 'proactive and straight talking approach.' He just did not fit the profile of an embezzling faker, nor of a man capable of disabling three hired thugs like Richardson and his two cronies. Or murder for that matter.

If, as Michael Richardson implied, Alex Harris had killed Redford to cover up his larceny, what was his connection to the Maureen Ladd case? Had it been Harris who had called him? If he had killed Redford, why did he leave Richardson alive to identify him? He was an enigma, and Duncan was no nearer to unravelling his mystery than he had been at the start of the day.

When Duncan opened his eyes, the train was pulling into Stockport. Another ten minutes, and he would be at Piccadilly station. He stretched out his long legs under the seat ahead of him and extended his arms to relieve the stiffness in his muscles.

His mobile buzzed in his pocket, set on silent, it vibrated against his thigh. He got up and went to the section between carriages just behind his seat, where he could take the call without the disapproving tut-tutting of the other passengers.

He answered the call before checking the number it came from as he went through the automatic doors.

'Yes.'

'It's your messenger here.' The voice was muffled and difficult to understand.

'I'm sorry. This isn't a good line, who is this?' Duncan thought he needed to buy some time, enter into a conversation, try and pick up some idea as to the identity of the person he was speaking to.

'I have sent you another message, a slightly more conventional message. You should get it tomorrow.' The voice seemed to be fighting to be heard against background noise, it was raised but not clear.

'Who are you? If you want to give me a message, why not just speak to me face-to-face?'

'Don't worry, Chief Inspector, that time will come. You will get my package tomorrow.'

Duncan hurriedly tried to prolong the conversation. 'Will it be a dead body again?'

There was a laugh at the other end of the line. Duncan listened intently; there was that flicker of recognition again. Like a spark off a flint, it shone for a second and faded instantly. 'I didn't send you a body. I just attached a message to it.'

'What do you mean, you killed Steven Redford. Why don't we get together and talk about it.'

'No, I just attracted your attention to it. Talk to the daughter. Ask her who killed him. Ask her why she was in hospital. She has all the answers.'

Duncan's mind was racing. 'Whose daughter are you talking about? Why don't you just tell me what you know?'

'Because I am a little preoccupied at the moment.' Duncan could almost hear the smile. 'Talk to the girl.

She will lead you to the killer. There's something else. Sunday morning, Dover, there is a lorry coming in with a huge shipment of cocaine. I can give you the registration number if you promise me that the driver, who is the person this information comes from, will be protected. He will testify for you, but you have to look after him.'

Duncan was leaning against the door to the toilet and fumbling in his pocket for a pen and his notebook. 'I'm not in the drug squad, or in Customs, why would I be interested in this?'

'Just take the details and do what needs doing and you'll see. Have a little faith.'

Duncan took the make and model of the vehicle and the time of the ferry crossing and the name of the driver and the location of the coke in the vehicle. He scribbled furiously.

When he had everything, he paused and tentatively put forward a proposition. 'Look, Alex, why don't we get together. I know you're a decent man, and whatever you've done, I will speak up for you.'

He heard laughter again at the other end of the line. It floated through his memory like a rare butterfly, and just when he thought he had it cornered, it vapourised. 'Nice try. I will be at the Lord Abercromby on Monday at two o'clock. You can buy me a pint. If you have anybody else there, I will just walk by, and you will never find out who I am and what I know. Speak to the girl.' The line went dead.

Duncan was flummoxed. The Lord Abercromby was pretty much next to Bootle Street station. Why would the prime suspect in your murder case arrange to meet you next door to the police station in a pub full of police officers, mainly off—duty? He had never known anything like this.

As the train pulled into Piccadilly Station, Duncan dialled Lynn's number. He needed to liaise with Her Majesty's Revenue and Customs, and he would get Lynn to organise that. He would speak to Charley Richardson in the morning. He felt that the case was coming to a head, but he was still fumbling in the dark, being played like a marionette, with no idea who was pulling the strings.

He stepped down from the train as he got the ringing tone from Lynn's mobile. Despite being under the cover of the roof of the station, he was drenched by the wind-driven rain, coming in sideways from across the other platforms. Welcome back to Manchester.

CHAPTER 26

SATURDAY, DECEMBER 10

THE CAST IRON FIRE ESCAPE was cold. But with his coat tied to the rails over his head in a makeshift tent, it was at least dry. The rain had not stopped, but the wind had died a little. The metal was unforgiving in transferring the cold through his clothing. Should anybody decide to look up into the rain, they would assume he was just another dosser trying to find a safe place to sleep.

He had been sitting on the fire escape attached to the empty building on the corner of Mangle Street and Dale Street since dawn. He had climbed from the pavement on to the railings covering the lower ground floor windows. From the top of the railings, it was a short step to the ledge of the ground floor window, and from there, he could reach the bottom of the ladder to the fire escape. He had situated himself on the third floor of the staircase from where he could look down Tariff Street. He could see the Maguire building and into the yard from this height. With his binoculars, he could clearly see who was coming and going.

It was surprisingly busy in there for a Saturday morning. Trucks came and went, the workshop seemed particularly busy. What was more surprising was the activity in the office building. He had seen Frank Maguire go in after his early breakfast at the Koffee Pot. Then he had seen Steven Holland and Ryan Maguire turn up. They had a fervent discussion outside the workshop. Holland left on foot shortly after.

At around 10.00 a.m., a black Mercedes pulled into the yard. Two large men in green quilted bomber jackets got out: one from the back and one from the front passenger side, and a thickset man with white hair was shepherded from the back seat, at speed, into the office block. He did not recognise the man.

He decided it was time to take a closer look to see if he could work out what was going on. He decided he would walk down Tariff Street, passing the yard, follow the road around to Laystall Street, where he would turn left, on to Great Ancoats Street and back to Port Street, which ran around the back of Maguire's yard. He would get a clear picture of the layout of the buildings and see if he could get in to have a nose around without being seen. From there, he would turn right on Hilton Street and back to Stevenson Square, where his car was parked.

He untied the sleeves of his parka from the fire escape and put his cap on. He climbed down the ladder and hung off the end letting himself drop to the street. Mangle Street was a backstreet with no shop or office fronts, just the sides and backs of buildings that were either empty or used as seedy nightclubs in the late evening. Nobody saw him.

He crossed Dale Street and walked slowly down Tariff Street. The rain blew into his face, and he pulled the tweed cap down low to provide cover for his eyes. He tucked his hands into the high side pockets of the US military coat, which was older than him, and made his way down towards the entrance to the yard.

The old building had boarded up windows on the ground floor, so nothing could be seen until he reached the open gate, which was wide enough for two articulated lorries to pass each other comfortably. He tried to gauge his speed so that he would have enough time to look in and yet be quick enough not to appear to be taking too much of an interest.

As he passed the gate, he saw the two bomber jackets outside the entrance to the office building. With cropped hair and thick necks, they did not look like a welcoming party. He could see into the workshop, but there did not appear to be anything amiss there. Garage workers were strolling around with various tools in hand on a shiny grey floor. One cab was over an inspection pit, but nobody appeared to be working on it.

Then he passed the gate. He picked up speed as he turned the right hand bend in Tariff Street and crossed over the Bridgewater Canal towards Laystall Street. Here he was exposed to the wind from the open spaces around him, which bit into him. He hurried on to Great Ancoats Street, which was busy, four lanes of traffic heading in and out of the city centre and to the central shopping park.

He got to Port Street and turned left, already looking ahead to see the back of the Maguire's compound. As he approached, he could see there were black wire gates. They were high, but he could climb them. Once again the ground floor was boarded up, and as he came to the gates, he realised he was around the back of the workshop. This gate was obviously used by the workers, who parked their cars in a line running up the side of the building.

He decided he had nothing to gain from climbing over the gate. He may hear what was going on in the workshop, but he felt certain the visitor to the offices was the reason for all the activity; he had no way of getting past the workshop and into the offices.

He decided he had seen but not learnt enough and headed back towards his car. He turned right on Hilton Street and headed on to Stevenson Square. His car was parked outside Habib House in one of only a few parking spaces on the square.

As he approached the car, he looked ahead and debated whether he should warm up in the Koffee Pot. His blood turned to ice in his veins. He quickly took out his keys and unlocked the car, slamming the door shut behind him and immediately firing the engine. He pulled away without putting the seat belt on and immediately turned right from the square on to Lever Street. He looked in his rear-view mirror.

Steven Holland stood at the corner of Lever Street and Stevenson Square holding a cardboard tray with four tall coffee cups and watching the back of his car, open-mouthed.

'Shit.' He banged the steering wheel. Alex could not believe he had made such a stupid mistake. Now they knew he was watching them, and worse, they could not fail to spot his Karmann Ghia.

'You really should be dead by now if you weren't my nephew, you would be.'

The atmosphere in Frank's office was tense. Frank was sitting behind his desk, wearing black shirt and tie with his black suit. It had seemed appropriate. Ryan perched on the edge of the desk to his father's right-hand side. He was wearing a tight turtleneck sweater, subconsciously hoping his physique would make him more intimidating. Sitting in the chair opposite the desk was the hulking frame of Jimmy Maguire. He had never been intimidated in his life.

'Come now, Jimmy, there's no need for that sort of talk, we are family.' Frank tried to relieve the oppressive atmosphere. 'Let us be constructive now, shall we? Ryan knows mistakes were made, but at the end of the day, Jimmy, he has been up front with you and kept you in the loop. It was his idea to ask for your help.'

'My help to recover my own fucking money and yours no doubt, Frank,' Jimmy's growl reverberated through the room, through Ryan's nerve endings. His father had told him not to speak unless spoken to and not to make excuses. Ryan was only too happy to obey. His trembling voice would confirm his fear of Uncle Jimmy if he were to talk.

'Once the money is returned, you will receive recompense for your trouble, you know that. You have the expertise, Jimmy. Ryan is still learning, he is hoping to learn from you.'

The three men sat in silence for a few seconds. Frank relaxed into his chair. He had always been the more astute of the brothers, the most persuasive. He had been the silver-tongued rascal in his younger days whilst Jimmy had been the harsh, aggressive, and fanatical sibling. He had believed in the cause. Something Frank had supported, but only out of conscience. He had no real desire to be political, no real connection with the land of his fathers. He liked Manchester, the place had given him a good living, and he had no desire to tear it apart.

When the IRA had bombed the city centre, Frank had been as appalled as any other Mancunian. He had given his workers a day off to help with the clean-up operation as a genuine gesture of togetherness with the city and its people, although the positive press he had received had not done him any harm.

Jimmy had needed a cause into which he could channel his energy. The fact that his energy was almost entirely destructive was a happy coincidence for those he served. Since the troubles had effectively ceased with the Good Friday Agreement, Jimmy had continued to do what he did best, but for his own ends. His cause was now his own self-interest. He was particularly dangerous as he was no longer interested in the money. He did what he did because he wanted to, because he had become used to being feared, and he needed to feed off that fear.

He enjoyed the fact that Ryan was afraid. He was irritated that Frank was not. There was no real love between the brothers. They had spent too many years apart. But the blood bond between them was honoured and always would be. Neither brother could be seen to break it. Jimmy would have liked to have Frank fear him.

Jimmy frowned; his grey eyebrows were meeting above his nose. 'All right. Tell me everything we know about this boy. We will find him, and we will get our money back. And we will be respected.'

There was a knock on the door and then it opened. Steven Holland appeared; his face was red, he was carrying the four takeaway coffees in a cardboard tray. He put them down on the desk and looked straight at Ryan.

'You will never guess who I just saw.'

Duncan was in his office. He was often in the office on a Saturday morning. He was conscientious and liked to set a good example. He was, however, completely alone.

His post had been left on his desk. He put down his coffee. He had treated himself to a real drink from the Costa on Albert Square. He could not face the vile liquid from the office when he was here on his own time. He had enjoyed a latte in the cafe whilst he watched the City Council workers putting up the huge inflatable Santa that would annually cling on to the side of the town hall clock tower. He had ordered a cappuccino to go and walked around the edge of the square to Bootle Street. The stage for the switching on ceremony for the Christmas lights was under construction, and he could not cross the square itself.

He thought to himself that he would have to be away from the office long before the minor celebrity arrived to flick the oversized switch, otherwise he would be forcing his way through crowds of people back to his apartment.

He left most of the mail and concentrated on the opened brown envelope, A4 size, which contained the discs. There was just a handwritten note with his name on it and two CD-ROMs. He put the first disc into the computer and waited for the virus scan to be completed. He sipped at the now lukewarm coffee, which was still better than he could get in the station.

The files opened on screen. He read through every document. There was no doubt that it had been thoroughly prepared. It contained details of all the cases that Hanson's had handled for Maguires—every payment made, every medical report produced, detailed notes of all conversations with the staff at Maguires. Duncan smiled. Steven Holland was in this right up to his neck. He looked forward to that particular arrest. He felt a dawn raid would be just the job.

File after file was opened and read. Duncan typed up his report as he progressed through the mountain of information. He would need warrants and quickly. He could see that the information in his possession could bring down the whole company.

It was all broken down in minute detail. The only thing missing was direct evidence of the involvement of Frank and Ryan Maguire. But that may come with the questioning of the people arrested.

Duncan came to the last file: the case of Steven Redford. He scanned the documents reproduced on his screen. 'Bugger me,' he reread the final payment made to Redford and the name of the bank it was paid into.

He heard the door to the Pit open and looked up. Terry Drew walked in, sat at his desk, and switched on his computer. Duncan peered through the glass. Drew sat facing him; his computer faced away from Duncan. Duncan stood up and waved.

'Don't normally see you in on a Saturday, Terry.'

Drew looked up from his desktop, relaxed. 'No, Boss, I don't usually, but I've a lot of paperwork to catch up on. I need to type up my report on the Redford case for you. I won't be here long though. I've got tickets for Old Trafford.'

'Who are they playing?' Duncan already knew. He wanted to see if Drew was really going to the game as he had never known him show any interest in football before.

'Wolves—should be an easy win. An old mate of mine has been invited to some corporate do and has a spare seat, so I get fed and watered and a comfy seat. Can't say no really.'

It was the right answer and a plausible explanation.

'Enjoy it. I fancy Rooney for a brace today.' Duncan sat down.

He had been in a good mood. The case was coming together. The motive for Redford's killing was becoming apparent. If his not-so-mysterious caller was right, money from the smuggling and sale of cocaine is fed into the insurance company, which then cleans the money by passing it through a number of offshore accounts. It is then paid back to the Maguires via the fraudulent claims being made, having passed through the solicitors' client account, further washing it.

The documents from Hanson's made two things clear: if Charley Richardson was right about the kind of money that Redford was coming into, then he must have been planning to do the dirty on Maguires and disappear with their cash. Only when they found him he told them that Alex Harris had already collected the money, according to Michael Richardson. If Harris did take the money, then he had set Maguires up for a fall, and, with the main protagonists inside, he planned to walk away with all their loot. It was a nice plan. But it wouldn't happen now. It was feasible that Harris had killed Redford to stop him talking to the Maguires. He clearly had it in him judging by the carnage found at his house. But something in the back of his mind told Duncan that was not the case.

It was clear that Alex Harris was the person who had been calling Duncan. Duncan grimaced at the idea that he was being used to fulfill the scheme of one criminal at the expense of another. He was determined that he would not be a pawn in somebody else's game. He would bring Alex Harris in himself, once he had cleaned up Maguires. Then he would deal with the problem that was ruining his mood.

There was a nagging sense of doubt at the back of his mind. He was uncomfortable with Alex Harris. He did not understand him. He thought his motive was clear—money. But this was a man making a good living legitimately. What concerned Duncan most of all was why, when he was clearly wanted for questioning by the police, would he make arrangements to meet in a pub around the corner from the station? Why meet at all? He could now let justice take its course, having set up the Maguires for a fall. And what made him think he would be able to walk away from that meeting?

His report was finished; he e-mailed it over to Detective Superintendent John Hall. He considered his next move. He did not like the idea of being led, but he decided it was time to go and speak to Charley Richardson.

'It's me.'

Alex was in his hotel room. His mobile had rung just as he had emerged from the shower. He had a towel wrapped around his waist. His physique was still good. There was definition in his abdomen and chest. He was heavier than he used to be, but it was muscle bulk rather than flab. He had powerful shoulders that were not obvious when he was dressed.

He held the phone to his ear and closed his eyes. 'Jules, I'm glad you called.'

There was a pause. Alex was unsure what to say. Did she want reassurance from him? Was the episode in the house the final crack that resulted in their shattered relationship? He had no doubt that she had never experienced anything even close to that in her life. He was not sure how she would react to seeing him commit acts of such savage violence.

There was no disguising the fact that he was now two different people. The trouble was Jules had fallen for the mild, affable lawyer. He had now uncovered the violent, ruthless animal that had always lurked deep within. Now that genie was out of the bottle he knew it could never go back.

'Alex?'

'Yes.'

'I'm afraid.'

He considered the statement. He anticipated that this was how the relationship would end. She would be afraid to commit to him, afraid that his other self would eventually take over.

'You don't need to be afraid, Jules,' he spoke as calmly as he could, hoping he could reassure her. He couldn't bear to lose her, and he knew that if he did, he would lose himself.

'Alex.'

'Yes.'

'I'm afraid here. I want to be with you. I will only feel safe if I'm with you. I know you can protect me.'

Tears welled in Alex's eyes. 'I can, and I will—forever.' He swallowed hard.

'Come and get me, Alex. Come and get me and let's just disappear.' He could hear the anxiety in her voice, pleading with him.

'Jules, I can't come today or tomorrow. I've got to meet the police and to try and get this all cleared up. I want us to be able to live without looking over our shoulders all the time. Give me two days, and we will be together.'

'Let me come to you then, Alex. I've got a bad feeling that I won't see you again. I want to be with you even if it is just for another day.'

'Look, Jules, it's just a reaction to what happened yesterday. Give it another day at least. You will feel differently tomorrow, not so anxious. Then, once I've seen the Old Bill, I will come and get you. Start thinking about where you want to go.' He could not handle Jules joining him in Manchester. As much as he ached to see her and to hold her, he knew that it was only a matter of time before the Maguires traced him now they had seen the car. He had to assume that they had his registration number and that they had the connections required to track him down. They had obviously already traced his telephone calls with Redford.

'Please, Jules, just give me another day or two, and I can have all this done.' It was his turn to plead.

'Where are you staying? I need to know that I can find you if I need you.'

Alex considered whether it was safe to tell her. He concluded that it made no difference. If they found Jules, it would be better for her if she told them where he was.

'I am at the Premier Inn on Medlock Street. Jules, I'm really glad you called. I just want you to know that if I didn't have you, I wouldn't be able to carry on. You are my reason for getting through this.'

He heard her sigh. 'Alex, will things ever be the same?'

'Are you kidding? No, they won't.' He left a pause. 'They will be so much better.'

'I love you, Alex. Please be there for me.'

She had put the phone down before he could reply.

CHAPTER 27

SATURDAY, DECEMBER 10

THE ROPEWORKS WAS A MODERN apartment block on the corner of Little Peter Street and Medlock Street. You could see the purple sign on the Premier Inn from the front door. It was pretty much on Duncan's route home from the office. As the name suggested, it was built on the site of an old ropeworks, but this apartment block was all new.

Charley Richardson had a top-floor, two-bedroom apartment with views over the old Central Station and across to the Beetham Tower with its bizarre step. Duncan remained convinced that the building would one day topple over in a heavy wind.

He studied the young woman before him. He was puzzled. She was immaculately dressed as before—tight-fitting black trousers that showed off the shape of her legs and the curve of her rear, a bright green T-shirt, also tight, pulled long over her bottom, accentuating those curves. Her waist was tiny, which Duncan had not noticed before as she had not removed her jacket. However, she seemed less confident and self-assured than she had done when interviewed at Bootle Street. The large blue eyes were clear but shifted constantly. She seemed reluctant to hold Duncan's gaze and tried to busy herself tidying the apartment when Duncan could see nothing out of place. The modern leather furniture was clear, no papers or magazines had strayed from wherever they were hidden. She seemed to be moving things around for the sake of keeping herself occupied.

'How are you then, Charley?'

'I'm fine, why wouldn't I be?'

'How is your dad? Have you heard from him?'

'He's alive.'

Duncan picked up on the terse response. It was time to start digging a little deeper.

'Your dad was sent to recover some money from Steven. We know that for a fact, seems odd for him to be sent to get money back from your boyfriend. A lot of money too.'

She turned to look at him, maintaining eye contact for the first time.

'Did your dad tell you he had been sent to collect the money?'

'No. He didn't,' she almost whispered her response.

'Why was that do you think?'

She just shrugged and bent over to fluff the cushions.

'Where did you go after the murder, Charley?'

She straightened up. 'You know where I went. I was in the clinic. I was . . . well, I was upset.'

Duncan could see he had found a weak spot—her slight pause, the anxiousness in her voice. The slightly upward glance as she fought to put forward a convincing performance.

'We know about the money, Charley. We know about the dodgy claim, the arrangement with Maguires to pay them back. We know that Steven was dealing. Did your dad know Steven was dealing coke?'

'What's all this about my dad? Does he know this? Does he know that. Who fucking cares what he knows,' she was shouting. Duncan knew she was close to breaking; It was time to throw a curve ball.

'How did they get you off the coke in the clinic, Charley?'

'What?' Her look told the whole story—the disbelief in her eyes, the anger, the flush of her cheeks and her throat.

'Come on. You went away, so we wouldn't see what state you were in. I can get access to your records, you know, if I have to.'

She sat down, put her hands together, and held them between her thighs as though if she let them go, they would betray her of their own accord. She looked at Duncan.

'He did it, didn't he? My dad.'

'It's a possibility we have to consider. Did he have reason to?'

She looked down, her shoulders slumped. 'He hated Steve. He hated him because he thought Steve had got me hooked on coke. He couldn't see that his baby girl already had a habit long before Steve came along. That might have been why Steve came along in the first place.' She looked up; her lips were tight, the strain showing in her face.

'He told me that he would straighten him out, that him and his boys would get to Steve and warn him off. He was told about the money and told to collect it. Steve had planned on using the money to finance a big deal, we could then disappear together. But Dad somehow got wind of it.' The first tear rolled down her cheek.

'He came here the night Steve died. He told me they had gone looking for him, and they had found him dead in Canal Street. I didn't believe him, and I slapped him and screamed at him. Eventually, he held me down, and they got me in the car and took me to the clinic, where they dried me out. He promised me he didn't do it.'

'But you think he did, don't you.' Duncan's voice was low, soothing.

'He had grazes on his hands. When they thought I was out cold, I heard them talking, those two losers that trail after him, about how Dad had knocked him out with one punch.' Her voice was quiet and weak. 'When I got to the clinic, I asked him outright, and he told me he didn't do it. But I could see it in his eyes.'

'Will you make a statement, Charley?'

She whispered, 'Yes.'

Duncan left the building to head back to the office. He had Richardson for the Redford murder. He should have been elated. All he could think of at that moment in time, however, was that Drew had been right all along. It left a very bitter taste.

The pub was full. It always was on match day. It was noisy. The bar was buried beneath bodies six deep, ordering double rounds so that they could get their pints in before heading off to the ground. Pockets of supporters sang songs raucously, occasionally bouncing up and down as they did so, like they were already in the stadium.

There was a mixture of good humour and tension in the room. The whole week spent building up to this afternoon. The result of the game would shape the mood of most of these men for the next two or three days and expectations were high.

Drew stood by the door to the ladies toilet, the quietest spot. He had his back to the wall, and he sipped his half pint of lager. Had those around him been interested, they would probably have realised he was a policemen, so incongruous did he look in his blazer, shirt, and slacks. But this was not a pub for the hardcore football hooligan, just the regular working man getting his release at the weekend. A few hours to let of steam, be part of the pack, and enjoy the spectacle.

Drew despised football, it's supporters and, more than anybody, it's players—pampered, spoilt prima donnas, one and all, in his opinion. The fact that they earned millions whilst behaving like children in a playground, he found particularly galling.

He waited patiently though. He would go to the game that day and enjoy the meal and the hospitality in the executive box. He had heard the wine was very good in the ground, and he could stay away from the baying masses, behind a glass window, enjoying the fruits of his labour.

The door to the pub opened, and he was there. Drew pushed himself off the wall and put his glass down on a nearby table as he walked to the exit.

When there, he shook the powerful, proffered hand; he was handed an envelope, which was unsealed. He flicked the envelope open and checked the contents, took out the credit card-style ticket, and closed the envelope, leaving the cash inside. He took a folded sheet of paper from his inside jacket pocket and placed the envelope where the paper had been, handing the paper over as he did so.

If anybody in the bar noticed the two men and their exchange, it would have looked like the usual ticket tout handing over his wares in return for payment. As a result, they were completely ignored.

They shook hands again.

'Enjoy the game,' said Jimmy Maguire as he left the pub.

Jimmy sat in the back of Frank's Mercedes. He unfolded the paper and took out his mobile phone.

'It is a red Volkswagen Karmann Ghia, 1965, registration number C111 AJH. I want everyone you have to scour the city centre for this car. You get a photograph of one on every mobile phone. I want people in all the car parks in central Manchester. He will be nearby. We find the car, we find our man. Nobody approaches him. When he is found, you ring me immediately, but you follow him if he moves, you understand? Good.'

He put the mobile in his pocket and sank back into the plush upholstery of the luxury car. 'Take me back.'

The car pulled out into the heavy match-day traffic, crawling along Chester Road and heading south towards Cheshire. The rain had started again.

The house was cold and dark. The curtains were drawn, and the light was switched off. The central heating was also off and the gas fire not lit. Money was tight, and there was no need to waste it on heat and light in the middle of the afternoon when a few extra jumpers would do the trick.

The radio was on, a crackly, dull signal transmitting on medium wave, BBC Radio Five Live. There was always enough electricity for the football commentary. It was one of the few pleasures he had left.

He limped from the kitchen to the living room, cup of tea cradled in both hands, giving off a little warmth. He lowered himself into the sofa; his thin frame was creaking as he did so. He winced as the pain from his back shot through to his buttocks and down his left leg to behind the knee. Regardless of the fact that he had pain every day for the last fifteen years, it still had the capacity to take his breath away.

He pulled the tartan throw over his knees and settled himself down to listen to the match. He closed his eyes and tried to picture the stadium, using the noise of the crowd on his radio as his guide.

He enjoyed his Saturday afternoons with his radio. It was, perhaps, the only chance he got to close his eyes and not think about them. He would enjoy that day's game. He was not sure that he would make it through to the end of the season in May, so he would savour every match between now and then.

The whistle blew, and the commentator announced dramatically that the game was underway.

Jakov drove through the Belgian countryside—flat, monotonous landscape and lines of tall beech and poplar acting as windbreaks or borders between the fields. He would be at the port by early evening and have a night in Calais before his crossing in the morning.

He would need to try to relax. He needed to sleep so that he would be able to think clearly when he reached England.

He had done everything he could to ensure things went according to plan. His preparations had been careful and secretive. His family had left their apartment in the middle of the night three days ago.

His wife had a cousin with a pension in Zakopane. At this time of the year, he was busy with the winter sports crowd and always needed a helping hand. His wife was an excellent cook, and his daughter would work as a maid and a waitress in one of the other hotels in the shadow of the Tatra Mountains. They would slip in unnoticed amongst the tourists at this time of year. They should be safe from reprisals, at least until he could get them to join him.

Everything had gone well, but now Jakov was relying on others to help him. People he did not know and had never met. He was nervous. He had nobody to trust.

As the long, straight road slipped away under the wheels of the massive Scania, Jakov wondered if he had done the right thing.

The clouds on the flat horizon were an angry grey and bunching together. They seemed to be a projection of his own foreboding. There was no doubt he was heading into a storm.

In the Premier Inn on Medlock Street, Alex sat on the bed with his new iPad on his lap. He had been forced to buy another as the old one had been left behind at Adelphi Street, burnt beyond recognition he was sure. He was on Google Maps, flicking between aerial photos and street view.

He switched between applications, making notes of what he had seen and then reverting back to the maps.

It was dark outside. His room on the second floor overlooked the car park. He could hear the wind rushing around the corners of the building. The flagpole outside the main entrance rattled, and rain lashed against the window. His TV was telling him that United had beaten Wolves comfortably, two more goals for Rooney. He would have liked to have had time to catch a game.

He got up to check on the position of his car. The car park was busy. Christmas shoppers could pay to park, which meant that there were cars in every bay and on every spare piece of ground between the bays. Cars were parked half up the walkways between the spaces, leaving just enough room for one car to get through the gaps.

The Karmann Ghia was parked in the far left-hand corner of the car park, where the lighting was poor, and where the car could not be seen from the entrance. He had considered parking it away from the hotel but decided he would then be unable to tell if anybody was watching the car. At least here, he could see any vantage point from which somebody may view the car park other than from inside the hotel.

The car was under its protective cover from the garage in Milton Keynes—waterproof, grey with an elasticated edge to grip around the bumpers and cotton on the inside to avoid marking the paintwork. A trained eye could see it was an old car underneath because of the size and unusual shape. Old cars are smaller and lower than modern-day vehicles due to the safety requirements of modern times—the wheels and tyres generally skinny by comparison. But in this weather and poor lighting, the grey cover made the car almost invisible.

He returned to the bed and looked over his notes once more. He ran through his sequence of events, checked his routes, and double-checked the traffic news.

Outside, the wind grew louder, the rain heavier. The windows were battered by the increasingly powerful gusting and pounding of the rain. The flagpole clattered and knocked constantly. The storm was building.

CHAPTER 28

SUNDAY, DECEMBER 10

THE SUN WAS SHINING, AND the grass was long and luscious green. She called to him, and he looked up from the picnic blanket. She looked beautiful and happy. He waved to her and called for her to join him, but she stayed where she was, by the huge oak tree, and smiled. He called again asking for her to come to him, but she didn't seem to take any notice; she smiled and waved, the light summer breeze rustling her hair. He called again, more urgent, and this time, she turned and looked away as though distracted by a noise.

He listened. He could hear it too, an insistent ringing noise. It started to grow louder, and he could see she was starting to fade away.

Alex opened his eyes. The telephone on the bedside cabinet was ringing. He wiped his eyes, which were damp.

He looked around the hotel room, then leapt out of the bed, and checked the window. He could see a taxi pulling away from the entrance to the hotel but nothing else. Walking back to the bed, he picked up the phone.

'I'm sorry to wake you, sir, but we have a visitor in reception for you, and they were quite insistent.'

Alex paused. 'OK, did they give a name?'

'Yes, sir, a Ms. Everett.'

Alex closed his eyes. 'OK, thank you. Can you send her up?'

'Well, actually, sir, we are not really . . .'

'Thank you.' The phone went down.

Within a couple of minutes, there was a tap on the door, and Alex opened it. Jules walked in and turned, waiting for Alex to close the door.

He let go of the door allowing it to slowly swing back. As the catch clicked, they embraced.

Jakov stood outside the cab. His rig was parked in a customs shed at Folkestone as men in dark blue boiler suits swarmed all over it like enormous flies on a forgotten picnic. There was banging and clattering of tools and shouts throughout the process.

Jakov was trembling. They had barely spoken to him since they pulled him over and not at all since the feverish work had commenced under the trailer.

'Here, have a brew.' Jakov jumped. A large man, with broad shoulders and a head so completely devoid of hair that it shone under the lights, proffered a plastic cup from the top of a flask. Jakov took it warily.

'Don't look so worried, my old son. All we are doing is sticking a tracking device and a listening device to the trailer. Then we can follow you from a safe distance, not to create any suspicion. When you get to the depot, we can remotely turn the listening device on and, bingo! We hear everything they say. All you need to do is what you normally do. Drive the lorry, then sit tight. You will be arrested along with everybody else, but that's for your own protection. When our boys come in, just stay still, don't move, definitely don't run.'

Jakov stared back at the man, unable to bring the words to the front of his mind. 'Do you speak Polska?'

'No, me, old china. Don't worry, Jakov, we will look after you. Just drive the truck.' He patted Jakov firmly on the shoulder and hot tea spilt over the edge of the cup burning the base of his thumb.

Jakov sipped the tea. It was milky and with full of sugar, and it was disgusting. He looked around for somewhere to put it down or tip it away, and, seeing nowhere, he decided he would have to open the door to the huge shed and tip it away.

As he made his way towards the door, he was stopped by the same man.

'Sorry, Chief, can't open the door. If they are watching you, they will be very suspicious if they see you drinking tea with us.'

It had never occurred to Jakov that he could be followed by the people who he was betraying. His legs felt weak, and he desperately wanted to sit down, fearing that he would pass out.

'Drink the tea, mate, it'll do you good.'

Jakov took another swig. It still tasted terrible, but the warmth inside him helped, a little.

Duncan was at his desk early on the telephone to the Customs' men, who had confirmed Jakov's truck had arrived on time and that it was certainly carrying the cargo that he had warned them about.

He typed his e-mail to Detective Superintendent Hall, enclosing his report of things so far and clicked send. He decided it was time to nip out for a coffee, before the fan was in need of a really deep clean, so he put on his coat and steeled himself against the wind and rain.

On his way through Albert Square, his collar pulled up high to protect his face from the stinging of the icy rain; he mulled over the content of the report. Richardson, who was to be released from Milton Keynes General that day, would be arrested and immediately driven back to Manchester, where he would be charged with the murder of Steven Redford; his two accomplices in the apparent raid on the home of the missing lawyer, Alex Harris, were still in no position to be released from hospital but were both now talking candidly with Steven Miles, who had extracted detailed statements from them that would assure Richardson's conviction.

Miles had excelled himself, using the information that Duncan had fed him to play each party against the other, until he had a full and detailed picture of what had happened and then laying his cards on the table with the two heavies, who folded under the weight of his knowledge of events. The report praised him for his interrogation technique and his astute use of the information at his disposal to build a watertight case against Richardson.

Costa was warm and welcoming. Duncan ordered his cappuccino to drink in and sat himself in his usual seat overlooking Albert Square. It was quiet at this time on a Sunday. The shops in the city centre were not yet open, and wouldn't be for a couple of hours, so the traffic, both pedestrian and motorised, was almost non-existent.

Santa was still clinging on to the side of the clock tower on the Town Hall and was looking a little the worse for wear. Last night's heavy storm had left him a little deflated, and he was almost bent double, his massive head facing down to the pavement. Like one of the many Saturday night drinkers whose body would now be rejecting the excess alcohol from the night before. Santa seemed to be right at home.

Duncan considered the rest of the day; his way of ensuring he had thought of everything. Jakov's truck would arrive around 1:00 p.m. That was the duty men's show, and he would be going along, with a small number of officers, to take part in the search after the seizure and arrests were made.

In exchange for his tip-off, it had been agreed that he would have access to the offices to go through the papers and to try and find anything that would help tie Ryan Maguire to the Redford murder or to cement their case against Richardson. Duncan was also hoping for something on the insurance scam that would help put Holland away and would try and connect that to the drugs. Harris's file suggested that the money obtained from the drug operation was being laundered through the offshore insurer and the bogus claimants, but the money trail was incomplete, and to get the bigger fish would require some evidential building blocks that may lie in the paperwork of either Ryan, Frank, or Holland.

The Serious Fraud Office had been notified and was hoping to review the papers once they had been through Duncan's hands, but he was keen to bring down Frank and Ryan Maguire himself.

The one connection between all threads of the investigation was Alex Harris. The lawyer could not be found. Lynn had researched his history and found a law-abiding man, never so much as a parking ticket, and no history of violence.

It was true he had a complicated life in his early years. His parents had both died young. His mother died from cancer when he was sixteen. His father, a respected architect living in Surrey but working in the City of London, was seemingly unable to cope without his wife, turning to drink and gambling, he lost a small fortune and his house and committed suicide two years later. Alex never took up his place at Oxford and went travelling. He was seemingly out of the country for three years before he reappeared at Luton Airport on a flight from La Rochelle. He claimed the remnants of his late father's estate and, it would appear, started working for an insurance company in London.

He subsequently moved to a law firm in the city and was then picked up by Hanson's in Milton Keynes, where he had remained until now.

He had the house in Milton Keynes and an ex-council flat in London, which had been bought with his inheritance. He owned two cars, a brand new Audi, destroyed by the fire at his home, and a classic Volkswagen, which, like its owner, could not be found.

He was a loose end, and Duncan did not like loose ends. Still, whilst the report was silent on his plans to apprehend Harris in the Abercromby the following day, Duncan was uncertain as to whether there were likely to be any charges brought against him. There was no doubt that his file and the information provided to Duncan, over his untraceable mobile, had broken the case. But he could not ignore his involvement in the Redford murder, the possibility he had acquired the illicit insurance money from the victim, or his intensely violent attack upon Richardson and his boys.

Duncan felt he was a good reader of people. His years studying psychology and teaching had developed the skill. But he had to admit that Alex Harris was unreadable—

both saint and devil. He was determined to find out which was the dominant trait.

The cappuccino was drained, and Duncan shrugged himself back into his overcoat. It was time to return and face the music. It was the final part of his report that would really put the cat amongst the pigeons. There was one final recommendation, one more arrest that he sought a warrant for. He expected his welcome to be about as warm as the rain on Albert Square.

As he walked in through the door to the Pit, Lynn was holding the phone to her shoulder. 'Detective Super wants a word, Boss, good luck.'

Duncan rolled his eyes as he walked past her and to his office, where the phone was already ringing. He took off his coat and picked up the phone without sitting down.

'Yes, sir, what can I do for you?' He regretted the question immediately.

'You know bloody well why I'm ringing, get your arse down here now and explain yourself.'

Detective Superintendent Hall was not a man to stand on ceremony, least of all for Duncan. Their relationship was one of thinly disguised antagonism on both sides. Hall felt Duncan was too keen to show how clever he was and too insubordinate, in short, a threat to his status. To Duncan, Hall was a poor excuse for a policeman. A glorified administrator who could no more do Duncan's job than Duncan would want to do his. If you looked up the term *jobsworth* in the Oxford English Dictionary, Duncan maintained, there was a picture of Detective Superintendent John Hall. He was the epitome of the career policeman. To Duncan, there was no more disparaging description.

'I will be there shortly, sir, but I am due to be at the Maguire's yard soon, so I don't have very long.'

'I will tell you how long you have. I am your commanding officer Duncan.' The phone was slammed down at the other end, and Duncan smiled to himself as he replaced his receiver.

He looked into the Pit. Only Lynn from his team was in the office, and he beckoned her in to his room. Sitting behind his desk he watched her stride across the floor.

'Everything OK with the super boss?'

'No. I have to go to Old Trafford to "explain myself" to Johnnie Boy. While I am gone, I need you to get on to the Excise boys and find out their ETA at the yard. I want you with me. We are going to search the offices.'

'No problem, what exactly are we looking for?'

'Anything that links the Maguires to Redford, Richardson, Harris, and the insurance company.' Duncan checked his watch. 'Is Steve back in tomorrow?'

'Yes, he is travelling back today.' She looked at her watch. 'He has left already and will be in the office first thing.' Lynn pushed her hair behind her ear as she spoke.

'Good. Tomorrow I want you and Steve to provide back-up. I have a meeting in The Abercrombie at two. The person who has been feeding me information, who I believe to be Alex Harris, has agreed to meet me there alone. I intend to bring him in for questioning, but he will be looking out for others, so you need to be very discreet. Can we rustle up a couple of uniforms, stick them in plain clothes, mess their hair up a bit so they don't stand out too much. I don't fancy taking this bloke on my own, he might still be carrying his toolbox.'

Lynn laughed. She had read the report of the 'Adelphi Street Massacre' as Miles was calling it. 'I can rustle up a couple of big boys to look after you. Why would he want to meet you there, it is basically next door?'

'Lynn, I have no idea. I just can't get a handle on who this bloke is. He is one contradiction after another. Right, I'd better go and see my doctor about a castration. Oh, and one last thing, nobody else needs to know about this, it stays between us. Make sure nobody will blab about this. It has to be as low key as possible.'

'Sure, I understand. Good luck.' With that, she was out of the door, and Duncan was two steps behind, picking up his coat as he left.

Alex and Jules were still lying in bed. Breakfast had come and gone. Alex had lain awake, listening to the gale blowing outside and Jules breathing. She had been in such a deep sleep that he had decided to leave her. He was running over things in his mind, trying to consider each eventuality.

His whole strategy was reliant upon his reading of Detective Chief Inspector Duncan and his reaction to their meeting the following day. If he was allowed to walk free of the Abercromby, then he would take Jules and just drop off the grid. If they tried to take him in, it would get messy, and his chances of disappearing to a quiet life were significantly reduced.

Jules stirred and reached her arm across his chest. Alex looked down at her whilst she slept. He contemplated just walking away from it all now, *Forget the meeting, forget the Maguires. Pack their bags today and just take off. Jules could help him forget.*

He sighed deeply. It would never work. He had to do this. He had to get this out of his system once and for all; then he could finally break away, relax within his own mind. He had realised over the last months how he had always had something gnawing away in his subconscious. He had buried it many years ago, but it was not dead. Like a rat eating its way out of a box. For him to be truly happy, for him to commit completely to the woman that he loved, he needed to resolve this one issue. He needed redemption, even if it destroyed him.

He told himself that his desire to meet Duncan had nothing to do with the excitement he felt. Since leaving Milton Keynes, his mind had been racing. He had felt it again, that old high, the adrenaline rush. He had replayed things in his mind, over and over—the swinging of the hammer and the indescribable thrill of combat.

He had contemplated whether it was an addiction. Was he any different to a junkie or an alcoholic? He decided, like any addict would, that he had it completely under control and that he could walk away whenever he felt like it.

'What are you thinking?' Her voice was thick with sleep.

'I was thinking that, after tomorrow, we need to be moving on. As beautiful as Manchester is,' he said as he looked at her with one eyebrow raised, 'it is not New York, Hong Kong, or even Wolverhampton.'

'I will have you know that Wolverhampton is a wonderful place, and if you are going to criticise it, you may have to find yourself another woman.'

Alex pretended to consider the proposition. 'Mmm, I don't think I can handle two women.' Jules slapped his chest. 'You know what I meant. Are you serious about moving on?'

'Yes. I should be finished with all this tomorrow. I meet the police in the afternoon, and by tea time, we can be on a flight to anywhere we want.'

She looked away as she asked, 'What makes you think they will let you just walk away from it all?'

'I have a secret weapon. Hopefully, something that the lovely chief inspector has not yet considered.'

'Will it really all be over, or is there something more you need to do?'

This time, there was no pretence as Alex considered her words carefully. He turned towards her and put his arm around her, pulling her close to him. 'There is. I will.'

She tilted her head back so that their lips were close. So close he could feel her breath on his mouth. 'It's for the best.' She kissed him slowly.

Dainius brought the Mercedes to the front door of Frank's mock Tudor house, precisely in the middle of the U-shaped driveway. He skipped to the double front door, between the puddles and light on his feet for such a big man, and opened it in order to wait in the cavernous hallway until the meal was finished. He picked out his usual chair from where he could see the kitchen door, so he could be on his feet with the door open before Frank reached the hall.

In the modern, gadget-laden kitchen, Frank sat at the table with Jimmy and Ryan. They ate their sausages, eggs, and bacon in silence. Toast was constantly added to a stack in the middle of the table by the cook, not Mrs. Maguire, who was still in bed, but Dainius's wife, Rasa. Frank called her Rose, but she didn't seem to mind. It was lunchtime, but Frank was very fond of his breakfasts.

Jimmy's mobile phone rang. He got up from his seat and walked through to the dining room to answer the call. Ryan and Frank exchanged looks but nothing was said. The sausages were good.

As Frank speared another poached egg, soft but not runny, just as he liked them, Jimmy returned and sat down. He took a huge gulp of his tea, served in an oversized mug, three of which were on the table. Frank liked to drink his tea from a proper working man's cup, no fancy bone china for him.

'What time are you leaving?' Frank asked, looking between Ryan and Jimmy.

'Are you not coming then?' Ryan looked concerned.

'This is not my show, Son, you and Jimmy sort this out. Besides, I need to stay here and pack. Me and your mother are off to Nassau to oversee the final stages of the house and start making our move. I expect to be gone for good first week in January. You need to chase up Holland on the paperwork for the business. I want it all signed and delivered before Christmas. I can then relax and enjoy my retirement.'

Ryan looked at Jimmy. 'The truck is not due for another hour, so we've got thirty minutes at least.'

Jimmy had polished off the last of his fried eggs and wiped around his plate with a slice of toast, mopping up any egg yolk and fat that may have been missed.

'I won't be going.' His voice was taut, his eyes flashed with anger. Ryan looked at Frank and back to Jimmy.

'Why not?'

'Because you are about to be raided, because there are customs men on the way waiting for you to unload the dope off the truck, because I don't want to spend my last years in prison. You have a leak in your organisation, Son, and this time, the damage is irreparable.'

Ryan felt sick. He had to fight the rising bile as the colour drained from his face. 'I don't understand. That's bullshit. How could you possibly know that?'

His head was spinning. He stood up and took his mobile from his pocket and started pressing buttons.

'Put that away,' said Jimmy. Ryan turned his back and lifted the phone to his ear. Jimmy jumped from his chair and slapped the phone away from Ryan's ear; it went spinning across the tiled floor, coming to rest against the kitchen cupboards. Rasa looked down at the phone and turned, leaving the kitchen and knowing it was no place for her at this time.

'If you warn anybody, they will know. They will know that you are involved. Do you think they won't be looking at your phone records over the next few days? Christ, they are probably already tracking your calls, you dumb little shit.'

'We can't just sit here and let it happen.' Ryan's voice had gone up an octave.

Frank jumped in. 'Jimmy's right. You stay aloof. The people who get arrested, they were working alone without the knowledge of the company. We look after their families behind the scenes, but they are going down regardless. If they stay quiet and take the rap, their families are taken care of. If they don't, well, their families are looked after by Jimmy.'

The two brothers looked at each other, and there was an almost imperceptible nod from Jimmy.

'But what about . . . we can't just . . . ,' Ryan stuttered over his words. 'I mean who . . . ?'

He looked at his father, unable to articulate his question, his brain stumbling over his inability to comprehend his demise.

Frank looked at Jimmy again. 'Alex Harris?'

'So I am told. He sent a file to the police.'

'That bastard. I'm gonna kill that fucker. I'm gonna chop him into little pieces.'

Jimmy sat back at the table and finished his cup of tea. 'I have lost a lot of money in this business with you, Ryan. I have killed men for less. Harris is mine, and he is mine until I get the money he has stolen. Then you can have what's left of him.'

Ryan threw his arms out wide. 'But we don't know where he is.' He articulated each word, accentuating the gaps, spelling it out as though Jimmy did not speak the same language. Frank winced internally. His boy was getting very close to some serious trouble with his uncle.

'No, to be sure, we don't. Not right now. But I do know where he will be tomorrow.'

CHAPTER 29

SUNDAY, DECEMBER 10

IT WAS LATE AFTERNOON. THE rain and wind had not let up all day, and now the sky was darkening just a little. It was an early dusk, and without any break in the cloud, it seemed like nightfall was just around the corner.

He looked out of the window, but up at the sky. He would need the light on soon, but not yet. Keep it dark for a while. He was comfortable in the shadows.

The radio was on. Another game would be on at four. He would have a listen, but it was not United, and he was not particularly bothered. He shuffled away from the window and into the kitchen to put the kettle on. A nice pot of tea would warm him before he decided to light the fire.

He emptied the dregs of cold tea from the pot and rinsed it around with clean water before putting in two spoons of loose leaf tea. He leant against the kitchen cupboard as he waited for the kettle to boil. His days were always much the same. He listened to the football at the weekend, and during the week, he would go for a walk around the estate in the morning. It was best to go in the morning, before all the youngsters were up and about.

He liked to keep out of their way. The tracksuited young men waiting for their benefit money, keeping a careful watch on any car, looking out for an unlocked door, like crows waiting for carrion.

In his younger days, Tommy was never anybody's prey, but the arthritis had weakened him severely. He was stooped and walked with a limp, but he told himself that he retained enough strength to look after himself if pushed, especially if he was carrying his stick. But he preferred to take the easy option and avoid any confrontation these days.

The kettle started to whistle, and he immediately picked it off the cooker and poured the boiling water into the pot. He put the pot on his wicker tray and covered it with a tea cosy and placed his newly washed cup next to it. He took the milk from the fridge and poured a little into the blue and white milk jug that Maureen had bought in Devon, what was it, thirty years ago? He picked up the tray and set off into the lounge to park himself in his chair by the window. He would watch the wildlife for an hour before concentrating on the football.

As he walked through the gloom of the unlit room, he picked out the shape in the far corner by the door. Tommy stopped. It was too dark to make him out, but it was definitely a man. Tommy froze for a moment; then straightened himself up to his maximum height.

'What are you doing in my house? You've got to the count of ten to get out before I call the police.' He kept his voice low and even, as threatening as he could be. Don't let them think you are sacred.

'I don't think you want to do that. It might be a good idea to get another cup though.' The voice was calm, well spoken, just a slight accent. Tommy tried to squint to get a clear look and then the man stepped forward, passing into the watery light from the window.

'It's me, Dad, it's Jack. I'm back.' The tea tray crashed to the floor.

'Christ, why the hell am I here in the pissing rain with a load of fucking grease monkeys and Neanderthals.'

Steven Holland was not happy. He had missed his son's rugby match; his wife would most likely not speak to him for days, let alone allow him any sexual favours, and before long Ryan would stroll in like he had all day.

At times, he hated this job. But what choice did he have? He had spent his entire working life struggling for the recognition and rewards that he deserved. After Cambridge, he had been called to the Bar and completed his pupillage in chambers in the Inner Temple. But he had found work hard to come by. His Head of Chambers had suggested that he may not be a 'good fit' for the profile of the set, and he had been forced to cast around and find whatever work he could.

He pitched up at Goldberg's, a medium-sized Manchester firm in their commercial litigation team. It suited them to have an in-house barrister, and it suited him to have a steady income.

He was already living the life of a successful barrister with all the trappings that entailed without the income. He was working on a contractual dispute for Goldberg's largest client when he was introduced at their Autumn Reception. He immediately struck up a relationship with Frank Maguire. After a few months, he had met Ryan on a marketing junket. He had tried to ignore Ryan hacking up the course at Royal Lytham, had plied him with drink, and had tried to develop some sort of friendship.

Eventually, they got to the thing they had in common—women. They both had, well, not a weakness, quite the opposite. The strength, as Holland saw it, to do exactly as they pleased with the weaker sex. They would find them and take them as they saw fit.

Obviously, they would stay within the realms of the professionals. Anything else was likely to result in complications. They had a similar appetite but differing taste. Holland liked them young, timid, and even afraid. Power was the greatest aphrodisiac. He loved having it and women loved him to demonstrate it, other than his wife. She was cold. But her family had breeding and old money and that was power and that was a turn-on.

Ryan, on the other hand, liked older women, experienced women, and other peoples' women. He liked the feeling of power but in an altogether more fundamental way.

Once Holland had understood this, he went about making himself useful in the procurement of appropriate partners, and together, they would spend evenings, sometimes weekends in unrestricted gratification.

Holland was seduced by Ryan's apparent lawlessness. He was like a gunslinger in the Old West. If he saw something that he wanted, he took it. He had no regard for the social conventions that everybody else adhered to. He was exciting. And Holland saw an opportunity.

He suggested that they should work more closely together and, eventually, he found himself employed by Maguires as in-house legal counsel and, eventually, company secretary. He had long been aware of Ryan's plan to exploit the business. They had discussed it over many a weekend in one sleazy bordello or another. It was only what Ryan's father had done in the early years, just on a larger scale.

It was Holland's role to ensure that there were no paper trails to create a plausible deniability for the Maguires and, of course, to share in the profits of his labour.

And what profits? His bank balance was very healthy indeed—healthy, untouchable and untraceable. His salary and share options made him a wealthy man in any event. But the 'bonuses' lifted him into a different league altogether—into the financial league to which he truly belonged. His in-laws and their old money would soon be looking to him to prop up their estate, and he would do it too, on condition that it became his.

Standing in this freezing shed on a grey, sodden Manchester Sunday was a small price to pay for all that.

He looked at his watch and called Ryan again. The wagon should have been here half an hour ago, fucking voicemail. Where was the stupid oik? Probably he was shafting some old bird from a council estate. You could throw all the money in the world at Ryan Maguire, and he would still end up crawling back to some saggy, old cow, who smokes twenty a day and tops up her benefits by taking the odd slap. The man had no class.

There was the sound of an air horn, and the large metal gates rolled inwards as the truck turned off Tariff Street, at last.

It rumbled into the yard and straight through into the workshop, where it sat dripping on the polished floor above the inspection pit. The door opened, and the driver jumped down from the cab and stretched.

'About fucking time, where the hell have you been?' Holland shouted angrily.

'Sorry, Boss, that M6 is a piece of shit,' Jakov replied in his broken English.

'Never mind that, just get yourself off to the hotel and be here on time tomorrow.'

'Sure, Boss.' Jakov pulled a heavy blue anorak from the cab and a small holdall and waved over his shoulder as he walked out through the main door. As he crossed the threshold, he heard the metal door starting to roll down from above him, and he turned to see the side doors of the workshop open and the mechanics heading in from their canteen.

He crossed the yard and went out through the gates, turning left on to Tariff Street to walk towards Piccadilly, where he would normally get a cab to the hotel.

He tried not to look at the vans parked either side of the gate, or the vans and cars parked all the way down the street. Just look ahead, they had told him, like there is nothing to see.

When he reached the crossroads with Brewer Street, he turned right and walked to Port Street. Before he turned left, he glanced right, down Port Street. He saw the white van parked at the rear of Maguires. He had been told not to look at it, but he could not help himself. He saw the aerials and a small dish on the top. He wondered what they were hearing inside.

He turned left and walked up Port Street. He knew he would be met by a police officer on Dale Street. He wondered if he could relieve himself without causing a scene. The stress was taking its toll, and he didn't want any accidents on the way to the police station. He decided against it, took a deep breath, and walked on.

Duncan was sitting in the back of a blue Ford Transit van. Lynn was beside him, Miles opposite, fresh from handing Michael Richardson over to the custody sergeant at Bootle Street. He did not want to miss anything.

Four officers from Her Majesty's Customs and Excise were crammed in amongst them, all appeared to be armed as though about to storm the Iranian Embassy.

Duncan had an earpiece and was listening to the transmissions from 'Houston' as the Customs men called their mobile operations and communications vehicle. He could hear the mechanics clattering around, cursing as they went. There was, however, very little in the way of incriminating audio. Duncan was straining to recognise any of the voices or to pick up the names. He had no real idea how many people were in the workshop. Jakov had told them that Ryan Maguire always supervised the transition from truck to vans for local distribution.

Duncan shifted uncomfortably. His long frame was not ideal for stake-outs. His thighs and buttocks ached. The back of his neck was raw and chafed by the armoured vest he was forced to wear.

'Why don't they just go in?' It was Miles, whispering.

The customs men looked straight ahead as if Miles were not there and certainly not audible.

'They want to get them loading the stuff into the vans, that way they can demonstrate they intended to distribute, and they can also be sure to collar all the drivers as well.' It was Lynn, also whispering. She also appeared to be both invisible and inaudible to the duty officers, all of which had earpieces of their own—none of whom had spoken since the three police officers got into the van.

Duncan looked at his watch. Then came the words over the airwaves, 'Go, go, go.' The customs officers burst out of the back of the van leaving Duncan and his team sitting with the doors open, looking at each other.

'Have the pubs opened?' Duncan said, smiling.

Holland stood at the door to the side of the workshop, checking the bags of white powder as they were passed from the underside of the wagon to the back of the van, mentally counting them off, making sure they were not short-changed and that all the merchandise reached the distribution chain. There was too much money involved to leave it to chance.

He heard the first shout and immediately knew. His self-preservation instincts kicked in. He turned and ran to the back of the workshop and into the small toilet there. Once inside, he locked the door behind him, climbed on to the lavatory seat, and reached for the small window high in the back wall of the building.

The latch was stiff due to lack of use, but it came free under his sinuous grip, and the window pushed open upwards. It was barely wide enough to get his shoulders through, but he squeezed and scraped until his upper torso poked out the other side.

He could see the rear car park; his own black BMW was parked near the gate, facing out. He could be out through the gate and into the Sunday shoppers in minutes. He pulled his hips through the opening and then, with too much weight outside the window, toppled forwards, somersaulting downwards and landing awkwardly on his lower back on the wet tarmac.

Pain shot through his spine, but he was up on his feet; his calfskin loafers with their wooden heels were clacking on the car park surface.

He got to his car, opening it remotely and starting the engine on the button. As he pulled out of his parking space, he pressed a button on his key fob which activated the electric gate, and it started to slide open.

He picked up speed as he approached the opening and then, too late, realised that the exit was completely blocked by a white van parked across the gate. The BMW careered into the side of the van, and Holland was thrown forward, his chest crashing against the steering wheel and his forehead hitting the windscreen. As his consciousness wavered, he cursed himself for forgetting the seat belt and wondered whether he could sue BMW for the failure of his air bag to deploy.

He was still sitting in his car, his aquiline nose dripping blood on to his Ralph Lauren shirt, the red polo player appearing to be fighting his way through a field of giant poppies, when Duncan arrived.

'Oh, dear Mr. Holland. I suspect you might need a good personal injury lawyer. Would you like me to recommend one?'

'Fuck you, Duncan.'

'Actually, that's Detective Chief Inspector Duncan. Miles, read this arse his rights and then stick him in the van.'

Duncan walked away with Melbourne following, heading into the offices. The keypad was hanging from the wall as he went through the opened door. He took the stairs two at a time and headed straight for Ryan Maguire's office. He called behind himself to Melbourne, 'Take Frank Maguire's office, and we will meet in the middle at Holland's office. Get Miles up here once he has Holland in the van, and he can go through the accounts.'

'Yes, guv.'

Duncan tore through Ryan's office. In less than five minutes, he realised that there was nothing there. Not just nothing incriminating, nothing at all. If he was involved in the running of the business on any level, you would never have known it from his office. There was barely a piece of paper in the place, two or three copies of contracts, mainly for maintenance of the trucks, a rota for the workshops and a list of conferences for the coming year.

'Shit.' Ryan was not on site as anticipated. Jakov had been adamant that he was always there. His office was virtually empty. Duncan looked at the computer, which was, frankly, the only hope he had of getting anything of evidential value from Ryan's office. But that would have to be carried away by the tech boys. He switched it on anyway, waited for the annoying 'Control, Alt, Delete' screen, and waited to see if it was password protected. It was. He cursed under his breath.

Duncan moved down the hall to Holland's office. Here he found an absolute mass of paperwork, so he settled himself behind the desk and started reading.

After an hour, men in white overalls arrived and unplugged the computer and carried it away. Duncan opened a vanilla file marked 'Investigation'.

Inside the file, the only page was a memo to Frank and Ryan Maguire, dated Friday December 8, 2011. It was headed, somewhat grandiosely 'For Your Eyes Only'.

Gentlemen, I have received word from one of the workers in the mechanics team, whose identity I shall keep to myself for reasons that will become clear, that there may be some illegal activity going on involving some of our workers.

I have no hard evidence at this moment in time, just the suspicions of one employee, but the accusations are serious and need to be brought to your attention immediately due to the implications it would have on the good name of your business.

The accusation is that certain employees have coerced the drivers from our Eastern European routes to engage in smuggling, that they bring in contraband, without our knowledge, and remove it from our vehicles in the old workshop on the Tariff Street site.

It is my intention to commence a detailed investigation into these claims, and I believe we should consult both our private security team and the Greater Manchester Police.

May I suggest that we meet to discuss this serious situation at the earliest convenience.

Regards,
Steven.

Duncan closed the file, which was otherwise empty. 'Crafty bastard.' He immediately went back to Ryan's office and went through every item of paperwork. Then he strode down to Frank's office and handed Lynn the memo.

'Have you found Frank's copy of this?'

Lynn read the memo. 'No, and to be honest I've found bugger all of any note and precious little of anything else. I'm assuming that Mr. Maguire is a very technologically minded CEO and that his office is run on a paperless basis because I've read just about everything.'

Duncan smiled. 'That Holland is a sneaky bastard. I am prepared to bet anything that he writes this memo every single day so that it has a fresh date on it, and when people like us come knocking on the door, he presents it as his magic bullet. Get on to the techies and get them to check his computer for old copies of this memo. I will not have that slippery swine get away with this.'

'Boss?'

'Yes, Lynn.'

'We have nothing on the Maguires as things stand. This is, potentially, a plausible defence and none of them were here for the raid as we were led to believe. It doesn't look good.'

'No, it doesn't. Give the station a call. I want uniforms at the Maguires' houses immediately. I want them in custody tonight, wherever they are. I'm heading back so that I can get Holland in for a chat.'

With that, he stalked out of the office and down the stairs, leaving Lynn thinking that she could almost feel the electricity radiating from him when he was about to lose his temper and knowing also that he would regain his composure on the drive back to the station.

Lynn took out her mobile phone and made the first of two calls.

CHAPTER 30

MONDAY, DECEMBER 11

TOMMY HAD BEEN UP EARLY.

He felt better than he had done in years. The arthritis that racked his joints seemed to have relaxed its grip, just a little. He had showered and changed into his best clothes, eaten a hearty breakfast of scrambled eggs and toast, washed down with orange juice and a cup of tea, which reminded him, he needed to replace the shattered teapot.

Despite the wintry, freezing rain that welcomed the daylight, Tommy had begun a spring clean. The curtains were opened, the old rug discarded into the green wheelie bin outside, and the carpet vacuumed, not once but twice. The whole house smelt of furniture polish and bleach—all because of Jack.

He still could not quite believe it. His son had come back to him, not to mock him or to punish him but to forgive. Or, if not forgive exactly, to reach an understanding, more to the point, Jack needed him. Tommy had not felt needed for nearly thirty years. He had started his married life thriving on the responsibility that came with it, but the loss of the first baby had broken him.

Somewhere deep inside, he had vowed that he would not leave his heart so exposed again, so that when Jack came along, he held back emotionally, for fear of being hurt once more.

Maureen had been strong enough, but Tommy felt it was different for a man to lose his child. He was the protector, the guardian for the fledgling family. Yet at the first hurdle, he had lost the most precious thing.

His life had spiralled out of control from that point on. When you don't feel like a man, it is impossible to act like one. He had faked it for years. His violence was a smokescreen for the inadequacy he perceived within himself. He drank to anaesthetise himself to the pain of his failure and found, like many before him, that the drink only served to magnify his moroseness.

The final humiliation was the beating he received at the hands of his teenage son. It took him many years to realise it, but it was exactly what he both needed and deserved. He had hit rock-bottom. It just took him another twenty years to pluck up the courage to face it, and only then, when forced to by Jack's return.

Tommy had looked his son in the eye, perhaps for the first time, he could not be sure, and he had wept. Like a child, his tears flowed uncontrollably but silently. He could not express his reasons; he was a simple working man of the old school. He would have liked to have told his son he was sorry, to have pleaded for forgiveness, and to have tried to explain that he was overcompensating for his perceived impotence. He could not find the words to elucidate his feelings, so the tears had done that on his behalf.

They had talked into the evening. They talked about the past a little. Jack was reluctant to go there, and Tommy had sensed he was becoming distant again, so they talked about the future. The future started today.

Tommy put on his best shoes, an old pair of brogues he had worn twice in the last ten years. They were a bit stiff, but they were nicely polished, *perhaps a size too big when they have loosened up,* **he thought,** *since I have lost weight.*

He had not mentioned his illness to Jack. It just did not seem important. He had a son, hopefully a proper son, for the first time, and he did not want his predicted demise looming over their relationship.

He put on his overcoat and fished an umbrella from the back of the under-stairs cupboard. He examined himself in the mirror and was pleasantly surprised to see an apparently well-dressed, middle-class retiree staring back at him.

He picked up the mobile phone Jack had left for him and the piece of paper with instructions of how to use it and the addresses he would need. Picking up his keys and wallet from the hallway telephone table, he took a look around the house and left double locking the door behind him.

Jules sat on the bed, flicking through the TV channels, not actually seeing any of them.

She switched the TV off on the remote and walked to the window. She was close to tears. She felt this way whenever she was without Alex. Ever since the incident at the house in Milton Keynes, she had struggled to be alone. In fact, it was not even being alone. She had felt the same at her parents' home. It was being away from Alex that was the problem.

Internally, she was unable to unscramble her feelings. She was, even taking into account her modesty, brilliantly clever. She had spent her whole adult life appreciating others for their intellect. She had never chosen a partner based upon physicality.

As a schoolgirl, she was not attracted to the sportsmen or the hard or rebellious boys. It was always the quick-witted ones. Her feelings were based primarily on personality. Of course, looks played their part, but if a man did not challenge her mentally and was not at least her equal intellectually, then he was not of any interest to her. Her needs and desires were more cerebral than carnal.

At least, that was what she had always thought.

Her relationship with Alex was always driven by the psychological reaction between them. His sharp humour had first attracted her; his slightly irreverent manner was sometimes bordering on the discourteous, often forthright and occasionally even rude but always with a charming sincerity.

He had a penetrating way of looking at you when asking questions that could be both disconcerting and intimidating, but, which, she had found challenging. They had sparred, verbally, for months before he had asked her out. Stutteringly, revealing a tenderness and vulnerability that had been supremely well hidden.

Now, however, she had seen the other Alex. She had witnessed the natural fluidity in his violence. She experienced the tranquillity that emanated from him after acts of terrible ferocity. More than that, she had seen the excitement in his eyes during the barbaric assault he had inflicted upon Richardson. It both terrified and excited her.

For the first time in her life, she was attracted by the most basic of animal instincts, power—the pack leader. She found the thought of it abhorrent. But, like a heroin addict, she could no longer imagine life without it, but neither was she sure that she could survive with it.

She turned back in to face the room. Her bag was packed, so was his. She checked the time on her watch and checked she still had the number she needed in her contacts. She knew she did, but she felt better for checking.

All she could do now was wait for Alex to return, or not return. She was not entirely sure which she was hoping for, and she expected to have regrets either way.

Alex had walked from Bootle Street to Cross Street to the bank. Having completed his business, he stood in the doorway, looking either side.

It was still raining. Light rain that sat on top of your clothes and gradually seeped through chilling to the bone. His old parka needed to be waterproofed again.

They were still there—two men across the street. They had picked him up on Bootle Street as he walked down and then back up, past the Abercromby, looking for exactly what he found. Men were trying to tail him.

He had considered running, but he wanted to know who they were, police perhaps. But he didn't think so. They looked out of place. No policeman would be looking out of place outside a policeman's pub and a police station.

He had decided to take them for a walk, to see if they tried to take him. If they were Maguires, they would stop him meeting the police. If they were police, they would just stay on his tail.

He turned right from the bank on to Cross Street and headed towards King Street, back towards Albert Square, Bootle Street, and the pub. He had ten minutes until his meeting.

He walked past Mr. Thomas' Chop House, checking in the window's reflection as the two men crossed the road to fall in step behind him.

His heart was beating faster. His mind raced assessing the possibilities. The clarity of thought was rushing back to him like an old reflex action. He had not felt this way for a long time. He picked up the pace a little as he came to King Street and turned right into the pedestrianised section. He sensed the increased movement behind him, caught peripherally as he turned the corner. He made a quick dash diagonally across King Street to Four Yards Alley, a narrow walkway running parallel to Cross Street.

As he nipped down the alley, there was a shout as one of the men notified the other that they had spotted him.

There was no pretence now, and Alex broke into a full on rundown Four Yards coming out on King Street South, sprinting across the narrow road, and on into Four Yards, which carried on towards John Dalton Street.

His time spent with his iPad was serving him well as he knew every alley, every bend, and how far ahead he needed to be to disappear from view as he ducked down another passageway.

Alex could hear the footsteps behind him but fought the desire to look back.

He burst out of the alley and into John Dalton Street, busy, as it was all day being adjacent to Albert Square and the Town Hall. Alex knew he had two choices: left to Albert Square, from there it was a sprint across the square on to Southmill Street and Bootle Street, and once on Southmill Street, the station would be his saviour; to his right, he could run the twenty yards south to Tasle Alley, an even narrower thoroughfare by the side of the New Church House bookshop and the Pig and Apple pub.

On the basis that Albert Square would be full of office workers heading back to their desks after a rushed lunch break, clogging up the pavements and slowing him down, Alex chose Tasle Alley. Hardly anybody knew it was there and even less used it.

He broke right and dashed across the road, darting just in front of a double-decker bus travelling south towards Deansgate. The brakes screamed, but Alex did not break stride. He heard the cursing behind him as his pursuers were forced to divert around the back of the now stationary bus.

He reached the entrance to Tasle Alley and bolted through. It was dark with high walls both sides and part covered by the fire escape two floors above. After only twenty metres, the alley opened out on to a dead end street. Left would take Alex back to Albert Square again but straight ahead was Mulberry Passage. The passage was only wide enough for two people abreast and completely enclosed above.

Alex hoped that he could split up his pursuers as in both cases he could be out of sight before they were clear of the alley. He careered forwards into Mulberry Passage, hoping that his echoing footsteps would not give him away, darting out of the dark on to Mulberry Street, beside St. Mary's Church. Alex turned right and considered ducking into the church but realised he had no way of knowing if there was another way out. To his left, opposite the church, was the post office building whose entrance was on Brazenose Street, another street running off Albert Square. Under the post office was an underground car park with a green wire fence around it.

You could easily drop from the fence down to the car park and get lost among the cars and the numerous exits. But Alex continued past the church. He could hear footfalls echoing in the passage, and he decided now was the time to disappear. On his right was the rear of a modern red brick office building. It had a narrow walkway to a service entrance between the pavement and the buildings' walls with a low retaining wall keeping the walkway enclosed. Alex hurdled the wall and lay flat against it.

It was no more than two feet high, but it had flagstones on top that provided an overhang that formed a recess into which he could squeeze.

It smelt of urine and kitchen waste, and the concrete path was cold and rough, but he could not be seen.

He heard a shout and cursing. An Irish accent? There was a quick debate, and steps went right past him, and the sound died away. But only one set of steps.

Alex inched out of the hollow and peered tentatively over the wall. One man stood with his back to him, holding on to the low wire fence and scanning the underground car park.

Alex checked to his right and, seeing nobody else on Mulberry Street, stepped quietly over the low wall. He walked, as casually as he could manage, towards the man, who was panting from his exertions. When he was no more than a couple of yards away, Alex sprang at him, grabbing both legs around the knees and lifting him, in one movement, over the fence and sending him spinning down into the car park.

He crashed on to the bonnet of a silver Ford Focus, and Alex heard a scream from the woman driver. The bonnet of the car crumpled, and the body lay twisted and groaning.

Alex ran to his left, through the pathway to Brazenose Street, straight across the gardens, passing the somewhat incongruous statue of Abraham Lincoln (he had no idea why Abe was in central Manchester) and on to Queen Street, turning left and coming out at the junction with Southmill Street and Albert Square.

Here, he slowed to a walk, pulled out his cap, turned up his collar, and made his way slowly to Bootle Street.

CHAPTER 31

MONDAY, DECEMBER 11

THE SIR RALPH ABERCROMBY WAS a small Victorian pub next to Bootle Street Station. It was three stories high in traditional brick. Sayers Court ran down one side but was closed off by high iron railings for security reasons as it ran between the pub and the police station. On the other side, a small terrace with wooden picnic tables and benches, with green parasols, were folded down in the rainy Manchester winter.

Normally only the smokers would be in this area on a day like today. Two men were sheltering under the awning: a young man in a green coat, with turned up collar and an oversized flat cap, pulled to one side of his head at a fashionable angle; and an old man in a brown overcoat, carrying his umbrella, stood close together, deep in conversation.

The sign outside was black with the name in gold letters. Brackets for hanging baskets were fixed above the name, but the baskets and the flowers had long since departed along with any widespread knowledge of the soldier whose name was bestowed upon the pub, or why a public house in central Manchester would take the name of a Scottish soldier who was once commander-in-chief of Ireland and who died during his successful attempts to remove the French from Egypt.

Not that Duncan was concerned with the origins of the name of the establishment as he entered the cramped bar for his meeting with Alex Harris.

Duncan had taken a small table opposite the door; his back was to the wall with a clear view to the bar on his left and the door to the outside terrace to his right.

He had arrived early and had looked around to ensure that his people were in place and that Harris was not there before him. He only had a basic description of Harris as he seemed to have avoided any photographs other than a twelve-year-old sample from his passport, faxed through by his new friends in customs and of poor quality.

Christopher Hanson had promised to send over some old publicity shots but had called back and sheepishly admitted that they had apparently been misplaced or deleted accidentally.

Duncan nodded at Lynn, sat on a tall bar stool with one of two officers seconded from vice. The other was standing over by the exit to the toilets, distractedly playing the fruit machine and nursing a pint of lager.

Miles was sitting at another table in the corner furthest from the door, away to Duncan's right, seemingly engrossed in his mobile phone. There were three men standing at the bar in suits, drinking Guinness and laughing loudly—one short and stocky, one medium height and thin with cropped hair, and the third also stocky with a Dublin accent and a booming guffaw.

Duncan had drunk his orange juice and waited and nothing had happened. The door had not opened. He checked his watch. He was five minutes late but that did not concern Duncan. It was an acceptable time lag allowing for the variance of different timepieces. But sitting still was difficult at times like this, so Duncan wandered to the bar and ordered another orange, deliberately not speaking to anybody and avoiding eye contact.

He collected his drink and turned back to his table to find a man in a green parka and flat cap, pulled low over his eyes, sitting in his seat. Duncan paused, trying to get a look at the face while glancing at Miles and seeing him looking back at him, giving an inquisitive look. Miles nodded towards the door to the terrace and lowered his eyes back to his phone.

Duncan walked slowly to the table and put down the orange juice.

'Would you like a drink?'

He studied the man before him. He was of a normal height; Duncan guessed five feet nine or ten, difficult to tell as he was seated with his legs crossed. He looked quite lean, but he was wearing his coat zipped high, the straight collar, like a military style, was turned up, and he kept his hands in his pockets.

The head moved slightly, as though to acknowledge his presence, but did not look up. The eyes remained hidden, the angle of the face downward so that Duncan could see only the cheekbone and the short stubble.

Duncan waited for his response. Just as Duncan was about to speak again, the head tilted back. The face was rounded, but not fat, the lips spread into a broad smile below a straight nose, and the unmistakeable piercing grey eyes. Then it hit him—the parka. Christ, it was the same bloody fishtail parka.

'Oh shit,' Duncan whispered. 'I knew it.'

Alex Harris took off his flat cap and placed it on the table. He ran his fingers through the light brown hair and ruffled it to relieve the flatness caused by the hat.

Detective Chief Inspector Duncan stared at an older but instantly recogniseable Jack Ladd. Then he pulled up a small stool and lowered his long, gangly frame down. Jack continued to smile.

'Hello, Joe, nice to see you again. Look at you, you lanky sod.'

Joe Duncan was lost for words, almost. 'You bastard.'

Jack stood at the door of the Abercromby and looked up Bootle Street. The fine drizzle was like a freezing gossamer veil over the city, gently soaking everything. The sky was getting dark, the clouds above seemingly one conjoined mass that looked ready to crush the buildings beneath should they lower themselves any further.

He had made his decision. He took his iPhone from his pocket and tapped in a message to Jules, that sent, he tapped in a message to Tommy.

He fished in his pockets for his hat and pushed the iPhone inside the sleeve of his parka. The cuffs had buttons on an elasticated strap, so that they could be tight or loose and he fastened them tight, so the phone stayed against the inside of his wrist.

With his flat cap in place and tilted, he took a deep breath and set off down towards Deansgate. He could see the two men in the doorway to his right, about twenty yards ahead. They were in discussion, one of them held a mobile phone to his ear, the other, the one who had recently been for a spin on a Ford Focus, stared directly at Jack, malevolence in his eyes. *Understandably so,* thought Jack.

The meeting in the pub had not been a resounding success. Yes, he had taken Joe by surprise, and, yes, it was great to see him again face-to-face, but it was not all good news.

Jack had begun by asking if the raid on the Tariff Street workshop had gone ahead.

'Yes, it went ahead. But I'm afraid it did not exactly go to plan.' Joe had lowered his eyes as he spoke. 'Ryan wasn't there, Jack. He never showed up.'

'What? He is always there, Redford told me, and I watched them. He takes control of the unpacking and the dealers in the vans.'

'Not this time I'm afraid. And it gets worse. I went through all the paperwork, and there is nothing, not only that, they may have a Get Out of Jail Free card.'

Jack glared back, incredulous. 'Why?'

'Their lawyer, Holland, it seems has been one step ahead. He had prepared a file that, when produced at court, will show that he was investigating the possibility of a smuggling operation in the firm, and he had the approval of the Maguire's to do so. It's all set up to give them plausible deniability, Jack.'

'Jesus Christ. So the old man has put the fix in again, hasn't he.' Jack was shaking his head in disbelief. 'Who is it, Joe, who is tipping them off?'

Duncan was riled. 'What are you suggesting?'

'Oh come on, Joe. Ryan does all the switches from lorry to van except the one when you are sitting outside waiting to catch him. Holland has a strategy in place to keep them free. Their boys are out there on the street now, they knew I was coming. I had to do a bit of dodging and weaving to make it here. The only people who knew where I would be today are you and me.'

That was not true, but Jack was in no mood to tell Joe that his father was outside on the terrace, and he certainly had no intention of mentioning Jules waiting at the hotel, not until he knew who could be trusted.

Joe looked around the pub. He was getting quizzical looks from Lynn.

'OK, look. We might have had a bit of a leak, and I froze one person out, but I know nothing about you being followed today, and the only people who know about our meeting are sitting in this bar now.'

'So that's four others then.' Jack couldn't resist letting Joe know that he had identified his team. 'So one of them is giving up what they shouldn't. I suggest that you find out pretty bloody quick who it is because my life is going to depend on it.'

Joe was taken aback. 'Hold on, what do you mean?'

'Joe, the whole point of this sorry exercise was to get Ryan locked up. The reason I came here today was to give you a message for Ryan, from me, so that he would know who and why. Then I was going to disappear.'

'With the money you stole.' Joe's tone was terse. Jack looked back at him for the longest second, the eyes burrowing straight through. But Joe had changed over twenty years, and Jack reached a hastily constructed wall before he got to Joe's thoughts.

'But now,' Jack continued, 'I have to finish this myself.'

'Jack, I can't let you do that. I can't sit here and let you walk out knowing that you intend to kill someone. I will arrest you right now. Christ, I'm a police officer, Jack, and you are not a kid any more. You have to let me do my job. I will get Ryan. The blokes from the workshop may yet talk, plus Richardson. What's more, you've destroyed the family business. The whole company is likely to collapse once this gets out. Come, Jack, give it up, you've done enough.'

Jack considered his options. Joe was right, he could walk away. He had a degree of retribution.

'Look, Jack. If you walk out of here and leave the Maguires to me my report will detail how Alex Harris stole their money and vanished without trace. You will be free. I can buy you some time to get your affairs in order, sell up and start again. But if you go down this other path, I won't be there to pick up the pieces again. I won't be able to avoid coming after you.'

The two old friends looked at each other.

'Do you see much of Ladyboy these days, Joe?'

'I saw him a few days ago, asked him what he knew about Redford. He's OK.'

Jack nodded. 'Tell him I always regretted getting him involved, will you? Next time you see him.'

'You could tell him yourself. He lives just up the road in Asia House. People call him the Queen of the Gay Village.'

Jack stood up, and Joe made to stand to block his path. Jack put a hand on his shoulder, a firm hand, pressing him back down into the stool.

'Joe, I'm going to walk out of here. I will leave the Maguires alone, but if they come for me, I *will* take my revenge. I don't want to cause you any trouble. You've done enough for me. Even if you have to take me in, nobody will ever know what you did for me. That's between you and me, and that's where it stays.'

Joe looked up at Jack. Was that an implied threat? He studied Jack's eyes for a clue. He found himself staring at the open face of the only close friend he had ever had.

'It was nice to see you again, Joe. It would have been nice to spend some time catching up, but I don't think that's likely now, do you?'

Joe saw himself on the top deck of the bus, wiping away tears as his best friend waved goodbye without looking back. There would be no tears this time, but he could feel the sense of loss in the pit of his stomach.

'Jack, I'm sorry it can't be better. Look, when all this is done, you can get in touch—e-mail or something. At least let me know you are OK.' He pulled a smile from his locker. 'Maybe let me have a cheap holiday wherever you swan off to?'

'May be, Joe, may be. Make sure your people don't stop me at the door. Oh, and buy a decent suit.' He patted Joe's shoulder as he walked away.

Now he was only five yards from Maguire's men. They shuffled their feet, widening their stance and readying themselves for his approach, unnerved by the fact that he appeared to be walking directly to them.

Jack stopped in front of the two men and, smiling, spread his arms wide. 'I come in peace, boys. Take me to your leader.'

'What happened? Why did you let him go?' Lynn sounded almost angry. Joe was still sitting in the Abercromby, only now he had a pint of bitter in front of him. He looked at the bronze liquid, with its perfect white head, and took a long, slow draught.

'Lynn, sometimes you have to be able to tell the good guys from the bad guys. That was one of the good guys.'

Melbourne looked confused. 'I don't know what the hell you are talking about. That was a guy who you think stole over a million pounds, was the last person to talk to Redford that we know of, may have been involved in a massive insurance fraud, may have caused Redford's death by hanging him out to dry, and, to cap it all off, put three men in the hospital. And you just let him walk out of here to God knows where. We haven't been able to trace him until now, and you let him disappear again. I don't understand, Boss.'

'No, that's interesting, isn't it? We couldn't find him until he came to us. With all our resources and all our manpower, not a sniff of his whereabouts. But Maguire's boys could find him. They knew he was coming here. How did they know, Lynn?' Duncan watched her reaction closely.

'I don't know, how could I?'

The necessary anger was there, but the slight tremor in her voice, coupled with the rapid eye movement, gave lie to the fear behind it.

Duncan took another long gulp from his pint. 'You told Drew.'

Miles had been watching the conversation between Lynn and Duncan, although he could not quite hear what was said. He strained to catch the drift of their angry words, trying to read lips and body language.

It was then that he noticed the old man. He came in from the terrace and paused at the door, looking around the bar. His tired, grey eyes settled on Duncan, and he paused before walking over to him.

Miles got up from his seat and intercepted the old man's route between the tables and chairs.

'Can I help you there?' he said, keeping his tone light and matter of fact. They were both stopped, and Miles looked into the haggard face to try to read his intentions.

'I don't think so, son. I need to have a word with Joe.'

Miles was taken aback by the familiarity with which the pensioner referred to his boss. Miles had worked with Duncan for the last two years and still never used his Christian name and had never even considered using it.

'Er, OK, what about?'

'When I said I needed to speak with Joe, what I meant was that I speak to him, and you fuck off out of my way, OK?'

'Whoa, hang on there, Grandad.' Miles reached into his pocket to pull out his warrant card—a little prop to support the forthcoming demand for respect.

'It's all right, Steve. I know him.' Duncan had stepped between them. 'Hello, Tommy, fancy seeing you here. Come and sit down.'

Duncan gestured for Miles to leave them, and he retreated to the bar, nursing a dented ego. Melbourne followed, staying silent, looking chastened.

'So he's roped you into this, has he? What's up then, Tommy?'

Tommy sat in a carver chair and was undoing the buttons of his overcoat.

'You need to go after him, Joe. He's in trouble.'

Duncan noticed that there was a slight shakiness about Tommy. An involuntary quivering when he tried to stay still. He looked unwell.

'Are you OK, Tommy?'

'Jesus, Joe, you're his friend. I'm telling you he is in trouble. I just saw him getting picked up by two thugs.

They grabbed his arms and carted him away down Bootle Street towards Deansgate.'

'OK. Where were you?'

'I was on the veranda, waiting for him to come out.'

'Why? Why are you here at all?'

'He asked me to come. He came to see me last night and told me he needed help. He said people were after him, and he thought they might try to grab him when he left. He told me you would be in here, and he told me to give you this.'

Tommy was pulling at his overcoat pocket, and eventually freed his hand. In his bony grasp was an iPhone. Tommy steadied his hand and pressed the menu button with his claw-like finger. The phone lit up. Tommy paused for a moment, then fished in his trousers for a piece of paper. He read the writing, in block capitals, and then swiped his finger across the phone to unlock it.

He held the phone out to Duncan. 'He told me that if they took him, this would tell you where he is.'

Duncan took the phone, noticing Tommy's cold, dry hand still shaking. He looked at the display, which read 'iCloud. Find My Phone.' He pressed the virtual button on the screen, and the image immediately became a Google map. A couple of seconds later, a blue circle appeared, pulsating as it moved, down Deansgate into Castlefield.

Tommy leant over. 'That's his phone. It's tracking his phone. Don't ask me how.'

Duncan looked back at him. Tommy was an old man. He was still recognisable as the hard drinking, tough mechanic Joe had known in his youth, but he was a skeletal reminder of that man and no more. But he looked content somehow. Agitated but at peace, if it were possible.

'What does he expect me to do?'

'He didn't say. He just said that if they took him, I should give this to you, and you would do the right thing. Will you do the right thing, Joe?'

'Christ. Don't I always do the right thing? You stay here. We are going after him.' Duncan got up and headed to the door. 'Miles, come on.' He looked at the undercover officers at the bar. 'You lads as well, this job isn't finished yet.' Lynn got up from the bar stool. 'Lynn, I want you back in the pit. I may need to call in for support. We might just have a way of getting hold of the Maguires after all.'

CHAPTER 32

MONDAY, DECEMBER 11

'THAT'S IT. WE'VE GOT THE fucker.'

Jimmy got up from his chair in the deserted office. He walked over to the window. The rain was not letting up, and the day grew ever closer to night. Frank and Ryan were standing at the empty desk.

'That's good then.' Frank shrugged on his camel coat. 'I've got a plane to catch. I will call you tomorrow.'

Jimmy sneered at Frank, 'You don't want to get your hands dirty then, brother?' Frank stopped by the door.

'This is your dirt, not mine, Jimmy. You and your money-grubbing scheme have brought this upon us. My business is ruined, for what? Just so that you can sit back in Belfast and show people what a bad man you are? Well, you can try and dig your way out of the shit on your own, Jim. I am flying to Nassau tonight, and I am out of the business as from now, you understand. If this lands on anybody, it won't be me.'

Jimmy looked at Ryan. 'Are you running off after, Daddy?'

'Fuck you, Jimmy. I'm staying here. I'm going to get my money out of this little shit, and I'm going to cut the fucker up.'

Frank gave a resigned shake of the head.

'This has already gone badly, Son, it can only get worse.' With that, he stalked out of the small prefabricated office, through the huge empty warehouse and into the waiting Mercedes, engine running, with Dainius at the wheel.

'We are meeting Mrs. Maguire at Ringway, Dainius, let's get there sooner rather than later, eh.'

'Yes, Boss. Bags are in the trunk, Boss, and the removal guy, he empties the house tomorrow and then me and Rasa get the flight, and I see you in Nassau tomorrow.'

'Good job, Dainius. Make sure the house is properly locked up and the security people organised. God, I'm looking forward to some sunshine and to get out of this godforsaken place.'

Frank sank back into the heated seat and closed his eyes. The business was finished, he knew that now. He had got out just in time, selling half of his share of the business to Holland and Ryan and a further 20 percent to the bank so that he only had a 20 percent share left, which would have paid him a steady income in his remaining years.

The rest of the money had gone to pay off the final installment on the house in Nassau and to be invested in the Cayman Islands. He would also get rental income from the mock Tudor house in Cheshire. The agent was hopeful that a new Italian footballer signed by Manchester City was going to rent the place. So even if the business went completely under, he would have enough to live comfortably, if not luxuriously.

As the Mercedes slipped through the growing traffic, Frank's only real concern was for the welfare of his son. He knew the noose was tightening, and he knew that Ryan would be a target for the police. But the lad had made his bed, and Frank had to let him be his own man.

It was odd. He had worked his whole life to build a business, had broken laws, people and promises along the way. He had fought for every penny. But now that his empire was crumbling before him, his greatest sensation was one of relief—relief that it was finally all over, and he could sit back and relax, relief that he could finally just be himself, and relief that the cold, damp grip of this city would be released.

As they hit the M56, Frank had started to nod off and was already looking ahead to the azure, crystal waters of the Caribbean.

Tommy stood in the reception area, feeling the oppressive warmth, and debated removing his overcoat.

He was nervous, and he shifted from side to side, just to keep moving as though to stay still would result in some sort of internal explosion. He glanced into the bar. He had not had a drink for a while, and he suddenly felt the pangs of desire. He looked furtively towards the staircase, already trying to assess if he had time to get into the bar, order and down a whisky, and get back to his spot in the foyer before she arrived.

The voices in the back of his head had just convinced him to skip out when he saw the feet, ankles, and then the long, slim legs descending.

She wore a tight, knee-length pencil skirt, dark blue, with a black cashmere sweater, fitted. She glided down the remaining stairs in her low heels, and as she approached him, he felt the dryness in his mouth and a tightening in his throat.

'Hello.' Her voice was perfect. She seemed able to convey intelligence and sophistication from the one word.

'Hello. I'm Tommy.' He was hesitant, and he knew that he had tried to cover up his thick Mancunian accent and felt just a little ridiculous. He was, after all, a septuagenarian.

'Hello, Tommy, I'm Julliette. So you are Alex's father. It is nice to meet you at last.'

'No,' Tommy growled. 'I'm Jack's Dad.'

'Of course, I'm sorry. His new, sorry, his old name is going to take some getting used to.'

Tommy flushed. 'No, love, it's me who should be sorry. You know him now. I don't. So I suppose he is Alex now.' He looked down at his shoes and noticed that he was hopping from one foot to another again.

'Hmm. I am not sure that he is just at the moment. But I hope he will be.' Jules stepped forward and looped her arm under Tommy's. 'Why don't we go and have a coffee, and we can have a proper talk.'

'Yes, I'd like that.' Tommy led her into the bar, feeling ten feet tall. He would be satisfied with a coffee after all.

Jack sat in the back of the car, the rear windows steaming up—a black Peugeot saloon. It had a number for a name, but Jack couldn't remember what the number was. His arms ached, and there was a growing pain in between his shoulder blades. His wrists chafed from the plastic tie, and his fingers felt numb, so he tried to shift his weight forwards.

They had not searched him, and his mobile remained in his sleeve. He prayed that nobody tried to ring him as he was not sure he had remembered to turn the sound off.

'Are we nearly there yet,' he asked cheerily.

The two men in the front ignored him. The car had crossed the bridge over the River Irwell, which meant they had crossed into the city of Salford. Most people outside of the Manchester area had no idea that Salford was a city in its own right, and it seemed bizarre that you could walk from one side of a road in Manchester City Centre to the other and be in a different city. Jack could not imagine that you could do the same in any other city anywhere in the world.

They had passed Peel Park, and the dated 1970s buildings of Salford University campus. Now they were on a trading estate—modern units that were car body repair shops, storage warehouses, and electronics factory units. They drove up to the gate of the largest building. It was painted in stripes—a deep blue at the bottom and gradually getting paler towards the top. The obvious intention was for the huge slab-sided building to blend into the sky. But this was the northwest of England, and they had not painted the building in varying shades of grey. The walls almost glowed against the backdrop of a yesterday's dishwater sky.

The huge metal double gates were open, and the sign at the side, almost hidden amongst the bushes, said KOTR Transport. The car bounced over a small speed hump and drove to the right-hand side of the blue monolith, where it parked in a marked bay beside a large Range Rover with blacked out windows.

As he was dragged from the back seat, Jack noted the number plate was KO1 TRT, which nearly matched the name of the business but not quite. The sort of number plate that made a statement about your status, you were nearly there but not quite.

He was manhandled towards a small door, painted to match the walls, and the taller of the two men, the one who had been for a short flight in the car park, stepped forward and knocked loudly on the door. The second held Jack by the upper arm in a vice-like grip.

With his hands close together, it was easy for Jack to unbutton the sleeve of his coat and let the sleek iPhone slip into his palm. There was a border around the building with low privet, no more than thirty centimetres high, which was only broken by the entrance they were standing at. Jack was hoping he could flick the phone into the bush without it being seen. He decided to wait until the door opened, and they were watching ahead.

The lock on the door made a snapping sound from the inside, and to Jack's relief, it opened outwards, meaning Focus man had to step backwards, making Jack step back and turn slightly, so his back was at right angles to the bushes. He immediately flipped the phone, using only the flexibility in his wrists, knowing that its flight would be masked by the door itself.

He listened for a bang as it hit either the wall or the floor and heard neither. He was then shoved unceremoniously through the door.

He found himself inside a cavernous workshop, which was almost completely empty. There was a small office in the far corner, basically made up of two thin plasterboard walls. Set in the middle of the open space was a table, the sort you might find in a woodwork class with metal legs. Around it were three chairs. Two matched the table and were placed either side, facing each other. The third set apart was an old-fashioned wooden chair with no arms and a tall slatted back—the sort your grandmother may have had in her dining room just before the outbreak of the Second World War. Jack realised straight away that the wooden chair was for him.

Leaning against the table was a bull of a man with white hair and a ruddy complexion. He was clearly in his sixties but the shoulders and upper arms looked powerful enough to do some serious damage. His neck was as wide as his head, and he wore a red check shirt with the sleeves rolled up above the elbow.

As Jack was pushed nearer, he saw tattoos on the forearms one of which read Oglaigh na hEireann in Gaelic, Irish Republican Army. Jack began to think that handing himself in may not have been his best idea today.

'Sit him there,' the Bull said, 'put his arms over the back of the chair.' Jack made note of the strong Belfast drawl and the gravelly, smokers rattle.

'So, Alex Harris, you're a difficult man to get hold of, so you are.' Jimmy moved so that he stood immediately in front of Jack.

'I've been very busy lately. Did you leave a message with my secretary inviting me to this interrogation because she never mentioned it?'

Jimmy Maguire smiled. His eyes glinted with the malevolence within. 'You are a funny guy.'

With that, he swung a haymaker of a left hand that blasted into the side of Jack's head and knocked him sideways, chair and all, crashing to the floor, his left shoulder hitting the concrete, preventing his head from cracking like an egg. Jack blinked furiously, trying to clear his head.

'Sit him up and get his clothes off. I want everything he's got on the table.'

Jack was hoisted upright, and he heard the chair crack as it was slapped back down on its rickety legs. Then he was pulled upright as his clothes were pulled from him and pushed back into position, arms over the back of the chair, completely naked. Jimmy looked through his wallet. 'No phone, no keys, no credit, or bank cards. No identity then.' He dropped the wallet on the table with an air of finality, and Jack understood the inference.

Goosebumps appeared on his arms and shoulders, and his buttocks felt the cold of the vinyl seat, shrinking his manhood. He realised that this was a tactic to intimidate him and make him feel helpless. He had seen the film *Rendition*. It clearly worked as that was exactly how he felt.

'So, Mr. Lawyer, this is a very simple matter. You tell me where the money is, you arrange for it to be transferred to me, and you walk away from here with your life but not much else. If you don't tell me quickly, the bank will be shut, and you will be here all night, and you don't want that because it will get very cold, and I will get very bored and angry, and you will suffer a great deal whilst I try to keep myself warm.' The words were delivered with slow menace. Jack saw the blood vessels, like mini-maps of the Nile delta, trailed across the nose and cheeks.

Jack cleared his throat. 'I have no idea who you are or what money you are talking about.'

Jack looked at Focus man. 'You seem to have forgotten the introductions, perhaps it was that bang on the head you had.'

He looked back at the white hair. 'I have never seen you before in my life, so how could I possibly know where your money is?'

He expected the swing this time and managed to roll with it as far as he could. He stayed upright in the chair, but his jaw throbbed, and he tasted the warm blood in his mouth. He swallowed it.

'If you are going to dick around like this, you will be half dead before you tell me, but you will tell me. You are a lawyer, so you must be pretty clever. Surely you can see that you are not in any position to play the smart arse.' Jimmy was growling, and the impatience was tangible.

'Tell me who you are, and I might be able to help you. Surely you can appreciate that I handle money all the time from numerous different sources.' A right hook to the ribs. 'And unless I know who you are . . .' A left across the mouth, splitting the top lip, spilling warm blood on to Jack's cold chest. ' . . . I can't be sure that I have even touched your money.'

Jack spat blood on to the floor. He looked up and saw the shoulders twist as another blow was aimed.

'Wait.' The right hand stopped mid-air. 'I will talk to Ryan. Get me Ryan, and I will talk to him. I will tell him everything but only him.'

'Son, you will tell me everything, eventually.' And the massive right hand crashed against Jack's eye and nose.

He slid away for a moment, his vision becoming liquid, like he was looking at the world through a lava lamp. When he returned, the pain came with him. His head detonated internally, and he let it drop forwards. Blood dripped from the end of his nose on to his thighs. He wondered if his nose was still straight. He felt nausea rising within him. He closed his eyes and tried to concentrate on one thing, *pick a subject and think only of that and the pain will become secondary*, he told himself.

He thought of Jules and realised immediately that was not what he needed right now. He thought of his mother. He saw her lying in her hospital bed. She was beaten and broken, and he was sitting beside her, holding her hand.

He took a deep breath and mumbled, 'You are right. I might tell you eventually. But if you get Ryan, although it almost certainly won't be as much fun, it won't take as long.' Jack smiled, revealing his bloodied teeth, giving him a grotesque, clown-like appearance.

Jimmy flicked his eyes to the far end of the building. Focus man set off at a slow trot.

'I will get my fucking money out of you, son.' And another series of crunching hooks from the ham fists pummelled Jack's ribs.

There was at least one crack, maybe two, and Jack's breath started to come in short, painful gasps. He put his head back and straightened his torso out to try and expand his lungs. He closed his eyes, and Maureen was still there. It was a bizarre, unconnected thought, but he remembered reading the autobiography of Muhammad Ali. The great fighter had explained that when he was dizzied by a blow, particularly by George Foreman in Zaire, he talked about entering 'the dream room', where he could go to recover himself. He visualised this dream room and saw himself entering and trying on the clothes that he found there until he was ready to come back to his reality. Jack realised he had done much the same thing in trying to fixate on his mother, and he decided to make his own way into this halfway house between the conscious and subconscious and let his senses go.

He stepped into his mind's vision and became enveloped by his memory. He was fifteen again; his mother had been brutalised, and she was dying in his arms. Jack embraced his wrath like an old friend. Inside, he was screaming, but the external pain was dissipated as the fury took over. 'This is why I'm here,' he told himself. This was what he had been building towards for the last six months of his life—no more pretending, no more self-delusion about walking away once Ryan had been arrested, and no more new life. Jack had been gradually and inextricably drawn to his own emotional wreckage that he had set aside whilst he masqueraded in the urbane, middle-class suit of Alex Harris. The realisation dawned on him that his subconscious purpose of this vision was for him to reabsorb his anger and his hatred, for these were the very essence of Jack Ladd, and it was time for him to be resurrected with all his rancour, antipathy, and, of course, all of his violence. Alex Harris had been a good friend, but he was finally laid to rest. Jack Ladd was now very much alive.

The suppurative rage, suppressed for twenty years, welled within him. His skin seemed to be burning with outrage; his breath came quicker and harder. There was no physical pain. His mind cleared. His vengeful passion did not. He opened his eyes, seeing everything in the glorious technicolour and wide panavision of his favourite childhood films, and before him stood Ryan Maguire.

CHAPTER 33

MONDAY, DECEMBER 11

THE VAUXHALL RACED THROUGH THE wet Salford streets, three other cars behind. The blue lights flashed, but the sirens were silent. Joe didn't want them to know he was coming.

He sat in the front passenger seat, holding the iPhone, with its map and it's blue pulsating dot, showing the position of Jack's phone.

What a stupid plan. What if they had just chucked his phone out of the car window? How would they find him then?

'Come on, can't this heap go any quicker?' Impatience was growing.

The driver looked sideways at his senior officer and decided to keep quiet.

Two cars back, Drew was leaning forward, between the two front seats of the BMW, watching the direction of the lead car.

Duncan had no idea Drew was with them. When he had rushed into Bootle Street demanding cars and men for an immediate raid, there had been no shortage of volunteers, and officers had dashed into the courtyard to fit themselves into the nearest car.

As Duncan's car had screeched out on to Jackson's Row, Drew had pulled rank and squeezed himself into the back of the last car.

They were weaving through the traffic on Regent Road. It was now clear to him where they were headed. Drew sat back and took out his mobile.

'Nice to see you, Ryan. It's been a long time.'

Jack was smiling. The blood in his mouth covered his teeth and lips made him look like a parody of Heath Ledger's Joker.

'What are you on about? I've never met you.' Ryan looked puzzled, and he glanced at Jimmy and then back to Jack.

'Like I said, it's been a long time. I think it's fair to say I knew your brother better.'

'What do you mean?' asked Ryan cautiously. Jack could see his was wary of the white-haired man, who was clearly the senior figure. He could use that.

The blood still dripped from his nose, and he shook his head to get a particularly stubborn drop from its resting place, flicking the blood inadvertently towards Ryan, leaving drops on his white shirt.

'Well, I guess it's been a long time . . .'

Jimmy cut in, 'Enough of this shit. Tell him where the money is now, or I swear I will break you in half.'

'OK.' Jack looked into Ryan's face and saw only confusion. What he needed was anger and chaos.

'My name is Jack.'

'So what?' Ryan spread his arms out. 'Come on, Uncle Jim, let's cut this twat. He's wasting time.'

Jack carried on, his voice low and quiet. 'We lived on the same estate in Haughton Green.'

Ryan looked down as though trying to place the bloodied face within his memory.

'I don't care.'

'I think you knew my mum. I'm sure you remember her. Maureen.' Just saying her name to her killer stoked the fire within Jack. He studied Ryan's face whilst he slowly flexed the muscles in his shoulders and upper arms, which were still around the back of the ancient wooden chair.

Jimmy stepped forward. 'Enough of this happy fucking families.' He threw his right hand, a long arcing punch from the side, aimed at the jaw, but Jack was alive to it. His reflexes were razor sharp. He had seen the punch coming, and he leant into it, taking the blow on the top of the skull, reducing the power by changing the angle of the blow.

'Shit.' Jimmy shook his hand and looked at his knuckles.

Jack looked back to Ryan. He had visibly paled.

'You remember Maureen, Ryan. You and Sean had a little party with her, remember?'

Ryan was staring at Jack now, his eyes betraying the uncertainty within. Jack still needed rage.

'Tell your uncle Jimmy about my mum, Ryan.' Ryan looked at Jimmy but said nothing. His mouth opened and then closed. He was lost and confused.

'OK, I'll tell him. He raped her, he beat her, and he killed her. And that, my friend, is why I took your money, all of it. And that is why I blew your little smuggling operation, and that is why I brought down your business. And that, my friend, is why I am going to kill you.'

'That's bollocks. Jim, I don't know what he's on about.' Ryan was looking around himself frantically as if searching for some comforting words of support. But his father was over the Atlantic, heading to Nassau.

'It's all your fault, Ryan. I will never give you that money back. I would rather die.' Jack smiled. Jimmy rolled his eyes. That was all he needed, a fanatic with a cause. This would not end well.

Jack continued in his threatening monotone, 'You kill my mum, and then you employ me to run your little money-washing scheme with the insurance company. How stupid are you?'

Jimmy's black eyes were now on Ryan.

'No, wait, it's not like that, Jimmy.'

'You invited me in, Ryan, despite the fact that I sliced up your queer little brother like last Sunday's roast beef.'

Bingo! There it was, right on the button. Jack had Ryan floundering, scared, and seeking approval, and then he hit him with the big one. As if turning his mad uncle against him wasn't enough, he now admitted to the murder of his brother.

Ryan had been struggling to keep a lid on things. He already knew what Jimmy thought of him. He already knew that he was a disappointment to his father who had washed his hands of him over this affair. He had lost the business, which meant that he lost the status that went with it—the girls, the respect, the gangster lifestyle, and now this!

He could not keep it within himself any longer. Ryan screamed and ran at Jack throwing punches and kicking out wildly.

'I'll kill you. I'll fucking kill you.'

Jack took the beating; there was no focus, no real power. He took the punches and waited for his chance.

The phone in Jimmy's pocket buzzed. He pulled it out and looked at the text message he had received.

He looked at Ryan, stood in front of the beaten and bleeding lawyer, panting after the exertion of his attack. He needed his answer right now, but he wasn't going to get it.

Jimmy had survived for over forty years in this game. He was cautious, some might say paranoid. He had the self-preservation instincts of the common brown rat.

He pointed two fingers at his two men. 'You two, with me.' He strode towards the door.

'What's going on, Uncle Jimmy?' Ryan was confused.

'He killed your brother, Ryan. This is between you and him. I suggest you finish him off and meet us in the car.'

Ryan looked back at Jack. It was his eyes, he thought later. He looked at the eyes, they were grey. They seemed even more striking as the rest of the face was red and covered in welts and blood.

But it was the look in those eyes that made him pause, that kept him motionless as the door closed behind the Irishman.

He was still transfixed by the eyes as Jack sprang to his feet, jumping backwards on to the chair, and then raised his hands over the slatted back.

He was crouched with knees bent and hands behind his back, but still, Ryan stood looking into the eyes that burnt with an icy fire.

'There, on the left, no, the big place, on the left, you moron.'

Joe was pointing, jabbing his long index finger towards the **KOTR** warehouse just as he saw the Peugeot start to move in the car park.

'Quick, get across the gate, they're on the move.'

The driver immediately accelerated hard, pushing Duncan back into his seat, and flicked on the siren. The car screeched to a stop blocking the exit, black smoke billowing from the tyres as Duncan burst from the passenger door.

Ryan turned, the sound of the siren breaking the spell of Jack's gaze. Immediately Jack jumped from the chair, keeping his knees bent and swinging his tied hands underneath his feet, like a skipping rope, before landing lightly, on the balls of his feet, with his tied hands in front of him. In the next movement, he had twisted and picked up the chair by the back.

The movement had caught Ryan's eye, and he spun to face Jack as he lifted the chair above his head and brought it crashing down. Ryan raised his hands to try and protect himself.

The sound of broken and splintering wood echoed through the huge empty building as the chair was hammered to the floor. Ryan had taken a couple of involuntary steps back, shielding his face with his forearm.

When he lowered his arms, he saw that Jack, naked, sweating, and bloodied, stood before him with a leg of the chair gripped in his bound hands. Each inward breath came with an audible, sharp wheeze. Jack was smiling; his eyes looked wild, and his skin glistened in the fading light as he took a lithe step forward.

Jimmy heard the siren and the screeching brakes. He left the Range Rover and ran to the back of the multi-blue building. There was a high fence all around the compound, but on this side, the fence backed on to private gardens, and there were trees to screen the factory unit from the kitchen windows of the semi-detached houses. The fence was high, and he was a heavy man, but he began the climb. Survival instincts were telling him this was the only way.

For a man in his sixties, he was astonishingly agile, but it was his brute strength that took him to the top of the chain-link fence, all his weight being pulled up by the massive forearms and biceps.

He reached the top, and without looking back to check whether he had been seen, he rolled himself over and fell into the trees, ripping his shirt and his skin and bouncing to the ground with shuddering thud.

Duncan was still running towards the Peugeot, despite it being obvious that they did not appear to be stopping. It was too late he realised that they intended to try and ram their way out of the car park, and he was between the Peugeot and the police car blocking the gate.

He stopped. It is often said that in your final moment's time appears to stand still and that dying men see their lives flash before their eyes.

Joe knew now that this was simply not true. There was no reliving of his past, no fond images of the lovers in his life, and no final, ecstatic revelation of what it had all been about.

What there was, was simple fear—uncomplicated, foul-smelling fear. He could see the faces of the men in the car, but their features did not register. He could see the ground being eaten up between them and hear the engine and gearbox whining as the wheels spun on the tarmac.

The human body is a remarkable thing. Whilst we walk around, smug in the knowledge that our consciousness and powers of reason have made us the most sophisticated and successful creature the planet has ever seen, we forget that it all started with an unbelievably efficient vessel within which to store all that sentience.

Without consciously making a decision, Joe jumped. His left shoulder bounced off the windscreen of the car, his back hit the roof and the boot, and he landed on his right side at the same point at which the car ploughed into the Vauxhall with a deafening bang, stopping the Peugeot with the engine revving high and hard.

The driver's door opened, and Joe was on his feet, dragging the shaven headed man to the tarmac and punching him, repeatedly, until he was pulled clear by one of the uniformed officers with his right hand covered in blood but not his own.

Joe's pulse raced a million beats per second. His heart pounded against the inside of his chest. He reached the black door and pulled it open.

'Jack!'

'You know it wasn't me. It was our Sean. Come on, it was Sean. I didn't touch her.' Ryan's voice was high-pitched. He was backing away from Jack, his arms out and palms up, in an unconscious gesture to demonstrate he was no threat.

Jack's guttural response was plain. 'That's what Sean said. He said it was all you. He was gay, Ryan, as queer as a bottle of crisps. Not the usual profile of a rapist.'

Jack was still walking forward; the veins in his biceps and forearms were standing proud as he gripped his makeshift club.

'Of course, he might have just been saying that as he knew I was going to kill him.'

Maguire stopped. He had reached the point where he would listen to no more. 'Well, you're not going to kill me. The police are outside, and I will just walk away when my lawyer gets here. Then I'll come for you, Jack Ladd. And you will go the same way as your mother.'

As the final word was uttered, Jack was already swinging. Ryan leant back to avoid the swing, and he felt the movement of air across his face as the chair leg swished by. But all his concentration had been on the immediate threat, as Jack knew it would be, and he was totally unprepared for the knee rising into his groin, crunching into his testicles, taking all the wind from his lungs.

His body convulsed forward to the site of the pain. Jack held the chair leg upright and jabbed, hard, under the chin.

Blood spurted from Maguire's mouth as he involuntarily bit through his tongue, his jaw having been forced shut by the blow. But the club was already coming back in a blur of movement and power; it slammed against the right side of his head.

Ryan's vision tunnelled. His motor skills seemed to desert him, his right leg involuntarily bent at the knee in a bizarre reflex action, and he could feel himself tottering, overbalancing when he tried to right himself. He knew he was going down when there was another explosion, over the left ear now, and the lights went out. He was already unconscious when he hit the floor face first, breaking his teeth and his nose.

Jack stood over the stricken body of Ryan Maguire, his own body streaked with blood and sweat. After all this time, he finally had him. He had taken a lot of pain to get to him, but once he had been given the chance, it had been disappointingly easy and quick.

The adrenaline does not wear off as quickly as it comes. Jack was still wired, his eyes alert, his body tensed and hard, and his mind cold.

It was time. It had been twenty years. At first, he thought the pain would kill him, but as the years passed, he had been able to put it to one side. Like his old parka, it was mothballed and left in the wardrobe of Jack's old self, whilst he adopted the new suit of Alex Harris. And for a while, it seemed as though he might never retrieve that old coat.

But now he had. He had gotten a taste for it when Richardson had attacked Jules, and now it felt like there was no going back. This is who he was, who he had always been.

He lifted the bloodied chair leg over his head, aimed to bring it down on the back of Ryan Maguire's skull, and put an end to all his pain. In his mind, he heard his name, screaming recognition of his resurrection.

He took in a deep breath, gathered his considerable strength, and brought down the weapon.

CHAPTER 34

MONDAY, DECEMBER 11

DCI JOE DUNCAN SAT IN his office, leaning over his desk, his head in his hands. He could hear the noises of celebration in the Pit, just outside his door, but he was in no mood to celebrate.

The same thought ran through his mind. Why? Why had he done it? He'd had a pretty decent life. He had a good job—one that he enjoyed. His future looked promising. Why would an intelligent man throw all that away?

Now it was going to be down to Joe to pick up the pieces. Good old reliable Joe, always there to make everything right, everything except his own life.

He went back to his keyboard to finish writing his report. He looked at the mobile phone on his desk that was in a plastic bag and tagged as evidence.

What a mess!

His whole body ached, no doubt from his run-in with the Peugeot. Two men were in custody but had so far refused to give their names, in broad Northern Irish accents, with an unfeasible amount of expletives thrown in for good measure.

They were going nowhere, though charged with attempted murder for trying to run him down. Plus the slightly less serious charge of dangerous driving. They may struggle to make a case stick against the passenger, but they would certainly be putting together a case for false imprisonment and assault provided they could get Tommy Ladd to cooperate.

Tommy would need to be picked up, and Joe knew he was at the Premier Inn. He had grilled him about Jack's plans before leaving the Abercromby, so he also knew about Jack's partner, Juliette, and Miles had informed him that she was a lawyer at Jack's or Alex's old firm. He had looked her up on the Internet out of curiosity and had studied her profile and studio picture on the Hanson's website. He had lingered on the photograph longer than would be normal for him.

Joe finished the report, the sanitised version of what had gone down, and forwarded it to John Hall. Once again he felt he had compromised himself for Jack's benefit, although now he was not sure why, it would make no difference to Jack. He debated waiting for the phone call, but decided to act now, whilst everybody was here.

He picked up the evidence bag with the mobile and left his office, entering the Pit, which was alive with people drinking champagne from paper cups, laughing and backslapping all round.

Miles sat at his own desk, feet up, quietly sipping his drink, watching the revelry. Melbourne was on the edge of a circle of officers, Drew at the centre, regaling those around him with his rendition of Duncan's attempt to leap over the advancing Peugeot.

Duncan looked at Miles and nodded. Miles got up, leaving his drink behind and sauntered casually over to the group, making his way behind Drew.

The conversation dropped as Duncan approached.

'Sorry, Boss,' said Drew. 'We were just discussing your gymnastics earlier.' A few sniggers.

'Terence Drew, I am arresting you for perverting the course of justice. You do not have to say anything, but it may harm your defence if you do not mention, when questioned, something which you later rely on in court. Anything you do say may be given in evidence.'

Immediately Miles pulled back Drew's hands and cuffed them behind his back.

'What's this? What the fuck is going on?' Drew was snarling at Duncan.

The plastic bag with the mobile phone was held up in front of his eyes, and Duncan allowed it to sway a little for added effect. There was now silence in the office.

'You left your phone on your desk. I already had a warrant from the Super. It is there on the desk. I don't think you've looked at it yet. So tell me about your connection with Jimmy Maguire, Drew. Tell us all, as you appear to be in story-telling mood, how much information you have given him during the course of this enquiry. Explain to your colleagues here why him and Ryan were not at the drugs raid, and how he knew Alex Harris was meeting me at the Abercromby.' Melbourne shifted uncomfortably in her seat.

'While you are at it, perhaps you should explain how this man managed to evaporate from the scene when we managed to grab everybody else? Could it be your last text that reads "Jimmy, we are five minutes away, get yourself out of there, leave us something to find." I think that might have had something to do with it.'

Drew stood open mouthed.

'You are too stupid to survive in this job. You didn't even think to delete the messages. Take him away, Steve.'

'Pleasure, Boss.' Miles yanked the cuffed wrists, making Drew wince. There was a stunned silence hanging in the room.

'You lads enjoy your champagne, OK. Lynn, my office.'

As she closed the door behind her, Lynn could hear the hubbub of conversation start up. She sat in the seat opposite Duncan and looked down into her lap, resigned to her fate.

'So what did you tell him and when?' Duncan's voice was hard and cold.

'Sir, he is my sergeant, if he asks me what's going on . . .'

Duncan interrupted, banging his palm on the desk, making her jump. 'I didn't ask why. I asked what and when.'

'I told him about the Abercromby meeting. I told him the day before. I was obeying an order, sir.'

'Anything else?'

'No, sir.'

Duncan sighed. 'OK, why did you compromise us, Lynn?'

'Sir, I was given an order by my DS to tell him what was going on. He told me that Detective Superintendent Hall was questioning the direction the investigation was going in and, to be honest, you were going into a meeting with a man who was one of our prime suspects without telling your superiors, sir.'

The flash of anger did not go unnoticed. Duncan raised an eyebrow. 'Is there anything else you want to tell me?'

Lynn looked down again, her shoulders, normally square and tight, slumped forward. 'No, sir, I've told you everything.'

'OK.' Duncan stood up and moved his long frame around the table. 'Do you have your warrant card?'

'Yes, sir, it's in my bag at my desk.' She got up slowly to leave. Duncan saw her eyes start to fill, and her determined jaw, muscles knotted, fighting back the tears.

'Then make sure you keep it safe. You came bloody close to losing it today. If you are going to stay working with me, Lynn, I have to know I can trust you.'

One large tear escaped over the lower lid of Lynn's right eye, leaving a track behind it as it rolled slowly down her cheek.

She reached out and held Joe's forearm. He felt his skin tingle under his shirt sleeve.

'Thank you, sir. I will keep it very safe from now on.'

Duncan opened the door for her to leave. She kept hold of his arm and looked up into the tired eyes. 'I do appreciate it, Joe . . . sir.' Then she walked back to her desk, picked up her bag, and left without speaking to anyone.

Joe shut the door and went back to his desk. He could feel his face was red, and he busied himself with paperwork to try and take his mind off it. Inevitably his thoughts meandered back to the events at the depot.

He had pulled open the black door and had seen Jack, naked and bleeding, his face bruised and swollen, kneeling over the body of another man, lay face down on the hard, cold floor. He saw Jack raise a thick piece of wood above his head, and it was obvious what he intended to do with it.

Joe had screamed Jack's name as the club arced downwards. Jack continued with his movement, and the wood crashed against the floor to the side of the prostrate Ryan Maguire.

Jack had looked up. He was barely recognisable from the man Joe had spoken to in the Abercromby such a short time before. His right eye was almost shut and was already forming a purplish hue around the lids. His nose seemed slightly off-centre, and his lips were fat and distorted.

Blood dripped from his nose and from one corner of his mouth, and there were splatters of red across his chest and shoulders.

Joe ran towards him and then stopped ten yards away when the wood, which he now realised was a chair leg, was raised above Jack's head again. The remnants of the chair were scattered behind Jack, by the table.

'Jack, don't do it, mate, please. Don't do it.' Joe had panted, the tension reverberating through his voice.

Jack had looked at his old friend, his battered face distorted in anguish, eyes still aflame.

'He has to die, Joe, you know what he did.' His words were muffled, almost incoherent, caused by the damage inflicted to his mouth. Joe could see he was bleeding badly, and he could also hear the rasping breath and see the red welts on his torso.

Joe pleaded, 'Jack, I can't let you do this now. Look at me, Jack, I'm a copper. If you kill him now, I can't let you walk away. Not this time, Jack. Things are different now.' Jack tilted his head to one side as though considering his options.

'Come on, Jack,' Joe continued. 'You've done enough. You ruined him and his business. He will have to live with the knowledge that you broke him for the rest of his life. Trust me, Jack, that will hurt him more than if you snuff out his miserable little life now.' Joe took two steps forward.

He could see Jack's good left eye was wide, pupil dilated. 'Jack, please. If you do this, you will spend the rest of your life in prison. There's police all around this place. I can't fix this, Jack.' Jack had begun to shake his head.

'No. No, Joe, he has to pay,' he shouted the last word, and its echo rang around the cavernous building.

'Jack, wait. Remember what you said to me the night after your mum died. We sat in your bedroom, remember?'

Jack nodded slowly.

'I said your mum wouldn't want this, and you told me she would, but she would want you to get away with it, remember?' Jack was now still; his one visible eye now gazed wistfully into the middle distance, at nothing in the physical world.

'Well, if she was here now, she would tell you to walk away, Jack. Don't let them ruin you. If you kill him, it's all over. You don't get Frank because you will be locked away.'

Jack stumbled over his words, like Charles Lawton's Quasimodo, not yet in tune with the thickness of his lips. 'Frank didn't kill her. Anyway, I've taken care of Frank.'

Joe made a mental note to check on Frank Maguire's welfare. But the look in Jack's face had softened. Joe felt he was bringing him around. It was time for him to surprise Jack for a change.

'What about Juliette. Where does she go once you bash Ryan's head in, Jack? Her career is knackered, you saw to that. Does she go back home and plan her prison visits, is that the life you want for her?'

Jack looked down at Ryan Maguire. He was starting to stir. Jack rolled him over. His nose was demolished and his front teeth shattered and sticking out through his top lip. He had a gash on the side of his head.

Jack looked back at Joe and sighed, wearily. 'Jesus fucking Christ on a moped. Does everyone know about me and Jules? I haven't seen you for twenty fucking years, and you know about my secret girlfriend. What a joke.'

He dropped the chair leg as he stood up.

'Jack, thanks. Let's get your clothes on. You've got a knob like a cashew.'

Jack coughed out a laugh. 'Thanks for that, Joe. It is pretty cold in here.' They walked to the table, and Jack started dressing, wincing as he moved; his cracked ribs were shooting sharp knives of pain through his body.

'What's happened to Frank, Jack?'

'Oh him. Not a lot. Don't worry, Joe, I've not topped him. But he has a nasty surprise coming in paradise.'

By the time Jack was dressed, the remaining officers had come into the building. Jack had looked at the two men from the Peugeot. 'What happened to Jimmy?' he had asked Joe.

'This is it, nobody else.'

'Ryan's uncle, Jimmy, from Belfast. He was the brains behind the drug smuggling, and he was the one who resurfaced my face for me. You need to get him, Joe, he is a crazy old bastard.'

An ambulance had arrived, and the paramedics had taken Ryan away on a stretcher. They had strapped Jack's torso before they left and encouraged him to go for a CAT scan, which Joe had assured them he would do once he had been in for questioning.

Jack had been gingerly sitting in the back seat of the police car, and Joe had driven. Jack had explained that Alex Harris was an old friend he had met in France, who had not made it home. He had skipped the details. Jack had assumed his identity (he skipped over the inheritance) so that he could start his life again.

He had forgotten about the Maguires until he dealt with a claim for an employee of theirs, a young man who had been catastrophically injured in a medical negligence case. It was just coincidence that he worked for King of the Road.

At that stage, he had started to check up on Frank and Ryan. He found out that Frank was planning to retire and decided he needed to act.

His client's mother had recommended Alex Harris to Steven Holland, and Holland had engineered a meeting at the Midland Hotel.

Jack had found that they were money laundering through the insurers, paying fraudulent claims and taking the clean money back. Jack maintained that he had only intended to bring the company down; hence he had produced his file that he sent to Duncan.

Things got out of hand with Steven Redford. Jack had decided to provoke the Maguires by 'losing' their money (again, he never actually came clean on the whereabouts of the money, Joe noted), and he had seen Redford attacked and killed by Richardson.

It was at that point he decided to bring Joe into play. He had 'dressed' Redford's body to send a message to Joe, with the thought that he would be the silver bullet that would bring down the Maguires, allowing Alex Harris to melt back into obscurity.

The fly in the ointment had been Uncle Jimmy and his pathological desire to make an example of Alex.

The real turning point in the plan was Richardson's attack on Jules. Not only did Jack realise that the Maguires would never leave him alone but it also reawakened his desire for a physical revenge—the realisation that he still had the proficiency to inflict corporeal damage to the murderer of his mother and the appreciation of his dormant violence and the thrill it dispersed within him irrevocably changed his plan. From that moment on, a confrontation was all that would satisfy him.

He had found himself spiralling back into his old self and enjoying the sensation, the risk and the promise of retribution.

Joe had listened patiently—the odd question here and there but generally filling out the blanks in his own knowledge of how things had gone down.

He stopped the car outside the hotel on Medlock Street and turned to face Jack in the rear seat.

'Why didn't you just come and see me when you came back?' He seemed genuinely hurt.

'I looked you up, Joe, but you were married, and you were off in Africa. I figured then that you had just moved on. When you came back, what was I gonna do? Pop round for tea? Hello, love, this is, Jack, I helped him dispose of a body when we were kids? I just assumed that if you never saw me again, it wouldn't weigh you down. Let's be honest, you being the filth now, it is kind of an elephant in the room. I thought I was doing us both a favour.'

Joe leant over and opened the rear door.

'Next time, Jack, let me do the thinking.'

As Jack struggled out of the car, he had chuckled quietly. 'That's twice you have saved me, Joe Duncan. I owe you everything. If you ever need help, with anything, I don't expect to be second or third on your list. Do you understand?'

He straightened up, grimacing as he did so. 'I'm going to be leaving, take Jules away for a few months. You should meet her, Joe, you'd like her. She'd like you. On the other hand, best that you don't, you don't want me to be jealous.' Joe smiled. 'I'll send you a text when I have a new phone, but I won't tell you where I am. I don't want you compromised.'

Joe had laughed. 'God forbid, Jack.'

As he put the car in gear, Jack tapped on the window, and Joe flicked the switch and let the window slide down.

'One last favour, Joe. Get me a message to Ladyboy. Tell him to enjoy the sunshine. See ya.'

Joe had watched Jack stride away, somewhat awkwardly, and laughed as Jack waved his right hand without looking back, just as he had done the last time he walked out of his life.

Now Joe Duncan sat in his office. The whole affair had caused him to doubt himself, to file reports that, whilst not strangers to the truth, were certainly not sleeping with it. Ultimately, however, it appeared it had done his career no harm at all. Sure there would be questions over the mislaying of Alex Harris, but he could deal with those.

Once it became known that Ryan was in custody and that Frank had bolted to the Bahamas, the mechanics hauled in by the customs had started to talk. They knew that their families were both safe and unlikely to receive financial aid from the Maguires.

The business would collapse within days. Once Steven Holland started to talk, and he would know that there was nobody to protect, the whole thing would unravel. Jimmy had disappeared, but they would be able to begin extradition proceedings for Frank once they had built their case. He would be the public relations coup that the boys down at Old Trafford were looking for.

Duncan decided that enough was enough; it had been a long day. He switched off his computer and picked up his coat from the back of the chair, where it had been thrown—time for a decent cup of coffee.

He groaned as he put on his coat. He was pretty sure he would be some interesting shades of purple under his suit following his run-in with the French automobile and decided to forgo the coffee and head back to his apartment for a long, hot bath. He would call in on the Queen on the way, to pass on Jack's cryptic message.

EPILOGUE

FRANK WAS INCENSED. HE WAS held back by Dainius as he raged at the petty official in front of him. Spittle flew from the corners of his mouth; his face was a deep beetroot colour, and it had nothing to do with the sunshine.

'You bastards. You ripped me off. You're all in it together. You bastards. You will pay for this. I know people. I have friends. Do you have any idea who you are fucking with?'

Dainius manhandled him out of the office. He had never seen Frank like this.

It had started that morning, when they arrived at the newly completed house, removal trucks and all, to find it already occupied by a large black American man and his extremely beautiful wife and three noisy children.

Frank had demanded that they leave immediately but only to be told that he should be the one leaving as he was trespassing in their new home. The police were called, and the American showed them the rental agreement to the house, which he retrieved from the safe that Frank had insisted, should be built into the floor of his dressing room.

The police had forced Frank to leave and directed him to the Town Planners Office who had confirmed every last detail of the purchase of the land and the permit from the Ministry of Works for the building. Every last detail but one, there was no Frank Maguire named anywhere in the paperwork.

Rasa had taken Mrs. Maguire back to the hotel. She could not understand the problem and just kept telling Frank to 'sort them out'.

Urgent calls had been made to Davis, but his number was no longer active. The bank were of no help, they had just sent the money to Davis to go into his account. It was obvious that Davis had used Frank's money to build the house and then sold it on to somebody else. Nobody seemed to know where Davis was. Back in the United States, it was suggested.

'I don't fucking believe it, Dainius, I'm ruined. Every last fucking penny, gone,' Frank continued to rant, whilst looking at his photocopy of the title deeds. His eyes were popping, and his breath was short.

'Boss, you need to calm down.' It was a sound advice but too late and unheeded. Frank Maguire started to cough. He felt the first twinge in his chest and then a shooting pain down his arm. His knees buckled, and he was on the floor before Dainius could catch him.

The loyal Lithuanian was the right man for Frank's crisis. He placed him into the recovery position before storming back in to the Town Planners office and demanding an ambulance.

Frank lay on his side in the corridor. He felt his energy draining away from him. After all these years, this was where he was going to end up? Dead from a heart attack and a million miles away from home!

As if to taunt him, the photocopy of the deeds lay beside his face. Before he lost consciousness, he wondered who the hell Raymond Ladyman was.

Jimmy Maguire sat in the back room of his terraced house. The curtains were shut. In the gloom, he held the phone in his right hand.

'Nothing fancy. Just make sure that it goes up and that nobody survives. You know what to do.'

He banged down the receiver. 'It's never over,' he muttered to himself.

The cover was pulled back from the glistening red paintwork, and he rolled it up and put it under his arm as he inserted the key and unlocked the door. The bodywork was so exquisite it looked like you would get a red hand if you touched it, as if the paint were still liquid, sitting on the car just because it looked good there.

He could hear the well-oiled lock tumble with the pressure applied. No fancy central locking in those days.

He opened the door and dropped the car cover on to the rear seat. He positioned himself in the driver's seat and altered the position so that he was nearer to the pedals. He adjusted the mirror and placed the key in the ignition.

He played with the gearstick to familiarise himself with the position of the gears and then dipped the clutch and turned the key.

The Karmann Ghia exploded in a ball of fire, the force of the explosion lifting it from the ground and smashing windows in the hotel and the cars parked around it.

It was completely obliterated, like the sad, painful life of Tommy Ladd.

It had been a long and tiring flight, but the weather had been a pleasant surprise as they had left the terminal building at Chek Lap Kok airport. It was warm and sunny, but a nice dry heat, like a September 'Indian summer' in England—a pleasant 75 degrees Fahrenheit, according to the pilot on their Virgin Airlines Airbus A340. The information was received in the opulent surroundings of their upper class seats.

A uniformed chauffeur had met them in the arrivals lounge and the dark green Rolls Royce Phantom and spirited them majestically through the New Territories to the Peninsula Hotel, on the Kowloon side of Hong Kong harbour.

Their bags were removed from the boot and taken straight up to their room whilst they checked in.

The stunning receptionist, with almond-shaped eyes, flawless skin, and perfect English, welcomed them, checked their passports, and handed over the key cards giving a curt nod as she did so. He had clearly lost weight since the passport photograph, but what perturbed her was the bruised and swollen face of Mr. Johnny Hayes. He obviously had the means as the room was paid for in advance on his debit card, and the Peninsula was far from cheap, very far. But she was sure that the maître d' would be seating them at a secluded table for dinner. He did not appear to be Peninsula class at all.

'On behalf of the management of the Peninsula, we hope you enjoy your stay, Ms. Everett, Mr. Hayes.'

Jules and Johnny thanked her and headed up to the Deluxe Harbour View double room, arm in arm.

The End